PAUL J. McAULEY

An AvonNova Book

William Morrow and Company, Inc.
New York

AVON BOOKS
A division of
The Hearst Corporation
1350 Avenue of the Americas
New York, New York 10019

Copyright © 1991 by Paul J. McAuley
Published by arrangement with the author
Library of Congress Catalog Card Number: 93-8064
ISBN: 0-688-12757-6

Library of Congress Cataloging in Publication Data:
McAuley, Paul J.
    Eternal Light/Paul J. McAuley.
        p. cm.
I. Title.
PS3563.C332E8 1993   93-8064
813′.54—dc20   CIP

First Morrow/AvoNova Printing: September 1993

AVONOVA TRADEMARK REG. U.S. PAT. OFF. AND IN OTHER COUNTRIES, MARCA
REGISTRADA, HECHO EN U.S.A.

Printed in the U.S.A.

ARC   10   9   8   7   6   5   4   3   2   1

Oh rosebud red!
Man's lot is of such extreme necessity,
of such bitter pain,
I had far rather be in Heaven.
I came upon a broad highway
when a little angel appeared and tried to send me back.
Oh no! I refused to be sent back!
I am from God and shall return to God!
Dear, merciful God will give me a little light
to light my way to everlasting bliss!

PRIMEVAL LIGHT
(from The Boy's Magic Horn)
KLOPSTOCK/MAHLER

In the realm of light there is no time.

J. S. BELL

CONTENTS

.\/\/\/\/\/\.

Prologue
Primeval Light

IT BEGAN WHEN THE SHOCK WAVE OF A NEARBY SUPERNOva tore apart the red supergiant sun of the Alea home system, forcing ten thousand family nations to abandon their world and search for new homes among the packed stars of the Galaxy's core. Or it began long after one Alea family had slaughtered most of the others and forced the rest to flee the core, when a binary star came too close to the black hole at the dead center of the Galaxy. Or perhaps it began half a million years after that, when Alea-infesting asteroids girdling the red dwarf star BD +20° 2465 destroyed a Greater Brazilian flyby drone as it shot through their adopted system. That's when it began for Dorthy Yoshida, for instance, although it happened a dozen years before she was born: the first act in a futile war of misunderstanding that ended in a gratuitous spasm of genocide.

There are so many beginnings to the complex weave of the secret history of the Universe. Causation chains merge and separate and loop like the stacked geodesics of contraspace that underpin the four dimensions of normal space-time. Half a million years ago, for instance, just after the double star encountered the black hole in the center of the Galaxy, the remnants of what had once been a minor moon of a Jovian gas giant, accelerated close to the speed of light, grazed the second planet of the star Epsilon Eridani. This, the end of the beginning of the shaping of modern human destiny, was the final spasm of an Alea family feud which Dorthy Yoshida would help close out in the fullness of time.

There is no end to beginnings in the unbounded multiverse, no particular beginning to its end.

A beginning chosen at random . . . ?

Freeze-frame that shattered world, half its oceans flung into orbit by multiple impacts, the remainder aboil and washing over its continents beneath global fire storms. Black clouds wrap it

3

from pole to pole, except above the places where fragments of moon impacted. Look down from orbit, through wavering columns of superheated steam to where white-hot magma wells up from the mantle. Now fast forward: half a million years.

People live on that world, now. They call it Novaya Rosya; their ancestors, nomenklatura fleeing an Islamic jihad, came from the lost nation of the Commonwealth of Soviet Republics, stacked in coldcoffins in the cargo pods of slower-than-light ramscoop ships. People have lived on Novaya Rosya for five hundred years, but it is still not much more than the wreckage of the world it once was, before one faction of a divided Alea family struck down the civilization it cradled.

An intricately braided ring-system tilts around its equator, debris flung into orbit by the impact: nuggets of water-ice and frozen mud; glassy beadlets of vaporized mantle; frozen gases. It is rumored that some of the ice nuggets contain perfectly preserved flash-frozen fish: a rumor which persists despite a couple of speculative and unsuccessful attempts to recover these fabled revenants. The world itself is still thermodynamically unstable, its climate fluctuating from searing summer heat, that at the equator volatilizes the shallow hydrocarbon-rich seas, to wolf-winter that freezes those same seas from top to bottom. What is left of life is confined to the mountains and altoplana of the south polar continent, surviving in the teeth of scouring hurricanes and rainstorms that last a hundred days, surviving earthquakes and vulcanism, spasms of fractured crustal plates adjusting to their new geometries.

Most people live in domed arcologies. Only zithsa hunters freely roam the crags and canyons of the catastrophic landscape, following the perpetual migrations of their prey; and zithsa hunters are regarded as a crazy kind of people by the rest of the population.

Sitting in his air-conditioned subterranean hutch in the middle of the secret excavation site on the flanks of Arrul Terrek, Major Sebastian Artemio Pinheiro wondered, not for the first time, if he was becoming as crazy as everyone said the zithsa hunters were. A tall, burly man, Pinheiro was perched on the edge of his bed, a square slab which took up most of the space in the little room, vigorously polishing his expensive zithsa-hide boots to the celestial chorus of Beethoven's *Missa Solemnis*—which was why he was thinking about zithsa hunters. And the reason why he was polishing his boots was the reason why he was wondering what he was doing out here in the lowlands, supervising a dozen mercenary archaeologists, most of whom couldn't speak each other's language, fenced in by continual perimeter patrols for as long as the excavation took to finish: yet again, one of his superior officers was coming to visit.

Pinheiro methodically polished away, absorbed in the little task, until Jose Carrerras pushed through the folding door of the hutch and told him that the distinguished visitors had just reached the guard post at the pass.

Pinheiro put down his boots and reached over to the little freezer set on the floor. He said to Carrerras, "Want a drink?"

"Are you crazy?"

"As a bedbug," Pinheiro said, and poured a shot of gelatinous vodka and tossed it down his throat. Then he pulled on his tight, blackly glittering boots, smeared blocking cream over his face and pulled up the hood of the environment suit, and stalked out of his room and through the commons beyond toward the airlock, Jose Carrerras tagging right behind.

The stocky drilling engineer said, "What it is, Sebastian, is I hope you'll remember to register my protest."

"The visitors are the last people you should pester, Jose. They are nothing but high level tourists, you know, come here to gawp. Put a hard copy of your complaint—"

"As I have already done, twice already!" Carrerras's luxuriant mustache seemed to bristle, so fierce was his righteous indignation. He pulled the airlock's hatch closed and followed Pinheiro up the helical stair, calling out, "I need assistants to help bring up the deep cores! I am a drilling engineer, not a laborer! The work they want of me is impossible in these conditions. More men on the site is what we want, not more guards!"

Stepping out of the shadow of the stairwell was like stepping into the breath of a blast furnace. The polar sun, a squashed disk of white glare, had circled nearer to the blunt peak of Arrul Terrek. Heat shimmered across the cindery floor of the narrow valley; the ragged hills which swept around to the left and right to enclose it seemed to shake above a rolling haze thick as oil.

The living quarters of the archaeology crew were sunk deep into the ground, covered and insulated by low mounds of dirt so that, save for the cluster of stubby shortwave antennae and the small dish aerial, they looked like the burial mounds of the North American Plains Indians, of Iron Age kings. Downslope was the excavation site itself, and beyond it Pinheiro could just see, through veils of heat and horizontal glare, the silvery bead of the crawler making its way out of the rocky throat of the pass a klick away.

Carrerras pulled up the hood of his environment suit and said, "How many guards do we have? Fifty? A hundred? Everything is ass-backwards here."

Pinheiro said, "It is the zithsa breeding season. They pass through this area toward the lowlands. Extra guards are needed to keep away any hunters who stray too close."

"Sometimes I think you believe all that shit."

Pinheiro shrugged, because he did believe it, more or less. The security was necessary, and it kept out of the way, and it wasn't an alternative to a large work force because even the dozen archaeologists already here were enough of a security risk that Pinheiro felt like the cork on a bottle of sweating nitroglycerin. He couldn't tell Carrerras that, but he felt that he owed the engineer something; Carrerras made a lot of noise, but he was a tireless worker.

"Be patient," Pinheiro said. "I will see what I can do. But I cannot promise I can do any good. Things would be better left in the ground than those outside our charmed circle find out that they are there."

"I know it. But if I don't get help, the deep cores will *have* to stay in the ground, okay?" Carrerras smiled again. "You try to do your best, Sebastian, I know. A hard place to be. But listen, don't drink too much vodka. It is not good for your liver."

"All you guys do is bitch when distinguished visitors are due, and when they turn up you can't get enough of showing off your work. Me, I have to act polite and charming the whole time, so I need something for stage nerves."

"You just tell them how badly we're doing here without proper backup. Breathe on them to get their attention."

They began to walk down the fossil beach where the camp had been sunk, around the lip of the stepped semicircular excavation the team called the amphitheater. Its patterned forest of encrusted pillars stood in shadow down there, webbed by the flickering lines of laser transects, Xu Bing tirelessly refining his coordinate pattern to the millimeter. The ground sloped down to the level of the amphitheater's floor. There was Carrerras's skeletal drill rig, a crisscross maze of trenches and a vast cat's cradle of transect lines and markers, randomly parked digging equipment, ragged heaps of spoil from the amphitheater. Excavations and building sites are mirror images, the same tape run backward and forward. Freeze the frame and you can't tell where the arrow of time is pointing.

Most of the crew were standing on the edge of the sudden steep slope that had once been a drop-off from shallow to deep water, a slope littered with half-buried rocks and weather-fractured debris. The crawler was close now, dragging boiling clouds of dust as it started up the slope. Its narrow windshield flared with reflected sunlight.

The paleobiologist, Juan Lopez Madrinan, came up to Pinheiro and said, "How many more circuses are there going to be, Sebastian? I've been here six months now. I've a mountain of data. I need to publish more than I need a woman!"

"There are people who have been here twice as long. Be patient, Juan. Nothing can be published until everything is finished. You know that."

"But you let these people know we're unhappy, okay?" Madrinan's fierce hawklike stare burned up at Pinheiro. He was the only one of the crew not to have pulled up his hood, and there was only a token smearing of cream on his high, angular cheekbones, startlingly white against his deep black skin. "You tell them we're all ready to run riot here."

"I always tell them that," Pinheiro said, wishing that he'd had two shots back in his hutch. Visits always brought the archaeologists' resentments into focus.

Jagdev Singh said, "All we want is a little recognition. They'll understand that." Singh was the chief excavator, a mild, uncomplaining giant of a man. If he was unhappy enough to speak up, then things really were going badly.

"I'll tell them what I always tell them," Pinheiro said.

"Tell them something new," Jose Carrerras said. "The same old song just doesn't cut it."

"I hear you! I hear you all! Now get to work. If they don't see you working, you don't get any favors. Work! Work!" Pinheiro shouted in half a dozen languages at the sullen archaeologists. By the time they had all moved off, the crawler had pulled up at the crest of the slope, and the distinguished visitors were clambering out of its rear hatch.

There were three this time. Admiral Orquito, a frail, white-haired old man, stooped and shaky on his feet, whose black eyes nevertheless burned with fierce self-will in his skull-like face. His aide, a cool, brisk, beautiful blond, half her face masked by green wraparound shades, alertly solicitous to the admiral's needs. And another woman, small, slight and subdued, her round sallow face almost completely hidden by the hood of her environment suit. Her handshake was brief and limp, and she averted her face from Pinheiro's scrutiny. Her name was Dorthy Yoshida.

"We want you to show us it all, Major," the admiral said, peering toward the lip of the amphitheater. "Perhaps we start there. You think so, Dorthy?"

"Whatever you like." The Yoshida woman was looking in the other direction, toward the low encircling hills.

Admiral Orquito said to Pinheiro, "She knows all about the Enemy. She will tell us if this has anything to do with them." And he laughed creakily at Pinheiro's open disbelief for, like most of humanity, Pinheiro knew that no one had ever so much as glimpsed one of the Enemy. Virtually nothing was known about them, except that they liked red dwarf stars, and that they could be implacably, insensately hostile. The asteroid habitats orbiting BD Twenty had been scorched without any-one's setting foot on a single one, and although there were rumors that an exploratory team had been sent down to the surface of the planoformed world that was the Enemy's only other known colony, they were rumors only. And that world had been under permanent quarantine since the end of the Campaigns. So Pinheiro was instantly and intensely curious about the small, unprepossessing woman, but there was the two-cruzeiro tour to get through before he could ask her any questions.

The trenches cut through the layers of fossilized silt that had been deposited by tsunami which had raced around the world after the bombardment, the topmost showing the ripples left by the receding floods. The sinkhole where hundreds of spirally carved bone rods had been found, subtly notched grooves that were some kind of written language perhaps . . . but only perhaps, Juan Madrinan said. And fossils everywhere, minute spiral shells ground to powder under each step, huge starbursts of spines pressed flat, the bones of fishes and things like manta rays. Once, this had been the silty bottom of an inlet of a rich polar sea.

The admiral smiled and nodded as the archaeologists explained their work, and became suddenly vague whenever the subject of publication was raised. Juan Madrinan made a little set piece speech about the importance of allowing other experts to think about the findings, and Jose Carreras made his usual demands about the need for more labor. "But you've made such progress," Admiral Orquito said. "It really is quite amazing . . . Now, Major, you were going to show me the amphitheater?" And he smiled vaguely at Carrerras and tottered off on the arm of his beautiful blond aide, and Pinheiro hurried after him to escape Carrerras's wrath.

More than anything else, the amphitheater was what all the distinguished visitors came to see.

Nearly as wide as the valley, it was a semicircular depression that had been scooped out of the bedrock of the prediluvian shore. The wide floor was studded with pillars, here clustered thickly, there placed in precise hexagonal patterns. Many had been broken or tilted by the force of the tsunami. All tapered up from a broad base, composed of thousands of intertwining strands of something like a woody kelp, those on the outside invariably bearing the shells of a sessile organism. Roughly the size and shape of a jai alai scoop, they were arrayed in intertwining helical patterns suggestively similar to the carving of the bone rods.

Xu Bing was eager to show off his measuring grid, to explain his theories of numerical distribution to Admiral Orquito, who, it turned out, was an orbital survey expert. Pinheiro left them to get on with it and went to catch up with the Yoshida woman, who had wandered off among the cathedral-like forest of fossilized pillars.

She was running a hand over a pillar's ribbed surface, fingering the curved projections of the scoops. Her nails, Pinheiro saw, were bitten to the quick. He asked her, "You truly know about the Enemy?"

"Orquito talks too much," she said. "He's allowed to; I'm not. This is strange stuff. Reminds me of seaweed holdfasts."

"Probably because that is what it is, more or less. When this was underwater, you can imagine long ribbons of weed trailing on the surface of the bay like a green roof." And for a moment, Pinheiro did see it: shafts of sunlight striking through the floating weave, catching the winding patterns of the living scoops, their shells iridescent as soap bubbles in the clear, calm, green water.

Dorthy Yoshida had turned to look at him. The silvery hood of her environment suit had pulled back from her face. Her black hair was unflatteringly cropped; it didn't suit her round, high-cheeked face at all. Her lips were slightly parted, revealing small spaced teeth white as rice grains. Her eyes were half-closed. She looked at once teasingly enigmatic and wholly vulnerable. She said dreamily, "Yes. I see how it could have been."

Pinheiro said, "If the creatures who built this normally lived in deep water, as I think they did, they would have needed shade when they came here. Unfortunately, we don't know what they looked like. There are plenty of fossils of large animals around, but nothing with a big enough braincase—"

Dorthy Yoshida had leaned back against the pillar, fitting herself among the fossilized scoop-shells. Now she cupped her forehead with a hand, and Pinheiro asked, "Are you all right?"

"It's just the heat," she said. And then she fell into his arms in a faint.

Admiral Orquito's aide came over at once. She told Pinheiro to lay Yoshida down, and then she knelt beside the woman and broke a capsule under her nose. Yoshida sneezed and suddenly

opened her eyes. "They were like spider crabs," she said dreamily, "many pairs of legs, some like paddles, some tipped with fine
three-part claws. And they were like manta rays, too, in a way I
don't quite understand. They swarmed through the shallow seas,
across the marshy shores, all one nation, their lives ruled by solar
tides. They tamed giant sea serpents and rode them across the
oceans; they mapped the stars and explored the system of their
sun in ships half-filled with water, dreamed of finding other
oceans to swim in. . . ."

And then her eyes focused on Pinheiro, and she asked, in a
quite different voice, cool and matter-of-fact, "What did I see
this time?"

"I have it recorded," the aide told her, and helped her stand.
"You didn't hear a word of this, Major Pinheiro," she said, and
glanced at a couple of archaeologists gawking from the top of
the amphitheater. "And they didn't see anything," she said, and
walked over to the Admiral, her long legs moving like scissor
blades.

Pinheiro looked after her in confusion. Something had happened, but he wasn't quite sure what it meant. The aide touched
Orquito's arm and steered him away from Xu Bing, talking
quickly and urgently.

Dorthy Yoshida leaned against the pillar, and Pinheiro asked
if she was all right.

"It will pass," she said, quite self-contained again. "Please
don't worry. Well, at least they got what they wanted."

Pinheiro would have asked her what she meant, but at that
moment he saw that the crawler was moving over the spoil
heaps toward the amphitheater. Singh was running toward it,
waving his arms, and Pinheiro started after him. Distinguished
visitors or not, they couldn't run all over the workings! As
Pinheiro came out of the shadow of the amphitheater's bowl,
he saw a dust cloud boiling out of the pass, and then the things
moving within it, dozens of huge animals lumbering across the
cindery valley floor.

Pinheiro stopped, staring with disbelief. The crawler was very
close now, diesel motors roaring as it started to climb the first
of the spoil heaps. Singh danced at the top, for all the worlds
like a matador facing down a bull and—and there was a flash of

red flame that rolled over the crawler and the top of the heap.
Something knocked Pinheiro down. There was a roaring in his
ears; the side of his face was numb. Things were falling to the
ground all around him, falling out of boiling smoke and dust.
Some of the things were on fire.

Someone grabbed Pinheiro's arm, helped him up. It was Jose
Carrerras. The engineer put his face close to Pinheiro's and
yelled, "You okay? What is this crazy stuff?"

Pinheiro could feel blood running down his neck. He couldn't
quite get his breath. The crawler was aflame from end to end, its
bones glowing inside the flames. "Zithsas," he managed to say
at last.

The creatures were coming on very fast. A hundred of them
at least; it was hard to tell with all the dust they were raising.
Pinheiro said, "I think we had better get underground."

"Where the fuck are the guards, Pinheiro? We can't keep
those monsters off by ourselves."

Pinheiro said, "I don't think the guards are in a position
to help anyone. Someone took out the crawler. They'll have
taken out the guards, too." Silvery figures were running up
the slope beside the amphitheater. Pinheiro started after them,
and Carrerras caught his arm when he stumbled dizzily, helped
him along.

Just as they reached the mounds covering the sunken living
quarters, the first zithsa threw itself over the crest of the spoil
heaps. It was twice as big as the still-burning crawler. Its flanks
glittered blackly; its great head, frilled by irregular spines, lowered as it looked around. Atop of its flat skull, the blowhole
distended and relaxed (*zith-saaaaah!*). Claws scrabbled among
sliding stones. Sunlight slashed rainbows along the black scales
of its back.

Another slid past it, and another. Dizzily, Pinheiro thought
that he glimpsed someone riding one of them, and then Carrerras
pushed him into the stairway.

Beyond the airlock, the commons was in an uproar. All of
the archaeologists were talking at once, shouting questions at
Admiral Orquito, at each other. Their voices racketed off the
curved, steel-ribbed ceiling. The Yoshida woman was sitting
off in one corner, serene and self-contained, the hood of her

environment suit pushed back from her round, scrubbed face.

Pinheiro's wounded head was throbbing; his mouth seemed to be full of dust. Jose Carrerras came back with a medikit. A little pistol was tucked into the waistband of his orange trousers.

"That popgun won't do any good," Pinheiro said, as Carrerras touched a little stick to his face; instantly the wounded side went numb.

Carrerras said, "They killed Singh. He isn't here, and was standing right in front of the crawler. . . . Just hold still, now."

The first wad of wet cotton he wiped across Pinheiro's cheek came away red. The next, pink. Pinheiro allowed Carrerras to spray the wound with dressing. He was remembering what had happened. It was becoming real. The crawler blown apart, the threads of smoke punctuating the rim of the hills. The zithsas. He brought his face close to Carrerras's and shouted above the din. "Has anyone called up the guard posts?" The spray-on dressing made his jaw feel spongy.

"That aide of Orquito's maybe. She's over trying to fire up the com net."

"I should do something about that, I think."

Carrerras grabbed his wrist. "You sit down, man. Nothing we can do down here except wait for the guards to come. We Brazilians should stick together."

"Keep that pistol in your pants," Pinheiro told the drilling engineer, and shrugged off his grip and pushed through the crowd, ignoring questions shouted at him from all sides. The blond aide was crammed into the communications cubbyhole in the far corner of the commons. She was fiddling with the controls, but the screens over her head were showing only raster lines of interference.

Pinheiro pushed in beside her, told her that she should let him do his job.

She looked up, something mean and unforgiving crimping one corner of her mouth. "If you know how to run this thing, Major, I want you to call Naval Headquarters."

"Just leave it to me, Seyoura. Please."

The aide relinquished the seat with an impatient gesture. Pinheiro ran through the shortwave—nothing from any of the guard posts: those thin threads of smoke: real—and then unlocked the little cover over the controls of the dish antenna, the emergency link via the transpolar satellite to the Naval Head-quarters at Esnovograd. But that wasn't working either. "Maybe the zithsas carried away the antennae complex," he said.

The aide said, "You will keep trying."

"Later, maybe. Why don't you go and look after your admiral there?"

"Oh, he enjoys himself," the aide said, but stalked over any-way, pushing through the people around white-haired Admiral Orquito, taking his elbow and saying something in his ear. The admiral looked over at Pinheiro, shook his head faintly.

Pinheiro had turned back to the useless com panel when he heard the burring vibration. The archaeologists' excited chatter died away; even the Yoshida woman looked up.

"Fucking hell," Jose Carrerras said. "That's my prolapse drill."

Pinheiro remembered the one thing he'd thought had to be unreal: the glimpse he'd had of a rider on one of the zithsas, back of the frill of horns around the beast's neck. The noise climbed in pitch, and the ribbed metal ceiling groaned. Everyone had moved to the edges of the room.

"Heads down," Carrerras said. He had taken his pistol out of his waistband. "When that thing holes through—"

It did.

Pinheiro instinctively clapped his hands over his eyes, but the light was still hurtfully bright; for an instant he thought he saw the bones of his hands against the glare. There was an acrid smell of burning metal, a brief fierce gust of air as the cool overpressured atmosphere of the living quarters equilibrated with the hot thin air outside. Blinking back tears, Pinheiro scrambled to his feet as the first of the intruders dropped through the smoking hole in the ceiling. Carrerras brought up his silly lit-tle pistol, and the man fired from his hip, a single shot that blew away half of Carrerras's head and knocked his body to the floor.

There were half a dozen intruders now, swinging easily down a rope ladder but careful not to touch the sides of the hole they'd drilled. Lean, wolfish-looking men, they all wore silvery cloaks over loose trousers and jerkins. Zithsa-hide boots, long hair tied back by red bandannas. Laser prods in wide, intricately braided belts. If they weren't zithsa hunters, they'd gone to a lot of trouble to look as authentic as possible.

The first was holstering his weapon, a pistol with a short, fat barrel and a grip of crosshatched bone. He looked around with a grin, his eyes icy blue in a lined, deeply tanned face. The little finger of his left hand was sheathed in silver; that made him either a hawker or a netter, Pinheiro couldn't quite remember which. If he really was a hunter. He said, in Russian, "Who here is leader?"

Pinheiro volunteered that he was. The aide was whispering in Admiral Orquito's ear. The old man nodded, looking not at all alarmed. "We're researchers, *gospodin*," Pinheiro added. "There is nothing of value."

"Do not worry, we come not to steal your data or relics of the mist demons." The tall man turned, flaring his silvery cloak with deliberate theatricality. His silver finger guard was pointed at Yoshida. "We have come for you, Dr. Yoshida."

The little Oriental woman stood, composed as ever. She said, "Did you really need to be so dramatic?"

"As needs must. We wish the Ten Worlds to know of this. You will come, please?"

"Yes, of course. I'm sorry," she said to Pinheiro, "about your friend. It's not the way I would have chosen."

"And the guards," Pinheiro said, burning with outrage. "They killed the guards too. More than fifty people, Seyoura!"

"Oh no," the zithsa hunter said. "Most ran when they saw zithsas coming; the rest are only disarmed and temporarily disabled, although we did burn their outpost. No doubt even now they are making their way into valley to reach you. Which is why, Dr. Yoshida, we must be going."

Pinheiro expected them to climb back up through the hole they'd drilled, but they filed into the airlock, the leader last of all, flourishing his pistol mockingly at the shocked archaeologists. But what was to haunt Major Pinheiro for the rest of his days was not the zithsa hunter's sly triumphant smile, but the Yoshida woman's calm acceptance of her kidnapping. As if it meant nothing at all to her; as if it were no more real than the vision she'd had in the ruins.

Part 1

ʌʌʌʌʌ

Bright
Fallen Angels

1

OUTRACING NIGHT, TALBECK, DUKE BARLSTILKIN V, flew by rented subsonic plane from Los Angeles to the spaceport at Melbourne, the third largest spaceport on Earth, where he parted company with his entourage of fixers, medical technicians, entertainers (even a sulky Talent), and secretaries. They raved through the warren of underground halls and corridors like a pocket riot, scattering ordinary passengers and dodging security guards, finally crowding onto a shuttle that went north to São Paulo, taking with them someone who looked remarkably like Talbeck: a burly, black-haired, blue-eyed man, half his face a raw sheet of burn-scarred skin. And the RUN Police tail went that way, too, while Talbeck caught a stratocruiser that arced high above the turning globe, a thirty minute low orbital flight that came down at the river port of Chungking, in the province of Szechwan in the Democratic Union of China, on the shore of the Yangtze Kiang.

It was raining, in China.

The gentle summer rain drifted through the indistinct light of a tropical dawn, hazing the signal lights of the high-masted ships that plied the broad, muddy river. Little stalls, sheltered by red and blue canvas awnings, lined the road out of the spaceport, where by the flare of glotubes smiling, round-cheeked schoolgirls sold oranges and incense sticks and wads of fake money. It was one of the many feast days of the lunar calendar, a time for obeisance to the myriad petty gods who ordered the daily lives of the peasants. Old women dressed in neatly pressed samfoos were lighting small pyres by the roadside in the soft rain, bowing to guttering wisps of smoke with intently devout expressions, splayed fingers pressed together in prayer. Old men knelt on wet grass before smoldering piles of incense and offerings of fruit or flasks of rice wine, or set fire to bright red, tissue paper banknotes, shaking ashes from horny-nailed fingers.

On impulse, Talbeck Barlstilkin asked his groundcar to stop. He bought wads of fake banknotes from an astonished girl and set fire to them with a chemical match. The old women and the old men looked at him sideways, puzzled by this exotic stranger who had stepped out of the groundcar's gleaming white teardrop. A big foreigner dressed all in black, his face half-ruined, eyes closed, lips moving as his offering burned out and its ashes fluttered up into rainy air. A grim unwelcome intrusion into the eternal unchanging rhythm of their lives, an implied menace that seemed to hang like a stain in the brightening air long after he had climbed back into his groundcar and disappeared down the road to the city.

Talbeck spent most of the day in Chungking, closeted with the chief of the local police until he was sure that he had not been followed. The police chief, whose brother-in-law was factor of the warehousing company which was a wholly owned subsidiary of one of Talbeck's transport companies, offered a full escort, but Talbeck refused as politely as he could—it took more than an hour—and flew the hired aircar himself to the house in the mountains.

The sky had cleared and the first stars were pricking through when he brought the aircar down on the house's pad—a clumsy landing that jarred the vehicle's frame; he hadn't flown anything for years.

The house was perched on a high crag, overlooking bamboo forest that dropped steeply into misty gorges. The bonded servant who tended it was waiting for Talbeck in the shade of the stand of tree ferns which framed the house's giant double doors. She was almost as tall as her master, ugly and impassive in loose black utilitarian blouse and trousers, hair swept back to show the small metal plates inset in each temple. The guest was gone, she told him, and didn't even blink when her owner's pent-up anxiety broke through for a moment and he slapped her hard on the face.

Talbeck was instantly calm again. "Where is she?"

"Three point eight kilometers northwest, in the forest. She is building a fire, and thinks herself unobserved."

Talbeck sighed. The news of Dorthy Yoshida's safe delivery had come just as the group of Golden he'd been traveling with had split up after one of them had got himself killed when a set piece involving an ephemeral and the bull dancers of Los Angeles had gone awry. When Antonio's medics had cooled his body and taken it away for repair, the others had gone their own ways. Talbeck had been about to return to his house in São Paulo—one of the houses that he allowed the RUN Police to know about—when he had received the message that Dorthy Yoshida had been successfully smuggled to Earth. Now, his body still working to a clock half a dozen time zones away, his mind seething with half a hundred possible calamities, everything was down to him.

"Get me a torch and a sonic caster," he said. "I'll track her down myself."

When Talbeck found Dorthy Yoshida it had started to rain again, hardly more than a condensed mist that seemed to hang between the swaying boles of the giant bamboos, pattering on their lanceolate leaves and dripping onto the rich mold of the earth. Dorthy Yoshida must have known that he was coming even before she saw the light of his torch, but she had not run. That was something, anyhow.

She had built a fire in the middle of a rocky outcrop. A bowl, cunningly woven of bamboo leaves and hung high over the flames from three bent poles, was steaming furiously. Dorthy Yoshida crouched over it, her back to Talbeck as he picked his way over mossy stones. Without turning around, she said, "It's almost ready, Seyour, if you don't mind sharing with me."

The bowl held a shallow bubbling broth of bamboo shoots and wild mushrooms. Talbeck switched off the torch and hunkered down beside her. "I had hoped that you would be enjoying my hospitality."

She said "I didn't ask to be brought here," and showed him the little pistol she'd concealed inside one baggy sleeve, its needle-thin bore aimed at his face.

Some client must have left it behind after a hunting trip. Talbeck bit down a spasm of anger, thinking, *be calm, be careful.* . . . He said, "Do you really think you'd be allowed to kill me?"

It was a cool lie, but he knew enough about her Talent to be able to conceal things from her scrutiny. In fact, no one but the bonded servant knew that he was here—and she was run by a computer, and hardly counted. His entourage was half a world away; he could die here and they'd never get to him in time. He grinned at the thought, though he wasn't ready for death, not yet. It was only just beginning.

Dorthy Yoshida laid the pistol on moss crisped brown by the fire's heat. Her smile was hardly there. Talbeck saw that she was holding herself very still. She said, "You're trying to confuse me, so you're probably lying. But what the hell, here we are. Who are you, anyhow?"

"My name is Talbeck Barlstilkin."

"Now, I know that name. Wait. God, yes. Duncan Andrews mentioned you in one of his wilder raps. You're Golden, like him. An agatherin grower from Elysium. A dilettante, he said."

"Perhaps it's true, but not the way poor dead Duncan meant it." His smile was cruelly distorted by the sheet of scar tissue that caved in the left side of his face. "Duncan actually had to go out and lead a scientific expedition to a wild, dangerous world to try and prove his worth, and he was killed for his trouble. I have been content to wait, to choose the time to act."

"You don't mind if I eat, do you? As I said, you're welcome to share."

"You know, my house has anything you could want. I'm

delighted that I managed to smuggle you to Earth, Dr. Yoshida, but I'm also a little insulted that you want to run away without even waiting to find out why."

"I've been the pawn of someone or other for so long now. . . . It was really good, to believe that I was actually doing something on my own. Five years of being debriefed by the Navy—that's what they called it, anyhow. There's stuff in my head, you know. The Alea put it there, when I was on P'thrsn. The Navy has been trying to get it out."

"I know."

"Of course you know." Her laugh rose in pitch and she bit her lip. "Otherwise," she said, after a moment, "you wouldn't have rescued me. But you see, even I don't know what the Alea did to me. On Novaya Rosya it gave me a vision of the deep past, of the time before the Alea destroyed a whole civilization. But I don't know *why*. When I was on P'thrsn, I became the unwitting participant in the suicide of the Alea family's lineal leader. She was so very smart, her collective intelligence went back a million years, and so full of guilt. Not for the civilization she'd destroyed so that her family could remain safely in hiding, but for the sisters she had to murder when they opposed her. She manipulated poor Duncan Andrews into a position where he had to kill her, and her retinue fell on him and tore him apart. But I was allowed to escape. I'm still in her grip, you see! I'm still not free! What's in my head—"

"What may or may not be in your head is only partly why you are here, as a matter of fact."

Dorthy Yoshida was calm again. "Yeah? Look, excuse me while I eat, okay? It's my first meal today, and I've been looking forward to it." She used two slivers of bamboo as chopsticks to lift steaming morsels from the bowl. Firelight struck under her chin, shadowed her almond-shaped eyes. Her black hair had been cropped so short that the bumps of her skull showed through. She chewed and swallowed. "I'm pretty good at this. Living in the wild. I have the pistol and a knife, a sheet of plastic to sleep in. I managed on a lot less, in a far stranger place than this."

"And what did you think running away would do?"

"People should know what I learned on P'thrsn. I made that promise to myself while I was waiting to be rescued. Not just a few politicians, a few of the Navy brass. But all the people on all the worlds. I guess I didn't get very far, huh? I mean, you own this mountain range for all I know."

"Just the house and a few thousand hectares around it. And I don't own it, or not directly. A rice-growing collective uses it to entertain business clients. I happen to be a major shareholder in the collective through a holding company based on Luna."

"Okay, I'm impressed. That means Navy security or the RUN Police won't catch us, right?"

"Not for a couple of days. The best estimate is sixty hours, actually, the worst slightly less than twenty." Talbeck Barlstilkin settled a little closer to the fire. It was cold, here on the dark mountainside, in the bamboo forest, in the gentle rain of Earth. "And what were you going to tell the people of the Ten Worlds, Dr. Yoshida? The peasants down in the valleys here, for instance. What *could* you tell people who don't care anything about the next province, let alone another world. They've lived the same way for three thousand years. Dynastic emperors, the British Empire, Communism, Noncentrist Democracy, it's all the same to them. What's important is getting three crops of rice a year. Did you think they would listen to a ragged Cassandra staggering down from the wilderness crying woe, woe, thrice woe! There are demons at the center of the Galaxy, coming for us!"

Dorthy Yoshida said, slowly and seriously, "They aren't demons, only a renegade family of the Enemy. And they might not be coming for us. They might have all died a million years ago."

"And then again," Talbeck said, "they just might still be alive."

"What do you know?" she said. Her gaze was suddenly intent. "You know all about P'thrsn, it seems. You know all that I know, or all that I've told the Navy at any rate, but you hired zithsa hunters to kidnap me on Novaya Rosya, you had me cooled down and shipped in a coldcoffin in some freighter's hold, flew me here in an unmarked 'thopter with a bonded servant as pilot. I mean, I appreciate the drama, but I'd like to know the reason behind it? What else do you know?"

"Come back to the house," Talbeck said. "I'm not as young as I once was. I could catch a cold out here."

Dorthy Yoshida set her face; she looked very defiant, and very young. "And if I don't? I can be bloody difficult, if I want to be."

"Oh, you don't really have a choice," Talbeck said, and shot her with the sonic caster, jumping up to catch her as she slumped over. The woven basket tipped wildly, and spilled broth hissed into the fire.

2

$\textbf{R}$IDING REAR GUARD HIGH ABOVE THE SKEWED DIAMOND of the other fliers in her combat team, Suzy Falcon saw the accident from beginning to end, a long minute in which her world fell apart.

Shelley was flying point leader, the psychedelic patterns on his wings vivid above Titan's rumpled red snowscape, the banner bearing the yellow and black chevron ensign of the team's owner snapping smartly in the -200°C tail wind. It was clear and calm, the sun almost vertical. Thermals rose straight up from the ridges and outcrops of black siderite which broke the surface of the Glacier of Worlds. It was a perfect day for combat.

The rival team had launched themselves from the platform only moments before, bright clustered dots spiraling high above the towers and domes of the city of Urbis which crowned the sharp ridge of the Tallman Scarp. In combat, height was everything. It meant superior vision; it could be converted to kinetic energy at the tilt of a wing, a steep stoop at just the right angle to drag the line of your tail-banner across your opponent's and cut it free. In the first minutes of combat, everyone climbed as fast and as high as he or she could.

Shelley had just begun the turn to catch the updraft of the next thermal when it happened. Suzy saw his left wing dip briefly, primaries glittering as they flew back along the control edge. For a moment she thought that he'd simply misjudged the angle of attack, too eager to start his climb. Probably impatient, always his failing, hoping to save face by finding that treacherous thermal instead of gliding down and picking up enough speed to tack against the wind. But Shelley didn't go into a glide. It was as if he couldn't bring his left wing down. It passed its critical stalling angle and lost all lift, slowing him further, pulling him sharply left, forcing his right wing up.

Something more than the airy thrill of flight yawned in Suzy's belly. The subtle tugs of pressure on primary vanes thrumming in her control-gloved fingertips, lift like a plucked bow thrilling along her spine, suddenly dwindled to the periphery of her attention. She was all eyes.

She saw Carlos Perez and Ana Lenidov split right and left, bright wings spiraling up the thermal in opposite directions while Shelley yawed wide, folding his right wing back to try and recover, to go into a dive to pick up speed and regain lift. Artemio Gonzales at trailing point swept below him.

And then Suzy felt the surging sideways slip as she caught the rising funnel of warmer atmosphere (relatively warm: but for her suit it would freeze her to her very marrow in seconds; it happened to fliers). The stall warning beeped briefly in her helmet and she flexed the lifting surfaces of her wings, spread the primaries to give herself a stable vector. The corduroy surface of the Glacier of Worlds tipped away far below as she circled higher. When she saw Shelley again, he was trying to come out of his dive.

Too late. Too fast. When Shelley tried to level out, the outspread primaries of his right wing jammed, rolling him right, pressure enormous over the wing's curved lifting surface—and something broke. The right wing was flung back, trailing. It must have broken his arm, must have. Someone was screaming. It might have been Shelley. It seemed to go on forever, while his bright wings folded up around him and he dwindled down toward final impact on the Glacier's dirty methane ice.

*   *   *

Much later, Suzy ended up in one of the practice rooms, the only quiet place in the whole of the fliers' warren. She was wrung out by the long, tearful recriminations and commiserations with the rest of her team, and she'd had to fight her way through determined newstapers when she'd finally left the staging area, after Shelley's body had been brought in.

The others had rallied around, declared willingness to fly one wing short. Artemio Gonzales swore that was what Shelley would have wanted; he was probably right, too. But Suzy knew what Duke Bonadventure would say to that. Wouldn't want to lose face by having his team wiped out in the next heat, so he'd want to withdraw. And Suzy knew, too, that the others weren't ready to hear that just yet, so she'd suppressed her opinions, made vague promises about recruiting a solo from the pool—which she would have to do anyway, even if only to get ready for the next tournament, when the city's perpetual Carnival came around to its beginning once more.

And then she'd tried to walk away from the whole mess, right into a gaggle of hungry newstapers. She'd knocked one on his ass, swatted one of the inquisitive remotes darting around her clean out of the air, thrown it over the railing of the companionway. Dumb, dumb, oh so dumb, Suzy! It had been on the net in a moment, a little extra live action for the *enthusiasmos*. It was a very comprehensive disaster.

Now she sat cross-legged beneath the simulator, blues rumbling in her ears, one hand wrapped around a tarnished silver flask, the other rapping rhythms on oily concrete. A tall, slender woman, in black jeans and a vest of supple black leather, head bent lower than the hump of grafted muscle on her back, her bleached hair in a ragged urchin cut, her muscular arms bare. The left was wrapped from shoulder to wrist by a tattooed dragon in polychrome gold and scarlet and green: its scaly tail curled around her biceps, its wide red mouth breathed flame across her wrist. She sat and listened to the music and sipped plum brandy. And tried not to think about Shelley's fall, and the fall of all her fellow singleship pilots during the Campaigns.

The past had a habit of sneaking up on her at times like this. The smell of the practice room, cold, filtered air feathered with oil and stale rubber, was the smell of the launch pod of the support ship. The tightness in her abdomen was the feeling she'd had on being woken the morning of each mission. Moonfaced Chinese steward gently shaking her awake, announcing it was oh six hundred. Forcing down the traditional steak breakfast, making strained jokes with the other jockeys of her wing. The gentle hands of her flight attendants as they eased her into the polysilicon holster of the combat singleship. Plugging her in, buttoning her up. Oil and warm rubber, the air plant humming back of her head, headup displays ghosting false constellations across the scape of stars.

She'd been the only survivor of the wing at the end, when the Navy had pulled back and torched the system clean of the Enemy. Keeping that thought in her head helped focus her anger, like the lens she'd used as a kid, focusing sunlight to an intense burning point, crisping ants with a minute satisfying sizzle.

Twelve missions, nearly a record. And then the one time after it all that she didn't want to think about. *Fucking Beta Corvus. No green world, no fortune. Slag time. Not even much of a science bonus.* Suckered by the percentages like most of the singleship veterans. Fame and fortune held up to her, and all she got was an exclusive one-time-only glimpse of a bunch of rocks and a gas giant so far out it made fucking *Pluto* look inviting. And the cartel that'd sponsored her had been nice about it, said look, we'll forget your debts. You just work Urbis a while, the combat teams, a different kind of flying is all. And that's what she'd done, first as one of the cartel's solos, then as team leader for Duke Bonadventure. For ten fucking years.

So Suzy sipped a little more brandy and got down with the music, growling out the lonesome lyrics, rapping out twelve beats to the bar 'til her knuckles started to bleed, and not even noticing.

And that was how Adam X found her, hours after the accident, tranced out on memories and music and high-octane brandy.

Glotubes flicked on high above as he stalked into the chamber, throwing the shadow of the simulator over sweating rock walls: its curved and recurved wings, the catenaries of the prone harness hung down like entrails. His steady footsteps echoed loudly, but Suzy didn't look up until he was standing over her.

"Christ," she said, "how did you find me?" The music was still playing in her ears, and with a sigh she took out the player and switched it off and set it beside her on stained concrete.

Adam X sat on the floor beside her. He was a tall man, massing close to one hundred fifty kilos, but he moved as sweetly as a cat. As if a pack of cards had been shuffled to reveal a new suit, he frowned and said solemnly, "Suzanne. I am so sorry."

"Shit, how can you be sorry 'bout anything. And don't you call me *Suzanne*. Call me Suzy, you got to call me anything."

Her name really was Suzanne, Suzanne Marie Thibodeaux. But that wasn't any kind of handle for a competitive flier, so she'd topped and tailed it and stuck it in front of her mother's maiden name. She was Suzy Falcon, now, the hottest and fastest combat flier on Titan, until time came for her luck to run out. It suited her fine. Suzanne Marie Thibodeaux had died a while back, in the last days of the Campaign, after the Final Solution run.

Adam X reshuffled his features, dealt her a smile. That wasn't his real name, either. It was Duke Bonadventure's little joke. Bonadventure owned Adam, just as (in a different way) he owned Suzy, the others in the team. When Adam leaned forward to take Suzy's hand with fake solicitude, light glinted on the little metal plates, one on each temple, that were half-hidden by his fashionably curled fringe. Suzy repressed a little shudder at his touch; those hands, white, long fingered, immaculately manicured, had taken apart at least a dozen children. His palm was smooth and warm.

He said, "I feel what I am allowed to feel, Suzy. At the moment I feel sorry about Shelley."

Suzy took her hand away and lifted her flask of brandy (her big, knotted elbow joint clicking) for want of anything better to do with it. She said, "I don't need your sympathy, seeing as it's all simulation." Brandy's fire hollowed the cave of her mouth, ran a hot wire down to the pit of her stomach.

But Adam X couldn't be insulted. He picked up the player and the aching music filled her ears again. His too, of course: like Suzy, he was wired for sound. He was wired for everything. His eyes lost focus as he accessed the computer in Duke Bonadventure's house, and in that moment Suzy saw him for what he was. A tool. A meat puppet, micrometer-thin pseudoneurons woven all through his cortex making his every move. Sometimes she wondered if anything of the mass murderer still lived. In the muscles perhaps, close to the bone, the way her body remembered the inculcated reflexes of flying a singleship.

The music went off and Adam X said, "Robert Johnson. Country blues, early twentieth century. Why do you listen to such music, Suzy? It is all about male sexuality and death."

"I like it," she said, and took the player from him.

"Johnson recorded that song just before he died. Poisoned by a woman, he died on his knees, barking like a dog. So much for art."

"Some people say he was poisoned *because* of a woman, given a bottle of poisoned whiskey at a party because he was coming on to the host's wife. Though maybe you wouldn't appreciate the difference."

"So much of the music you listen to is about death, Suzy. It is worrying."

"I suppose that you're going to tell me that people talk about my . . . my *musical preferences*. Let 'em gossip; I don't care." But she knew very well what the other combat fliers said: that she was flirting with the idea of death, had been ever since the end of the Alea Campaigns. For why else would she still be flying at age twenty-nine? Truth was, she didn't fly to court a flier's death (the sudden rippling collapse of Shelley's wing, his death wail all the way down to the unforgiving ground). No, not at all. It was simply that there was nothing else left to her.

She said, "Just quit playing at being a person and tell me the message you're here to give. Okay? 'Cause I don't much feel like company right now."

"Duke Bonadventure sends his condolences, Suzy."

She knew what was coming. She felt as though she were free-falling right there on the dirty concrete floor.

"Of course, the accident means that your team will withdraw from competition."

As though her insides had been cleanly haled away, and air was rushing through the hollow space.

Suzy got to her feet, fists clenched. She said, "There must be a hundred solos looking for team action. Jesus Christ, I know most of them; I know two or three who can fit right in. I can audition tomorrow, have them run through our moves—they'll have watched us; they'll know what's on. I can do it in a week, and we've two. . . ."

"And exhaust yourself and the rest of the team. No."

"That's your fucking cool computer speaking, right? It don't know about it. All it knows is how to play it safe."

"You are tired. You are upset."

Suzy was so mad she could have torn those metal plates right out of his head. Instead, she shoved a hand into one of the control mitts of the practice rig, balled her fist, and brought the wing that arched above Adam X's head swooping down. She felt the impact in the tips of her fingers as primaries rattled against concrete.

But Adam X didn't even blink. "Please," he said, calmly looking up at her as if nothing had happened. "I know of the bond between the four of you. I know you will want to honor Shelley's memory by still trying to compete. But I know, too, that it is not possible to integrate a new member into your team in such a short time."

"I'll see Bonadventure. I'll make him understand."

"That is good. Because he would very much like to see you, Suzy. He has a proposition for you. He needs a pilot."

"Go ask a freespacer. I retired from that a long while ago."

Adam X said "He needs someone with combat experience." He said, "He wants someone who can fly against the Enemy."

3

D ORTHY YOSHIDA WOKE WITH A PARCHED MOUTH AND a headache. She was dressed in white linen trousers and a white linen tunic belted with a wide black sash, and lying on a bed, as big and soft as a cloud, that seemed to stand in the middle of a rocky clearing in a sunlit pine forest. A huge, red silk banner, painted with yellow Han ideograms, slanted a dozen meters above, glowing with the late morning light of Earth's sun.

A spring bubbled up from beneath a tilted slab of granite. Dorthy drank with cupped hands, splashed cold water on her face.

The water, the rocks, the soft turf: those were real, at any rate. It was difficult to tell where the room ended and the hologram of the pine forest began, and it took her a while to find the way out: which was to follow the little gravel-bedded stream fed by the spring. It ran between two towering pines which faded away as Dorthy passed beneath them into a still bigger space roofed with the interlocking triangular panes of a geodesic dome. The panes were tinted bright blue. Across a hectare of emerald green turf, half-hidden by a stand of (real) pine trees, a waterfall cascaded down a high rock face into a huge circular pool. Dorthy crossed the red-painted wooden bridge that arched over the water, pausing to look at the huge koi carp which sculled above clean white pebbles. The planks of the bridge vibrated gently beneath her bare feet. She nodded to herself and went on.

A dank mossy tunnel opening onto a conservatory pierced the rock face behind the pool. Raked gravel paths looped around stands of fruit trees under more blue-tinted glass. Munching sweet peach flesh, Dorthy pushed through the curtain of ivy

32

that shrouded the only other doorway, and found herself waist deep in drifts of stars.

Talbeck Barlstilkin turned toward her across a hundred thousand simulated light-years, his mutilated face grotesquely underlit by the bright, close-packed stars of the Galactic core. "Come and see, Dr. Yoshida," he said. "I'll explain everything!"

He must have been waiting for her, Dorthy thought, but how had he known she would find her way there? Posthypnotic suggestion? With a moment of vertiginous panic she wondered just how deeply she was trapped, just what was wanted of her. Perhaps none of this was real. She could be asleep; she had spent so much of the time after P'thrsn asleep, dreaming under compulsion. Perhaps that was why she had accepted what had happened to her so easily. After so many years of dreaming, nothing seemed quite real any more.

Still, the orrery compelled attention. Hung right in front of her was the Galaxy's familiar triple spiral, stars like packed diamond dust winding into the lanes of dark gases which shrouded the glowing nucleus where Barlstilkin stood. The thing that lived inside Dorthy's head stirred. She could feel it, nothing more. Without counteragent to the secretions of her implant, her Talent was little more than an unspecific low-grade empathy, and the Navy had never allowed her access to counteragent, not since P'thrsn. But that didn't stop her trying to probe her guest, as her tongue might return again and again to an aching tooth.

"Known space," Barlstilkin said, and the glittering tinsel of four hundred billion stars vanished in an eye blink. A few hundred points of light filled the orrery now, most of them dim red dwarfs. Barlstilkin was a shadowy sketch, black on black. He said, "Altair. 1745. BD plus twenty degrees 2465. Procyon. Sol." And each star brightened in turn: a brilliant blood-red ruby; two dull spots of carnelian, close together; a sapphire; a diamond. Sol was in the center.

"Very pretty. Really, I am impressed. But why are you showing me this?"

"Two more steps," Barlstilkin said, "then we'll be there. First of all, I'm widening the frame."

All around, other stars seemed to drift into the oval room; and the bubble of known space shrank until it was lost in an ocean of stars.

"Now we run proper motions backward from the present, about a thousand years per second in real time." Barlstilkin's voice was cool and controlled, with the faintest upward lilt at the end of each sentence. Dorthy couldn't see his face and, with her deadened Talent, could do no more than sense his presence.

Stars began to drift like motes of dust in a sunbeam, some moving faster than others, some swirling counter to the general motion, but most slanting from left to right, sinking toward the floor.

"That's the proper motion in this part of the Galactic arm," Talbeck Barlstilkin said, "but of course there are rogues. Here's Barnard's Star, for instance. . . ." And a faint red point moving three or four times more quickly than most of the motes flared so brightly that it illuminated Barlstilkin's forefinger.

Dorthy said, "Proper motion of about ten arc seconds. All this is well-known." Yet the display was compelling. It aroused an atavistic oceanic feeling, of self dissolving out into the boundless Universe. But she couldn't tell if that was her true self, or what she had come to call, privately, her guest.

"To be sure. I know, of course, that you were studying to be an astronomer, before the Alea Campaigns. But please now watch this point—" and another star flared, dirty green-white. It was moving counter to the general motion, like a streak now it had been brightened; in a few moments it had flown out of the frame.

"That's real?" Dorthy felt a kind of sick eagerness that was not excitement, that was more than yearning. The closest she could come to defining it was the dependency burned into every cell of a drug addict, so strong she'd felt a ghost of it days after the few times she'd skimmed the minds of such people in her salad days at the Kamali–Silver Institute—a desperate need to know everything about this, without knowing why she needed to know.

"It's about seventy light-years away right now," Barlstilkin said. Dorthy's eyes were becoming accustomed to the velvety, star-spattered dark. She could make out his bulk, looming against drifting stars like a vast dust cloud, like one of the gods with which humans had once populated the heavens. He said, "When the first comprehensive catalogs were being made, seven hundred years ago, it was about one hundred and ten light-years away, coming toward us out of Sagittarius. By us, I mean the Solar System. Extrapolation shows that it will pass close to Sol in twelve hundred years, perhaps so close that the orbits of the planets will be perturbed. The difficulties of measuring the proper motion of something that's heading right down our throats leave a wide margin of error, as you may imagine. In fact, the star is listed in a couple of the old catalogs, but no one noticed how unusual it was."

"Hardly the word for a star moving at what, about six percent the speed of light?"

"Indeed. With a relative proper motion of close to seventeen thousand kilometers per second, it is the fastest star in the Galaxy. It is a very strange star, too. All sorts of odd metal lines in it, and it seems to be rotating very quickly, enough to distort it into an oblate spheroid. Almost enough to tear it apart. If it was on the main sequence, it would have been torn apart long ago, in fact, but of course white dwarfs have a nicely dense uniform structure."

Dorthy had been working something out in her head, a conclusion so fantastic that she had to run through the figures again. She said slowly and reluctantly, "It came from the Galactic core, then, about half a million years ago."

"Oh yes. I know something of that story already, Dr. Yoshida, from the same source that told me about the fastest star. Half a million years ago, the Alea who planoformed the world we call P'thrsn, refugees from a civil war in the Galactic core, discovered that there was an interstellar civilization emerging on the second planet of Epsilon Eridani. The Alea were worried that this civilization would attract the attention of those from whom they had fled, and so they fired off a small moon at close to the speed of light. It more or less disintegrated when it crossed the dusty gravity well of Epsilon Eridani, but enough fragments hit the second planet to ruin its biosphere forever. Well, I need not tell you any more about Novaya Rosya, I think. You have been there, after all."

"But the family which destroyed the civilization of Novaya Rosya never had the kind of technology that could accelerate a *star*! And there was no kind of civilization at all on Earth then, nothing to destroy!"

"Of course not. But who did the Alea family flee from, Dr. Yoshida? Who was the enemy of the Enemy?"

"The marauders," Dorthy said. "You think they did this? That they could see into the future?"

"I don't know. But there is something *you* should know, Dorthy. There is at least one planet orbiting the hypervelocity star. Who would put a world around a weapon?"

Later, they sat on a terrace that seemed to overlook crags and terraced bamboo forest tumbling down into an ocean of mist. The impassive bonded servant set down a lacquer tray bearing a teapot and porcelain bowls so thin that they were translucent, stepped backward to wait silently by the rough rock wall.

"Jasmine tea is a weakness of mine," Talbeck Barlstilkin said, as he poured.

Dorthy, looking out across simulated kilometers of mist toward rounded mountaintops, took her bowl of tea distractedly. There was even a bird circling in the middle air, sunlight flashing on its wings as it widened its gyre. She watched the illusionary bird circle higher and higher, sipped scented tea, and thought about all she'd been shown.

There had been a projected simulation of how the runaway star had been accelerated. A pair of white dwarf stars swinging in close to the black hole at the center of the Galaxy, one star captured, spilling its guts across the sky in a nova flare, the other gaining its partner's momentum and flying away at a tangent: gone in the blink of an eye. Impossibly, it had taken a gas giant with it, something Barlstilkin's simulation couldn't explain. The orbits of the binary's component stars had been so close-coupled that neither partner could have had a planet—and besides, any planet would have been lost in the Newtonian encounter with the black hole.

And there had been a simulation of what would happen if the hypervelocity star passed close to Sol. Cataclysms as tides pulled apart the outer planets and stripped away their moons; the orbits of the myriad asteroids in the Belt collapsing sunward; the orbits of Mars and Earth widening eccentrically. Measurements of the hypervelocity star's relative motion were still unrefined; it was as likely to miss Sol by a light-year. But close encounter was a possibility. It could happen, and it would be a thousand times worse than the ruin of Novaya Rosya. And if the knowledge became public, no one would stop to think about probabilities, or even that the disaster wouldn't happen for twelve hundred years. . . . Dorthy felt as if she had been maneuvered into a corner. Trapped. The way the Navy had trapped her, used her for her Talent and then imprisoned her because of what had happened on P'thrsn, because of what was inside her head. She'd been freed for the same reason, but she didn't know *why*.

Barlstilkin had been watching the view quietly, sipping tea. Waiting for her to speak, Dorthy realized. She asked him, "Why are you doing this?"

"Look at my face, Dr. Yoshida. Go ahead. I'm not embarrassed by it."

"I was wondering why you haven't had it fixed—"

Her bowl shattered against the stone flags of the terrace. Barlstilkin had reached across the little table and grabbed her under the chin with a square, strong hand, pulled her head around until she was looking right into his face.

"Look at it!" His fingertips were bruising her gums through her cheeks.

She looked.

Shiny scar tissue sheeted the left side, pulled down the corner of his mouth. The eye was half-hidden, a lashless glittering crescent. Under the cap of his straight black hair, his left ear was a knob of tissue twisted around its hole. Dorthy held his gaze with her own (it hurt her more than his grip), feeling the swirling storm of his emotions. A castle on fire high above a raging sea, flames flapping up hundreds of meters, flung away by wind into the night. . . .

"You see. . . ." His voice was softer; his grip relaxed.

Dorthy pulled back. She couldn't tell if it was his anger that she was feeling, or her own.

Barlstilkin said, "It happened before the Federation of Co-Prosperity. Not long after the phase graffle was invented, and the Re-United Nations sent expeditions to find out what had happened to the old American and Russian colonies. They set up a puppet government on Elysium, decided to take control of agatherin production. When they began to force all the growers to join the Fountain of Youth Combine, my father decided to resist. He hired fifty or so mercenaries from Earth, but the RUN had a bottomless purse: they hired a fucking *army*. Their troops sacked the castle, killed my father. I escaped them, but only because I was so badly hurt they didn't recognize me. Afterward the RUN pretended to be kind, to placate the other growers. They did not steal my inheritance, and they allowed me to sit on the Combine's Council. Their mistake. It gave me money enough to do what I want. To pursue this. The Re-United Nations has kept what happened to you on P'thrsn secret, even from the other governments of the Ten Worlds. But I found out. And they've kept the hypervelocity star secret, too, even though they've already sent an expedition out to it. I'm going there too, and I want you to come with me, Dr. Yoshida. You wanted to tell all the peoples of the Federation the truth about the Alea. I want to find out the *whole* truth."

"So do I," Dorthy said, and was pleased to see his surprise. It gave her, for a moment, the feeling of being in control, ahead of the game. Trying to keep him off-balance, she asked, "But aren't we already on our way?"

Talbeck Barlstilkin smiled and waved a hand. Mountains and misty sky blew away like rags. There were only the myriad pinpoint lights of the stars, hard and bright against interplanetary night, sweeping very slowly and imperceptibly up from the balustrade.

"I should have known I couldn't fool a Talent forever," he said.

"Oh, I've been on a ship like this once before, when I was a working girl. Really, an air plant would be simpler than your greenhouse and waterfall and pine trees."

"Simpler, but not as elegant. I have . . . appearances to keep up. This ship is a lot bigger than you think it is. A relic, rather like me." He was only a bulky shadow against the stars, but Dorthy knew that he was smiling.

"And where are you taking me?"

"Why to the hypervelocity star, of course. But first, to Titan."

"Titan? But intersystem ships are only allowed to depart from Luna orbit."

"Exactly. It will take us two more days to get there. We have to pick up our pilot. Some old friends of mine are arranging that. I am no solitary schemer, Dr. Yoshida. There are almost a dozen of us engaged in this. The others look for profits to be made from exotic technologies. Ostensibly, so do I. Meanwhile, I suggest you enjoy the rest of the trip."

Dorthy knew, because she had made the journey from Earth to Titan once before, that it took a lot longer than two days. "You put me to sleep again," she said.

"I'm sorry. It was a necessary precaution, even though I had laid a false trail. I got you to Earth from Luna because the Luna port is too closely regulated. Too much Guild traffic, too much Navy. Chungking is the most obscure of all the obscure ports on Earth, but still . . ."

"I'll help you, but I won't be fucking patronized!" This time her anger was all her own. "I'll do it because everyone on Earth, everyone on the Ten Worlds, should know about what I found out on P'thrsn. Not because you want to play at revenge!"

He made hushing noises. "Of course, of course. That's why I knew you would help me. I am running in a desperate game, Dr. Yoshida. Despite my precautions, the RUN Police almost caught us as we were leaving Earth orbit. One of their ships is tailing us even now, and it will take a good deal of luck to pick up our pilot and avoid whatever reception awaits us at Titan."

Dorthy's anger had blown away. She smiled at his stilt-ed, archaic Portuguese. "If you're more comfortable speaking English," she said, "it's my second language."

"A native Australian, of course. I could be related to you, Dr. Yoshida. Many of the original colonists of Elysium were from the fifty-fourth state of the U.S.A. Now, please, have some more tea. Enjoy the view. Look, now. There. Do you see?"

Dorthy turned, and saw.

Rings tilted about his banded globe; Saturn was rising beyond the balustrade.

4

U RBIS HAD BEEN FOUNDED BY A CARTEL OF GOLDEN WHO
had intended it to be an exclusive resort, sited at the bottom of
the only permanent clear spot in Titan's smoggy clouds. That
had been thirty years ago, and in that time the cost of intrasystem
travel had plummeted. Urbis was no longer exclusive, merely
fashionable: the original arcology was lost beneath clusters of
domes and towers that climbed up and down Tallman Scarp's
sharp ridge; the bedrock was combed through with hydroponic
tunnels and reservoirs and generating plants. To escape from the
crowds and inconvenience of the perpetual Carnival, the rich
had moved out to extravagant homes in the chaotic landscape
north of the Scarp.

Riding Bonadventure's private line, Suzy watched icy pinna-
cles spin past outside the transparent wall of the little car, picked
at the tufts of the hand-woven rug on the floor with her long,
double-jointed toes, and generally tried to ignore Adam X. He
sat across from her, still and upright, hands on his knees, face
slack: no more company than a corpse, and as disturbing.

She'd given up trying to find out anything from him, was
trying to figure it out for herself. Just this one time, Suzy, think
about what you're getting into. It wasn't easy.

The Enemy. . . . They'd been burned in their asteroid habitats around BD Twenty, but there was another nest of them
not five light-years away, some ratty, marginally planoformed
world quarantined by the Navy. No one knew where they'd
all come from. They'd settled those two systems a million years
ago, could be all through the Galaxy. So, maybe some singleship
explorer had stumbled across another colony. You couldn't deal
with the Enemy—they were instantly, implacably, unrelentingly

40

hostile—but if you could torch them without destroying their stuff, it would be worth a planetary fortune. If their primary was a cool red dwarf, you could put an intersystem ship in orbit a thousand klicks above the photosphere, turn on the phase graffle, and blow up a mother of a flare. That's what the Navy had done at BD Twenty, fused all the asteroid habitats to so much slag. But if it was a planet. . . . A flare would rip a biosphere apart, but it wouldn't destroy everything. Yeah. She'd like to do that. Ants under a lens.

Suzy took a swig of plum brandy. The flask was almost empty, though she didn't really feel drunk. Just . . . disconnected.

High crags fell away as the car swept around a long curve in the elevated line. The reticulated surface of an ice field stretched to the close horizon, where streaks of altonimbus feathered the pink sky. Ahead was the singular jagged peak where Duke Bonadventure's house perched.

Once, Suzy had gone to a party there with someone she'd picked up in the city, an astronomer from Fra Mauro University who'd had a passion for twentieth century moving picture dramas. Movies. When he'd seen Bonadventure's house, suddenly revealed by the curve of the line, he'd drawn a breath and blurted, "Count Dracula's Castle!" Later, he had shown her flat, grainy, black-and-white images from one of his files, and Suzy had sort of understood what he'd meant.

Perched atop the steeply rising rock, its high crenellated walls built of massive blocks of stone, towers with tiny slitted windows at every corner, Bonadventure's house *did* look like its make-believe counterpart, even down to the huge arched gate through which the car plunged, slamming Suzy back into her seat as it slidingly decelerated into a vast marble hall.

Across from her, Adam X blinked, and slowly worked his mouth into a smile.

It was a long walk from that marble hall, along corridors wide as Age of Waste freeways, up sweeping stairways that only led to yet another corridor, through big rooms with nothing in them but huge dark paintings on the walls, and once across a transparent walkway bent over a hundred-meter drop to broken rocks and ice colder than liquid oxygen. Adam X walked quickly and

Suzy marched behind him, getting madder and madder, hardly noticing the only person they passed in all that time, a mechanic who grinned and winked at her as she hurried after Adam X. By the time they reached the room where Duke Bonadventure was waiting for her, all Suzy's caution had been burned away. Show her one of the Enemy and she'd like to rip its head off with her bare hands. If it had a head.

The room was tall and wide, big as any mall. From floor to high ceiling, white silk banners rippled over rough stone walls. Suzy padded across what seemed like a couple of hectares of deep, white carpet to the knot of people by the cavernous fireplace at the far end, where blue flames roared over a heap of simulated tree trunks—on Titan, not even Duke Gabriel Bonadventure II could afford to burn wood.

Bonadventure was standing with his back to the flames, a gorgeously embroidered gold on red silk robe slashed open over his chest. A couple of medical technicians were fussing over the readouts of a portable autodoc they'd set up on a black oak table that looked to be a thousand years old, more like stone than wood. Leads trailed from it to the diagnostic cuff around Bonadventure's arm.

"He'll talk with you in a moment," his secretary told Suzy, having intercepted her a good thirty meters from the Duke. A courteous, white-haired man in a discreetly expensive green suit, the secretary ushered her to one side of the fireplace and crooked a finger at one of the flunkies, who brought over a silver goblet on a silver tray.

Suzy sniffed at the stuff inside, clear as water, and sipped. The liquor seemed to evaporate on her tongue, tasting of cold sea air, of winter in a pine forest just after the first snow has fallen. Its bite was a moment of fire that faded to a lingering glow.

The secretary smiled. "It is a polytrophic, from Serenity."

"Yeah?"

"Which means simply that it is whatever you think it should be. Please, relax, Seyoura Falcon. Allow me to tell you what will happen. The Duke has ten minutes to give you his attention today. He will ask you if you will pilot a special expedition. Very dangerous, but very rewarding. At least, potentially. If you agree, you will be given the details."

"The Enemy," Suzy said. "I was told it was about the Enemy."

"Perhaps. We are not certain. But the probability is very high."

"I'll do it," she said, and knocked back the rest of the cool firewater.

The secretary's mild expression didn't alter. "Of course. That is why we asked you. You will rendezvous with your ship in just over a day, when it passes by Titan."

"Passes by?"

"The RUN Police are already aware of our . . . plans. We are having to be more circumspect, now."

Suzy had a sudden drunken insight. "I'm not the first you asked, am I? This is so important, you wouldn't want to get it going from ground up inside a day. Unless you didn't have a choice."

The secretary touched his silky white beard with two exquisitely manicured fingers. "I admit, Seyoura, that you are quite right. Our first pilot was arrested at Luna, as he boarded the liner for Titan. The second was arrested here, in Urbis, just yesterday."

Suzy decided to face it out as best she could. "Yeah, well I've been in retirement, so I guess I'm no prize. But I want a chance at this. At the Enemy."

The secretary smiled. "You are our last hope, Seyoura, if I may say so. Indeed, you should not really be here, but the Duke wished to talk with you before you left."

"That's good, 'cause I got a whole lot of stuff to ask him."

"Wait. Seyoura. He is not ready—"

But Suzy was already stalking across to where Bonadventure stood. One of the medics was slowly running something like a silver wand over the Golden's chest; the other was studying the fuzzy pulsing red on red pattern on a little holostage.

"You wanted to talk," Suzy said.

The secretary tried to get between Suzy and the Golden. "I am so sorry, Gabriel. She is impatient, I fear. Seyoura, you will be able to talk in a moment."

"Let her talk now," Bonadventure growled, pushing the medic away and pulling his silk robe closed. He was a short, stocky man, ugly as the pit bulls Suzy's father had bred for fighting: a grim, muscular set to his wide jaw; small, close-set eyes under a ridged brow. His scalp, fashionably depilated, gleamed in the firelight. Dataspikes were clustered in a socket behind his right ear. He was so fabulously old that his brain wasn't large enough to hold all his memories. He clapped his hands and suddenly two people were standing on either side of him: one a bare-chested fat man with a jaunty black beard; the other a woman as thin as a rail, with eyes cold and hard as any stone on Titan. Golden, for sure.

Bonadventure said to Suzy, "Two of my associates. Go on, girl. You say your piece."

"I want to know what I'm getting into, that's all." Despite the dizzy, numbing haze of alcohol and polytrophic, Suzy was beginning to feel intimidated. She'd met Bonadventure a couple of times before, but with the rest of her team, on brief formal occasions at the end of the combat tournaments. Never like this, one-on-one. She could feel the weight of his authority, his age. It was like trying to face down some elemental force, a thunderstorm, a solar flare. She said, "I mean, I want to fly against the Enemy for you. I want another chance at them. But I want to know what it is I'm getting into."

Bonadventure held out a hand, and someone put a silver goblet into it (a stunningly beautiful woman, black hair piled high and threaded with little lights, a small calm face and perfectly white skin setting off the silver mesh of her dress: it was as if she'd winked into existence when she stood beside Bonadventure, less real than the projected Golden on either side of him).

"What you are getting into," Bonadventure said, "is something highly illegal. Some might even consider it to be an act of war against the Federation."

The fat man said, "I would agree with them. It *is* war. That's the point." He had a high reedy voice, the trace of a lisp. He smiled right at Suzy. "After all, my associates and I control economic empires larger by far than many countries on Earth. We are monarchs ruling over countries without boundaries, over subjects who are all working entirely for our exclusive benefit. Yet those countries are inside the Federation. That's what makes this all so dangerous, my dear."

Bonadventure said, "Right at the end of the war someone turned up a new way of mining orthidium, knocked the price of catalfission batteries through the floor, and the price of intersystem and intrasystem travel with it. We sponsor a dozen singleship explorers. Already we have rights to a world as good as Elysium, maybe even better. Small colonies are on it right now, groups that have paid us for the right to settle there, groups that are doing the hard work of establishing beachheads, finding out whether the native biosphere has any traps. Out beyond the jurisdiction of the Federation, do you see? In fifty years we will control more worlds than you can dream about!"

The fat man said, "We are entering a new age, Seyoura Falcon. We are leaving behind the old Marxist-Democratic era where the individual counted for nothing, where history was determined by mob psychology that swept so-called leaders along."

Bonadventure roared, "A new age, Suzy! An age of empires, of emperors!" He drank off what was in the goblet, slammed it on the antique table. His face gleamed in the leaping light of the flames that roared in the huge fireplace; his eyes glittered. He said, "And you are wondering what this has to do with you, with the Enemy."

"Yeah."

Bonadventure smiled, showing small, widely spaced teeth. Bud implants, taken from a cloned embryo. The full medical programs that were part of the longevity treatment maintained half a dozen decerebrated clones for spare parts. Suzy's old boyfriend had been right: Golden were somewhat like vampires, except that they were feeding on the undead, not the living. Though it was rumored that some illegally brought their clones to term, let them grow up ready for brain transplantation. Longevity not enough, immortality the thing, riding body after body. Yeah, vampires.

The beautiful woman handed Bonadventure another goblet, and he told her to give Suzy a drink, too. It was a black, fuming wine, bitter as gunpowder. Its heavy smoke stung her nostrils.

Bonadventure toasted her with his own goblet, sipped, and said, "The Enemy. Did you ever think, Suzy, where they came from?"

"Originally, you mean? I guess we used to talk it over some-times, but it was only like guesses. No one knows."

The fat man said, "Someone does. She found out all about the Enemy on the other colony. P'thrsn." The sound he made was like a cross between a spit and a sneeze. "Not a precise translation, of course, but it is what the Enemy there call their home. There was an expedition to the surface, you see. The Enemy were quiescent, at first. Not like those at BD Twenty. They are not normally intelligent, you see, not in the way we define intelligence. Only when under threat, or in hostile environments, like the asteroid habitats."

On the other side of Bonadventure, the woman with the cold eyes yawned ostentatiously, but said nothing.

Suzy set the goblet down on the table and rubbed her shoul-der, the tail of her tattooed dragon moving under her right hand. "Someone went down on that planet? It isn't in quarantine?"

"This was *before* the quarantine," the fat man said. "Almost all of the expedition were killed after the Enemy were, let us say woken, by the intrusion. Only two survived, and one of the survivors found out the story of the Enemy. You have heard bits and pieces, because some facts, selected facts, were leaked by the Navy. The rumor that the Enemy eat their children, for instance. It's true, up to a point."

Suzy said, "I don't need a fucking biology lesson. What I need is to be told exactly what I'm getting into."

And then she was seized, crushed against Bonadventure's silk robe, held at arm's length with his eyes staring at hers. They were blue, with little flecks of yellow in them. She'd never noticed that before.

Bonadventure said, "What I like about you, Suzy, is that you aren't like other ephemerals. You know my power, but you aren't overawed."

Suzy tried to shake free of his grip, but he was strong, stronger than her enhanced musculature. Kick him in the balls? Oh, sure.

Bonadventure showed his baby teeth again, let her go. On either side of him, the secretary, the gorgeous woman, the two meditechs, the other flunkies, were all not quite looking at him, at her. Suzy was suddenly, acutely aware of that. As if she were sealed inside a security bubble with the Golden. That was his power: the power to be invisible in a crowd of his own employees, the power to inculcate that obedience. She said to the projected image of the fat man, surprised at how steady her voice was, "You were going to tell me where the Enemy came from."

"They're old, you know. Very old. They came from the center of the Galaxy a million years ago, but they're much older than that. Two million, ten million. A billion. Think of what they might have discovered in all that time, Suzy. That's the prize, you see. The Re-United Nations, Greater Brazil, can't be allowed to steal it all for itself."

"I know two things about the Enemy," Suzy said. "They don't have the phase graffle, only slower-than-light. And we beat the shit out of them at BD Twenty. So how smart can they be?"

"One little colony," Bonadventure said. "Where you're going, girl, is going to be a lot hairier than the Campaign around BD Twenty. That I know for certain."

The cold-eyed woman said, "In the wrong hands, advanced technology stolen from the Enemy could be highly destabilizing. That's the point."

The fat man said, suddenly angry for some reason, "She doesn't need to be told that."

"These are dangerous times, Suzy," Bonadventure said. "They scare all of us. That's why we're relying on you."

Suzy saw the secretary make a slight, discreet signal to his employer, and realized that her time was up. She blurted out a final question. "So what is this place you want me to go to?"

But Bonadventure had already turned away, and in the same moment the projected images of the other Golden winked out. The white-haired secretary said, "Seyoura Falcon? Please come with me. I will show you what you need to know."

5

THERE WAS ANOTHER TALENT ON THE SHIP.

Dorthy Yoshida was sure of it, in spite of the numbing fog of biochemicals her implant continuously leaked into her bloodstream. She hadn't dropped a tablet of counteragent in all the time she had been a 'guest' of the Navy, had become accustomed to dulled, low-grade empathy instead of scalpel-sharp penetrations of other minds. As with living with bad eyesight and no lens implant, eventually you get used to blurred light.

Until now, now that she needed to focus and remembered how badly she was crippled.

She had tried zen meditation, the trick she had always used to calm herself, to find the echo of other voices at her still center, when she'd been a working girl. But it had only given her the odd, inverted feeling of someone more aware of her than she was of him, as if she were his glimpsed reflection in a mirror at the far end of a long, dark corridor. A Talent somewhere on the ship, but why was he there? Talents were rare, and expensive to hire. Why did Talbeck Barlstilkin need two? Despite his assurances, did he really trust her?

There was no one to answer her questions. She hadn't seen Talbeck Barlstilkin or his bonded servant since the interview on the balcony, a day ago. And although she had spent much of that time exploring the ship, she had no more than glimpsed anyone else.

The ship was that big.

It was a little like a wreck she had come across when snorkeling off the Great Barrier Reef. Australia. The Pacific. Vertical sunlight burning out of the vast blue sky, striking through blood-warm water to coral ridges. At first she had thought that the wreck was just another crest in the reef's topography. And then she had been able to make out the line of portholes through which brightly colored fish swam, the broken superstructure clad in white lime, a stretch of rail trailing seaweed banners in the current . . . everything overgrown and intermingled, encrusted by the purple and brown and white limy architecture of the patient coral animicules. It was a remnant from the old wars, the ones that had ended the global dominance of Russia and the United States and ushered in the Interregnum.

Barlstilkin's ship was as old as that reef-bound wreck, a conglomeration of at least half a dozen vessels sunk into a tunneled core of lunar slag, overlaid with lifesystem blisters and a modern reaction motor. Maybe it had started out as an arcology, one of the so-called independent habitats which had once hung in the L5 point out beyond Luna. That would explain the rocky core, a place of refuge from solar flare radiation.

Once or twice Dorthy encountered members of the crew, small, deferential men as shy and agile as wild monkeys. Dressed in tight, black one-piece coveralls that left their hands and feet bare, heads shaved, with skin the tone of dull bronze and epicanthic tucks in the corners of their eyes, they all looked the same to Dorthy, odd little dwarf aesthetic monks, living on sunbeams and the steam lifting off freshly boiled rice. Maybe they were clones, raised in tanks, educated solely by hypaedia. They spoke no language she knew, neither Japanese nor Portuguese, English nor Pan-Polynesian. She even tried out her smattering of Russian. But they only smiled, and bowed, and sped off down twisty corridors or into narrow ducts, performing amazingly precise zero-gee maneuvers Dorthy couldn't begin to follow.

Only the lifesystem blisters had generated gravity. Inside the conglomerate ship's rocky keel, Dorthy could fly effortlessly through the maze of corridors, over catwalks laced through huge empty cargo holds, around tanks that rang to the touch. At the center of the keel, safe from mutating radiation, in a pocket cavern with spotlessly clean walls of sprayed white plastic, rows of algae-tinted tubes bubbled in the glare of piped sunlight. Beyond, parts of an incredibly ancient shuttle were embedded in a stratum of dirty slag, its tubular cabin lighted by feeble yellow fluorescents, with a double row of seats whose clunky plastic fascias crackled under Dorthy's fingers. Neat blocks of *kana* and *kanji* script spelled out obsolete zero–gravity instructions for the benefit of long dead passengers. Mitsubishi-Nippon Orbital Services . . . from before the loss of Japan; it brought tears to her eyes, unexpected nostalgia for a glory she had only heard of through the idle boasting of her father.

It was always there, all of it. It would all come back if she let it: her brief childhood in the little Western Australian whaling town; the spartan company apt blocks; her father, bitter because his family had spurned him for marrying a *gaijin*; her mother, worn out by poverty and her husband's impossible demands; weak, drunken Uncle Mishio; poor Hiroko, twice-lost sister. . . . When Dorthy had come down from orbit at the end of her contract with the Kamali-Silver Institute, she'd been twenty years old, and her childhood had long ago ended, sometime after her first suicide attempt during the controlled wakening of her Talent. She'd been vain, self-assured to the point of arrogance, her whole future mapped out: a year or two as a freelance Talent, and then the Fra Mauro University and a career in astronomy, escape into the vacancies of deep space. . . . But first she'd gone to visit her family, or what was left of it after her mother's death, and plunged straight into nightmare.

Her father had used the money from Dorthy's indenture to the Institute to buy a cattle station in the Outback, but drought and hangers-on had bled his capital dry. Dorthy had rescued Hiroko from Uncle Mishio's incestuous clutches, found her an apt in Melbourne, set up a credit line, and left her to begin her career as a free-lance Talent. Three months in Rio de Janeiro, and at the end of it, Dorthy had returned to find Hiroko gone, returned to the wretched cattle station with only a cryptic note by way of explanation. *I cannot live among strangers.*

Dorthy had never seen her again, had been too proud or too cowardly to confront her family again. She'd graduated, started her research career, and been shanghied by the Navy to join the expedition exploring a world of an insignificant red dwarf star thought to have been planoformed by the Enemy.

In the shuttle's dingy cabin, Dorthy thought that it was so easy to let in the past. It was always there, waiting to ambush her—her own past, and the secret history of the Enemy, the Alea. Poor Hiroko probably still alive, and nothing Dorthy could think to do for her, nothing she *could* have done after the Navy had taken her. And now Talbeck Barlstilkin, and perhaps a chance at redemption.

Tears had swelled in her eyes, huge in microgravity. "Damn," Dorthy said, and dashed them away. She swam dimly lighted air into the shuttle's flight deck. It had been gutted, restrung with webs of cables. Hung in their center, like a shiny black brooding spider, was the polycarbon casing of a megacee computer, illegal for anyone but the RUN or the Federation Navy to own one in these post-Interregnum days. The plot was deeper than she had thought. Its cameras swiveled to follow her, but it wouldn't or couldn't answer any of Dorthy's questions and she fled the spooky chamber and its ghosts, real and imagined.

As far as she could determine, the ungainly conglomerate structure was still accelerating. In the keel, gravity's ghost pulled away from Saturn. Obviously, the rendezvous Talbeck Barlstilkin had promised wouldn't be in orbit, but during flyby.

Dorthy revised her estimate of how long she'd been in coldcoffin sleep. Ships like these were so clunkily fragile they couldn't accelerate at anything much more than a twentieth of a gee . . . given continuous acceleration, with no turnover, then at least four days would have been shaved off the usual trip time. Barlstilkin was in a hurry, and with good reason: there was a RUN Police ship on his tail, and who knew what reception awaiting him at Saturn.

As Dorthy explored the ship, there was always the feeling that the other Talent was watching her from inside her own skin. Once, as she sat in the orrery contemplating the simulated Galaxy's winding lanes of stars, she thought she heard a faint humming hiss, and ran after it through the conservatory, over the bridge that arched above the waterfall's pool, chasing the sound down the corridor that sank into the empty spaces of the ship, growing fainter, gone. Only her breath, the whir of ventilators, the tingling continuous rumble of the ship's reaction motor.

Unwilling to chase ghosts, Dorthy returned to the orrery. She had spent half a dozen hours there, running through scenarios for the acceleration of the hypervelocity star. She changed and changed again the parameters of the binary white dwarfs' encounter with the black hole, trying to see if the marauders could have got planets accelerated some way—but in every case worlds were spilled across the sky, most torn apart by tidal gravity and vanishing into the black hole's flickering event horizon. Rocky planets, with or without molten cores, gas giants, even a sphere of pure iron; none had enough cohesion to withstand the terrific tidal stresses. Atmospheric gases were stripped away in a nanosecond; rock flowed like water. Only the neutron-neutron forces found in white dwarf stars could withstand a close encounter with the black hole's tides.

It took Dorthy hours to work out that the marauders could have added planets after the star had been accelerated, using the same anti-inertia drive that the Alea of P'thrsn had used to spin up a tide-locked world of a red dwarf star to make it habitable, to rip a moon out of orbit and aim it across light-years to keep themselves safe. It needed incredibly fine maneuvering, but it was not impossible.

That, at least, was reassuring. It gave the unknown a sketchy metrical frame, a possible face.

When Talbeck Barlstilkin reappeared, Dorthy was on the balcony, eating one of her irregular meals. She didn't see him at first, engrossed as she was in contemplating Saturn, grown huge beyond the balustrade.

The rings were tilted like a delicate white bow around the banded, slightly flattened globe, cut by its shadow. A thousand jostling lanes of dirty icebergs forever pouring around the equator, grainy white either side of the Cassini division, were just beginning to show their complex braided structure. From Dorthy's vantage, they stretched across most of the sky. A couple of moons cast perfect black shadows on turbulent salmon and ocher bands. Another was a bright, steady star, hung beyond the end of the ringbow.

Rhea, Iapetus, Tethys, Dorthy thought to herself. Dione, Enceladus, Mimas. And Janus and Hyperion and Phoebe. Not to mention half a hundred flying mountains catalogued only by date of discovery. And largest of them all, bigger than Mercury: Titan—a solar system in miniature, a perfect Newtonian toy.

Talbeck Barlstilkin coughed politely, and Dorthy whirled, heart suddenly leaping with fright.

"Well," he said, smiling his cruelly distorted smile, "I never did expect to be able to sneak up on a Talent."

Just behind him, no taller than his waist, a little boy nervously pushed unruly black curls back from his smooth round forehead. Then his hand crept down his plump cheek and his thumb socketed in his mouth.

Dorthy said to Barlstilkin, "What do you want with another Talent?" But she was looking at the boy.

Seven, eight? Sucking his thumb, he returned Dorthy's stare with solemn equanimity. He wore bib overalls, striped pale blue and white, with large, bright red plastic snaps. Barlstilkin put a hand on top of the child's mop of curls, but he moved out from underneath at once.

Barlstilkin pretended not to notice. "Diemitrios was lent to me by the Kamali-Silver Institute," he said. "By Isidore Silver herself, as a matter of fact. Yes, she's in on the plot, too."

Dorthy had forgotten how ghastly his smile was, pulled tight as a skull's rictus grin by silvery scar tissue. He was dressed in loose black pants and a crewneck jersey that defined the drum of his chest, his muscular arms. Zithsa-hide boots glittered dully in Saturn's curdled light.

"Bad woman," Diemitrios said suddenly.

Barlstilkin knelt so that his ruined face was level with the boy's. "What's bad about her, Diem? She's going to help us."

"Something wrong. Something wrong with her head, like a thing riding deep inside her."

"I know," Dorthy said. "What does it look like? Can you tell me?" She thought that she knew, but until now she had never had a chance to find out. It was a sick eagerness in her, almost like lust, crowding out caution, crowding out every other question.

Diemitrios's mouth widened around his wet thumb. His blue eyes widened too, so that white showed all around their blue pupils. "Light," he said, "too much light." Then his eyes rolled up and he collapsed in a heap on the floor.

"Jesus Christ!" Barlstilkin pawed at the boy's neck to check his pulse, peeled up an eyelid. Still kneeling, he turned and looked up at Dorthy. "What did you do?"

"Nothing." And when he glared at her: "No, really. Your boy wonder went straight at my passenger without even the most elementary precaution." She crossed over to the boy, only faintly alarmed. This kind of thing happened all the time with novices at the Institute. She had lost count of how many times she had been overcome during even the simplest probe in her days there.

Diemitrios was breathing shallowly but evenly, as if asleep. Probably he was, a simple fugue he'd soon come out of. Dorthy took his thumb out of his mouth, settled his lax limbs. His skin was soft and warm, and a smell like stale milk and honey rose up from him. "He'll be fine," she told Barlstilkin. "He's a little young to be brought on such a chancy affair. To be prying where he's no right."

"He isn't going all the way. Only as far as Saturn. He is the best and most experienced Talent the Institute has. Or that's what Isidore told me, anyhow."

"Then he probably is." A thought shook her. "You had him look inside my head when I was in coldcoffin sleep, didn't you?"

Barlstilkin stood, brushing at his wrinkled pants. "I know that you have a passenger Dorthy. I know the Navy had no luck trying to understand it. I thought that it was worth trying out Diemitrios. You want to know about it too, am I right?"

"Of course. Of course I do. That's not the point. It's the way you go about things. The way you leave me feeling used, no better than when the Navy had me. I want to be here, I want to go to that star. But on my own terms."

"I suppose I have treated you badly. I apologize. But time is short, shorter than I'd hoped it would be."

Dorthy said, "The Navy tried everything they could think of to get at my passenger. I'm not surprised your little boy there couldn't do any better. When he wakes up, he won't remember what he's seen. I know that much."

"What else do you know?"

"I know that it's there, but not what it is. I became aware of it shortly after I was rescued from P'thrsn. It has to do with what happened down there."

"The neuter male."

"Female."

"There is a difference?"

"Normally, Alea are barely sentient, male or female. But their children metamorphose into short-lived, intelligent, neuter males when the radiation flux increases. An evolutionary development to cope with the drastically erratic star of their home planet. The family that colonized P'thrsn had created neuter females, very long-lived, very intelligent, to keep a pocket of civilization intact at all times. Your briefing didn't tell you about this?"

"Perhaps. I forget. I forget a lot of things, once I'm sure I don't need the facts anymore."

"You'll need them if the Alea are behind the hypervelocity star."

"Then I'll relearn them, if we get there. That's what hypaedia is for. So. This neuter female did something to you, to your mind?"

"I think she's put a part of herself, or rather, *herselves* in my head. She was cunning, clever, incredibly old. She could have done it. Her mindset was unmistakable, like a swarm of burning bees. When the boy comes around, I'll ask him about it. But he won't remember."

"Diemitrios," Talbeck Barlstilkin said. "His name is Diemitrios." He seemed to have lost interest in what had happened, and strolled over to the table by the balustrade, picked at the food Dorthy had left there. "Lord," he said, after a moment. "What is this you're eating?"

"*Shiitake no tsumeage.* You're supposed to dip the mushroom in the sauce there, and eat it with the radish. In one respect you make a better warden than the Navy; their messrooms were strictly Greater Brazilian."

Barlstilkin popped a morsel of mushroom into his mouth, and said around it, "Speaking of the Navy, I am reminded why I came to see you. We have confirmation of a reception awaiting us at Titan. Computer, show us the interceptors."

Three red dots bloomed beyond and a little way above the leading edge of Saturn's rings. They formed a perfect equilateral triangle.

"If you look closely, Titan is in the middle," Barlstilkin said. "We were due to go into orbit in eighty-four hours, but we're somewhat ahead of schedule now. We've been accelerating instead of braking, a slight change of plan. From what my spies have told me about the capabilities of police singleships, it should be enough to outrace them. If they can't match our delta vee, the only way they can stop us is shoot us out of the sky—and that is not politically acceptable. It will create difficulties for the rendezvous with our pilot, but I am sure a way will be found. I have no connection with the people on Titan who are organizing that, but I am confident in their ability to carry out their part of the plan."

"I wondered about the acceleration."

"Of course, you have been floating about the main body of my ship. A quaint vessel, don't you think?"

"That's one way of putting it. I saw your megacee computer, too. Is that what's working out your strategy?"

"Oh no. I do that. The computer is running a simulation of *police* strategy, to try and outguess what they will do." He ate another mushroom, dipping it in sauce and taking a little of the grated radish. He seemed to be far too calm for the situation—with RUN Police interceptors closing on his ship and complex plots meshing invisibly around his head. There was something of the extreme solipsism of the Golden there, the invulnerable, immutable confidence that was their armor against entropy.

"You seem very sure of yourself," Dorthy said.

"I have to be. Ah, Diemitrios, you are with us once more."

The mop-haired little boy scrambled to his feet, glared at Dorthy when she turned to him. "Bad woman," he said. He was burning with shame and fear. "I hate you! Hate the thing in your head!"

"What is it? Do you know what is, Diemitrios?"

But Diemitrios wrenched an airstick from where it leaned beside the door, straddled it, and sped off with the breathy hum Dorthy had so often heard without knowing what it was.

6

SUZY FALCON WOKE WITH THE INSISTENT PAIN OF A HANG-
over prying behind her eyes, a warm shape pressed along her
length . . . and something new inside her head, the sense of
the iron star that was her ultimate destination tugging at her
through Titan's mass, across seventy light-years. The man beside
her—blue-veined feet sticking out from under one end of the
quilt, a cap of glossy black hair from the other—only stirred
slightly when she got up and went to the bathroom cubicle.
She emptied her bladder, drank about half a liter of water, and
felt a little better.

Something was askew, though, leaving a kind of unbalanced
feel, as of something missing from the setup she'd been dragged
into. Except she didn't know what it was. She sat on the
toilet and massaged her scalp, trawling through the events of
the day before, trying to think them through, make sense
of them.

Shelley's death. No sense to that. Adam X finding her, handing
her the proposition so neatly. One thing, then the other, some
connection between them she couldn't quite see. Like that interview with Duke Bonadventure, and the other Golden. Something missing there, too; she was sure of it. But there was nothing
wrong with the mission profiles; she'd know if there were.
They'd been drilled into her under hypaedia, tested out on a
simulator in the bowels of Bonadventure's house, hour after
hour. And Adam X had taken her up to the spacefield,
shown her the craft—mean little thing, more missile than
ship, mostly reaction motor, lifesystem a kind of cramped
coffin bolted on as an afterthought—she'd use to rendezvous with the ship she would pilot on the mission, some-

where beyond Saturn. Not much preparation, considering how important the Golden had said all this was. But maybe they didn't want her to know too much, just enough to fly the mission. Maybe they trusted her to do the right thing.

Sure, Suzy. Drink some more water. Take a pill to blow away your hangover. She discovered bite marks on her shoulder, scratches up and down her thighs, and long parallel welts (twisting to see herself in glaring mirrored light) across the humped muscles of her shoulders. Shit, they'd gone at it last night, she and Xing.

After Adam X had turned her loose, she'd wandered through the Carnival crowds, looking for a last good time on Titan. She remembered joining a theater performance in one of the lesser malls, actors mixing with spectators, and people taking turns at a bank of percussion instruments, from tambourines to a gong as tall as the tall woman who beat it. They made a roaring, pulsing thunder. Suzy beat a kettledrum with her palms ("Go ahead," the man who'd pulled her out of the crowd urged, "just find your own beat!"), while the principal characters, dominoed and in voluminous black or white, prinked and whirled about each other, mimed threats which grew ever more extravagant until a long multiple balletic sword fight was ranging up and down the length of the mall while the crowd clapped in counterpoint to the drumming. The acrobatics grew more frenzied, and holographic projections of fire roared higher as the drumming rushed of its own accord to a climax, a welcome catharsis that left Suzy breathless, her palms filled with an electric tingling that took hours to fade.

Afterward, she'd helped the actor pack away the kettledrum, suggested they go and find something to eat. He'd looked around at the other actors (stacking boxes of percussion instruments and the equipment which had generated mood-altering ultrasonics, folding up black and white gowns, rolling up light cables which had projected the closing flames, the earlier images of skyey clouds, of leafy branches and dappled sunlight) and shrugged and smiled, said, why not, he'd never met a flier before.

He had a sudden toothy smile, small, live black eyes halved by neat epicanthic folds. His eyes and mouth were ringed with white greasepaint; Suzy wiped it off for him. Not the type she usually went for—she preferred compact, muscular, hairy men—but he'd woken something in her, or just happened to be there at the right time, at the end of her long, weird day.

His name was Wu Xing.

They had eaten at a restaurant overlooking the Glacier of Worlds, an expensive place cantilevered high above the city's staggered tiers where you cooked your own food, meat and vegetables threaded on long skewers, turned over a bubbling lava pit to crisp. The maître d' knew Suzy, of course, and she and Xing were given one of the prime tables, beside the thick glass window. Far below, slopes of bare water-ice and fields of slushy hydrocarbon snow the color of old, dried blood stretched away to the clustered cones of ice volcanoes. Cumulus feathered the clear pink sky two or three kilometers up. Saturn was a thin crescent, rings like an arrowhead fitted to his bow.

Titan. Suddenly, Suzy wanted to be very far away from it all.

Tourists were staring at her flier's black leathers, but none dared approach, not even the *enthusiasmos*. Especially not the *enthusiasmos*, who would know that she was the leader of the team who had lost one of its members to a fatal accident that morning.

Suzy ignored the tourists' stares as best she could, but she knew she wasn't being very good company. Xing didn't seem to mind, and kept up a steady stream of anecdotes about his performance troupe, occasionally reaching across the table to pat her hand, something she would normally have found irritating but which, now, was oddly reassuring.

Suzy smiled and nodded as Xing prattled on. It was kind of comforting, but her head was full of knife-edge trajectories, the warp of gravitational tides and orbital parameters. When she pressed the side of her face against the window's thick, slightly greenish glass, Titan's poisonous atmosphere centimeters away, she could see all the way down to the nursery slope where tourists' deltakites, leaf shapes in bright primary colors, spiraled down the constant thermals. And saw over again the beginning of Shelley's stall, that bright instant when his left wing had flung back. She was beginning to wonder, through the fog of all she had drunk, if it had been an accident at all, when Xing patted her wrist, asked her what was wrong.

Somehow she had got through the meal without noticing; coffee was cooling in a thick china cup before her. She apologized for her inattention, but the actor brushed it aside.

"I know how much trouble you have, Seyoura Falcon. I only hope I help a little."

"More than a little," Suzy said, spilling a heap of cinnamon and chocolate flakes on her coffee and then downing it in one, licking the mustache of foam from her top lip. She had the table flash up the bill, inserted her credit disk and watched coolly as an incredible number of air-hours was deducted.

"I do not think I help as much as that," Xing said, fascinated by the long string of numbers.

"Take me to a bar you like," Suzy said, "and buy me a brandy. Plum preferably."

They'd ended up barhopping, she remembered, as she fixed her makeup in the bathroom's glare. Taken a vertical slice through the city, from a greasy maintenance crews' dive she liked because nobody there ever paid her any attention, through a bland tourist place with much running water and bad holography, where they were thrown out for making too much noise, and on through several others to a bar at the top of one of the city's spiky towers, spare and expensive, overlooking the spaceport.

The infolded patterns of the fluxbarriers and bafflesquares were like a flock of gray sails: the noses of the ships rising amongst them (her own was out there: the thought was like the airy thrill of flight); a tramp freighter accelerating up the faintly blue tunnel punched by gravithic generators, dwindling into the neon pink sky.

Suzy didn't remember getting back to the capsule hotel and her spartan, permanently booked room. But she did remember slow comfortable lovemaking that had turned fierce and frantic for her in the middle . . . then maybe she'd passed out. Or slept, anyway. She had a feeling she owed Xing a debt of kindness, and the only way she could repay it in the little time she had was with her credit, which she would never be able to access once she left Titan. Use it or lose it, yeah. . . . She woke him with a kiss, suggested they go out and make a day of it. To her surprise, he agreed at once.

★　★　★

There was a newstaper waiting just outside the hotel, a portly man in a very fashionable, searingly colored suit. He hurried after Suzy and Xing as they headed for the transit line, his remote wallowing through the air ahead of him. The third time he called her name Suzy turned and stopped, and he trotted up to her, gullible, innocent, wide open.

He said breathlessly, "Just a word to your fans, Seyoura Falcon. I'm sure that many of them are worried that you might be thinking of quitting tournaments completely, after your recent close brush with death. I wonder—"

That was when Suzy kicked him under his left kneecap. The 'taper went over in an untidy heap, howling. She stamped on his hand, kicked the control pad for the remote over the edge of the walkway, grabbed a handful of his dry, silver-colored hair, and pulled. His face was mottled white and red, eyes wide with fear.

The pop-eyed lenses of the remote glittered in the corner of Suzy's eye and she swiped at it; but the thing swooped out over the railing, some homeostatic preservation program. So she smiled at it and twisted the 'taper's hair so he howled some more, and said loudly, "My fans will be real happy to know that my reflexes are as keen as ever."

Then she turned on her heel and stalked over to where Xing was waiting for her. He applauded her softly, his wide smile closing his eyes to slits. He said, "Some show."

"Just what the little fucker wanted. I shouldn't have lost my temper. He'll make a week out of that, at least."

"Still, do you feel better?" Xing fell in with her quick, angry stride, head bent to her so the fringe of his cap of black hair fell aslant.

Suzy examined her feelings: rage, self-loathing, barely controlled laughter.

She laughed. "Yeah, a little."

"I find you a few more 'tapers. Good therapy for you, they make a profit. All happy." Smiling, he rubbed finger and thumb together. "On Titan it is always money."

"Xing, what I want to do now is get something to eat. But first I want to go check something. You ever seen the fliers' warren?"

*   *   *

Xavier Delgado, the chief hangar mechanic, was a grossly fat man bloated by appetite and too many years in low-gee environments. He bounced up and down on the balls of his feet, a tethered balloon barely stuffed into his bib coveralls, as he explained to Suzy that it was probably fatigue in one of the spars that had brought Shelley down.

Suzy felt a measure of relief. "So it was an accident."

"Maybe. There's fatigue and then there's fatigue." Delgado joggled a hand, palm flat, at the wreckage of Shelley's wings, laid out on the oil-stained concrete floor of the cavernous hangar. Broken polycarbon spars outlining the once-proud sweep of the lifting surface. The tattered straps and control wires of the prone harness. Scraps of colored mylar stained by the intense cold of the Glacier's methane snows. A horrible, pathetic relic.

"What you trying to tell me, Xav? It wasn't an accident?"

Delgado sucked loudly on the hollow stick which jauntily stuck up out of his meaty lips; along with everything else, he had a bad nicotine habit. "All I'm saying is it's not possible to be certain, just by looking it over. The spreader spars of the primaries are thin, you know that. And polycarbon is a bit like glass, strong in one direction, brittle in the other. If a spreader spar was slightly out of alignment, then it would have been under stress. Would have broken eventually. But there's other kinds of fatigue, like I said." He mimed twisting a wire back and forth between his hands. "Do that to the spar before you fit it, get the same result, right? Or there are ways of attacking it chemically. I even heard there's something like a virus, gnaws at carbon-carbon bonds." Delgado shrugged, a movement as monumental as an earthquake. "Maybe half a dozen other ways to sabotage it. All I know is, right now, that Shelley was a kind of wild guy, but he knew how to check over his equipment."

Suzy balled her fists, felt her nails bite into her palms. The dumb certainty of it cut into her, cold as one of Titan's zephyrs. She would have gone anyway, tournament or no tournament, but it was just like a Golden to be absolutely certain, make sure all the bases were covered. That had been one of the meaningless folk sayings her father liked to use.

She said, "You can test for this, Xav? How long would it take?"

Another monumental shrug. "I guess X-ray crystallography would show whether the spar'd been artificially stressed. Chemical tests would take longer. And that virus. Well, I only ever heard about that, never had any experience of it." Delgado sucked on his stick, narrowed his piggy eyes judiciously. "Take maybe two, three days. To be sure. I need your say on it, too. Need you to authorize the credit."

In two days she would be a long way from Titan. Suzy flexed her arms, the hump of grafted muscle shifting on her shoulders. "No," she said. "No. . . . I guess I'm just being paranoid. It's not as if anyone would really gain anything from it, right?"

Delgado shifted his stick from one corner of his mouth to the other.

"Goddamn," Suzy said. "Xing! I'm all done here!"

A long way down the cavern, the actor turned from where he had been staring up at stacked wings which rose up toward the naked rock and constellations of glotubes of the cavern's ceiling. Delgado dropped a hand on Suzy's shoulder. He said in a dainty whisper, "You be careful now, Seyoura."

"Hey, Xav. Come on. I'm still here, aren't I?"

Delgado took the hand away. A heavy, hard hand, its nails broken and rimmed with oil. "I hear talk you're moving into a different league now. Grace and speed to you, if you need it."

It was an old freespacer's phrase, a formal benediction at the parting of the ways. It touched Suzy in a place she thought had long ago hardened over, so that when Xing came up, cheerfully animated, saying something about fighting kites, her eyes had misted over, and she turned away abruptly to hide her weakness.

Later, they were standing at the rail of one of the balconies of the topmost circle of the Central Stack, a shaft half a kilometer across which pierced the levels of the city from top to bottom. The Carnival was getting into its stride for the day, a hundred thousand people crowding runnels and malls and corridors in search of the perfect sin or the perfect lover, or maybe just the perfect fantasy about one or the other.

The Carnival wasn't just about combat flying, although the tournaments had been the seed around which it had grown, larger with each cycle it seemed, like a wax flake growing around the initial speck of a polymer chain as it descends, kilometer after kilometer, through the clouds that shroud Titan everywhere except the Clear Spot over Tallman Scarp. There were theatrical events ranging from a single actor in a bare room to a performance troupe like Xing's that took to the crowded malls and public spaces of the city and made everyone it touched a participant. There were masked balls, group sagas which threaded their hermetic, twisty plots through the Carnival's seethe, food from all the Ten Worlds and (so the saying went) from some even God hadn't visited yet, the full spectrum of legal drugs, total environment chambers where solipsists could lose themselves in private fantasy. . . . In short, it had everything to cater to the ritual letting go of the company people, the government people, the people who spent their lives tuning the circuits of human civilization.

"Termites," Xing said, looking over the rail.

Each slightly bigger than the one above, circle after circle dropped away toward the floor, where crowds of people, looking no bigger than insects, surged among plashing fountains and explosions of greenery. Someone had set up a huge holographic projection in the middle air of the shaft; it flamed and flared to the cascading rhythms of bocksa, that year's popular dance music.

Suzy was letting herself become spaced-out by the music and the noise of the crowds that rose on the heated air. She would have let go completely if she could, but the absolute sense of the iron star was tugging at her, and she could feel slabs of implanted data settling into the basement of her brain. In a handful of hours it would be time to go. It was getting late in the day, her last day on Titan. She still had her farewells to make, if she wanted to, and would have to get a couple of drinks inside her to find that out.

"Or ants, maybe," Xing said, when she didn't respond.

"Ants? No ants on Titan. Cockroaches, that I know about. But no ants." Truth to tell, she was growing a little impatient with Xing. After they'd had lunch in a noodle bar she'd asked him point-blank whether he shouldn't be rehearsing or whatever it was his troupe did to get ready for its performance, and he'd smiled and said a shade too quickly that it was a day off. Maybe he was happy basking in the reflected light of the attention she got everywhere, Suzy Falcon the famous flier; maybe it was just that he liked her. But he was beginning to weigh her down. She'd needed company last night but now, on the edge of Bonadventure's mission, she needed some space.

But Xing only smiled now and said, "By ants I mean the people down there. I mean there are too many to think of them as individual people."

Suzy held her half-empty drinkbulb over the rail. "If I let this drop, do you think it would kill someone?"

"Sure. Gravity is low, but we are high up. Oh, wait—" Because she had, for a moment, made as if to open her fingers.

"See," Suzy told him, "you care. Me, I could drop a fucking bomb from off the top here, and not give a damn."

"Fliers need audiences."

"You clowns need audiences. We just need wings and a good steady thermal." Suzy turned from the rail, eyeballed the people who wandered the gallery. Mostly garishly suited contract men on company holiday bonus, accompanied by wives in close-fitting dresses of what looked like multilayered metal foil, flashing like copper, like gold, like bronze. One breast left bare or sheeted by translucent stuff, breasts being in fashion this year. Hair teased high in lacquered stacks—how did they *sleep* like that, Suzy suddenly wondered. Maybe they didn't; maybe there was a switch at the back of the neck that you flipped, turned off and left until day began again. Rings on their manicured fingers, bangles and bracelets that clattered at their fine-boned wrists, were a complex code signing social and financial status—not necessarily the same thing, these days. Here, at the beginning of a new century, a decade after humanity had fought and won its first war against aliens, making Earth the center of an interstellar economic alliance of the Ten Worlds, there were still women in Greater Brazil who were no more than appendages of their husbands, accessories whose dress and culture denoted their owner's wealth and taste. Some glanced at Xing and Suzy (especially at Suzy: her mugging of that newstaper was already all through the net)—shy, sidelong glances, like those of gazelles nervously wondering about the lions which happened to be sharing the water hole. Even fewer studied the violent murals some artist had scrawled across sandblasted rock walls.

Xing was talking, something about overloading the city's environmental systems. "Too many people in Urbis for Carnival now. That is the point. Purging plants work at full time to clear ketones and butyrates from the air. If one breaks down, the whole city smells like an old shoe in a day. Heat exchangers the same, though at least they generate electricity."

"Yeah," Suzy said, thinking it was a funny thing for an actor to be concerned about.

A handful of Golden were moving through the crowd of ordinary tourists, each gorgeous and singular, like flamingos strutting amongst a flock of house sparrows. There was a man with a metal helmet wrapped around his entire head, fretted into a dozen or more thin rings that Suzy realized must be meant to represent the rings of Saturn. Someone else moved inside a twisting column of bloody vapor, a dark knee, a hand, visible in momentary rents in the carnelian fog. A girl in a pleated sarong, round breasts bare and sprinkled with sweat, danced a few steps with a leonine young fellow in coveralls that churned with storms of clashing colors, then linked arms with a bearded boy in a shimmering toga. Someone threw a ball up which exploded when it touched the luminous ceiling, releasing a snow of golden flakes and a scent like burning geraniums.

Xing watched Golden jostle each other at the escalator's maw. "People like that think they get away with anything. Releasing proscribed narcotics into atmosphere."

Suzy breathed deeply, feeling blood vessels in her face dilate, air suddenly turbocharging the jelly in her skull as if she'd taken a draft of pure oxygen. "Maybe they just want to cheer up the suits there. Make their day."

"In twenty minutes we could be foaming at the mouth with withdrawal symptoms. Golden have a funny sense of humor."

Suzy looked at Xing. Whatever it was in the golden flakes, it was powerful stuff. Things were suddenly coming together in her head, like machine parts sliding together on friction-less oil.

Bonadventure. Levels within levels.

She said, "You don't like the Golden?"

"The older ones, I think, are growing beyond humanity." Xing spoke slowly and carefully, as if he were holding some-thing in his mouth he had to get the words around. The stuff had got to him, too. "They don't see us as human. Our lives are too short to count for anything. I had a dog. When I was a boy. On Earth. She died when I was fifteen, of old age. I loved that dog, but I never confused her with a human being. That's how it is with us and the Golden. Why do they watch fliers so avidly, Suzy?"

"You're going to tell me, right?"

"They fear death and are attracted to it at the same time. The more you have, the greater even the vicarious thrill of loss becomes. We are all players in their games, in Urbis. I don't know, maybe the drug makes me run on like this."

Suzy looked at him. Tall smiling man, cap of glossy black hair, a rooster tail scuffed up at the back. An actor talking about atmospheric recycling, a stranger who had suddenly glued onto her life, right at this critical minute. . . .

She said, "Who are you? Who are you really?"

His smile did not waver. "I don't understand what you mean."

"I mean who are you working for? The Navy? RUN Police?"

People were looking at her. "Please," Xing said, "not so loudly. We don't want a scene." He grabbed one of her wrists, and she found she couldn't pull away from his grip; he was stronger than he looked. His face was centimeters from hers. He'd shed his accent, looked ten years older all of a sudden. "Just keep quiet, Seyoura Falcon. You will be all right. You are just a pawn, not a player. There will be no real trouble. We just need you to play out your part."

"You fucking set me up, man." As if she were standing outside herself, amazed at this.

"Just a little pheromone transfer, nothing permanent. It's already wearing off. Trick of the trade. I've been working deep cover for years now, watching those Golden you work for. Service engineer, go anywhere, see everything. What I know, Seyoura Falcon, is that your life is in danger. Bonadventure's plan is not all it seems. He's a front for a cartel of Golden that want to use you to get at Barlstilkin. They want stability. They want to eliminate Barlstilkin without fuss, without scandal." Xing took Suzy's hands, a strong grip. "You're a pawn sacrifice, but I am here to help you."

Suzy kicked out, but Xing danced back neatly, swung her around and put his forearm across her throat like a bar of iron. That was the wrong thing to do. Suzy flexed her grafted muscle and sent him sprawling. She kicked him in the throat, yelling, "Bastard! Bastard!"—hurting her toes on his skull. He was curled up, eyes rolled back, as he tried to breathe. Suzy said, "I should throw you over the fucking rail."

But she saw a couple of cops running around the gallery's circle, red uniforms flickering through the crowds—must have come up on the escalator—and she took off in the other direction, dodging around astonished tourists. A mass of tanglewire shot past her, hit the rail, and threw out a hundred writhing threads. Suzy saw a service corridor and went down it. Wrong move. It was a dead end.

She turned, saw one of the cops coming toward her. His pistol was held up by the side of his head. He was smiling. And then something dropped on him from the high ceiling and he collapsed under it, yelling and kicking. Cybernetic cross between a spider and a scorpion, moving with swift sinister grace, the thing pinned the cop with its jointed legs and sprayed him with stuff that looked like blood. It darkened his red tunic, puddled all around him.

Behind and above Suzy, a voice said, "This way Seyoura. Quickly now."

A knotted rope dropped from a ventilation shaft as tanglewire erupted in a frantic dance around the robot and the cop it pinned. Suzy, seeing the second cop take aim again, grabbed the rope and swarmed up it. A hand reached down and helped her over the edge into murmuring, dusty darkness.

7

SHE WAS IN A NARROW CRAWL SPACE, CROUCHING
face-to-face with the guy who'd hauled her up. He was the
mechanic she'd glimpsed at Bonadventure's place, tall and
incredibly thin, his head shaved except for a crest of spiky
blond hair, the front part flopped down over washed-out blue
eyes. Black pants, tight as hell, bare-chested under a black leather jacket, the left sleeve torn away to show off his augmented
arm.

While Suzy got her breath back, the mechanic pulled up the
rope and fixed the grill back in place, the elongate multijointed
digits of his prosthetic hand blurring over the fastenings.

Suzy said, "I guess I should thank you for saving my ass."

"Don't thank me until you know what I want." He had a
loop of braided wire in his prosthetic hand. "You hold still a
moment," he said, and waved the wire up and down Suzy's
body.

Her implanted speakers jabbed painful spikes of pure noise
into her ears: she clutched at her head, but the sound was gone.
She said, "What the fuck did you do?"

"Just a precaution." The mechanic's eyes seemed to film
over for a moment. "Yeah. They're all running now." His
wide happy smile showed a scattering of brown teeth in pale,
pulpy gums. "Man, I've been waiting to turn on this town my
whole life. They run. . . ."

"Hey," Suzy said, and shook him by his meat arm. "Those
cops out there have friends, okay?"

The mechanic looked through the grill. Light and shadow
shifted over his thin white face, his spikily crested, shaved scalp.
Old scars seamed the left side, as if someone had once tried to

take his head apart. He said, "My little helper down there is kind of blocking the way. But you're right. We go get a ship now."

"You want a ride. I got a ship, but I don't think you want to go with me. No way I can fit in a passenger, anyhow."

"I'd go anywhere. Been in this town too long, me. But you don't want Bonadventure's ship. Leastwise, not the one his friends want you to ride. I know all about that, and we'd better find us another. You come on with me."

There was a long and dirty scramble through a maze of ducts and crawl spaces. Suzy learned that the mechanic called himself Robot; he was a good old boy from Galveston, not two hundred klicks from where she'd been raised. By the time they'd quit the ducts for a cableway where they could at last walk instead of scrabbling along on hands and knees, they had switched to English; five minutes more, and Suzy remembered why the name was so familiar.

"You're that artist! The one that set that machine on . . . who was he?"

Robot smiled at her, pushing at his spiky crest. His pants were held together with a piece of twisted wire. A seam had gone along one thigh; pale moments of flesh glimmered between taut strands of thread. "Some old dingbat used to be RUN representative for Elysium."

"It was an advertisement? I kind of remember."

"It was what back in the twenty hundreds they used to call a snare. Bundle you into its sensorium, give you the hard fast sell, let you go. Mine were kind of like that, but mobile, and they reacted to the way you reacted to them. This old dingbat started arguing when it tried to sell him its religion, so it argued right back, and that made *him* yell louder. . . . Well, I think he'd be there yet if the cops hadn't busted him loose. They broke the damn machine, too." Again, his eyes seemed to film over for a moment. "I got better ones working now. Been planning this since I went freebreather."

"I thought they deported you."

"Tried. I persuaded their prison to let me go. They took my arm, see, but Machine could talk to the prison circuits, and they couldn't take *him* away from me. Got my arm back and been living in the walls since then, and you'd better believe I'm not the only one. We better keep walking, I reckon."

"All you have to do is take me back to Bonadventure's house. Don't tell me you don't know the way, 'cause I saw you there."

"I've been working for him and his friends, which is why I know you don't want to be flying that ship. Ever heard of the pyramids?"

"Just take me to his station then. I guess I can manage to ride a car out there."

"You got things to learn. Bonadventure's house is the last place you want to go. For one thing, Bonadventure's gonna be hard put to help himself. He was close to bankrupt, you didn't know that? Too much investment in exploration that didn't pan out, too much in conventional orthidium mining; he lost heavily when the price went through the floor. His friends were propping him up, which is why he was front man for this thing. What you and I saw of his partners were only simulcra. I bet they didn't even look like the real people."

Suzy said, "Hold on now. Bonadventure's bankrupt?"

"You probably got more hours than he has. And the other reason you don't want to go to his house is the cops'll be busting him now they know they can't get anything more out of you. I'll bet they planted a homeostatic circuit in you, by the way. That's why I ran the superconductor loop over you. Induced flux will've shut any transmitter down."

"I'm wired for sound, you jerk! You're out about a hundred days you fucked that up."

"You can try get it, but the only air I own is in my lungs. Flux shouldn't hurt speakers anyway. We don't have much time. You coming?"

"Well shit, what choice do I have."

"None that I can see," Robot said.

They went down a steel ladder that seemed to drop a vertical kilometer through the service levels, stepped off after about ten minute's descent into a duct between looped pipes, part of the heat equilibrium system.

A glimmer of bright light a long way ahead. Sounds of a crowd, muffled and botched by metallic echoes.

"I just want to eyeball a few things," Robot said. "Seems it's going well, though."

"You sure the cops aren't following us? I'd just as soon get to the port, if it's all the same to you."

"Honey, I'm the center of the biggest piece of interactive art you can imagine, and I want to give you at least a peek at it, y'know. Don't you worry about the cops. I'm keeping watch on them." Robot gestured with his augmented arm, a weirdly balletic movement, and Suzy saw a little rat-sized machine, bristling with sensors fore and aft, clinging to the ribbed steel roof of the duct. "I'm plugged into half a dozen like it," Robot said, "and I can tell you the area's clean. You come on now. This won't take long."

The little rat-machine followed them with the dumb persistence of a pet animal as they went down the dark tunnel, its clawed extensors ticking and scratching overhead. Suzy felt a kind of dreamy floating detachment, as if she were plugged into a saga instead of real life. Robot's stories of people living in the ducts, a marginal alternative society largely propped up by Golden who came slumming in search of illicit thrills, were fantastic yet immediately credible, like the parameters of the most expensive kind of saga. Freebreathers, Robot called them.

"On Earth we say free as air, but out here breathing time is the economic medium. So it's a seriously radical thing, being a freebreather."

"You sound like you approve."

"Sure. Not that I didn't have a choice, y'know. But yeah, it's ideologically correct as far as I'm concerned. Urbis is super artificial, everything human-made, regulated. Every plant in the city has a machine code, you know that? No wilderness, no *randomness*. That's what my machines are for, especially the predators. Put some adrenaline surge into the routines, some unpredictability. We've three levels in our brains, we should use them all."

The clarity of the Golden's drug was leaving Suzy, burned off by adrenaline maybe, and she was confused by Robot's talk, half street slang, half artistic theory, switching from Badlands drawl to something close to no accent at all and back again. It was as if he were trying to sell her something, or convert her to an obscure faith. She said, at random, "Predators?" And remembered the machine that had jumped the cop.

"That's what we're going to see. Hear that noise ahead? It's started. I started it back when I picked you up."

Suzy had to run to keep up with Robot's eager lope. Light and noise grew. They came out onto a narrow balcony, squeezed beside the humming, multigridded maw of an air recirculator. Three floors below was the vast circular floor of the Central Stack. People sat at clusters of cafe tables, wandered like grazing animals between market stalls. Suzy and Robot were at about the same level as the tops of the tallest of the pulsing fountains which spouted here and there from sprawling free-form pools, higher than the crowns of clipped bay trees scattered across the paved plaza.

Robot pointed with his augmented arm. "Over there," he said.

Suzy barely glimpsed it, an elusive star of light in the middle air far across the plaza. It drifted down as lazily as a snowflake, kissed the blue water of a pool—and exploded into a vast bank of white foam that spewed across the entire surface of the pool in a moment, was sucked into the fountains and spattered high into the air. Faint shrieks, mostly of laughter, as people scrambled out of the way of foam spilling over the banks of the pool, spreading its white tide across the plaza's multicolored tiles. Other pools were erupting in banks of froth too; the air was suddenly full of drifting foam, like a blizzard of sticky snow.

"Little machine, no bigger than your hand," Robot said. "Catalytic." He touched Suzy's arm, pointed.

But Suzy had already seen the human-sized metal spider skitter out of one of the runnels that punctured the rim of the plaza. People scattered before it: then it pounced, caught and cradled its victim with its forelimbs and squirted her with symbolic blood, dropped her, and went after new prey. There were other spiders in the plaza now, sending colliding wave fronts of panicky people tangling and untangling among foamy pools, sliding and slipping, swallowed by burgeoning banks of bubbles.

"We can go now," Robot said, and clipped something to the rail, a little spool with a kind of grip protruding from it.

"Monofilament," he explained, clambering over the rail (his split pant leg splitting further), "so take care." And then he fell toward the plaza, swaying to and fro on the invisible line. When he reached the bottom he let go of the grip and it shot back up, clattering against the rail. Suzy followed him down, her whole body a tingling target. The cops had to be somewhere about, and none of this was exactly inconspicuous.

When she got down, Robot was talking to a s&v remote that hovered a meter in front of his face like a huge hypnotized insect while he rambled on about some kind of art theory until Suzy lost patience and struck at the remote, which promptly shot up toward the distant ceiling of the stack, vanishing amid the storm of slow-falling flecks of foam.

"I was just signing the piece," Robot explained. He was looking around at the chaos with a kind of idiotic satisfaction.

"This is some kind of *art*?"

"Sure. I call it *Urban Terrorism*. Back in the twentieth century, when technology was spreading like ghostweed through every layer of society, individuals suddenly found that they had the power to subvert the status quo. One person could hold a whole city to ransom if he was fanatical and cunning enough. You had every kind of splinter group resorting to violently aimless protest, from groups which believed that animals had the same civil rights as human beings, to tiny religious sects who figured it was better to blow infidels to bits than waste time converting them. Of course, that wasn't really art. For one thing, they mostly never gave proper attribution to their work."

"This is great. I guess I'm not going to escape, but at least I'll have plenty of time to check the critical reviews of this thing. If I'm allowed net access after they sling me in jail."

"No, it's okay. Listen, this thing here is just part of what's happening all over the city. The cops won't even think to start looking for us yet; they've enough problems with keeping the tourists calm."

Suzy backed off a couple of steps. This guy really was crazy. She said, "Forgive me for not appreciating this thing of yours, but I'm in kind of a hurry, okay?"

Then she ran, heading between two swelling towers of foam. And one of the spider things burst out of a foam bank not ten meters in front of her and reared up as her boots slipped on wet tile and she went down ass over tit. Breathless, she looked up as glittering forelimbs palped the air above her. Then the thing swiveled and scampered away, and Robot reached down to help her up.

"I am sorry," he said, no accent again. "You must stick with us. We ought to be getting along."

Suzy considered throwing him into one of the pools. Sure, and then get turned into chopped meat by the spider-thing. She ignored his hand and got to her feet. "You really plugged into those things?"

"Of course." Robot spun a little white and green disk in the air, caught it, and slapped it on the back of his prosthetic hand. "We'll go that way. This thing isn't over yet. We have a ship to catch."

As they walked down the runnel, Robot told her how he had subverted an autodoc into doing a little rewiring—his term— of his brain, the kind of thing that was done to brainwiped criminals like Adam X. "Circuits in the left hemisphere to take care of routine, to free the right side, the creative side. Let me dream all I want. Say hello, Machine," Robot said, and cocked his head and said in his other, his neutral voice, "We've talked, Seyoura Falcon, but I haven't had the opportunity to introduce myself before."

"No shit."

"No shit," Robot said, and explained that he had a little biopowered transmitter under the skin at the back of his neck, too: it kept him in touch with his creatures through the city Net. They had their own pseudoreflex routines, but he could tap into any one of them, take it over or simply take a peek through its sensory array.

Robot seemed to be proud of what he'd done to himself, but Suzy thought it was a little creepy, morbid even. Like mutilation cults, or the kind of gothic pre-Interregnum technology that had nearly destroyed the Earth. Machines and humans weren't meant to interface so closely, so permanently. It was kind of obscene.

Still, Robot's piece of terrorism, or art, or whatever it was, seemed to be keeping the city cops busy. If they were still looking for Suzy, they were looking in the wrong place. Suzy and Robot rode a capsule all the way to the spacefield administration complex without seeing a single redskin, and then they dived into the service levels again. Robot jiggered the lock of a maintenance hutch with his prosthetic hand, and they put on pressure suits and cycled through the airlock into the tunnels that threaded beneath the spacefield itself. The little ratlike machine perched on the ribbed shoulder of Robot's p-suit, cozened up to his helmet as he led Suzy through chamber after chamber where gravithic generators sat in ceramic-sealed pits. Then a shaft to the surface, out among the gray sails of bafflesquares folded like the corolla of a flower around a singleship poised at a steep angle on its pad.

A delta-shaped lifting surface flared out from its narrow wasp-waisted body, its nose sculpted to accommodate air-breathing ducts: it was the model of singleship used by the new breed of explorers, capable of atmospheric flight. Even with a dozen fat chemical boosters strapped around its drive assembly, it was the most beautiful thing Suzy had seen in a long time.

Robot said over the common channel, "Before we go in, something I want to show you."

"Tower'll hear you, man."

"That's the point. Look." Robot held a little widget in his gloved hand. He gestured grandly with it, aiming off to where Saturn was setting beyond the spacefield's flocks of bafflesquares and fluxbarriers.

A star grew at the edge of the spacefield, hurtingly bright. A moment later, Suzy felt the polycarbon blocks begin to shiver beneath the cleated boots of her p-suit. The star was a ship, lifting on chemical boosters. She could hear its roar now, a basso profundo rumbling across a sudden chatter of panicked voices on the common channel.

Robot jacked a com lead into Suzy's p-suit, spoke to her directly. "That's the ship Bonadventure's friends wanted you to use, the ship that was going to take you to your rendezvous with Talbeck Barlstilkin. I rewired it for him, but I added a couple of things of my own, too."

"They fry your head for less than this, man! Flying a fucking ship by wire, using chemical boosters inside city limits—"

"Don't you get it? Barlstilkin would have had both of us killed. Me because I know too much. You—you watch the ship now, you'll soon see."

The ship's white star climbed quickly, doing eight gees at least, scrawling a ragged black contrail across the pink sky. Suzy tipped her head back, working against the resistance of the p-suit, as the star raced past zenith, so small now, yet still so bright—

And then it suddenly blossomed into a flower of light that for a moment was brighter than the shrunken sun. The babble on the common channel was cut by a howl of static. Suzy whirled away, a spot the size of her hand darkening her p-suit's visor. Everything was shadows and white light. And then the light began to fade. The voices came back, screaming at each other. Suzy dialed them down. She felt like hitting something. That thing that she'd missed when the Golden had interviewed her. Like she was the center of a joke she didn't get. So dumb. So trusting. So fucking trusting.

Robot said, "Rigged so the catalfission batteries would release all their energy at once. Supposedly when you made your rendezvous. I kind of changed it around a little. Bonadventure and his friends—"

"I fucking get it! You want to steal a ship? Let's do it." And Suzy jerked out the com line, turned around, and marched up the mesh ramp that curved above a thick tangle of power cables to the singleship's hatch. Punched the release so hard she thought she might have broken a knuckle or two; the pain was small compared to her rage. The airlock was so small that there was only a pressure curtain on the other side, its invisible embrace tugging at her as she scrambled through.

And came face to face with Adam X, who body slammed her against a padded bulkhead and twisted off her helmet. She managed to get a knee to his balls, but it didn't make any difference. Above them in the tilted cabin, Duke Bonadventure turned in the gimballed pilot's couch. Half the access plates to the control panels hung down around him. He said, "Things are going very badly indeed. I'm disappointed in you, Suzy."

"That's something." She'd gone from rage to fear in a flat second, trembling from head to toe with adrenaline that suddenly had nowhere to go. Adam X's warm hand pushed her face hard against quilting, so she could only just see Bonadventure out of the corner of her eye. The nostalgic tang of oil and resin and ozone filled her nostrils.

Bonadventure suddenly had a pistol in his hand. He said, "You aren't supposed to be here, Suzy. Ah, nor you, Robot."

Oh shit, Suzy thought. *He could at least have had the sense to stay outside.*

Robot said calmly, "You promised me passage off Titan."

"Did I? Details like that slip my mind. I think you'd better kill them both, Adam."

"Think again, man," Robot said in his lazy drawl.

Two things happened at once. Suzy glimpsed a flash as Robot's augmented arm flipped out the monofilament line they'd ridden down from the balcony. Its grip caught around Bonadventure's wrist, and his hand and the pistol it held fell away. And just as Bonadventure started to howl, Robot's little rat-machine dropped onto Adam X's head.

The bonded servant convulsed violently. One of his knees drove into Suzy's stomach; an elbow caught her under her right eye and everything went red, then black. And then his weight eased; Robot had dragged his dead bulk sideways, jamming him the other side of the airlock's hatch. The little machine dropped from Adam X's scalp to the rim of Robot's open helmet.

It took Suzy two or three tries to get the question around the choked knot that had been rammed into her throat. "You killed him?"

"We overrode everything, no time for any fancy stuff."

Suzy looked up at Bonadventure. The Golden was crammed as far back as he could go, halfway up the narrow angles of the controls. He was still wearing his p-suit, and it must have clamped down on his severed wrist; only a little dark red blood oozed from the clean-cut stump.

She said, "Thing is, what are we going to do with this cunt?"

"He can fasten up his pressure suit."

"And walk away? He could try breathing methane."

"That would be murder. The cops will get him, Suzy; for him that'll be worse than any clean death. Way I figure it, he was being used as a front by the people who saved him from bankruptcy; you can't get at them, but the cops might, if they can get Bonadventure to talk."

"Fuck. You killed Adam X, why stop now?"

"What we did to Adam X was damage to property, not murder, Seyoura Falcon. Legally, he has not been human since his personality was wiped from his brain. Add that to the other counts of property damage we have accrued, but not murder."

"That's Machine, right? Being so fucking reasonable." Suzy glared up at the Golden. "I should kill you. You know that."

Bonadventure didn't move, except for a couple of muscles shifting around his mouth. It was as if his smooth, young man's face had peeled away to show the frightened old man beneath, skin gray, bloodless. Like peeling bark from a log to show the termites seething underneath, the secret pattern of their tunnels through rotten wood that a moment before had seemed whole.

Robot said, "We'll put on the rest of your suit, Duke Bonadventure. Be good now. We're just going to deal with your servant here. Come on Suzy."

The bonded servant's sphincter muscles had all let go when he had been overridden; a terrible odor rose from him, like death. Grappling with the limp body was like an obscene little dance in the confined space; it took a lot of hard work to get him to fall back through the pressure curtain, through the hatch that was still open beyond it. Suzy looked away. She didn't want to see what happened to the body when Titan's freezing atmosphere hit it; she had never seen a dead person before, for all the Enemy she had killed. It had all been at a great distance, all over in a flash of light.

When they were done with Adam X, they had Bonadventure seal up his p-suit. The Golden was shaking, going into shock, so in the end Suzy had to do most of it for him. Got blood all over herself fitting the glove where his hand should have been. Robot had already thrown that out the lock. For a moment, she was tempted to rig the Golden's life-support so it would give out after a couple of minutes, let him strangle in his own breath. But better to let the cops get hold of him, let him spend the rest of eternity in jail. Or as some other Golden's bonded servant.

Just as Suzy was about to latch his helmet shut, Bonadventure stayed her hand. He said, "You're making a mistake, Suzy. Barlstilkin wants to tear the Federation apart. That's why we wanted to stop him."

Robot said, "You want it to fall apart, too. But gradually, not suddenly. So you'd have enough time to build your personal empires, each and every one of you."

"You can be part of that, Suzy. I own a world, a whole world! I can give it to you, if you'll just take me there!"

"What the fuck would I do with a world?" Suzy pushed Bonadventure's gloved hand away, dogged his helmet latches. He was still speaking, lips moving behind the gold-tinted visor. But Suzy wasn't listening anymore. She said into her p-suit's microphone, "Listen good. You get out the hatch, you start running. Get a good long way away, or the boosters will fry you good!" Then she hauled back, braced, and gave him a kick in the pants that sent him halfway through the pressure curtain. He scrabbled the rest of the way out in a frantic clumsy dance, and the hatch whined shut behind him.

"Okay," Robot said, "I guess I'm going to have to ask if I can hitch a ride here. I can't hide out against the cops and Bonadventure's friends, both. Now what do you say?"

"First you better put back those panels, being as you're the mechanic."

"And replace the circuits I took out. That's what Bonadventure was trying to fix."

"You planned this good, didn't you?"

"Machine worked out most of it. But we couldn't have done it without *Urban Terrorism*, so I guess we did it together. What do you say, Suzy? Do we get our ride?"

8

DORTHY WAS ASLEEP WHEN TALBECK BARLSTILKIN CAME for her. She first saw him in her dreams. He was running down a corridor between high stone walls. A single point of red light floated behind him, pacing his headlong flight with smooth, silent ease. When he burst into the courtyard, the light threw his shadow a long way across wet cobbles. He stopped three paces from the door, trying to catch his breath. On the far side, people were trying to clear a tangle of carts around the gate, shouting at horses and each other. A pennant streamed in the sea wind above the gate's tower, luminous against the night. He was looking up at it when the curtain wall blew out a solid sheet of flame; he just had time to scream before a ton of fire fell over him.

He sat up, silk pajamas soaked with sweat. No. She was Dorthy. Her name. Dorthy Yoshida.

Talbeck Barlstilkin held her shoulder for a moment; then she shrugged free of his hand. The ruin of his face, the pine-circled grove, were lit only by the frosty glimmer of the stars that spread beyond the hanging banners above her bed.

"It's time to go," Barlstilkin said, and without waiting for Dorthy's reply he turned and hurried down the dry streambed and into the darkness between the tall pines.

Dorthy followed, still half-gripped by the dream. When she stepped between the projected trees she had a moment's queasy sensation of déjà vu, expecting wet, firelit cobbles beyond the door's oval arch. Only starlit grass; and the stars above, hard and sharp beyond the shadows of the blister's skeleton. The pool was drained; the waterfall dry. A tremor shook the bridge as she ran across its arch to catch up with the ship's shadowy master.

"They've matched our delta vee," Barlstilkin said, although she had to ask him twice to get an answer. They were hurrying through the conservatory. He reached up (how did he see in the dim silver twilight?) and plucked something from a tree without breaking his stride, pushed through hanging ivy into the orrery.

Light dazzled Dorthy, white light bouncing off smooth white walls. It was like the inside of a porcelain egg.

"Computer, open the hatch," Barlstilkin said, and a perfect circle dropped out of the floor at his feet. "Gravity shaft," he said, and dived headfirst into the space.

Dorthy, more cautious, sat on the edge. Something pulled on her feet, and she surrendered to it. Anything seemed possible, most of all that in a moment she would turn over and wake in the ordinary bedroom of the suite of rooms that for so long had been her prison.

She fell past bands of metal that alternated with bands of softly glowing, semiopaque plastic, fell at a steady rate for fifteen heartbeats (she counted them). Then she simply stopped falling, and was floating free. A hand reached into the shaft and drew her down into a vast space glaring with industrial strength light. An upside-down metal catwalk lanced through the glare. Dorthy felt, rather than heard, a slow strong vibration pulse through the air. A breeze picked up suddenly, plucking at her pajamas.

Barlstilkin turned head over heels in midair; then he kicked against the end of the tube and grabbed Dorthy's waist as he shot toward the far end of the cargo hold. "I've always loved secret passages," he said. "Not far now."

"Where?"

"Our ship. The *real* one. And we must move quickly. The atmosphere plant can't make up the loss much longer. We're making our move before the cops board us. And *that* won't be long. The computer underestimated them. I don't know if we'll get our pilot now. I'll have to do it myself and trust in the Lord."

"What are—"

The catwalk passed beneath them. Barlstilkin reached out with his free hand and caught its rail, and light and shadow did a slow stately somersault. And then they were clinging not to a catwalk, but a ladder.

"What are we doing?"

"Escaping, of course. And starting off on the first leg of our journey to the hypervelocity star. That's it. Climb."

Dorthy climbed. Once, she looked up and saw a ceiling of black metal curving away; it was the keel of a cargo tug. It eclipsed most of the light. Once, when the wind suddenly doubled in strength, she looked down and glimpsed, past Talbeck Barlstilkin, a rift in the rocky floor. Only a glimpse, but at the bottom of the rift she thought she saw stars. The ship was breaking apart.

9

IT SEEMED TO SUZY THAT ALL HER LIFE SHE'D BEEN FORCED into one corner or another by circumstance, never by choice. Even her brief career as a singleship explorer had been a statistical inevitability: most freespacer combat pilots had signed on for that gig after the Campaigns because it had seemed such an easy way to get rich. Like Suzy, hardly any of them had bothered to check their contracts; like Suzy, most had ended up indentured to the cartels which had sponsored them. Long-range telescope surveys only held out hope, no more; when you got down to it, there just weren't that many point nine nine Earth-normal worlds. She'd been suckered by percentages.

So it was now. For Bonadventure, or for the Golden he was fronting for, she'd been sucker bait, a dupe, a Judas goat. For Robot, she was a way out of Urbis's prison.

"Mars is fine," he said, as he fixed up the controls. "Or Earth. Anywhere but Urbis. Urbis, I'm *persona non* 'til the Sun freezes over."

"We're stealing this ship, remember? So we can't go to Earth. You crazy?"

"Yeah. That's why I put Machine in my head."

"Maybe Mars," Suzy said.

But she knew that she wanted something for herself, wanted to get out to that fast star, bring back whatever she could find, and blow it through the Federation's circuits. See how the Golden, who wanted everything to stay the same, or to change slowly enough to suit them, see how they liked that. And maybe make a pile of money, too; she remembered what the fat simulacrum had said about the incalculable value of ancient alien technologies. Call it revenge. For Shelley, for herself.

The spacefield's gravithic generators had been shut down after Robot had blown the rigged ship halfway across Titan's sky, so the only way to get off this rock was by using chemical boosters inside Urbis's city limits. But since Suzy was about to commit the capital crime of piracy, she wasn't about to break into a sweat about violating city ordinances.

She was lying flat on her back in the wraparound gimbal couch, still in her sealed pressure suit. She'd flooded the singleship's lifesystem with impact gel, as much to protect Robot, who was braced in the narrow sleeping niche, as herself. The ship was beginning to shake with building thrust. The roar of its boosters filled the cabin, more physical force than sound . . . and only a thousandth of the noise it was really making, back of her tail. At least it drowned out the squawking of the spacefield administration tower.

Vibration sent weird pressure patterns racing through the faintly blue gel pressing against her visor, but Suzy was only vaguely aware of them. Her senses were flayed open, merged with the ship's systems. She felt thrust building as if she were lifting her own mass on her fingertips, saw in crystal clear, three-hundred-sixty-degree vision great plumes of vapor flapping across the crowded gray sails of bafflesquares and fluxbarriers. The panorama was overlaid with the fine print of the myriad readouts of the ship's systems, any one of which zoomed into legibility if she turned her attention to it. She had turned the ship's computer off, in case the field's tower tried to override it somehow. She was flying by the seat of her pants, the way she had on the cusp of combat, the vital few minutes when her singleship's orbit had intersected with that of an Enemy habitat.

Floating right in the center of her vision was the thrust read-out. It was creeping toward equilibrium, the point at which the ship's mass was balanced on the compressed, superheated steam of its booster's hydrox fuel . . . wavering on the line . . . there!

Suzy kicked in the ship's reaction motor. White-hot fire seared away the fog. For a clear moment she saw bafflesquares fly away in every direction. And then the ship was rising, rising smoothly and achingly slowly, boosters almost exhausted, only scant minutes left to them as the ship rose, restraining pins flying away, methane in the freezing atmosphere smelted into carbon and superheated steam by its fire, a dense black fog boiling up as the ship rose higher, higher than the knife-edge peaks of Tallman Scarp, Urbis a glittering toy draped across them, ice volcanoes distinct cones printed on the horizon line. . . . And then the horizon tilted away and there was only clear pink sky as the ship burned in its slanting trajectory, airbreathers cutting in as soon as velocity passed the critical point, ramming a tonne of methane a second and flaming it out behind, a burning spear aimed at Saturn's serene ringed disk.

Suzy was too busy watching flickering blocks of numbers and icons to notice the view. Acceleration pressed her deep into the couch, a wrinkle in her suit cutting into her left buttock, *gonna be a hell of a bruise*, gel stiffening around her arms and legs, vibration grinding deep into the marrow of her bones. Fracture patterns ran like blue lightning through the impact gel. She had time to notice a fluffy cloud deck below her, red-brown color of dried blood, and then the airbreathers cut out. Titan's smog too thin now. The whole ship shuddered, like a salmon making its final leap, and the reaction motor and the exhausted boosters cut off. They'd made orbit.

"Jesus Christ," Robot's voice said weakly.

Suzy asked if he was all right, tuned down his chatter after he said that he was. There was a really strange signal coming up over the horizon, maybe twenty thousand klicks out and going past like a stone dropped from infinity, radar dense objects fleeing a fuzzy expanding center, their trajectories defining a parabolic curve: all headed toward Saturn.

Sure.

Suzy set the ship's optical system to track at maximum magnification, and was rewarded with a view of all kinds of debris expanding away from riddled slabs of, what? Laser spectrography told her there was olivine and diopsite, asteroid stuff, mixed with a variety of alloys. . . . She looked away from the lengthening list and it shrank back to a point. Fragments twinkled as they tumbled in raw sunlight—were those trees? Yes, broken pine trees spinning away among all the junk.

Backing down magnification, Suzy tracked half a dozen exhaust trails on infrared, radiator fins of the reaction motors of intrasystem cargo tugs, according to the identification key. If the computer had been locked in, maybe it could have told her to whom the tugs belonged, but instinctive caution clamped down on the impulse. Hard to say what had happened, but she was sure that the debris was what was left of Barlstilkin's ship.

Suzy smiled inside her helmet. Tricky son of a bitch, he'd be on one of the tugs all right, but they were *all* aiming for slingshot encounters with Saturn. In less than a day they'd be spread across half the sky, vanishing in radically different directions. *Follow that!* Her gut reaction was confirmed a moment later when she spotted the neat formation of three singleships vectoring down on the wreckage. RUN Police without a doubt. Then the tableau set below the horizon of Titan, and she turned her attention back to her own orbit.

And saw the singleship dawning over Titan's muddy limb, right on her tail. She kicked in the reaction motor, and its flare burned across the ashen light that sullenly limned the nightside.

Robot was demanding to know what was going on, and Suzy told him that a ship had come up after them. They were moving into a higher orbit, easier to break out when the time came.

"Hey, but where are we going? Won't he be able to catch us?"

"There's maybe one place he won't follow us. You're not gonna like this, Robot, but there's no way we can even get close to Mars with him on our tail. Now pipe down, I've got some figuring to do."

Which wasn't really true, because she wouldn't be able to figure the fine vectors until she got there. For now, it would be strictly line-of-sight navigation, aiming at the biggest target in the sky. But she wanted time to think, and she didn't want to argue with her passenger. Let him figure out what was happening; by then it would be too late for him to do anything. She hoped.

The tailing ship had matched her new orbit, Suzy noted, no real surprise. Adrenaline was thrilling in her blood. The real thing, the true high—kite flying no substitute. They were coming around toward Titan's dayside now, the shrunken point of the Sun dawning a few minutes before Saturn himself rose, a winged half-sphere almost as big as the turning globe beneath her.

Soon be over Tallman Scarp, Suzy figured. *Well, hell, aim and point, right?* She fired up the reaction motor again, acceleration pushing her back into the couch with slightly more than Earth's grip. Her pursuer was hidden by the glare of the reaction motor's photon wake, but she knew that he would be accelerating too.

Out of Titan, bound for Saturn.

Think of two fixed points either side of an ocean, on a planet so huge that surface curvature is negligible. Obviously, the shortest distance between them is a straight line. Now fling one point away at a thousand kilometers per second, so it describes an orbit, an ellipse, around the first; and for good measure have both points fly off in some arbitrary direction, the first revolving around the second, both revolving around a common center. Now it's not only a question of distance, but of velocity, of time. In space, the shortest path between two bodies is always a hyperbolic curve.

"See, if we aimed straight at Saturn, we'd miss because we still have Titan's orbital velocity. So really, we're slowing down relative to Titan, 'cause we're going in the opposite direction."

"Even though we're going faster all the time."

"We're accelerating to slow down. We were traveling even before we left Titan. Titan is moving around Saturn at a particular orbital velocity. Well, see, that's what we're shedding, to get into a lower orbit."

"I don't know," Robot said, for maybe the fifth time. "It all sounds like some koan to me."

"So sit back and enjoy the view." They'd been batting the concept of intrasystem navigation around for more than an hour and Suzy was more than a little tired of it. She'd set up an internal link between Robot's implants and the ship's optical system, so at least he could see what was going on around them. But was he satisfied?

Next he asked, "What about the cop?"

"I guess he's still there. But I'd have to switch off the drive to see him, and I'm not about to do that."

"So he could be catching up. Or he could fire something at us, a missile maybe."

"A missile wouldn't match our acceleration for long. Anyhow, it would burn up in our exhaust. No, thing I'd do if I was him would be hang in there, wait until Saturn's pull begins to make a difference. Then ease off and overshoot, turn the ship, let his exhaust cut us in half. Think of a reaction motor as a really big laser."

"So while we're falling like a stone from an infinite height,"—which was how she'd first tried to explain the transfer orbit to him—"we could get sliced in two by a thousand-kilometer-long plasma jet."

"Photons. I've seen plasma weapons. Believe me, they're a lot worse." Down in the gravity well of BD Twenty, this tremendous hot glare coming at you at a fraction under the speed of light, naked quantum particles boiling away your hull in an instant. *Ffffp!* Ant under a lens. Suzy said, "Keep quiet a while, I've got to fine-tune vectors."

"What you're planning is illegal as all get-out, isn't it? I mean, it's a protected astronomical—"

"Think of it this way. You're going somewhere no one else has been for more than five hundred years. Now I really got to do some figuring."

"Aye-aye, Captain," Robot said.

Suzy chipped into her player and selected a random couple of hours' worth of twentieth century blues, then got down to the business of working through the encounter. The sooner she could make the final, delicate changes in the ship's hyperbolic trajectory, the easier it would be. But there was so much *stuff* down there. . . .

★   ★   ★

Hours slid by; Suzy hardly noticed as she ordered and reordered matrices, sliding them through a hundred different solutions to the problem. All had to have the same outcome: the summation of deflections of the singleship's course should give it the velocity, and more importantly, the relative proper motion, to match its next target, the neutron star whose absolute position, like all the rest of the crazy mission profile, had been burned into her by hypaedia. For momentum is conserved during translation through contraspace, and just as planets and moons sweep out orbits, so do stars.

Saturn grew beyond the grids of Suzy's calculations, but she had eyes only for a single bright point near the Cassini division, which halved the lanes of the rings. Everything but that point and the sliding calculations receded to the periphery of her horizon: the lonesome voice of some wailing Louisiana bluesman; the continual rumble of the reaction motor; the fug of sweat and rebreathed air in her suit; the tug of the suit's relief junction; the cradle of couch and impact gel; the itch of her bruised hip.

Music and mathematics flowed through her, a pure oceanic feeling. Fucking three-body problem, just the kind of thing she'd sweated over in the Academy. Boltzmann derivations hairy with four-space integers, little knots of figures like black holes in her consciousness. But she had to admit she'd missed this stuff.

Her passenger was, thank Christ, quiet. Thing he'd said back before she'd taken the ship up, when he'd been curing his sabotage. But for your tattoo, Seyoura, Robot might not have come, but we admire the impulse behind it. *Es muy simpatico.* Thought it matched his own mutilations, maybe. Doing that to your brain. Christ. Stone Age stuff, like trepanning. Except he was letting evil spirits *in.* Still, maybe handy for math. There were times when she was almost tempted to turn on the computer, risk being overridden by the cop on her tail.

And so time passed until, the rings huge and close now, showing grainy structure within their shining lanes, the ship's s&v system flared with whiteout and a hideous siren. Music and ringscape vanished. Suzy turned everything down, cut in aux-iliary channels so she could see and hear again; but she couldn't turn off the voice that was suddenly on every channel.

"You are approaching the boundary of the Saturn Astronomical Conservation Area," the voice said. It was a woman's voice, sibilant and sweet, speaking a pure, unaccented Portuguese. *"Please adjust your orbital trajectory at once. Trespass within five thousand kilometers of the mean orbital path of the ring system is strictly forbidden."*

Robot said over it, "This is the cop?" His voice pitched high with fright.

"Hell no. Just a warning buoy. And how did you tap into this channel anyway? I thought I'd turned you off."

"Your ship has been identified as Intersystem Singleship MV 397E222894. Please be advised that a record of your course is being recorded and transmitted to Urbis Traffic Control, Titan. Trespass within the proscribed boundary of the Saturn Astronomical Conservation Area will result in subsequent confiscation of your ship. This announcement constitutes sufficient warning under RUN Human Rights Charter 2698."

"Robot is not bound by machinery. Robot *uses* machinery."

"You are approaching the boundary of the Saturn Astronomical Conservation Area. . . ."

And then the voice faded to a whisper. "There," Robot said, sounding insufferably smug. "No laws, right?"

Suzy chipped into the ship's internal s&v for the first time since they'd lifted off from Titan; a bright blue-tinged window hung before Saturn's rings. Robot was crammed inside the sleeping niche, all right, strapped up in a crash cocoon as snug as a bug, but he was surrounded by a kind of web of cables and wires and jacks that snaked through the impact gel and mostly disappeared behind a padded panel pulled out from the wall. His little rat-machine sat inside the web in a kind of bubble in the impact gel, limbs folded like a dead spider.

Somehow, Robot had managed to subvert the buoy's broadcast, something which was, theoretically, impossible. Still, he hadn't managed to cut it off altogether, which meant that there were limits to his powers. But it was too late to worry about him. At long last, it was time to make a move of her own.

Suzy accessed the ship's library, cued the selection she'd been saving for this moment. Something with real *kick* to it.

The first notes of the guitar bent in; then the voice, hectic and hoarsely mannered, with an accent lost to history:

> *I got to keep movin'*
> *I got to keep movin'*
> *Blues falling down like hail. . . .*

Yeah, it was the story of her life. And here she was, hung on the very edge. Let's see the cop follow *this*.

The rings filled her vision now, the Cassini Divide an aching vacuum between. She called up a cursor to bracket the fleck of light that was her target.

"You fly a funny ship," Robot said in her ear.

"You don't like it, where we're heading there's plenty of rock to sit on and wait for another ride."

> *And the days keeps on worryin' me*
> *There's a hellhound on my trail. . . .*

"Robert Johnson," Robot said. "'Real gone blues.'" Check that I know my history. We access a gigabit memory, Seyoura. Robot offers it to you, should you need it."

"Christ, and you think I'm strange. Now keep quiet, huh? Enjoy the ride. We're coming up to a little course correction, and I want to see if that cop can walk the edge. . . ."

Her bracketed target was growing closer, right at the edge of the rings' braided river of billions of nuggets of ice and rock and primeval carbon left over from the solar system's condensation, too close to Saturn's bulk ever to collapse into a proper moon. But there was order in the apparent chaos. Small shepherd moons rode shotgun on the two dozen subdivisions of the rings, each balancing the teeming orbits of a million nuggets against Saturn's pull. Suzy had bracketed one of them, a ten-million-tonne flying mountain. The singleship was accelerating straight at it.

> *" . . . is strictly forbidden.*
> *Your ship has been identified. . . ."*

The rings were like a solid plane beneath her now, a shining tilted surface skimming past. She feathered the ship's attitude, a final adjustment, risked breaking her concentration by looking back, but saw no sign of the cop. Hanging right in there, in the glare of the reaction motor. Well, now she'd test his nerve to the limit.

"Oh man," Robot said, "we are truly in the groove."

"Keep quiet, for Christ's sake."

> *It keep me with ramblin' mind, rider*
> *Every old place I go. . . .*

Seconds now. They were plunging at an acute angle toward the seemingly hairline crack that divided one lane of debris from the next.

> *"Please adjust your orbital trajectory at once.*
> *Trespass within five thousand kilometers of the mean*
> *orbital path of the ring system . . ."*

"I am going to fucking adjust it," Suzy muttered.

"Man, this is just *crazy*. . . ."

"Quiet!"

Proximity warnings lighting up all over Suzy's wraparound vision, strays above the ring plane. Thin seething impact of dust on the hull, molecule-sized grains scattered one to every cubic centimeter. It hissed through the singer's wailing voice. Suzy could see the *structure* of the rings now, grainy and three-dimensional, and then the timer closed on zero and she cut the motor, praying that the cop had chickened out because this was his chance to overtake and blow them out of the sky. Robot said something she didn't catch because she was too intent on the churning edge of the ring; actually glimpsed the tumbling cratered target. . . .

And then it was past, just like that, and they were flying *beneath* the rings, kicked into a new course by the close gravitational encounter with the shepherd moon, angled down toward Saturn's wide curve and the next course change.

And Robert Johnson sang:

All I need's my little sweet woman
And to keep my company.

And then there was silence.

One by one, proximity alarms faded to green.

There was no sign of the cop. He hadn't followed.

Suzy couldn't resist letting loose a whoop of triumph. Robot said, cool and ironic, "You realize, Seyoura, that the mass difference between the ship and that moon is not so great that the slingshot encounter will have no effect. I calculate that in a couple of billion years the moon's orbit will have changed enough to break up the section of rings it is presently shepherding."

"The rings will have broken up long before that anyhow. They're not stable."

"That's the point," Robot said, and laughed, the first time she'd heard him laugh. It sounded like some ancient ventilating machine, a regular creaking gasp repeated half a dozen times and then shut off. "So," he said, "where are we heading?"

"Right now we've got another course correction. Using Saturn this time."

"But what's our destination?"

Might as well get it over with. Suzy said, "I'll tell you, Robot, there's no way we can rest easy on any of the ten worlds after this shit. So I'm going for broke here, like it or not."

"Kind of audience that would appreciate me can't be found on any colony world, Captain."

"Quit calling me that! We aren't headed for any colony world, anyway. After Saturn we've really got to jack up our velocity. We're gonna do a momentum transfer around a—"

Robot said, "Hey, now wait. Wait a moment. You think I'm crazy?" He was squirming in his crash cocoon, but couldn't move more than a centimeter each side.

Suzy said, "You should have asked me, man, before you hitched your ride. Just calm down, let me fly the ship. I got us this far, didn't I? So, hey, trust me."

She tried to tell him about the stuff they might find, that might make them both richer than the luckiest singleship explorer who ever lived, but he kept yelling back at her, or quoting chapter and verse from the laws against piracy and kidnap in Machine's neutral voice, so she switched off the internal s&v and turned her attention outward. Let him work out for himself that he really didn't have a choice.

The rings were far behind them now, swallowed by the shadow of the planet. Bands of cloud wider than Earth's diameter streamed below the ship. Salmon, umber, ocher, edges peeling away, mixing in complex scrolls, diminishing toward vast, dim hexagonal patterns at the pole. And then the terminator swallowed them and the stars came out. Ahead, the shadows of the rings cut a narrow ellipse out of their drifts.

Saturn's cloud streams were still faintly visible, limned by luminescent nodes and curlicues. Far across his dark curve, a faint flickering marked the top of an electrical storm at least as big as Titan.

Suzy snatched an hour of sleep, woke to the buzzer of the alarm. Sour, furry taste in her mouth that she washed away with a mouthful of water from the tube inside her helmet while looking around at the vast panorama of the nightside of Saturn, the stars beyond. She couldn't see her target, of course, but she knew where it was. And felt the complex contraspace coordinates begin to surface. . . .

Robot was immobile inside his cradle of cables. Sleeping was Suzy's first thought; but when she zoomed in to look at his face through the helmet's visor she saw that the weird omega-shaped spectacles he'd put on before zipping up were filmed over. A private movie, or maybe it was a dream, externalized, turned into a movie. . . . Whatever else might happen, having Robot aboard was going to make this a strange trip.

The rings were edge on, a line of black so thin against the starscape that it was impossible to trace, rushing past as the ship shot through the three-thousand-kilometer-wide gap of the Cassini division, proximity indicators smearing across Suzy's vision for an eye blink, gone.

Rising into the light of the Sun again, with added velocity borrowed from Saturn's orbital momentum. Figures unreeling in a grid off-center of her forward vision, countdown to reignition of the reaction motor. It had been unreeling ever since she'd shut down the motor before the first slingshot encounter, but out of habit she'd ignored it until it started to become critical. Now she saw nothing else as figures flung themselves back to zero. The couch slapped her length; impact gel gloving her body made a fist. Robot didn't seem to notice. *Well hell, let him be.*

Ahead, she could see those cargo tugs scattered all across the sky, Doppler signatures telling her that they were all receding at incredible velocity in half a dozen different directions. They had been falling a long, long way before they had encountered Saturn.

The cops wouldn't know where to begin chasing them down, but Suzy knew at once which one had to be piloted by Talbeck Barlstilkin. Because it was holding exactly the same course as her own ship—it was her ship now: she had already grown into every corner of it—receding out toward the point in Sol's gravity well where a ship could safely drop into contraspace. By the time she reached that point she would be matching Barlstilkin's delta vee but he would be long gone, three days ahead of her at least, on his way to the next target. And Suzy would follow, to the neutron star and beyond, and if she was still sucker bait, she wouldn't find out until they reached the hypervelocity star.

Part 2

⋀⋀⋀⋀⋀

Iron Stars

1

IT HAD ONCE BEEN AN ORDINARY, MAIN SEQUENCE STAR, twice as big as Earth's Sun, hotter and bluer, stabilized at a point where the pressure of radiation driven outward by the temperature of its fusion processes balanced the compressive potential energy of its own gravity. It had burned that way for perhaps five billion years—long enough for life to have evolved on one of its planets, if it had had planets; long enough for great and glorious civilizations to have risen and fallen, or to have ruled for longer than any human dictator has ever dreamed of ruling. . . . But nothing is forever.

Every second of its existence on the main sequence, the star had burned prodigious amounts of hydrogen, fusing tonnes per second into helium and a smattering of carbon and oxygen. That was all right. It had plenty of hydrogen, enough for sixty billion years. But as hydrogen fused into heavier elements, the density at the star's core increased; and at higher densities it was more difficult for radiation to escape. Slowly, at a rate imperceptible on any human scale, the core temperature rose, until about ten percent of the hydrogen had fused to helium and the first critical point was reached. For now the star's contraction had raised its core temperature to a point where less efficient burning cycles could take place: carbon to helium and neon and magnesium; oxygen to helium and silicon and sulfur; silicon to nickel. Like a metastasizing cancer, these reactions spread out from the core. The star grew bigger, inflated by radiation pressure into a red giant (vaporizing those marvelous, hypothetical civilizations and their hypothetical planet). A kind of feverish oscillation set in, cycles of contraction and expansion interspersed with unstable flares when radiation pressure grew so great that shells of unburned hydrogen and helium were ejected from the tenuous outer atmosphere.

This, too, could not last forever. For all thermonuclear reactions lead inexorably to iron, and ordinarily, iron (as the architects of Dis well knew) will not burn; the energy needed to convert it to any other element is greater than the energy released by the reaction. In the outer layers of the star, the nuclear furnaces, banked with slag, grew ever dimmer. Yet, paradoxically, the core temperature rose higher than ever, heated by gravitational contraction as more and more iron accumulated and it grew ever denser. And so the second critical point was reached, when the temperature at the core reached such phenomenal values that iron nuclei spontaneously broke down into helium, absorbing prodigious quantities of energy in the process.

In an instant, the core temperature plunged by a billion degrees. It no longer radiated enough energy to overcome its own gravitational pull. Gravity had at last won over light. The star collapsed in a catastrophic cascade of X-rays as electrons and protons were crushed together to form neutrons. It was all over in a handful of days, an eye's blink in the star's long lifetime. All that was left was a perfect sphere twenty kilometers across, a thin crust of iron and degenerate matter covering a superfluid of bare neutrons, protons and electrons and a core of solid neutronium, the densest material in the apprehensible Universe: the corpse of a star at the bottom of an immensely steep gravity well, spinning at a tremendous rate because it still retained the angular momentum of the very much larger body it had once been.

But even spin is not forever.

Three hours and ten million kilometers out, the ship's optical systems were at last able to detect the ancient neutron star.

Dorthy was watching it on the bridge, leaning forward in the middle of the huge wraparound command couch, chin resting on her doubled fists, elbows resting on knees as she stared intently into the navigation tank.

There was little to see. The neutron star was a dim, evenly red circle like the last ember of a dying fire. From the warping of its magnetic fields through the tenuous gas shells which still surrounded it, Dorthy had calculated that it was spinning very slowly for an object of its class, once every 3240 seconds. Every so often a star drifted behind it, and then a perfectly circular flash limned the dim red disk as its gravity lensed light in every direction. That was what Dorthy was watching. No human eye had ever seen it before, for no one had ever dared fly a ship so close to such a dangerous object.

Barlstilkin had told her that he had spent a year's income finding the ancient neutron star. He'd had a gravity telescope built at the outer edges of the Oort Cloud, half a light-year from Sol, where a billion cold comets eternally orbit and Sol's gravity well is so flat that it is virtually nonexistent. A research team of half a dozen astronomers had been put together (Dorthy recognized most of the names; she had studied at Fra Mauro with two of them, until fate and war and her Talent had plucked her from her budding career as research astronomer, set her down on a dry planoformed world inhabited by the Enemy). In less than six weeks the team had pinpointed a transfer point for the hypervelocity star, a binary system of white dwarf and ancient, slow-spinning neutron star which, by a fortunate coincidence, was one hundred fifteen light-years from Sol, and in the rough direction of Sagittarius.

The original plan had been for a double flyby, looping first around the white dwarf, flipping back into contraspace and crossing the quarter light-year gulf before flipping out again, diving close to the neutron star and gaining enough of its store of kinetic energy in the momentum transfer to match the hypervelocity star's runaway proper motion. A tricky, complex maneuver, but safer than trying to gain velocity from the neutron star alone, which would take the ship very close to the gravity well's tidal limit. But that was what Barlstilkin now proposed to do—take the quicker course even if it was more dangerous.

In that respect, at least, he was like his friend, Duncan Andrews: reckless, impatient, brimming with misplaced confidence, seeing the Universe an endless playground. Dorthy knew better. It was, in part, the message she had brought back from P'thrsn. The Galaxy was not virgin territory ripe for conquering, but a palimpsest overscribbled with the histories of other intelligent species. Humankind was merely the latest player on that crowded stage, a cocky newcomer dazzled by the lights, unaware of the audience waiting in judgment beyond the glare. She herself had been a witness to a final act of a family drama that had taken more than a million years to play out, that had incidentally destroyed a rising civilization on Novaya Rosya and would have destroyed human civilization too, but for a great deal of luck.

Like all Golden whom Dorthy had ever known, Talbeck Barlstilkin was indifferent to this kind of lesson in the dangers of hubris. He planned to live forever, and at the same time he burned with impatience. Revenge is a dish best served cold, and he had brooded for sixty years on the real and imagined wrongs done to his family, spent half a dozen more fitting together the elements of his vengeance. But now that his plans had come so close to unraveling, he would take every risk necessary to keep them running.

Dorthy was musing over that paradox and watching starlight flash around the ember of the neutron star, when Barlstilkin surprised her. She had grown so used to his presence in the ship's cramped quarters that she didn't realize he was there until he spoke. In the days between the encounter with Saturn and reaching the point where the Sun's gravity field was flat enough to allow transition into contraspace, Dorthy had taken to putting on a pressure suit and drifting out from the ship on a kilometer-long tether, until the vessel was just another point of light among the massed stars. It had been a welcome release from the itchy awareness of Barlstilkin's suppressed rage, the dead mind of his bonded servant. Transit through contraspace had been an almost unbearable trial, despite the fact that her implant was blocking all but the faintest activity of her Talent.

One hundred fifty days locked in a tiny ship with an animated corpse and a Golden with an urge for revenge so strong it bordered on the psychotic. Dorthy had lapsed into her old prison habits with an ease that frightened her. Reading, eating, sleeping. Mostly sleeping: after ten years of the liberty of prison, even Shakespeare had lost his savor. She'd done some cold sleep, too. And now they were traveling too fast, and there was too much gas and too much radiation for escape by space-walking.

The only escape was to stay inside her own head as much as possible. So when Barlstilkin spoke, Dorthy gave a little jump, and he chuckled, pleased to have startled a Talent.

"There's but two hours 'til transit," he said. "We should repair to our coffins soon. But before we do, something you should know." He reached over and spun the ball that controlled the ship's visual cluster, bracketed the volume of starry space sternward. The green-white point of the white dwarf was off to the edge, the planet-sized iron corpse of a star too small to collapse all the way to neutrons, mere electron degeneracy able to balance gravity's compression. "Computer, run back visual record thirty-five minutes," Barlstilkin said.

Something glittered in the center of the tank, fading before Dorthy could be sure she'd really seen it. Barlstilkin said, "False photons. Another ship just made transit."

"The Navy?"

"Perhaps. Although it's a singleship, civilian registration. It's taking the fast route too, but we're several days ahead of it." Talbeck Barlstilkin was feeling a kind of grim satisfaction: this was retroactive justification for the risk he was taking.

Dorthy twisted to look up at him. Shadow and the dim light of the bridge conspired to mask the livid ruin of the left side of his face. He looked broodingly noble, a resurrected ninja bent on revenge according to an ancient, atavistic code of honor. . . .

Dorthy said, "It could be those friends of yours from Titan."

"I suppose that would be better than the Navy or the RUN Police. But not by much."

"Well, I suppose we'll find out when we reach the hyper-velocity star."

Barlstilkin looked down at her. "You are so very calm about this, Dorthy. Detached. As if you aren't really living through it, just watching. We could die in a couple of hours, you know. There is a distinct possibility that the ship will be torn apart by the neutron star's gravity. We have to go very close to the Roche limit."

"I haven't been brought all this way to end up as a hoop of disrupted molecules in orbit around an ember."

Barlstilkin was remotely amused. "The thing that is in your head tells you this?" It was not as important as his revenge: nothing was.

"I don't know," Dorthy confessed, for perhaps the tenth time. "I've been living with it so long now that I can't tell what's me, what isn't. I've been probed by half a dozen Talents, when the Navy had me, and they couldn't crack it either, but I'm not surprised. She was very old, very cunning."

"The neuter female. Who killed poor Duncan."

"Andrews killed her. She wanted it. But I suppose she killed him, too, in a way." Memory of the strange plaza was suddenly strong . . . the dim light of the bridge was very like the light of the red dwarf sun of P'thrsn. Rows of Alea watching her like shaggy monks, narrow faces hidden in their cowls of naked skin. The neuter female reclining like an obscene parody of Buddha, the cloud of the residual selves of her sisters, whom she had murdered and absorbed, whirling in a double lobe.

"Whatever she did to me," Dorthy said, "she did for a purpose. Maybe she knew about the hypervelocity star. She had a radio telescope. Maybe she knew that the marauders were coming all along. . . . Shit, Barlstilkin, I don't *know*! Parts of her were a million years old, and she was alien, so very alien. I *thought* I knew, then. But maybe that's what she wanted me to believe."

Dorthy was shivering, suddenly. Barlstilkin laid a hand on her shoulder. It was the first time he had touched her since he had woken her, back on the ancient composite ship. He said, "We ought to set ourselves for the transit."

The ship, originally an intrasystem cargo tug which had spent half a century hauling cargo pallets from Earth to Mars and back, was a battered old workhorse with the bare minimum of living space. Barlstilkin's renovations had left even less room.

The commons was a bare volume of about a hundred cubic meters, curved in a horseshoe around the pod which housed the power system and the spine of the phase graffle. Steel mesh floor, unshaded glotubes, a scattering of functional furniture. The bonded servant was collapsing couches and fastening them down as Barlstilkin and Dorthy came down the helical stair. She didn't pause or even look up as they went past into the crawlway down to their cabins, little asymmetrical cubicles jammed in the spaces left over between the reaction motor and the environmental recycling system and the phase graffle.

Barlstilkin paused at the parting of the ways, and for a panicky moment Dorthy thought that he was going to hug her. His ruined face was centimeters from hers in the confined crawlway. Pinpoints of sweat stood out on his unscarred skin; Dorthy could faintly feel the feathering touch of his fear. She didn't feel afraid at all. But all he said was, "I'll see you in a few hours," before turning and going on toward his cabin.

A little holostage jutted out above the acceleration tank. Sunk in impact gel, cold metallic air hissing through her facemask, Dorthy could watch the dim disk of the neutron star grow beyond the bow wave of Balmer series emissions made by the ship as it plowed remnants of ejected helium. It was traveling very fast now. Generated gravity was flatlining more than twenty gees of acceleration; figures in the status indices, projected to one side of the view, were in constant flickering ferment. Dorthy was wondering if the light of the stars beyond the neutron star were beginning to be blueshifted when Barlstilkin unexpectedly spoke up, his voice horribly intimate in the facemask.

"I was just thinking about orthidium. Do you know how catalfission batteries work?"

"I don't know. Something to do with changing neutrons into gamma rays."

"Not exactly. A molecule-sized bit of orthidium is caught in a magnetic pinch, surrounded by a paint-thin coat of U_{238}. The uranium emits slow neutrons as it decays, and some of these are filtered into the pinch to react with orthidium's naked quarks.

Trapped neutrons decay into more orthidium and release gamma rays, which the battery converts to power. So eventually you end up with more orthidium than you put in; it takes a century or so to double the amount."

"I don't see—"

"I own, used to own, a share in an orthidium mining company working the Trojan asteroids of Procyon. Before the People's Islamic Nation Party on Novaya Zyemla confiscated all private companies when it tried to break away from the Federation. After the Federation deposed that government, after the Campaigns, of course it did not return confiscated property to the original owners. . . . Do you mind if I talk?"

"Shouldn't you be flying the ship?"

"The computers are doing that now. But I was thinking, just now, what would happen if you injected a bit of orthidium into yonder star?"

"You're the expert on orthidium." Dorthy was faintly amused by his reversion to archaic word selection.

"It would turn the whole star into orthidium. Of course, you would have to get it through the crust. And stand a long way back: the gamma ray emission would be rather unhealthy. The only drawback is, how would you get the orthidium up from the bottom of the gravity well? If I could figure that, I could recoup the cost of this adventure a trillionfold."

"You're not serious." Dorthy was beginning to feel a little dizzy, as if her feet and head were trying to go in opposite directions. More than fifty gees now, half a dozen gees above the limit of generated gravity. Best not to think what would happen if it failed.

"But it is an interesting thought, is it not? If we survive this—"

"We will." It's the tide, she thought. Her feet were a meter and a half closer to the neutron star than her head, and in its steep gravity well their orbital velocity was correspondingly a little greater: the closer the orbit, the faster you have to go. The stars around the neutron star were faintly elongated, no longer points but radial lines, all drawn out toward that even red disk—a fiercer red now. They were close to perihelion, and the tide. . . .

Talbeck Barlstilkin began to say, "I'm not sure—" and the red disk suddenly filled the holostage.

For a moment Dorthy felt as if she were being drawn apart on a rack. Even the impact gel started to deform, flowing toward her feet. The ship rang like a bell. And then the neutron star was past. The ship was tumbling. Stars pinwheeled crazily across the holostage. It was the last thing Dorthy saw before the acceleration tank injected something into her thigh that instantly knocked her out.

2

GUILD CAPTAIN CARLOS ALMONTE HAD NEVER BEEN AT ease with the traditional ritual of dining with first-class passengers each evening. He had worked his way through the hierarchy of the Guild from the very bottom, and because his career had been accelerated by the Alea Campaigns, he had not had time to learn the necessary social graces. The tactful pause. The diversionary question. The ability to dissemble to pompous and/or intoxicated bores. As a result, his table was often subject either to long, sticky patches of silence when he should have been elaborating some witticism or overblown, but nevertheless elegant, compliment, or to domination by some argumentative, self-opinionated person less sensitive even than Guild Captain Almonte to social niceties.

But this time it was not entirely his fault, for seating Professor Doctor Gunasekra at the same table as the Reverend Carlos Erman Rodriguez, S. J., had created an explosive mixture that even the most tactful and diplomatic captain would find hard to moderate. The professor doctor was ridiculously young for his eminent position, barely in his thirties and looking like a teenager, with plump cheeks and bright, black, inquisitive eyes and glossy black hair down to his shoulder blades. He kept leaning forward and jabbing a finger at Father Rodriguez as he made his points, and if Captain Almonte had learned anything about the autocratic ship's chaplain, it was that there was nothing worse than that kind of breach of manners to inflame his temper.

Still, for the moment at least, Father Rodriguez seemed to be more amused than angered by Gunasekra's peroration. Perhaps as much by the professor doctor's ridiculous, shrill, excited voice as the arguments themselves. Captain Almonte had stopped trying to follow them after the first few minutes. Another social grace he had still to learn. But who cared, really, where the Universe came from, and whether there had been a First Cause and a Prime Mover, or if the whole thing had somehow or other just happened? It was here: surely that was enough for any sensible man. Leave the rest to Rodriguez and his kin.

Down the table's lane of white linen, foaming with flower arrangements (the ship had its own hothouse), glittering with silverware and crystal, those of his guests who were Navy staff seemed to share Almonte's opinion; two were even conducting a whispered, private conversation at the far end, a breach of manners almost as bad as Gunasekra's obsessive boorishness. The scientists, though, seemed content enough to listen; and the exobiologist, Martins, chipped in now and again with some obscure point of his own, although both Gunasekra and Father Rodriguez were more or less ignoring him.

Guild Captain Almonte surreptitiously crushed the hanging edge of the linen tablecloth with one hand, his smile painfully fixed, praying for the advent of the next course and fixing a complicated curse on the purser's inexorable rota system which every evening dealt a new combination of passengers to his table. And all of them first-class, too! No hard-class! The coldcoffin hold had been stripped out, turned into a low gravity recreational area to help ease the boredom of the long voyage.

Transit through contraspace was the least of this problematical voyage. There was also the runaway star's tremendous proper motion to match: the liner had reentered urspace far ahead of the star's path, had been accelerating ever since, almost three months with the rumble of the fusion flame penetrating every centimeter of the ship's fabric, nothing to see of their destination but a green-white fleck sternward, steadily growing brighter, but seemingly no bigger, as the star bore down on the liner.

No other way around celestial mechanics, but Captain Almonte should have forestalled the fiery conjunction between Gunasekra and Father Rodriguez. If he had had the necessary social acumen, he would have seen it coming; and if he could have had his own way, he would have had all the passengers cooled down to twelve degrees centigrade for the duration of the voyage.

At least Professor Doctor Gunasekra had finally made his point, whatever it had been. He looked around at his peers with the satisfaction of one who has incontrovertibly won the argument; he took away his finger and leaned back in his chair (a genuine wood imitation of some spindly seventeenth century design: Captain Almonte, who was a big, bluff man, bigger even than Father Rodriguez, scarcely dared move a muscle for fear his would collapse beneath him).

Captain Almonte saw his chance to turn the conversation away from cosmology, but before he could even open his mouth, Father Rodriguez leaned forward, jabbing *his* forefinger across the clutter of silverware and translucent porcelain. His elbow upset a finger bowl: rose petals spun away on a sinking tide of lemon-scented water.

"You still cannot deny the central argument," Father Rodriguez told Gunasekra with suave rumbling confidence. "That because our very existence is so unlikely, there must be a special cause for it. If life is so very common in the Universe, as you claim, where are the other intelligent species? Would they not already have colonized this Galaxy—every galaxy? I am not a physicist—" which was not quite true: Rodriguez was an expert on the topology of contraspace and could act as intersystem pilot in an emergency—"but I do know that once started, a wave front of colonization will spread very quickly. A million years at the most, to colonize every star in the Galaxy. Yet where are they?"

"B-but they are here," Martins broke in eagerly. "Where do you think we're going, Father?"

One or two people laughed, but the priest just raised his shaggy eyebrows, the ghost of a contemptuous shrug. "The Alea are not truly intelligent, that is surely beyond discussion. They emulate intelligence, when need arises, but otherwise they are simply animals."

"Classified," someone called out, but Gunasekra smiled at her. "Are we not all equals here?" His smile included Guild Captain Almonte, who felt the delicate heat of a blush touch the rims of his ears.

"Perhaps the Alea have suppressed intelligent life throughout the Galaxy," Martins said. "The way they did on Novaya Rosya."

"The way they tried to suppress us," one of the Navy officers said.

Martins said, "They're supposed to be all through the Galaxy, if what that Yoshida woman reported is true. Refugees from a war, wanting to stay hidden, making *sure* they stay hidden by killing off anything that might uncover them. If they're all through the Galaxy, Rodriguez, why is it that God should be so concerned with us? Why not with them?"

"Because we won the war." There was laughter, and Rodriguez waved a hand, as if flicking away a mosquito. A rose petal clung to the elbow of his frayed black sleeve. "More importantly, because they do not have souls, as the Diet of Brisbane so recently proclaimed. But this avoids the central question. The Universe is old enough to have supported carbon-based intelligent life for at least a billion years. Long enough for it to have spread to every star in every Galaxy. Yet why do we not see any sign of it? I will tell you: because it is not there. Now, I have studied enough cosmology—" he smiled at his self-mocking modesty—"to know that if even one of the fundamental properties of matter and space-time was even the slightest bit different, we could not exist. No carbon-based life could. The helium resonance for instance, that ensures carbon and oxygen is preferentially produced in stellar fusion processes. Or the size of the Boltzmann factor, that determined excess abundance of protons over neutrons after the Big Bang, so that hydrogen dominates the Universe.

"There are thousands of other examples, some trivial, many deep. If physics has told us anything in the past five hundred years, it is that God's signature is immutably woven into the fabric of the Universe. And you say, Gunasekra, that there is no such proof. I say you have done nothing to refute it."

Gunasekra's smile widened. He held the pause for a few moments, playing the table, then said in his high clear voice, "But my dear chap! There is *nothing* to prove! All I hear is a string of tired old coincidences. I do hope God would be more subtle than that, for all our sakes. You see, it is very simple. We are here not because the Universe was subtly constructed to accommodate us. Think, gentlemen! Four hundred billion stars in this Galaxy alone, a trillion galaxies just like it . . . and fifteen billion years of unrecorded history so that stars could cook up all the ingredients to furnish our brief lives." He picked up a knife and rapped the table with its haft. "Stars exploding in supernovas, simply to provide me with the means to cut up my vegetables."

There was laughter, and Gunasekra smiled broadly as he looked up and down the table. His plump cheeks were flushed to deep mahogany; sweat glittered on his unlined forehead. He said, "No, no. That takes too much pride in ourselves to believe it is true. No. We are here because if the Universe was not the way it is, why then, we would not be here. All this is very old stuff. The weak anthropic principle, a thousand years old I suppose. More recently, as you may know, Father, as you seem to have *some* knowledge of physics, despite your modesty, more recently, much progress has been made on the many worlds hypothesis. It is almost certain that there are an infinite number of universes besides our own, that there is a metaspace in which every universe is only a bubble. A bad metaphor, but vivid. It is something I have dabbled in, because of course the mathematics are contiguous with the problem of the geometry of our own space-time. Do we postulate a God for each of these universes, Rodriguez? Or is ours the only universe touched with divinity, as we are the only animals with immortal souls? Do we require a plenitude of universes as well as of stars, of time, to justify our existence? Pride indeed!"

Father Rodriguez said, "I've read your paper on the subject, not without interest. *Toward a formulation for local boundary conditions in an N-dimensional unbounded superspace.* I enjoyed your flights of fancy, Professor. They had the beauty of economy. But let me say this: to assign your own professional prejudices to a personal conception of God is the first step on the dark road to blasphemy."

"Oh, blasphemy. I'm not sure I completely understand the term, my dear chap. I was brought up as a Buddhist, after all."

Farther down the table, a dim, sallow-faced man, something to do with interservice liaison, Almonte recalled, asked if they could fly to other universes through contraspace. Gunasekra turned to him, perhaps glad of the opportunity to get away from an argument he considered he had won. "Contraspace is part of our own space-time continuum," he said patiently. "It is not contiguous with other universes. Why, it is quite possible that many do not have contraspace. Mathematically, there is no objection to a universe with only four dimensions—or even three, which I would guess is the irreducible minimum. As for travel between universes, the only conceivable route would be through the singularity of a black hole—provided it was rotating, of course. Or through a rotating naked singularity. What has been called a wormhole." He shrugged. "An old idea, but still a hypothetical concept."

"And besides," Captain Almonte put in, "I would hate to contemplate the navigational problems." He smiled, pleased to have at last contributed to the conversation.

But the scientists all more or less ignored him, while a woman at the end of the table, her plain, scrubbed face round as a full moon and framed by strawlike hair, started talking rapidly about evolution of all intelligent races toward God, or perhaps *into* God. It was difficult to follow what she was saying because she was both excited and nervous, something shiny about her eyes, the fanatical light of a recent convert. There was a badge on her lapel, a cheap hologram of the Galaxy's pinwheel . . . one of the Witnesses, then. There were so many of them on the voyage, amongst the humbler scientific staff . . . some political maneuvering there, apparently. All Almonte knew about them was that they hung around spaceports, handing out data cubes to anyone who made the mistake of paying them even the slightest attention. The wretched woman was someone's aide, no doubt, out of her depth and knowing it, too, but without the sense to keep quiet. At last, she stopped talking, or at least ran out of words, and there was an uneasy silence at the table, a bubble of embarrassment in the huge domed space while all around a hundred conversations at other tables chattered above the rumble of the reaction motor.

Almonte was just about to say something—anything—when he saw one of the stewards coming toward him. He was wanted on the bridge to check crew rotas, a phrase that meant a serious problem had arisen. Still, Almonte felt a clear measure of relief as he bowed his apologies to the table, and left on the heels of the steward.

The liner was making its final approach to parking orbit, only thirty-odd hours away, now. The methane gas giant that was its destination loomed huge, half-full and splattered with dim, swirling greens. Its single moon, Colcha, was on the far side, and so the research ship which attended it was out of radio contact. For the moment, the problem was entirely Guild Captain Almonte's.

He gripped the chromed edge of the navigation tank while his first officer, Manuel de Salinas, a calm capable Brazilian, had the computer run through the sequence. The ship—incredibly, it was an intrasystem tug—had phased in a cascade of false photons right at the equilibrium point: a few thousand klicks farther in and it would have been too deep inside the star's gravity well and ripped apart by equalization of the energy levels of urspace and contraspace through its phase graffle. It was already traveling at a velocity more than matching the proper motion of the hypervelocity star: it would have had to kill some of that to achieve orbit. But that was impossible, for the tug was also tumbling uncontrollably, a highly eccentric nose-over-tail rotation with a period of less than a second. Its image sparkled dizzyingly in the navigation tank.

"It was even worse when they phased in," de Salinas remarked. "The pilot used up all his attitude thruster reaction mass to get it down to what you see now."

"How did it happen? And how did an intrasystem tug manage to achieve six percent light speed, for the sake of God?"

De Salinas smiled. He was enjoying himself. Light from the tank struck under his chin, making his thin, craggy face look incredibly sinister, filling each pit in his acne-scarred cheeks with a half-moon of shadow. "The pilot says he did a flyby momentum transfer around a slowly rotating neutron star. But it went wrong, radically wrong. He went a fraction too close to the neutron star, and ended up with spin as well as velocity."

"And he can't stop the spin. He's lucky torque hasn't ripped his ship apart. Can we do it? No, we'd have to spin the ship up to match him, and she wouldn't take it. Perhaps one of the *Vingança*'s tugs . . . ? I assume he wants to be rescued. He must be a criminal *and* a madman, to be here."

"He's willing to be retrieved." De Salinas's smile grew wider. "He has no alternative, of course. It is very lucky for them that we are here. In less than two hours the window for retrieval will have passed. But as it is, it will be a simple matter of matching velocity and sacrificing one of our maintenance drones. I'm running a simulation to see if we can pack enough reaction mass into a drone so that it can spin itself up and then cancel the spin after it attaches to the tug."

"And how will that affect our schedule?"

"Add almost fifty hours to it, I'm afraid."

"We might have to leave them," Almonte said, turning over in midair so he would not have to look at the tank. He needed to think it through, and the familiar scene of the bridge provided minimal distraction. Free-form redlit space, half a dozen crew members webbed in acceleration slings, faces hidden by hookups and display hoods. No sound but the faint hum of the environmental conditioning, the hushed air of concentration . . . like a church. . . .

Normally, Almonte would not have hesitated. Disaster in space was usually comprehensive and beyond redemption, rescue ruled out by distance and radically differing velocities. Any chance to save someone was therefore precious, not to be squandered. But there was the consideration of security. Beyond those already here, only a few high-ranking Naval and Guild officers and the Security Council of the Re-United Nations knew about the hypervelocity star. The mining tug was not on any sightseeing tour. Rescue, therefore, would be to aid and abet an unknown trespasser. But the decision was Almonte's to make. By the time Colcha and the *Vingança* came around the gas giant, the tumbling tug would be beyond the range of any help Almonte's ship could offer.

"Well," Almonte said, "who is the liaison officer among our passengers? I suppose he will have to know."

He was the sallow-faced man who had been dining at the Captain's table, who had asked the dim question about navigating between universes. His name was Alexander Ivanov. Horribly uncomfortable in the bridge's traditional microgravity, he clung to the navigation tank with a desperate grip as de Salinas explained the situation. Ivanov's lank black hair kept drifting over his eyes, and when he shook it back with a toss of his head the motion twisted him away from the tank, so Almonte doubted that he was taking in very much of de Salinas's soothing talk.

But when the first officer had finished, Ivanov said, "There really is no way to make contact with echelon?"

"The ship will be beyond the range of any rescue attempt we can make," de Salinas said patiently, "by the time Colcha's orbit brings the *Vingança* into view."

"But the gas giant has a couple of monitoring satellites in orbit around it, and they are in contact with the *Vingança*. We can patch in through them."

"As a matter of fact," de Salinas said, "there are three satellites. But we aren't allowed to interrupt their data streams, Seyour Ivanov. Continuous monitoring is too important to be interrupted."

The liaison officer tried to turn to Almonte, almost lost his grip on the tank's bar, and kicked his legs in the wrong direction. De Salinas gripped him by the vent of his brocade jacket just in time. The man swallowed, sweat standing out on his pasty forehead, and for a dreadful moment Almonte thought that he was going to vomit. But the spasm passed. Ivanov said grimly, "The risk of compromise is too great, Captain. You will attempt no rescue."

"I invited you to the bridge for your opinion, Seyour Ivanov. I am not under your command."

"Echelon would make the same decision; I know it. You'll let them go on their way. No rescue. There's no telling who they are. Novaya Zyemla insurgents, most probably. Let them onto this ship, and next thing you'll be under *their* command."

"There are only two aboard," de Salinas said. "Oh, and a bonded servant. Besides, I understand they are in a bad way. Only one is awake, and even he is sedated. The effect of their eccentric motion. . . ."

"*They* say only three," Ivanov said.

Guild Captain Almonte asked de Salinas. "How long until they're out of range?"

"We would have to start our burn within twenty minutes to match their velocity. As I have said, it will add fifty hours to our rendezvous with the *Vingança*. We will have to perform a flyby braking maneuver around the gas giant."

Guild Captain Almonte said, "Manuel, you will start our burn, and break out a maintenance drone. Have them suit up and ready to leave the tug once we have matched their velocity and killed that absurd precession. That way they will not be able to try anything foolish. Make sure they understand that. They can come across into one of the auxiliary airlocks, one by one, before we secure their ship. No, Seyour—" Ivanov had started to splutter something about aiding and abetting unfriendly powers—"you must remember that this is not a Navy ship. When I was given this command, the Navy neglected to reactivate my service rank. I serve the Guild only. We are not at war with anyone, and besides, neither the RUN nor any other sovereign government has laid a formal territorial claim to this system. There is a ship in distress, and I am in a position to help it."

Ivanov said, "You force me to notify you that I shall draw up a formal report, Captain Almonte."

"By all means. For now, please restrain your impulse to spew on my bridge." Almonte beckoned to the steward who had escorted Ivanov. "Take this passenger to his cabin. And why aren't you working on my orders, de Salinas? Time's running out."

Later, Almonte watched the navigation tank as the maintenance drone slowly approached the long axis of the tug's tumbling, blunt arrowhead. Drone and ship, only feebly limned by the white dwarf's tarnished light, were both rotating now, so rapidly that the strobes of the drone seemed to describe bright arcs, throwing random reflections off the tug's nose assembly. Then, with a kind of lurching motion, the two latched together, and the drone's angled thruster began to pulse in counterpoint to the swift erratic spin, an almost subliminal blinking.

Floating beside Almonte, de Salinas sighed and said, "There is going to be trouble over this, isn't there?"

"Undoubtedly."

After that, the bridge was quiet for a long time. The tumbling spin of drone and tug slowed imperceptibly.

Guild Captain Almonte said, "Do you know something? I haven't felt such satisfaction for a long time. If they do take away my command, this is what I'll miss. Not acting as host to a lot of puffed up functionaries."

Drone and tug had almost stabilized, turning very slowly end for end. Beyond, the dim green crescent of the gas giant was tipped against the stars, freighted with mystery.

Guild Captain Almonte said, "We're lucky to be here, Manuel. One more thing. As we have an emergency on our hands, I feel I ought to spend more time on the bridge. You may tell the purser that from now on I will take my meals right here."

3

HER FIRST MORNING ABOARD THE *VINGANÇA*, STILL
dazed by a vivid dream, Dorthy took the wrong turning
outside her cabin and within a minute was lost in the warren
of interconnected accommodation modules that battened onto
the research ship's kilometer-long spine like barnacles to a rock.
Only a small part was in use. The rest was unheated, lighted
only by the dim, spaced stars of emergency phosphors. The air
thin and stale and cold. Linear perspectives of corridors, shafts,
intersections, falling away in red light and shadow. Hundreds
upon hundreds of cubicles held nothing but a silting of dust
and the peculiarly poignant ghosts of those who are not dead,
but have simply moved on.

Originally an intersystem freighter, the *Vingança* had been
commandeered and converted by the Navy to serve as the
main operations base for the Alea Campaigns. Stationed half a
light-year from BD Twenty, safely out of reach of the Enemy's
strictly Newtonian ships, it had been the launching platform for
half a dozen wing squadrons of singleships, home for more than
a thousand personnel. There were fewer than two hundred
aboard now. Dorthy wandered the empty modules a long time,
enjoying the cold silences outside and inside her head—the
hydra-headed babble of the mob shrunk to a remote whisper—
and trying to remember all she could of the dream.

She'd dreamed that she was on P'thrsn, climbing the forested
lower slopes of the gigantic caldera. Poor dead Arcady Kilczer
was somewhere near. She couldn't see him, but knew that he
was behind her, in the shadowy tangle of trees hardly lighted
by the dim red glow of P'thrsn's red dwarf sun. There was
someone else, too: Dorthy heard high excited laughter, once

or twice glimpsed a girl in a white dress, bare legs flashing in the stygian gloom as she skipped away between scaly trunks, mossy rocks. When Dorthy tried to run after this apparition, her limbs seemed weighted with more than fatigue, but somehow she burst out of the forest onto the bare shore of a lake. Its calm black water spread out to mirror the huge, flecked disk of the red sun, the dim day stars. A little girl stood on a shelf of crumbling black and red andesite that jutted out over the water. Three, four years old, dressed in a white dress with a red checked blouse, long black hair wound in an oiled pigtail that reached halfway down her back. She waved as Dorthy looked up at her.

"I know who *you* are," the girl called, "but I don't know your friend. Who is she?"

Dorthy looked back at the forest margin. A shape too big to be Kilczer moved in the shadows beneath the trees.

The shock had woken her. As she had splashed water on her face and run her fingers through her cropped black hair, she had realized that the girl was still with her: she was her own childhood self, from the brief age of innocence before she'd been indentured to the Kamali-Silver Institute. Now, as Dorthy wandered empty, echoing corridors, she realized that she knew what the watcher in the woods was, too.

It was the thing that had imprinted itself on her, the thing that lurked in the muddy sediments of her hindbrain like a grandfather carp, the thing that made her crave the sharp illumination of her Talent. She was beginning to suspect that at last it was where it wanted to be, and now it wanted to act. It wanted to unlock the doors of perception. Suddenly, Dorthy wanted company again, human noise. She had grown out of her need for solitude in prison; she was only just beginning to realize that.

Some of the terminals were still working in the abandoned modules. Dorthy accessed the ship's net and had it spin a thread to the nearest refectory.

She was still in the bleak crew lounge, working on her third cup of coffee, when the scientists found her. There were two of them, men Dorthy knew from her days at Fra Mauro, her aborted career as a research astronomer: plump, nervous Estaban Flores; lean, elegant Luiz Valdez. Dorthy had had a brief fling with Valdez, but then, she'd had brief flings with more than a dozen men at Fra Mauro, scandalizing many of the Greater Brazilian students, who believed that seduction and sexual promiscuity was the prerogative of the male.

The pair took their time coming to the point. Dorthy heard out old gossip about her ex-classmates, and was circumspect about her role in the Alea Campaigns, giving the impression that afterward she'd gone back to being a Talent. She didn't yet know if she could trust them with what she had learned.

"The crux of the matter is that we are living on top of a bomb here," Luiz Valdez said at last. "There could be anything inside Colcha. The Navy is too chickenshit to send a probe into one of the shafts, and we've learned all we need to know about the outside." He made a languid gesture, as if to dismiss the Navy from the bounds of discussion.

Across the table, Estaban Flores, who'd grown even plumper in the years since Dorthy had last seen him, said uncomfortably, "We aren't really supposed to be talking about this. Not here, anyhow." Flores, Dorthy remembered, always had been neurotically anxious about transgressing unwritten codes of behavior back at Fra Mauro. A company man through and through, dogged and patient, and quite without any spark of originality.

Valdez said, "Flores, everyone is in everyone else's pockets. For instance, everyone knows about your sordid little affair with that technician despite the absurd lengths to which you go to hide it. She's a Witness for God's sake," he said to Dorthy. "I worry that she'll convert Flores."

Flores said, "You don't worry about anyone but yourself." He was blushing.

"Oh, Flores, if you started praying to the center of the Galaxy, who else will I find who has the patience to beat me three times a day at chess? And don't blush so. Sex is healthy. With the right person."

There had always been that sharpness to Valdez, Dorthy remembered, a dangerous impulsive edge. The seventh son of some minor industrial baron, his profile keen as a coin's stamped portrait, hair slicked back with something that made it shine like polished wood, mustache waxed to fine points. He was smiling at Dorthy, and she said, "What are these Witnesses? The people with the funny pinwheel brooches?"

"Dorthy, where have you been?" Valdez's surprise was genuine.

"Novaya Rosya. Traveling."

"Not on Earth for a while."

"They are millenarians," Flores said.

"They are crazy. They think that somewhere in this Universe, at the center of the Galaxy, down in the shafts of Colcha too, I suppose, there are wise, ancient aliens who will presently make themselves known, who will come to save humanity from itself. And when these paragons appear, they will, of course, take only the Witnesses. It's a sort of cargo cult."

"There's more to it than that," Flores said.

"Careful, Dorthy. He'll give you a data cube any moment."

Flores said, "The Witnesses believe that our kind of intelligence is only the first step in evolution toward a pan-Galactic, a pan-Universal, intelligence. They believe that the existence of the Alea means that many other alien civilizations must exist. If that's the case, then some must be very old, millions, perhaps billions of years old. They believe that we don't see evidence of these older civilizations because mechanical conquest of the Universe is just the first step, one soon abandoned."

"We'll all of us become angels," Valdez said, "flying through the Universe on wings of light. Or something like that. Witnesses think the hypervelocity star is a kind of message. That's why there are so many of them here. That, and the fact that Gregor Baptista is the brother of the Greater Brazilian Police Minister. They're not really interested in discovering the truth, because they believe that they already know it. They sit on their fat asses and wait for truth to shine through like a rare good deed in this naughty Universe of ours. They get in the fucking way, to be frank."

"Well," Dorthy said, "they might be right, in a way." Memory of the vision she'd been given on P'thrsn was sudden and vivid: vast structures abandoned around the black hole at the Galaxy's core, the source of the technology appropriated by the marauders for their war against the other Alea families.

Valdez leaned forward and said, "What do you know, Dorthy?"

"I really don't think we should talk here," Flores said. He was looking around the brightly lighted lounge, at its scattering of tables and its battered treacher, at the knot of people in the far corner, leather-jacketed mechanics, stewards with the high collars of their dress whites unfastened, scowling at the cards fanned in their hands. The permanent floating poker pool: apparently it had been going ever since the *Vingança* had phased out of the Solar System. Flores said, "We shouldn't even *be* here, strictly speaking. Isn't there somewhere else we can talk?" Sweat glittered the little mustache Flores had cultivated on the plump slope of his upper lip (which, paradoxically, made him look even younger than he had at Fra Mauro, a fat, tender mooncalf).

"I prefer it to the officer's wardroom," Dorthy said.

"Well," Valdez said, "this is more fun than the wardroom. Even you gotta admit that, Flores." He squeezed Dorthy's shoulder. "The Navy officers look down their long, aristocratic noses if we even hang around there, let alone start *drinking*, and all the fucking stewards will serve us is dilute reconstituted freeze-dried piss. Navy, y'know?"

"Yes, I know all too well."

"Yes, you and P'thrsn. I heard a little bit about that."

"I was beginning to suspect that you did." Dorthy was wondering, but didn't dare ask, just how much he knew. Presumably not that she had been held by the Navy in the years after P'thrsn, certainly not that she had escaped only with the help of Talbeck Barlstilkin. No one on the ship could know about that: it had happened long after the liner which had rescued her and Barlstilkin had set out for the hypervelocity star. And if they did know, then she wouldn't have been allowed on the *Vingança*, and neither would Barlstilkin.

"I'll tell you what," Valdez said, "we'll trade secret for secret. Navy thinks we can all work in tight little waterproof boxes. Security. Can't even access the ship's net directly."

"I know all about that, too," Dorthy said.

"He tried to get around it," Flores explained to Dorthy, "and now he has to have this supervisor ask questions for him. I mean, it's his own fault."

Dorthy smiled. "Valdez, do you still play those kinds of games? I remember you ran all our grades back to zero once."

"Yeah, childish, isn't it? But listen, Dorthy, if we can get you talking with some of the heavy duty people the liner brought, we might crack it. Don't you think? Then it won't matter *how* we did it, we'll be such big heroes. Defusing the Enemy's big weapon, maybe even turning it against them. And if we can get you into the research program, maybe we can cancel your ticket back on the liner. And get that new security slimeball off your back. He's a RUN Police spy, is the scuttlebutt."

Dorthy shrugged out of his loose embrace, picked up her beaker of strong, black java. Actually she felt a certain stirring in her blood. She had always liked slim, raffish, slightly dangerous men. That they weren't predictable, even to themselves (*especially* to themselves), was spice. And she had fond memories from Fra Mauro, too. She said, "It sounds good. But I think this isn't a weapon, and it certainly isn't anything to do with the Alea. Not directly, anyway."

"You do, huh? So what is it, then, and if it isn't the Enemy, who is it?"

"When I was on P'thrsn, I learned one or two things about the history of the Alea. You were probably told some of what I learned, what I told the Navy," she said, "although I bet you didn't know how they had come by the information."

Valdez smiled, but said nothing.

"Well, I thought I would be able to tell everyone once I got back to Earth, but the Navy wouldn't let me." Suddenly, Dorthy was acutely aware of her passenger, and wondered if she was about to have another attack, something that hadn't happened since Novaya Rosya. When she set down her beaker, coffee splashed onto the greasy, green plastic tabletop. Flores looked at her, concern in his moist spaniel eyes. "I'm okay," she told him. "I just get these flashes. Another legacy of P'thrsn."

Valdez said, "Yeah, you had it tough down there. So tell me what you think it is."

Dorthy said, "Valdez, you'll go far. Because you don't give a shit about anyone but yourself. How much do you know about me, anyway? Where did you find it out?"

"Not so much actually. More than I'm supposed to know, which is the crazy thing, considering where we are." Valdez was amused.

"I don't like this Navy bullshit any more than you do. They've got worse, since BD Twenty. The hand-tailored uniforms with all that gold braid, dress swords, sword belts with diamond and silver inlays. The cost of *one* of those uniforms is more than my father ever earned in his lifetime." *Including what he took from me and pissed away on that no hope cattle farm in the Outback.* Her anger was sudden and fierce; the feeling that she was going to get one of her soothsayer fits vanished under it. She drained her coffee and threw the empty beaker toward the recycling bin, contributing to the litter around its maw. "Listen," she said, "I'll go in with you because it's too important to be compromised by Navy politics. This is part of a story that's been spinning out for millions of years. It's not just the Alea, although I think they precipitated it. After the family nations had to flee their home system for the Galaxy's core, one of them stumbled upon old technology abandoned around the black hole there. Do you know all this?"

Flores shook his head. "I don't know if it's a good idea if you told us, either. A little knowledge is a dangerous thing. I mean to say, is it relevant to the chaotic geology of Colcha, or to the hypervelocity star? That's what we're here to riddle, not some half-baked ancient history."

Dorthy said, "It is the truth. It is what happened, Flores. You had better start facing up to it."

Flores's cheeks darkened with a flush of anger. "I remember that snooty way you had of pronouncing on people, prying into their heads. Drifting around Fra Mauro with your cute nose in the air, spouting Shakespeare at the drop of a hat. None of that made you any better than anyone else. What gives you the right to tell me what to believe?"

Dorthy said, " 'A friendly eye could never see such faults.' But you're right, Flores, I was a little shit back then. And you don't have to believe me now. But you're here to learn the truth about the hypervelocity star, and you should listen to what happened to me. You don't have to like it, and I don't ask you to like me. But what has that to do with anything?"

She held Flores's gaze until he looked away, and immediately felt ashamed at the cheap trick.

Valdez said, "Don't mind Flores. He can always run off and do experiments on interstellar grain impacts. That's the kind of thing we're doing, stuff the Navy can appreciate. Not the deep questions."

"Fuck you," Flores said. "All this talk of truth, and all you really want is glory."

"If we play this right, there'll be enough for everyone," Valdez said. "I only want a share. Now listen," he told Dorthy, "what you should do is tell your story to Gunasekra. From what I understand, he doesn't like the Navy at *all*, doesn't like the team leaders either, or any part of the system that's going here."

"The vacuum topology man? He's here?"

Valdez said, "He came on the liner that rescued you and that crazy Golden. You can tell me that story, too, when we've some spare time."

"Let's start at the beginning," Dorthy said. She told them about the Alea's home world, orbiting a brown dwarf which itself orbited an insubstantial red supergiant within the gas clouds that shrouded the Galaxy's heart, renewed by infall of hydrogen as it passed through belts of gas compressed by supernovas among the core stars. She told them about the Alea, the ten thousand family nations of hunters and their flocks of children, who metamorphosed into intelligent neuter males whenever the giant sun went through a periodic eruption of flares, jerry-rigging technology that would protect their dumb, indolent parents from radiation flux, warring with other families, dying away when danger had passed. She told them about the supernova whose hard radiation had brought about the slow death and dissipation of the supergiant star, the flight of the Alea families inward to find new homes among the packed stars of the core, the emergence of long-lived neuter females who would keep the families safe in the centuries it took to planoform suitable worlds—worlds of dim, red dwarf stars. She told them about the marauders, a family nation which had pirated technology abandoned around the black hole at the Galaxy's dead center, which had waged a relentless campaign of genocide on the other

families, of the arks which had fled the marauders and the core
to hide among the four hundred billion stars of the spiral arms.
She told them about P'thrsn, about what had happened to her
there, about the passenger inside her head.

It was a long story that took a couple of hours and several
cups of coffee to tell. At last Dorthy said, "That's why I'm here.
I don't know if it's my compulsion or hers, and it doesn't much
matter, anymore. When I was at Fra Mauro, I was trying to
make a normal life for myself, after the years I'd spent as a
Talent. It wasn't to be. There was P'thrsn, and . . . afterward.
I accept that, now. I want to make the most of what I've got.
That's why I'm here. So are you guys going to help me?"

Valdez said, "Tell me what you want."

"I want to know what's going on here. The gas giant, the
funny moon with the holes in it. I asked the captain, when he
had his little talk with Barlstilkin and me, but he wouldn't be
specific."

Valdez laughed. "You asked the captain! That's good! He
doesn't know anything, Dorthy. He just runs the ship. I can
tell you *all* about Colcha. Better still, I can get you a ride to
see Colcha from close orbit. What do you say, Flores? You're
always having stuff collected from those interstellar grain traps
of yours. One, two flights a day, right?"

"It's possible. But I say that we should get clearance for
it first."

"And I say fuck that. What's your authorization code—don't
worry, I know it already. Come on, Dorthy. Let's go hitch
a ride."

The surface of the gas giant's moon was a crazy collation
of a hundred different geologies, hazed by freezing wisps of
methane and drifts of dirty ammonia snow. On the way back
from sampling Flores's experiment—a kilometer-wide silvered
mylar target hung in orbit at the gas giant's trailing Trojan
point and given just enough spin to keep it rigid—the pilot
of the tiny orbital tug skimmed the edge of the exclusion zone
to show Dorthy one of the hundred or so enigmatic shafts
that pierced the moon's chaotic surface. It was a ragged circle
like a drug-dilated eye at the bottom of a smooth crater fifty

kilometers across. As Dorthy stared into it, this vast enigmatic eye seemed to blink, as if momentarily sealing over with a ghostly landscape.

"A gap in reality," Valdez said. He was shoulder-to-shoulder with Dorthy. They had to take turns to look out of the triangular port, clumsily bumping into one another in their pressure suits. The cabin was that small. "In the early days, some of the physicists lowered telemetry packages into the shafts. They're still trying to understand the readings. Everything changes down there."

"What are they for, Valdez?"

"Gates to somewhere else, is the best guess. Permanent phase points, wormholes . . . no one really knows." His shrug moved them both in the tug's microgravity. "If there was a black monolith, maybe we'd have a better idea."

"Do you still watch those old films?"

"I was wondering if you remembered that."

"I remember," Dorthy said. She watched the dim moonscape unravel beyond the port's thick glass. A rumpled surface, so thickly pocked with craters that they overlapped, abruptly gave way to a plain scored with straight, parallel ridges. Something stirred through her body, a tide wakening in her blood. She said, "This is it, Valdez. This is where I have to go."

The pilot, a rangy, green-eyed Iraqi Jew from Bombay, said, "I cannot take you. There is someone who goes down to Colcha; she services the monitoring stations. She's crazy enough to let you hitch a ride, certainly. But even she walks softly, down there. Don't want to wake anything up, you understand."

Valdez said to the pilot, "Amish, how about if we go into orbit?"

"You know that isn't allowed."

"Not even one low altitude pass? Dr. Yoshida here has a special interest in Colcha."

"I can ask traffic control. But they will say no."

As the pilot had switched channels, Valdez asked Dorthy, his lips so close to her ear they tickled, "This does something for you?"

"I do think I need to go down there. I told you about my passenger. Mostly, she's inaccessible to me, but there are cues that bring her into the foreground of my consciousness, that give me access to what she knows. Perhaps there are cues on Colcha. You're the planetologist, Valdez. Tell me what I'm seeing. Could it have been shattered by a collision, and reformed by gravity drag?"

"The rocks are different ages. The youngest is a billion years old, the oldest eleven billion. A record, by the way. There's what looks like a fossilized sea bottom, even down to wave ripples. It's mudstone, and there are microfossils in it. They're going back on the liner for classification. They just look like forams to me, but what do I know?"

The mesh floor vibrated and the reaction motor made a basso profundo rumbling. Gravity's ghost tugged at Dorthy.

Valdez said, "Amish, what is this? An insertion burn?"

"We must go back, Dr. Valdez. There is an intruder, traffic control tells me, that has just phased into the system. We have a stage one alert."

Dorthy said, "A singleship." A double star, the *Vingança* and the liner, dawned above the ragged horizon. The moon's enigmatic surface was dropping away. It would have to wait.

The pilot said, "How did you know that?"

Valdez said, "What do you know, Dorthy?"

"A singleship followed us around the neutron star. That's all I know. As for who is on it, ask Talbeck Barlstilkin. It's his plot. I just came along for the ride."

4

=

SUZY CAME OUT OF CONTRASPACE IN A BLAZE OF FALSE photons, her every nerve pressed raw against the singleship's inputs. Just like combat, phasing in at the very edge of the gravity limit, wired to the back teeth and ready and willing to deal a shit-load of trouble to anything that so much as blinked. A barrage of information downloaded across her wraparound vision as a dozen different displays lighted up at once. Radar and radio, overlays of ultraviolet and infrared on the wraparound visuals, not to mention impenetrable data tables from the weird sensors that had been bolted onto the standard package. A neutrino detector for instance, fizzling with signals from the shrunken star and from discrete point sources in orbit around the gas giant; a gravity wave meter; something that measured the quantum strain of the vacuum, more like a goddamn physics experiment than anything a pilot would want.

Robot, or rather, *Machine* (Suzy still wasn't used to making the distinction), had flanged up their specs from stuff he'd found in the ship's library, had had Robot's little rat-machine put them together. Designing the esoteric detectors had been something to occupy the dead time of transit, Machine had said—apparently he wasn't at all interested in sex, which was how Robot and Suzy had occupied a lot of *their* time.

Machine'd been a bit vague about just what he wanted to detect with his funny little devices, and Suzy was damned if she could understand most of what they were trying to tell her. Pepped to the eyeballs with adrenaline and cortical stimulants, she simply let all the data streams wash through her, retaining only what made sense.

It was just like combat, except . . . there was nothing there. Just a feeble little burned-out white dwarf, no bigger than the Earth but massing as much as Sol . . . and a gas giant . . . just a single moon. . . . A handful of discrete points around the gas giant's moon were lighting up the neutrino detector, but they had to be the Navy; the fusion generators that were putting out the neutrinos were burning the same lithium: deuterium mix as commercial reactors, according to the detector's hillocky little three-dimensional plot. Nothing alien, no other activity of any kind, unless it was hidden deep in the electrical storms and frozen methane clouds of the gas giant.

Nothing at all . . . not even dust grains, which was kind of weird, nothing but a thin rain of molecular hydrogen, the interstellar medium through which the hypervelocity star and everything attendant on it was plowing, whacking past at roughly six percent light speed. If it hadn't been for that, Suzy wouldn't have been able to tell just how fast the ship was traveling just to keep up with this drab little system. Not like the time they'd whipped around the neutron star. A dull red ember, bedded in a well of refracted blueshifted starlight, throwing itself straight at her face—gone! Just like that. Gravity generator redlining, impact gel suddenly rigid as concrete, her ribs trying to do open-heart surgery, as momentum exchange flung the ship out, so fast that in less than three minutes it was a hundred million kilometers from the neutron star, far enough out of the gravity well to phase into contraspace. Call that flying, and no one to see it but a spaced-out weirdo who half the time thought he was a machine.

Suzy ran the sweep again, distantly aware of Robot plugging into it through one of the connections his pet had lashed up. Like someone riding your viewpoint when you're inside a saga, reality intruding with heavy breath on the back of your neck. He was bundled tight in the crashweb; Suzy had insisted.

"Okay," she said after a while, "what do you think?"

"Well, gee, I didn't know I was allowed opinions."

"Maybe one. If it's good."

She'd survived the Alea Campaigns, she reckoned, by *not* planning ahead, by taking everything as it came in the few hectic minutes at the bottom of the orbit, on the cusp, when she'd shot past whatever infested slab of rock had been her target. Think too much about what might happen, and you get caught up in your own scenarios. Reality is the only movie, as that astronomer she'd once hooked up with had liked to say. What was it? Yeah, everything else is shadows.

But by expecting at least some kind of undefined strangeness, Suzy had been tripped by the absence of anything she could target. She was ready to go for anything that looked remotely like it had the stamp of the Enemy on it, and there was . . . nothing. A burned-out star, a gas giant which could have been Uranus, if you didn't look too closely. A no-account moon orbited by maybe one big Navy ship, half a dozen or so small ones. Difficult to tell: the neutrino detector wasn't all that sensitive, and none of the ships were putting out any sort of identification. Slag time all over again, the story of her life.

She said to Robot, "Are you gonna talk or what? If it wasn't for the Navy there, I'd've have thought we hit the wrong star. Come on. What are these weird detectors trying to tell me?"

Machine said, "That everything appears to be normal, Seyoura." And Robot added, "Don't listen to him, he's got no soul."

"Machine is right, you ask me. Nowhere is *exactly* where we are. The interstellar equivalent of downtown Outer Mongolia on a slow night. I thought it was supposed to be full of the fucking Enemy, I mean that was the point, right? Why I'm here? See one white dwarf you see 'em all, even if it is moving faster than anything else in the neighborhood."

Robot said, "That's the point. Think about it, Suzy. What a fucking statement of intent! By its very presence, it illuminates and changes us. It is its own message, see, packed down to the minimum. Like the works of the Abstract Monumentalists in the twenty-first century, at the end of the first Space Age. They'd build a cairn on some remote asteroid, nothing more. Or on Mars, select stones of a certain size, arrange them in a wide, perfect circle. Or the Moon, this I've seen, Mare Serenitatis, they dug a pit, a perfect hemisphere, exactly 3.142 meters in diameter, its deepest point exactly half 3.142 meters below the surface. It will outlast all other artifacts, most human artifacts. Yet so simple. A perfect statement of will, of intent. As is this. What more do you want?"

"A target will do, for a start."

"You want to make your fortune, but have you really thought what you'd do with all that credit? You don't have the infrastructure to look after it; someone's bound to take it from you. See, credit's not the point. If you're clever enough, you can subvert the system, like the freebreathers."

Suzy said, "Like a bunch of parasites." They'd had this conversation about a million times, and here it was again.

Robot said, "Parasites are always one evolutionary step ahead of their hosts. Let me tell you about the gene-for-gene hypothesis sometime. So which is more advanced? Forget credit, Suzy. Live in the moment. I'm in love, here. If I could get out of this cradle one second I'd give you a kiss to remember, this is so perfect."

Suzy said, "Men, they hack their brains in half and still all they can think about is sex." But she was smiling.

"There is something interesting about the moon," Machine said.

"Yeah?"

It was too far away for the ship's visual system to yield anything but a featureless crescent, dawning beyond the slanting rim of the gas giant. The tracking subroutines she'd initiated by reflex had been locked onto it long enough to calculate its unremarkable posigrade orbit, fairly regular, with an eccentricity of 0.03, a sidereal period of just over a thousand hours. That would mean for most of the time it was sheltered by the star or by the gas giant from any junk zipping through the system. Small, its diameter not more than a thousand kilometers; that and its orbit gave it a low density, less than water, though it wasn't cold enough to be a compact snowball of frozen gases, like Charon, for instance.

Suzy saw all this at a glance. "I don't see anything too strange," she said.

"You should deal with your machines more directly. Interfaces get in the way of thought processes. They are barriers—"

Before Robot could get another art critique rolling, Suzy said, "So why don't you tell me what your superior senses show up, huh? If I'm going to make orbit, I have to adjust our delta vee inside a couple of hours."

"It is quite simple," Machine said. "The moon is full of holes."

"Show me."

Suzy looked at the graphic a long time. A shadow sphere whose surface was punctuated by holes, *shafts*, more than a hundred of them. No pattern to their distribution, but they were all the same size. "Okay," she said, "I'm doing the burn."

Robot didn't say anything, before or after the couple of minutes of low acceleration that altered the singleship's fall through the system by the small amount necessary to bring it close enough to the gas giant. The silence stretched, so long that Suzy thought he'd switched out again, flashing over high art or simply switching himself off, as he'd done from time to time while the ship plunged through the nonlinear architecture of contraspace. It was a trick Suzy envied. Sagas, listening to the blues, even playback sleep (which always gave her technicolor nightmares), only stretched the long hours after a while, instead of helping them pass. If Robot had been awake all the time, she supposed she might even have grown tired of sex. . . .

Indicators were lighting up. The Navy appeared to have spotted the singleship at last. Cautious nanosecond low-power radar pulses were probing it; there was a brief, crude attempt to interrogate the switched-off computer.

Suzy ran through the checklist of the singleship's meager and entirely illegal arsenal. If there truly was nothing here, then she wasn't going to let herself be caught by the Navy. Plenty of places to go these days if you were a renegade with a stolen spaceship. A dozen new frontier worlds, for instance, the oldest not three years settled, and by barely more than ten thousand people. No questions asked out there, which is why the Federation wanted to restrict exploration, power like light subject to the square root law of diminishment with distance. . . .

Machine's uninflected voice surprised her. "Seyoura Falcon. I believe that there is something else you should know. Are you receiving any transmissions?"

"Navy's probing us. Not trying to talk. Not yet."

Machine said, "Well, I don't really understand this, but something is trying to talk to me."

And Suzy said, "Wait. You said some*thing*?"

5

TALBECK BARLSTILKIN SAID, "I SUPPOSE YOU HAVE COME to tell me about your little trip around Colcha."

"How did you know about that?"

Barlstilkin only smiled his crooked smile.

"All right," Dorthy said. "I suppose that's another of your secrets. But what *do* you want me to do if I can't use my Talent? You want to find out the truth, don't you? It's simple. Have one of the lab people synthesize the counteragent to my implant's secretions. Then I'll have my Talent, and I can find out what *she* knows."

Barlstilkin considered that for a moment. His bonded servant stood patiently just behind him, eyes on infinity. They were sitting in a corner of the wardroom, away from the others. A serial light fantasy played on the screen that filled one wall edge to edge. On another level of the huge room, a white-jacketed steward was bringing a tray of drinks to a table where off-duty officers lounged in their elegant, gold-trimmed dress blues.

Barlstilkin said, "If it were that simple, I would not have needed to come here. Do you really think that you can succeed where Diemetrios, and all the Talents employed by the Navy, failed?"

"She wants to talk with me. She's in my dreams, and that's something new. She's real, Talbeck, more real than a memory. I just need to bring her into the foreground."

"By going down on Colcha, perhaps, and triggering a cue?"

"You really have been busy."

"I so find it odd that a Talent should resent even a small amount of . . . prying. I need to know what you are doing, Dorthy."

Dorthy took a cinnamon oatcake from the pile on the crested plate, but put it down again after breaking it in half. She said, "I have the feeling that she knows about Colcha. She comes right into my dreams, shows me glimpses of herself. Last time I was back on P'thrsn, climbing the forest on the outer slopes of the caldera. . . ."

And for a moment she was there again, on the slopes she had climbed alone after Arcady Kilczer had been killed by one of the Alea neuter males. Climbing steep rocky slopes among sparse, wind-sculpted trees, blue-green pines whose ancestors had been taken from Earth a million years ago, when the Alea had ransacked nearby worlds to repair the biosphere of their new, planoformed home after it had been wrecked by civil war. The dark sky sprinkled with glimmering daystars, dominated by the glowering face of the red dwarf sun. Wind lifting the clean scent of the pine forests that tumbled away toward the dark eye of the lake she and Arcady had crossed, using a boat stolen from a gang of newly transformed neuter males. Dorthy had been happy then, despite losing Arcady, despite being lost herself, separated from the main expedition, alone on a wild alien world. Perhaps she would never again be so happy.

"What are we going to do without my Talent?" she asked Barlstilkin. "I've looked around, and I don't like what I see. They aren't trying here. On P'thrsn it was the Navy being cautious; here, it's the scientists. They don't want to know, most of them. They want to be shown; they sit around and wait for a revelation."

"Witnesses," Barlstilkin said. "And besides, they are a long way from home. And they have all the time they could possibly need, or so it seems. There is nothing to challenge them, not as it was on P'thrsn, or more especially at BD Twenty. There is no war, and so no urgency. No doubt the Navy, or the Navy's masters, want it that way."

"It must be frustrating for you, coming all this way and finding this. This shabby, run-down ship. . . ."

"But Dorthy, it is perched on the very edge of mystery. I am playing this by ear—" one of his curious archaic expressions— "and when I see the chance, I'll take it. There are certain . . .

disaffected elements here that I can make use of. You'd better be ready."

"Has this got something to do with the singleship?"

"I don't know anything about the singleship. Really, I am telling the truth. It may have something to do with those who I fondly believed were my collaborators. If it does, then I must move as quickly as I can, before things become too complicated."

"What are you going to do, steal a ship? Is that possible? Suppose I don't want to come?"

"You've come this far," Barlstilkin said at last.

"If I'm going any farther, I can think of better pilots."

"But we are here. I admit that I could have managed the slingshot maneuver better, but it worked."

"Only because the liner just happened to be in range of us when we phased in here." Dorthy was stung by Barlstilkin's imperturbable confidence, the boundless faith in permanent good fortune that was characteristic of all Golden.

"We were lucky: I admit it. But what does it matter now we are here? Keep your eyes open, Dorthy, and be ready to act on the instant. The singleship . . . yes, it will almost certainly complicate matters."

"So you want to run back and tell everyone, and get your revenge. Don't you think it would be just a 10 days' wonder?"

"At the moment, yes. But the science team has only just begun its explorations."

"It seems to me they've stopped before they've begun. The shafts are the obvious starting place, and yet they have given up on them. No one goes down to the moon, now."

"But you will go, perhaps with your Dr. Valdez. You will try and get counteragent if I do not help you. You will get down there any way you can. Oh, please Dorthy, don't be angry all over again! You need me as much as I need you. I will do my best to help you avoid the attentions of Seyour Ivanov, for instance. He seemed pathetically eager to show me that we are both subject to his surveillance."

"We're not playing the kind of games you Golden play among yourselves. The stakes are much higher. It isn't enough to sit and make clever remarks."

"Ah, Dorthy, Dorthy. I apologize. Be patient with me. I'm an old man, after all, still recovering from my recent brush with death. Yes, it has shaken me, more than you realize. I know you think all Golden are too confident, but remember: I no longer have my entourage, my medical backups. I have hung myself on the edge and so I move cautiously. You are impatient with me. Have you thought that it might be because the mindset you acquired on P'thrsn is driving you?"

Talbeck Barlstilkin smiled his crooked smile; then his eyes widened a fraction as Dorthy pushed up from the plush couch, so quickly that she almost knocked over the lacquer table and its silver breakfast tray. Her hands were shaking, although she felt very cool inside, quite separate from her anger as it boiled to the surface.

"Fuck your word games!" she said, saw the bonded servant shift very slightly. "And tell your fucking robot that I'm not going to hurt you!"

"I don't think," Talbeck Barlstilkin said, "that we should be causing a scene."

Dorthy looked at the table of officers, who all looked away from her. One said something, and the others laughed.

Talbeck Barlstilkin said mildly, "Do sit down. We don't know who might be listening."

"I'll sit down if you'll tell me what you're planning."

"Then run along. I do not play those games."

"I'm part of it. I ought to know."

"The less you know the better. Let's pretend we're here for different reasons, Dorthy. You go down to Colcha. I will—"

Music shut off; the light fantasy faded; a voice spoke out of the air, harsh and urgent. "Stage four alert!" it said. "All hands to posts! Stage four alert!" The Navy officers ran for the door, and Valdez pushed through their bedlam. He shouted to Dorthy over the relentlessly repetitive announcement, "There's something fucking strange going down!", and kicked open a section of the wallwide screen, started to fiddle with the controls.

The screen lit up as Dorthy joined him. The tipped crescent of the gas giant, spattered with swirls of green on green, filled more than half of it. Colcha, the patchwork moon, was a tiny, perfectly circular shadow against the gas giant's perpetual storms.

"I can't get much from this," Valdez said, hammering at the keyboard. Sweat beaded his forehead. "I can only plug into unrestricted data streams. Here, this is coming down from the high polar satellite." Clusters of picts and pointers flickered across the gas giant's intricate patterns as he scanned through channels.

"Hold it there," Dorthy said, standing back so she could get a better look. "There. What's that?"

A fine straight line of yellow light speared across the gas giant. Flickering, everchanging indices ran along it. Above, an inset showed a concatenation of slim shards of silver and shadow that after a moment Dorthy recognized as a singleship.

"The Navy will be upset," Barlstilkin said. He had brought his cup of tea, and looked across the cup's tilted rim as he sipped. Green light did strange things to his scarred face.

"Not necessarily," Valdez said. "See that delta vee?" His finger stabbed through ranks of yellow figures, small and sharp, in the holograph projection above the keyboard. "Whoever is flying that has to be some kind of suicide jockey. Relative angular momentum is too great to achieve orbit."

"It is going down into the gas giant? Dorthy, here is a pilot even worse than me."

"It's going to impact on Colcha," Valdez said. "In a shade under ten minutes, too. Watch the decrement there—"

And then his finger, his arm, his whole body was washed in light. Dorthy screwed up her eyes against the glare which beat through her eyelids, beat across the entire room. Valdez and Barlstilkin and the bonded servant were shadows in a storm of light that suddenly cut off as the screen stepped down its intensity. The projected flight of the ship, the attendant indices, the inset view, had all vanished. There was only the serene crescent of the gas giant, the shadow spot of its enigmatic moon. The ship was gone.

6

SUZY WAS DOZING WHEN THE REACTION MOTOR FIRED up; though it woke her, she wasn't sure at first what had happened. She swam up from uneasy dreams of falling to the familiar enclosed vibration of the ship, the glare of the cabin lights, the intimate stink inside her pressure suit.

"I think," Robot's voice said in her ear, "we may have problem."

That was when she realized that the vibration was the reaction motor, which she'd shut down after the brief insertion burn. Somehow, it had been switched on again. And after five minutes it was clear she couldn't turn it off. Her first thought was that Robot had been futzing around with the command sequences, but he blandly protested his innocence, and added that it was nothing to do with the ship's disabled computer either, which had been *his* first thought.

Suzy looked over the ranks of indices projected against her three-hundred-sixty-degree view of frosty starscape. The dim green crescent of the gas giant was directly ahead. "I guess maybe the Navy inserted a parasite command sequence. They've been probing us on and off ever since we phased in."

"I thought of that, too," Robot said. "They've done that, they're more subtle than Machine. And I don't think that's too likely."

"I wish I had such a good opinion of myself."

"The Navy isn't interfaced. It's still third millennium in its outlook. I'm not."

Suzy sucked water from her suit's nipple, studied projected vectors. "We keep this up, our orbit will widen enough to get us really close to the Navy's parking orbit around that funny little moon. You still say this isn't the Navy's doing?"

"The Navy isn't the only thing happening out here," Robot said.

"Machine's still hearing those mysterious voices, huh?"

"Not right now."

"He does, you tell me right away. Better still, get him to try and track where they come from. Knowing that would suit me just fine."

"They spoke to me directly, Seyoura Falcon."

"Then *ask* them. Jesus Christ. And Robot, you make sure you stay in that crashweb with your suit sealed up. You hear me? There's no more impact gel, so the web's all the protection you've got."

Suzy spent the next hour checking through the singleship's weapon systems, while the reaction motor rumbled unsettlingly and the gas giant's crescent swelled across her vision. Whatever had reached into the ship to jam on the reaction motor hadn't disabled the one-shot X-ray lasers, or touched the homeostatic cluster missiles: their tiny, paranoid minds were still dreaming of violent trajectories down in their launch tubes. Suzy ran through the indices with a feeling of cool nostalgia, repeating ritual preparations she'd performed so many times during the Campaigns. No anticipation, only the moment. Like a zen koan, it emptied her mind of everything but resolve.

So when Robot interrupted her, chipping into her data streams down the bootleg lines Machine had installed, it was as shockingly intimate as a stranger's unwelcome caress.

His voice came out of a picture that rippled open across the swirling vista of the gas giant's frigid storms. It was a picture of the little moon, patchwork globe crazed with jagged dark lines and spotted with holes, *gaps* . . . like a clay ball shattered and clumsily put back together, with some of the pieces missing.

"We've been studying this," Robot said. "No way is it a natural body. Someone made it."

The inset picture jumped into false color, like an illustration of the four-color map problem. It began to spin, blocks of graphemes flashing over various jagged boundaries. "Apart from the holes—" Machine's cool voice now—"there are many other anomalies. There are sedimentary rocks, impossible on so small a worldlet. What looks like an extinct volcano—again impossible. It is too far away from its primary for its core to have been heated up by tidal drag."

"Maybe it was closer, once. Where did you get all this stuff?"

"There's a mapping satellite looping around the moon. I tapped its memory dump."

"Fucking hell, I guess you didn't stop to think the Navy could tap you by the same route? Was this before or after the motor fired up?"

Robot said, "Hey. Trust Machine. It was a very simple nanosecond burst interrogation, and I swear it wasn't compromised."

"Don't you guys try anything else, okay? I don't give a fuck about that ball of dead rock. The Enemy is somewhere out there. I can taste it. That's what *I* care about."

"It's sculpture," Robot said. "Very large scale, high aesthetic content. It is wasted on the Navy."

"Yeah, well it's very pretty and all, but stay clear of my inputs, okay? I don't need distractions. This is the Enemy we're dealing with here, not a gang of fucking artists. You came all this way to look at the scenery? Look at it."

The inset picture faded. "Robot thinks you should make sure they are the Enemy before you use those pretty weapons. I knew a woman once, a mechanic. You know about mechanics?"

"They do their job. I do mine."

"When they have the operation to replace one of their own arms with the augmented prosthesis, they are given conditioning to accept it as a part of themselves." Robot's voice had flattened out again. It was the left side of his brain speaking. Machine said, "It helps healing and helps them to learn how to use it as quickly as possible. Robot programmed something like that into ourselves, when we sculpted his modifications. The woman he knew . . . something had gone wrong with her conditioning. It was too strong. She would talk only to machines. She talked to me, for instance, but not to Robot. She understood the difference on a level she couldn't explain. It was burned into her brain."

"This is a parable, right?" Suzy's father had been big on parables. Reading every Sunday from the big leather-bound Bible that to Suzanne smelled faintly but unmistakably of something long dead and dug up. Pages brown and crumbling at the edges but the ink still clean and sharp, the colors of the illuminated letters at the head of each book unfaded. It had been in the family a long time, hundreds of years. From before the wars, before what the colonists called the Interregnum. Her father's only real possession, more real than his wife and kids, maybe. Certainly more real than the decaying mansion which he'd been given as living quarters, better than the prefab shacks of the workers, but only just. Most of its rooms empty, its wooden foundation riddled with termites, spray-sealed with polymer to hold it together. Cheap homeostatic furniture, a huge Stone Age environmental conditioning unit that was always breaking down. Just thinking about that Bible brought back the claustrophobia of her childhood, the half-ruined mansion and the shacks with their strips of corn and vegetables and sugar cane, the encircling forest of genemelded pines that ran in precise rows from horizon to horizon: and everything, mansion and shacks and forest, owned by the Lusitania family, remote and powerful as gods.

Machine said, "Did you ever think the Navy conditioned you when they were training you to fly combat singleships?"

"I know what you mean, but how could I know? It would be part of the conditioning that I didn't know. Now shut the fuck up and let me get on with what I need to do."

But she was lying, because she knew damn well that he had guessed the truth. She'd been honed to a weapon, back in Galveston. They all had. Half of the singleship jockeys who'd come through the Campaigns had committed suicide within the year of the Final Solution; most of the rest were like her, looking for death and pretending they weren't. If there was some way of deprogramming combat singleship pilots, the Navy hadn't bothered to let on about it.

It had become so that it didn't matter to Suzy anymore. She was what she was. Suzanne Marie Thibodeaux was dead. She had begun to die back in Galveston, in the long waking dreams of the hypaedia. The end of the Alea Campaigns had finished her off. She'd died and been reborn, but as someone else.

The singleship drove across the darkside of the gas giant. Horns of weak light widened across the planet's wide limb; the white dwarf, when it dawned, was no more than the brightest star among the millions scattered over the deep black of space. The moon rose after the white dwarf, grew from brilliant point to featureless crescent.

The neutrino detector could now distinguish between the fusion generators of two ships that hung in synchronous orbit beyond the patchwork moon. Messages were cluttering the radio frequencies, most of them mechanical recitations: warning her to shut off her reaction drive; warning her not to attempt to gain orbit around Colcha (which she guessed had to be the moon toward which her ship was still accelerating), to stand by and await capture. Robot was reciting some kind of art critique back at the few human voices in among the endlessly reduplicated warnings.

Suzy let him get on with it. She could just about eyeball the ships now, even though they were no more than a few pixels at this range. One was unmistakably a Guild liner; the other had started to broadcast its call sign. With a shock, Suzy realized that it was the huge converted freighter that had been the launch platform for her singleship wing. The *Vingança*. Just seeing the familiar, half-forgotten binary string run off beneath the blurred mosaic of the support ship's long, blistered spine brought back the stale smoke and brandy fumes of the wardroom, endless white corridors and unrelieved glotube glare, Wang Ling's imperturbable moon face, first thing Suzy saw ("Oh si' hun'ed.") the morning of each mission. Jesus Christ. All there in front of her, only now her ship was its focus, its target. She was almost tempted to break silence then, explain that she was helpless, possessed. Sure. Do that and more than likely they'd shoot her out of the sky right away, because she was telling the truth, or because they thought she had to be crazy.

So Suzy kept quiet, listening with only half an ear to Robot's crazy monologue while she rechecked the weapon systems. If something was dragging her in, it was in for a shock, just as soon as she got close enough to figure out what it was and where it was. She didn't notice exactly when the reaction motor cut out. She was so intent on status checks, and she'd grown so accustomed to its rumble, that it took her a few seconds to figure out what was missing.

Robot was asking her what it meant, but she told him to shut up, sweating over vectors, trying to balance the ship's delta vee against the complicated three-body interaction of the gravity wells of Colcha, the gas giant, and the white dwarf. The weird thing was that, according to her calculations, they were still accelerating but, according to the ship's instruments, they were at rest.

Robot came to the same conclusion. "We're picking up speed, but Machine says there's no evidence of acceleration. Something has a grip on every molecule of the ship, is the only answer."

Suzy watched the *Vingança* and the Guild liner and half a dozen small ships rise above the curve of the patchwork moon. An unstoppable flood of messages and warnings was pouring in. Several were ominous countdowns. That moon was growing so fast! She was still trying to figure out just what would happen to the ship—surely it wasn't going to crash!—when one of the small ships that were deployed beyond the *Vingança* fired a missile.

Suzy immediately set off countermeasures: scattered a dozen autonomic beacons to distract the missile's homicidal mind; targeted a MIRV'd countermissile to the attacker's intermittent radar pulses. All this in a handful of seconds, before Robot had time to speak up.

"I guess we got them mad."

"Don't worry about it. I—"

A ragged blossom of fire blotted out the patchwork moon, fading even as it expanded.

"Bravo," Robot said.

"But there wasn't time. It wasn't—" Suzy was looking for her countermissile, which couldn't possibly have had time to reach its target. It wasn't on its track, and it took her a long minute to find it: drifting along parallel to the ship about a hundred klicks out. Caught by the same force that was dragging the singleship toward the moon.

Suzy and Robot fell silent as the singleship arched around the little moon's crazed, pockmarked globe. It was moving fast enough to slingshot away from the moon . . . but it didn't. Impossibly, unbidden, it performed a neat about-face in pure vacuum, nose down toward the moon's darkside. Only it wasn't exactly dark. There was a glow down there, spreading in slow ripples from a single point, unfolding complex wings. Rippling curtains, waves, and velvety folds of white light spurted up around the singleship. Nodes brightened where folds intersected, flared and shot away. It was as if the singleship were standing on its nose above a funnel where racing points of light converged into a black hole.

One of the gaps, Suzy realized. Radar told her it was maybe a kilometer across . . . shit, something wrong with the range finding. No way could it be infinitely deep. Something was fucking with her here. It was going to regret that. She called up the target display.

Robot said, "You shouldn't be doing that."

Suzy laid the grid over the scape of rippling, racing light, locked coordinates to the hole she'd been pointed at. She said, "I'm gonna see what a low-yield fusion pinch inside that thing does for us." She felt very cool, no fear at all, only a weirdly aloof sense of precision.

"Your other missile did not do its job, Seyoura. Really, I don't think—"

The missile told her it was ready to go; she let it.

Radar showed it snarking away through veils of light, down the funnel defined by bright descending nodes. But then it wasn't accelerating anymore. It slowed, came to rest relative to racing lights, then appeared to begin to rise toward the singleship. But it wasn't moving. The singleship was.

Suzy watched the missile's slim barracuda shape drift past, a shadow against curtains of light. Then it was above and behind, receding with the countermissile as the singleship began its slow plunge. Concentrated points of light shot past on all sides. The hole that was their center seemed to rise up toward her. Robot shouted something and then everything—his voice, the ship's displays, her suit's intimate embrace—seemed to fly away in every direction at once.

There was an interval of darkness.

7

A FULL WEEK AFTER WHAT HAD COME TO BE KNOWN AS the Event, the unofficial group of scientists organized around Dorthy and Professor Doctor Abel Gunasekra had been winnowed down from the more than two dozen who had, at one time or another, stopped in for an hour, a watch, a day, before dropping out, to a cabal of seven. Valdez was still among them; as a planetologist he had little to offer, but he was unwilling to let slip his chance at glory. Flores also hung on, taking copious notes and saying little; there was lean, copper-skinned Jake Bonner, an expert on particle splitting and partial to the more outré cosmological theories, who alone among them could keep up with Gunasekra's pace; and another mathematician, Seppo Armiger, who wore his coarse black hair greased back in a thick pigtail, and always the same canvas many-pocketed pants and a kind of quilted waistcoat open over his smooth bare chest. And there was the exobiologist, Martins, who had an amateur interest in cosmology and nothing better to do, saying very little most of the time but occasionally rousing himself to make an acerbic— and usually acute—criticism of Gunasekra's more vivid flights of fancy.

Dorthy apart, they were all men.

They had taken over one of the cabins in the empty accommodation modules, furnished it with a datanet terminal, the whiteboard which Gunasekra liked to use, a handful of molded chairs filched from one of the commons. In the center of the room there was a projector, on which the same looped tape was always playing. There was a hot plate and a beaker for making coffee and a dozen grimy cups, and that was all.

Dorthy and Abel Gunasekra probably spent more time there than anyone else; the others had their official projects to work on, reductive splinters of the grand vision they hoped to capture in that scruffy, cold little cabin.

Despite all the time she'd spent in his company, Dorthy still knew hardly anything about Abel Gunasekra, except that he was as brilliant and erratic as everyone said, the texture of his thoughts like lava spilling down a steep mountainside, hot and bright and swift, prone to unexpected explosions or diversions, and quite unstoppable in full flow. Unlike many of the scientists, he had not come to the hypervelocity star in search of fame, or confirmation of faith (it was surprising and disturbing how many of the scientists wore the tacky pinwheel badge of the Witnesses). Gunasekra already had fame in plenty, and at an incredibly early age, when he had shown that the density of matter in the Universe was precisely equal to the theoretical value needed eventually to halt and reverse the expansion of space-time; and he had quickly followed that coup by producing a seventeen-hundred-line equation which completely described the infolded topologies of urspace and contraspace. As near as Dorthy could judge, Gunasekra was here because he felt that he had exhausted the mundane universe. To him, the hypervelocity system was a laboratory, an ideas generator for higher levels of truth. Like the others of the little cabal, he was not interested in the Event and its aftermath in itself. It was a springboard for deep speculation concerning a particular obsession of Gunasekra's, the many worlds hypothesis and the structure of the hypothetical hyperuniverse.

Mostly, the math was over Dorthy's head, and math was what it was mostly about. She spent her time playing chess against herself or Valdez, who, although he wouldn't admit it, was floundering almost as often as she, or watching the patterns of light unfolding above the gull wing of the projector, the glory of the Event and the near-identical display that had been evoked when a probe had been flown into another shaft (it had accelerated at a vastly improbable rate, dropping millions

of kilometers through a moon only a thousand kilometers in
in diameter, its telemetry dopplering down the spectrum and
disappearing entirely a moment before the shaft and a hundred
square kilometers around it had been replaced by a chaotic
terrain of water-ice covered in sooty interstellar grains).

But Dorthy was not wanted for her mathematical insights.
The men were hoping for a vision from her, a glimpse of the
mystic she was certain was locked inside her head, the clue that,
when it did come, did not arrive from the rarified atmosphere
of mathematical speculation at all, but in a dream.

That particular day, the going had been heavier than usual. It
was late in the evening, and Gunasekra was holding forth as he
so often did. He'd taken over to clarify a point Seppo Armiger
had made, and branched out and branched out again until the
original kink, long ago abandoned, was lost in the welter of
scribbled equation lines and pothooks and modifiers which, in
green and yellow and purple ink, covered the whiteboard from
edge to edge.

Like a mountaineer working a traverse foothold by precari-
ous foothold, Gunasekra had been working his way toward
what he considered to be the main problem, the source of
the immense energies which had briefly torn space apart when
the wormholes—no one disputed that what the shafts led into
were shortcuts punched across contraspace—had closed around
the fugitive singleship and the probe. The effects of the displays
were still running down, dragging through local space-time
like the wake of a ship through water. Strange particles were
bursting into being, seemingly from nowhere, pairs of highly
energetic photons, multibillion volt gamma rays containing as
much energy as a chlorine or argon nucleus, hotter than anything in the known universe, hotter even than the primeval
pinpoint fireball from which it had inflated. In almost every
case, each photon annihilated its twin in the instant of their
creation, like the virtual electron/positron pairs that continually
blink in and out of existence everywhere in the Universe, an
ocean of momentary sparks whirling in and out of the grainy
foam of naked singularities (smaller than the Planck length
and, therefore, immeasurable) which underlie the structure of
space-time.

But not all of the ultrahigh-energy photon pairs canceled each other out; if they had, no one would have known about them. Instead, one pair in every billion or so avoided mutual suicide, and promptly decayed. Popcorn photons, one of the science crew had named them, so short-lived their existence had to be inferred from the cascades of particles their decay produced: electrons and hadrons—mesons, protons, neutrons—combining into atomic nuclei; and a zoo of particles never before observed outside of the vast particle accelerators which had dominated physics in the late twentieth century. One science team had deployed gravity sink collectors to sweep up some of the decay products. Mostly hydrogen with a leavening of deuterium and helium, the stuff of the first instant of creation, but spiced with highly improbable, incredibly short-lived isotopes of heavier elements—carbon 17, iron 62, gold 290.

Gunasekra's contention was that the popcorn photons had been dragged across from another universe, one only a few light-years in diameter and so with a high-energy density. This was what had powered the change in vacuum energy states during opening and closure of the wormholes. It was a solution that was both elegant and unprovable, because it would mean that the only signature left by the Event could not be read this side of Heaven, which was precisely the case. It was like a koan: crack it open, and it vanishes.

Now, Gunasekra was scrawling out a proposal for boundary conditions that would make such a transferal possible, something Dorthy recognized as a derivation of the classical deWitt solution:

$$\Gamma'(R=0, \tau) + \alpha\Gamma(R=0, \tau) = 0$$

"You've introduced a new constant in there," Bonner said after a moment. His long legs were stretched in front of him, crossed at the ankles. "Are you saying any condition is possible in the other universe? If so, you can't prove or disprove anything, and we might as well get on with something else. Besides, if your undefined constant, alpha, is measurable on the other side, then it must be measurable on this, also, or congruence won't be preserved and your boundaries won't cross at all."

"Quite right," Gunasekra said, smiling happily. His even white teeth gleamed. "So what we have to do is set α at 0, which I think you must agree obtains at the singularity, so we get—"

$$\Gamma'(R=0, \tau) = 0$$

"—which can then be incorporated into the wave function of our universe." He turned to the whiteboard again, and symbols flowed across it in the purple ink which stained his thumb and forefinger to the knuckles:

$$\Gamma'(R,\tau) = [3i/4Lp \sin\tau]^{\frac{1}{2}}\exp[(3\pi/4i)(\cot\tau)(R/Lp)^2]$$

"If Lp is the Planck length," Bonner said, uncrossing and recrossing his legs, "what's to say it's the same on both sides of the boundary? You might say the same goes for pi, too, or any physical constant you introduce."

"No, no," Gunasekra said, long hair swinging as he banged the purple pen against the whiteboard. "If both universes are quantum in nature, then all solutions must pass through the singularity $R=0$ when $\tau=0$. The singularity always dominates. It is the beginning of things and the end of things in a quantum universe. In those conditions the appropriate Green function can be derived which is congruent under the deWitt boundary conditions, and so constants are canceled out. There can only be one solution on both sides."

"He's right," Flores said, looking up from his tablet.

"Which is all very well," Martins said, "but I still have the feeling that you are arguing for the existence of a conjuror's hat from the *a priori* observation of a rabbit."

"Perhaps we should look for other rabbits," Armiger said, looking around at everyone with a broad smile. "Perhaps we should think about other sources for the popcorn photons, sources inside our own Universe. Discount the obvious before climbing onto the rotten ice of unprovable hypotheses. Otherwise we will all end up speculating about ghosts or God or something else equally implausible." *God* hung heavily in the air for a moment.

"Some of the mechanics claim that they've seen ghosts, here on the ship," Dorthy said, but as usual no one took any notice of her.

"When you eliminate the possible, then only the impossible is left," Gunasekra said, his smile broader than ever. "I misquote my favorite fictional character, but it is a maxim that applies here, I think. Not even the emissions of Seyfert galaxies can account for the energies we must attribute to the source of the particles observed to be created around the moon. And we must remember that we do not know if any Seyfert galaxies survived into this era of the Universe's evolution. Unlike astronomical images, any source of the particles in this Universe must be contemporary. Or are we to violate causality?"

Dorthy said, "I think we shouldn't throw out the idea right away. After all, we don't have any other alternatives to the mainstream of thinking here. Do you want us to stop trying to be radical, Martins?"

The exobiologist twirled his pen in his fingers. "I don't want us rushing out with something that will be torn to pieces, all at once. Unless you know something we all don't."

Dorthy said, "You'd know if you'd triggered off the mindset. No, I'm speaking for myself. I think we've done enough talking about this; it's time we *did* something. If I could go down to Colcha. . . ."

Valdez said, "If I had some eggs I could have eggs and steak for breakfast . . . if I had any steak."

Everyone laughed.

"Undirected action is of less use than undirected words," Seppo Armiger said. "We need a direction to move in."

"Goal-directed," Valdez said. "Martins is right. We'd look like damn fools if we tried something and fell flat on our faces in front of the Witnesses."

"Well, I didn't come all this way to sit on my hands," Dorthy retorted. "This whole system is a set-up, in the most obvious way imaginable. If we fail at understanding it, then we don't deserve to advance any farther. Instead of picking holes in this idea, perhaps we should be thinking of ways to test it. Perhaps we can open another wormhole and follow and follow wherever the probe and the singleship went."

"If they weren't destroyed," Armiger said. "I'm still not entirely convinced that we aren't dealing with the Enemy."

"We're not," Dorthy told him. "Believe me. If the Alea family that took over the center of the Galaxy, the mauraders, were responsible for this system, then we would surely know it. The marauders were a hundred times more than hostile than the Alea of BD Twenty. After all, those Alea were the losers in the war. They fled the marauders, who would not merely pick off one errant singleship and leave it at that. They would have destroyed the *Vingança* long before it had reached orbit."

She repressed a shiver at memories she had been fed on P'thrsn, so bedded in her psyche that she could not even find their boundaries any more, despite the analytical skills she had been taught at the Kamali–Silver Institute, in her salad days as a budding Talent. A trillion sentient carnivores sweeping through the Galaxy's core like a blood-crazed pack of sharks, suns flaring at their whim, driving all that they did not devour before them. . . . And the marauders had conquered the core more than a million years ago; what had they become, since?

Jake Bonner said to Dorthy, "So what do you suggest we do? Should we start chasing these ghosts the mechanics think they've seen?"

"It might be a start," Dorthy said.

"If we do not know where to look for ghosts," Gunasekra said, "and we are not interested in them, we will say ghosts do not exist. But if we are open-minded, we would devise a ghost trap. You look angry, Dorthy. I don't mean to joke. Let us suppose that the shafts are indeed haunted by those who made this system. Certainly, something must remain, to direct the destruction or abstraction of the singleship. The shafts are as good a place to start as anywhere else. And if we find ghosts, why then we can ask them for answers to our questions."

Valdez said, "The shafts are such an obvious place to look, so obviously weird, that there's a mass of data been accumulated about them if you all care to look at it. No answers, though, and no ghosts either."

"Because no one was looking for them," Dorthy said. "I'll tell you all what I'm going to do, anyhow, and that's try and get down to the surface of Colcha, prohibition or not. Perhaps that will trigger something, the way my visit to Novaya Rosya did. Don't scowl, Valdez. You promised to get me a ride down there at the beginning of this."

"No one goes down there," Valdez said. "Not after the Event."

"You can speculate all you like," Dorthy said, getting to her feet. "I'm going to take a look with my own two eyes at what's really there. That's what I came for, after all, not seminars in advanced cosmology. No offense intended, Professor Gunasekra."

Gunasekra bowed slightly, black eyes twinkling. "None taken, Dr. Yoshida."

Valdez said, "Dorthy—"

But she was already gone.

Dorthy had reached the main cross-deck upshaft when Valdez caught up with her. He took her arm just as she was about to step onto one of the endlessly rising disks of golden polished wood.

"Hey, babe, you're not really running out on us?"

"Don't worry," she said, "I'll try not to have any visions while I'm away. And if I do, I'll tell you all about them."

Valdez smiled. "Huh. Well, it's not me, you understand, but one or two of the guys think you may have been holding back—"

"You tell them it isn't true! Why do they think I came here in the first place, Valdez? You tell them that!"

"Okay, okay. Christos, take it easy."

Dorthy drew a deep breath, another. Calm, calm. Find the center. She said, "You're right. But it's difficult, you understand. Do you know the term breakout? It's not something Talents like to talk about. When we do what you call mind reading, the deep probing kind, we get a kind of model of the subject's thought processes and pathways, her mind-set, fixed inside our own skull. Usually, it is only a temporary electrical pattern transposed on our own neural pathways. Sometimes, very rarely, it gets fixed, an electrochemical fixation. Even more rarely, it takes over the Talent's own personality. What I have is a transfer made on me without my knowledge, back when I was on P'thrsn. I didn't even know about it, although it started changing the way I thought straight away. It was fixed not in my forebrain but much deeper, down in the archipallium, the innermost primitive reptilian layer. And it isn't human, but a fragment of a collective alien mentality a million years old. Of course I'm fucking frightened of it."

Valdez took both her hands in his. "You're worried something might trigger it and allow it to take you over. Jesus Christos, Dorthy, you only have to tell them. They'd understand."

"Would they? Do you know what it's like, having someone else thinking with a part of your brain? It's more deeply intimate than what we get up to in bed, Valdez, more deeply intimate than carrying a fetus for nine months, I'd guess. Maybe that's why most of the Talents who do go crazy are men; I'd not really thought of it before. Men reject the other, carry their sense of self like a shield. I know all about that, believe me, about the selfishness and vanity of men. Don't try arguing, Valdez, it will only prove I'm right."

Valdez laughed. "That's as twisty as asking me if I've stopped beating my wife yet."

"Have you?"

"Why don't you and me go somewhere else a while," Valdez said. "It might do us both good, huh? It's really late, and you've been in there all day."

Dorthy said, "It's like I can't stop. I do need to know, Valdez."

"Maybe that's just the thing you have. Your passenger, this mindset. Maybe it wants you to keep running, so you won't have time to think why."

It was a deep, unexpected insight. Valdez had surprised her again, and she admitted that it might be true.

"I think you're caught between a rock and a hard place. Your passenger, and Seyour Talbeck, Duke Barlstilkin V."

"Talbeck is doing his own thing with the younger Navy officers, stirring things up, waiting for something to happen. I have not learned much about him, but I do know that he is both immensely patient and an opportunist. Until something does happen, I don't think he cares what I do."

"Oh, he'll know all about you. And forget the Navy; word is that he's getting into something with the head of the Witnesses."

"The man who looks like he's just brought the tablets up from Hell?"

"Down from the mountain, is what I think you mean. Yeah, Gregor Baptista."

"I know what I mean: I've seen him. He makes my skin crawl, Valdez."

"We have every kind out here, babe. You, me, Abel Gunasekra. . . ."

"Barlstilkin, Baptista. . . . If the marauders are out there, we'd be a real pushover. That's so funny it might be true. Take me away from all this, Valdez, before I get hysterical."

8

THAT NIGHT, DORTHY DREAMED OF P'THRSN AGAIN. IT was an edenic vision of P'thrsn as it had been a few thousand years after civil war had decimated its newly planoformed biosphere. On Earth, the ancestors of modern humanity had yet to migrate across the rift valley that would later become the Mediterranean. On P'thrsn, the circular scars of asteroid bombardment had vanished beneath a tide of life imported from the worlds of a dozen nearby systems. Dusty grasslands, punctuated by small, shallow, freshwater seas, spread from pole to pole: vast ranges for the feral, nonsentient Alea and their herds of larval children, voracious herbivores, like a cross between a giant slug and a decapitated walrus, which during their unceasing migrations carved wide swathes through the grasslands, tracks red as blood in the furnace light of the red dwarf sun.

Dorthy dreamed that she was moving fast and high above

a grassy plain, a bodiless viewpoint zooming in toward one of the shield volcanoes which, during planoforming, had poured billions of tonnes of carbon dioxide and water vapor into P'thrsn's thin atmosphere. The volcano's slopes were cloaked in pine forests, rising sheer above the plain into the fleecy clouds which shrouded its peak.

Without transition, Dorthy was standing on a wide stone platform that jutted from a crest of bare, black lava. On one side, clustered collapse craters and smoking fumaroles tumbled down to the caldera's rumpled floor; on the other, the whole green world fell away to the horizon, where the vast disk of the red dwarf simmered, spotted with clusters of black sunspots. A cold wind whipped around Dorthy. It clawed at the coarse material of her gray uniform coveralls, seethed and hissed like static in her ears.

A figure sprawled at the edge of the platform, silhouetted against the gigantic setting sun. It leaned on one elbow. A hood was raised around its head. Without words, it told Dorthy to come to her.

Then it was night. Stars flung thickly across the moonless sky; the edge of the platform cut across the hazy arch of the Milky Way. The hooded figure was an indistinct shadow that grew no clearer as Dorthy walked across the platform, her boots clicking on smooth stone flags. It was bigger than she was, bigger than any human: a neuter female Alea, but not the old, grossly corpulent neuter female Dorthy had met on P'thrsn. This one was slim and lithe, coiled like a snake at the very edge of the platform, hood of naked skin flared out around her small, feral face so that all Dorthy could see of it by starlight was the deep-set glint of her huge eyes.

—No, the Alea said, in a way I am a part of her. A very small part by the time she captured you, but re-created here.

"You're one of her ancestors."

—One of her younger selves, to be more precise. I remember the flight out from the core at only two removes, and I do not bear the guilt of massacring my sisters, of destroying Novaya Rosya. That has yet to happen. It seemed suitable to us that I should talk with you.

Dorthy sat zazen on cold stone before the reclining Alea. She was aware, somewhere in the back of her mind, that this was a dream, and so she accepted without fear or question what was happening. Perhaps that was the point. She asked, "How many are there of you in my head?"

—I do not know. I would guess that there must be at least five, because that is the minimum number to form a stable consensus.

"You know you aren't real."

—Feel the stone. Go on.

It was polished and dry, so cold it stung Dorthy's palm.

—The nerve impulses firing in your cortex at this moment are identical to those which would have occurred had you touched the actual stone on P'thrsn, vanished thousands of generations before humans arrived there. Is it less real because it is happening only inside your head? I know that I am only a construct, my incarnation an imposed standing wave in a cluster of neurons inside your brain. But I do not feel any less real because of that knowledge. I feel that I could walk from this platform if I so wished, and walk through the youth of my world. Perhaps I am dreaming, and you are the one who is not real.

"Do Alea dream?"

—It is one of the few things that we have in common with humans, although our dreams are very different from yours. You dream of the past, filtering events to try and make sense of your lives. You strive always to impose patterns on the flux of the Universe. We dream only of the future, of the possibilities always opening up before us, of actions we may have to take to preserve our bloodlines, of actions we must not take in case we endanger them. That is why I can believe that you have fallen into my dream, for you come from a time when my world is dying because of the mistaken actions of one of my later selves. Here, the world is everywhere alive. The brothers and sisters of my bloodlines have yet to be confined to the Holds, those few islands of life in a planetary desert. The grasslands breathe oxygen across the face of the world; it is not yet necessary to turn our clean, clear seas into dense cultures of oxygen-generating bacteria. For after the crime of my unborn self, nothing will be done to stop the slow degeneration of our handiwork, the escape of water from the atmosphere which will cause the spread of the deserts, the thinning of the atmosphere itself, the return of the world to its tide-locked state. I live here in the beginning of the end of paradise. The seeds of paranoia are already sown, but have yet to germinate. They will come into full and terrible flower only when one of my unborn selves detects the use of faster-than-light physics near the star you call Epsilon Eridani.

"Do you feel guilty, about what you will do? You'll destroy an entire world to try and save yourself . . . and you won't even succeed."

—I will not do it, Dorthy. I will be dead thousands of years before it happens, no more than the most dissipated mote in the consensus mind of my unborn sister. Only a few live in me; I cannot imagine what it will be like, to be the vessel of a thousand remnants of previous selves. I know of what will happen, but it is as if I have read it in the spiral histories of our people that have yet to be written on the towers that will be built down in the caldera.

"So you can wash your hands of it."

—I do not understand.

"I'm sorry. It's a figure of speech. An allusion."

—I find your language difficult to follow at times. It is so reductive, so compressed, every word echoing a dozen others, echoing the ghosts of those meanings from which it has arisen. Our language has not changed for as long as we can remember, a million generations at least. Each word stands for the one thing for which it has always stood, no more. You understand that I have no access to your chemically encoded memories, nor to your own self. We must meet here, at this tenuous bridge.

Smooth cold stone under her buttocks; the starry sky; the windy, windy night, clean cold air smelling faintly of the pines on the slopes far below the platform. It was so detailed, so real, that Dorthy doubted very much that all this information was compressed into those few subverted nerve cells in her limbic cortex. In some way, templates had been unpacked into her sensorium, creating this entire fantasy as dreams re-create the known world. The Alea was lying when she said she had no access to Dorthy's higher brain functions, but the thought did not stir panic in Dorthy. There was no room for panic in this dream.

—I have been chosen to talk to you because I am the oldest of the consensus that you met on P'thrsn. Here, in my time, we live as we lived in the old world, before we had to abandon it and find new homes among the stars of the core. It is a time of peace, of dreaming. There is no dissent, no need to decision. Those sisters whose rebellion almost destroyed us all have escaped to another system where they will live in perpetual hiding, fearful that energy squandered during the planoforming of this world will be detected by the renegades from whom we fled.

"The marauders."

—Yes, the eaters of all children, whose crimes are so much worse than those of my unborn sisters. After we destroy Novaya Rosya, and slaughter those of our sisters who will fight against the genocide, we will give up hope. We will have been committing suicide long before you arrive and become the final instrument of our death. That is why we will do nothing when humans begin to travel between the stars, not because we will be without a weapon. We can always fashion weapons, if we need to. But here, at this moment, the world is as we willed it to be, while we were still falling through the spiral arm toward this star. It is paradise, and I am part of it, Dorthy. I still want my brothers and sisters to live. I wish to preserve my bloodlines.

"Is that why you wanted me to come to the hypervelocity star? Is that why you want me to go down to the patchwork moon? What's down there? Where do the wormholes lead?"

—There is much we do not know. When my ancestors and all the other families began to settle the core, we blundered into a secret history of the Galaxy—perhaps of the Universe—that had passed over our little world in the gas clouds.

"Yes, yes, I know the marauders appropriated technology abandoned around the core's black hole. But the moon, the hypervelocity star. Are they the work of the marauders? Where do the wormholes lead?"

The Alea's hood of skin flared out around her face. The blunt claws tipping her three-toed feet rasped against stone as she drew up her legs.

—Half a million years after the death of this incarnation, the star will be launched inward to intersect the galactic orbit of the star of your home world. You will have no civilization when the star is launched, no faster-than-light physics to betray your existence. I do not think it will be the work of the marauders. But I cannot know.

"Then what are you trying to tell me?"

—We think that we were infected, when we came to live on the worlds of the stars of the core. We took genetic templates of plants and animals from worlds of stars close to the star of P'thrsn, to restock its biosphere after the civil war. On three of those worlds, intelligent species arose soon after. My unborn sisters will destroy the species of Novaya Rosya when they begin to explore the near stars; another species, the aborigines of Elysium, will fail in themselves; and finally humans will almost destroy us. It is likely that we were the unwitting agents of a paradigm that kindles intelligence. For otherwise, given the proximity in time and space of all three species, the Galaxy, the Universe, should be swarming with spacefaring civilizations.

"How could you carry an idea? Like a virus, you mean? There were things like that in the last years of the American and Russian Empires. Loyalty plagues."

—No virus could infect species of different biological clades. We do not understand it ourselves, except it is the most likely solution. An idea may not need a physical location. Is an idea truer when written on stone, or when it resides in the twisted RNA of your deep memory? When you do not think of the idea, does it still exist? If the stone is destroyed, if the brain dies, does the idea die? We are a stupid species, Dorthy. We care for knowledge only if it aids survival of our bloodlines. We will only know of this possibility when it will be raised by the computers my unborn sisters will build to watch the species they will murder. Perhaps humans have an answer. It is one reason why I was given to you.

"Perhaps. But it sounds to me that it is touching upon gnosticism. Secret knowledge written into the fabric of the Universe, waiting to be expressed when suitable complexity of mind is achieved. . . . Laws and conditions exist, it's true, but they exist whether or not we know about them. They don't reveal themselves. Or at least, I don't think they do. I was trained as a scientist. As an observer, not a philosopher. Others may know the answer."

—You must ask them, Dorthy. It is important, so very important.

"Yes. I will ask them. But you haven't answered my question about the wormholes. I must know where they lead, before I can persuade—"

The Alea reared up as swiftly as a striking snake, a shadow twice as tall as Dorthy silhouetted against sudden red light. Was that the dawn? Surely, Dorthy thought, the sun had set in that direction. But the light was growing brighter by the second. The Alea seemed to be fading into it. Dorthy could scarcely make out her muzzled face, deep in the shadow of her flared hood. Her larger pair of arms was flung wide as if in entreaty; the small secondary pair was tearing at the bristly pelt of her chest.

—And ask them too if I am only an idea. I cannot remember all that I once knew, it seems, and yet I do not know what I have forgotten. Ask them, Dorthy! Ask them!

The light was brilliant now, too bright to be P'thrsn's dim red dwarf star. Dorthy twisted her head from its pulsing brightness and awoke on the narrow bunk of her cabin.

Valdez slept on beside her, one arm around her hips, his face so close that his slow breath mingled with hers. The light was merely the one light that couldn't be switched off in the cabin, an emergency glotube that flickered with age. Dorthy slid out of Valdez's embrace and quickly dressed, still half-asleep. But she knew where she was going, even if she didn't know why.

The docks ran the length of the *Vingança*'s keel, a kilometer of launch cradles and graving pits strung out beneath a maze of catenaries and catwalks and railed platforms and lifting gear, even single-story, metal-walled offices. It seemed to run on forever, a narrow, linear, metallic universe dwindling away in a cross-hatching of glotube glare and slabs of granite shadow. There were only a few craft in the launch cradles, mostly singleships and suborbital tugs; Dorthy glimpsed the bulbous nose assembly of Barlstilkin's ship as she went down a helical stair, lost sight of it as she followed a crosswalk toward the sound of metal ringing against metal. She stepped around a bundle of cables, each as thick through as her thigh, that ran over the edge of an empty graving pit. On the far side, a couple of figures moved behind a great fan of golden sparks that guttered down into darkness, where a robot welder was sealing up a seam in the black hull of a combat singleship.

As Dorthy walked toward them, the welder stuttered to a halt. One of the figures called, "The fuck you think you're going? Oh, Seyoura Yoshida, it's you. I didn't see. We are honored, eh, Ramon?"

They were a couple of the mechanics she'd spoken to a few times in the crew commons; sitting off to one side of the permanent floating poker pool, they would give her a rundown of the latest gossip while she sipped scalding oily java one of them ("No, Seyoura Yoshida, please, you sit down. It is no trouble at all.") had, with elaborate courtesy, fetched from the treacher.

These two went through a parody of that routine now. Ramon vanished around the blunt, bristling prow of the singleship and came back with a plastic cup of thin coffee (a black thumbprint on one side of the rim), while the younger man, Joao, found Dorthy a place to sit. "You look sad, Seyoura," he said. "A woman as young and as pretty as you should not look so sad."

"A woman so young and so pretty should never have a reason to be sad," fat, florid Ramon said. He was jacking his augmented arm into the welding robot: the torch stuttered into life and sparks arced out again, hissing as they fell through black air. "Nor," he added, "should she be wandering down here, strictly speaking. A dangerous place if you don't know it. Many of the pits are in vacuum. The pressure curtain wouldn't stop you if you fell in."

"Thanks for the warning. It seems so empty down here. Like so much of the ship, I guess."

Ramon said, "In the old days—" and Joao said, "We all know about the old days, more than those who were there, I imagine. But, Seyoura, surely you didn't come down here to visit us. If so, we are greatly honored."

Ramon said, "You spend too much time with the scientists. Up there, they worry over what they must do, endless worry."

"And down here you don't worry? This is a dangerous place for everyone, not just the scientists."

Ramon said, "If the Enemy was here, we would know it. I served on this ship when it was fighting the Campaigns at BD Twenty. I know all about the Enemy, Seyoura. That light show, nothing but automatic defenses." On the ball of his shoulder, the tattoo of a naked woman stretched bonelessly as his augmented arm swung up and back. High above his head, the welder's slave arm aped his motion. "The way I see it, we don't worry because if they hit us it will be all over before we know anything. I don't mean to alarm you, Seyoura, of course."

"I'm not alarmed. Actually, I came down here to find out more. There was a pilot who gave me a trip around Colcha. Does he hang out down here?"

Joao exchanged a glance with Ramon, and Dorthy knew that her transparent piece of misdirection had been seen through. There was something going on she couldn't quite grasp. Joao gestured with his augmented arm and said, "If you want to know anything about Colcha, you talk with Ang Poh Mokhtar, Seyoura. She did the maintenance runs, before the Event."

"She goes down to the surface?"

"Before the Event, sure. Someone has to look after all the stuff the scientists left behind." Ramon turned away to watch the welder's arm slowly track across the singleship's hull. He added, "It kept her out of the way, at any rate."

"She is a strange woman, Seyoura," Joao said. "You be careful, now."

"I'll bear that in mind," Dorthy said. "Where exactly is she?"

Ang Poh Mokhtar lived on her ship. It was a surface-to-orbit tug, a cluster of spheres studded with thruster pods, bristling with antennae. Perched in its cradle, its three articulated legs swung up above it, it looked like a huge insect struggling to free itself of its cocoon. Its pilot was a slim woman with a lined, hawkish face and thick iron gray hair pulled back from her forehead. A glittering spiral brooch pinned the high collar of her tunic. She said, "You want to go down to the surface? If you're brave enough for it, we shall go right away. You're as small as me, so there is no problem with pressure suits. Come on, now! Or are you really not so brave."

"I'll come," Dorthy said, surprised by the woman's directness. "Of course I'll come. Are you sure that it won't get you into trouble?"

Ang spat red juice into the black pit below the catwalk on which they both stood. She was barefoot, the wrinkled skin on the tops of her feet crawling with blue veins. "The time is right. We want to help you in any way we can, Dorthy. Don't you worry, my dear. I live in a comfortable little niche down here, and no one fusses much over what I get up to. And we Witnesses have been waiting for you to make this move."

"Really? Then I suppose I should count myself lucky that you didn't just kidnap me."

Ang said, "We want to help you. If you had talked with Dr. Baptista, all would have been clearer. Which reminds me that I have to give you this."

She held out her hand. A round white tablet lay on her palm's scribed lines. "It's the drug you want," Ang said, after a moment.

Chills snarled at the base of Dorthy's spine. "Counteragent? Where did you get it?"

"The medical technician is one of us, Dorthy. Dr. Baptista says it's a token of our goodwill."

Dorthy's hand snatched the tablet up, crammed it into her mouth. Light dazzled her as she tipped her head back to swallow, and she was suddenly herself again, felt the tablet's hardness as it went down her dry gullet into the darkness of her metabolism.

Ang spat another stream of red juice over into the pit, wiped her chin, turned and started up the curved side of one of the tug's blisters, gripping inset rungs with hands and feet. Dorthy followed, finding that it was easier than it looked. Gravity here was only about half of what it was in the main part of the ship. As they swung, one after the other, into the tiny cabin, she asked the pilot, "What is it you're chewing?"

Ang said, "Betel. My only bad habit, but at my age I guess I'm allowed one. That and chasing the boys, which is a lot easier here. I'll say this for letting the Greater Brazilians more or less run the Navy: at least it means the sex ratio is in my favor. Only competition is from those fluffy little aides some of the ranking scientists have brought along, and you can bet they don't share their favors around. Oh, I'm sorry, I'm embarrassing you. I forget you Chinese don't like to talk about that kind of thing."

"I'm Japanese, well, half-Japanese actually."

"Really? The other half Australian by that accent. Well, I'm sorry. I'm just an ignorant old Nepalese woman who should by rights still be walking a plow behind her cow in her stony fields halfway up the Himalayas. Here, now, put this on and stay out of my way while I get us into vacuum."

"This" was a one-piece pressure suit. Dorthy stripped off her tunic and loose trousers, wriggled into a liner and clambered into the pressure suit's stiff embrace, while Ang talked to someone ("One of ours, dear, don't worry.") about clearance, using a patch microphone she'd fixed to her scrawny throat. Meanwhile, the hatch whined shut and various servos and fans whined into life, and a fine continuous trembling thrilled in the little craft's entire structure as it was woken up. Dorthy squatted down to test the seals and indicators of the life-support pack, difficult in the cabin's dim red light. When she straightened, the gas giant's turbulent green light filled the triangular cutout ports.

9

IN MUCH THE SAME WAY THAT DORTHY YOSHIDA HAD become the center of the cabal of non-Witness scientists, and despite the beady regard of Ivanov, the interservices liaison officer (as fancy a term for a security cop as he had ever come across), Talbeck Barlstilkin had managed to gather a number of disaffected Navy officers around himself. Greater Brazilians to a man, they were mostly younger sons of impoverished aristocratic families whose estates had dwindled to a shabby town house in the capital and a *fazenda* with a few thousand viable hectares in the provinces. No career was open to them but the Navy, except the diplomatic corps if they were particularly intelligent, or the church if they were pious.

In many respects, they were like Talbeck's younger self in the bitter years after the Federation had put down his father's stubborn isolated rebellion. They were proud and resentful, kicking ineffectually against the unfairness of the Universe in general and being posted to the hypervelocity star in particular. It was demotion in all but name, usually the result of some transgression of the complex rules of Naval etiquette and deference. It was consignment to certain boredom and the ever-present risk that the meddling of the scientists would awaken the Alea that (all the officers were convinced on this point) were slumbering inside the patchwork moon. Chafing under the slack leadership of the ship's captain, a blandly affable bureaucrat seldom seen in the officers' mess, they hankered after action and glory, a chance to reforge their slighted honor in the fire of combat. That was the way they talked, and Talbeck played up to them, although to begin with he hadn't even the ghost of an idea what to do with them, except to lend them his bonded servant to slake some of their physical frustration.

No matter. Something would turn up. The confidence that Dorthy suspected was a facade in fact had deep roots. After all, Talbeck had led a charmed life. Because of his father's murder, he was by far the youngest director of the Fountain of Youth Combine. The rest were revenants from the time before Earth had returned to Elysium, preserved by agatherin and elevated by the wealth it brought, but still basically motivated by reflexes learned when each had been Duke of a minuscule kingdom: tiny islands of civilization in a sea of barbarism, spearleaf only a weed in the saltwater rice fields, and the disease it nurtured in the nucleus of each of its cells, the basis for agatherin and the longevity treatments, quite unknown. Talbeck had made his mark in the Combine by sheer force of will, and because he was virtually the only director willing to travel to the other worlds of the Federation . . . but he had tired of the Combine when he had realized that it would never be anything other than a figurehead, a puppet for Federation interests.

The realization had sharpened Talbeck's sense of superiority—he saw through the charade of self-governance, while the other directors, those crudely cunning self-serving revenants of a lost age, were content to follow the directives and recommendations of the Combine's officers so long as doing so guaranteed the continued accumulation of fabulous wealth—and it had deepened his thirst for revenge. Like his scarred face, his hatred of the Federation set him apart from the Golden with whom he'd spent much of the rest of his life, the perpetually frustrated heirs of undying Lords and Ladies, of immortal self-made tycoons. Self-mockingly, he had taken to dressing in black, to affecting an air of remote disdain for the elaborate pranks and *bon gestes* of the others of his set as he flitted with them from world to world, looking not for entertainment but a lever long enough to overthrow the governments of the Earth.

Talbeck did not delude himself that it would be an easy task. He soon ran through fantasies of uncovering or setting up a scandal that would overthrow the Security Council of the Re-United Nations, or of financing a rebellion that would split apart the contrary loyalties of the Ten Worlds (it was not that scandals were rare—it was that they were too commonplace; and while there were plenty of rebel groups, most were fighting lost causes, and most of the rest were too unstable to be worth the risk). He had run arms, very discretely of course, to the revolutionary People's Islamic Nation Party of Novaya Zyemla when it had attempted to secede from its treaties with the Federation; but the Alea Campaigns had put an end to that and, after the razing of BD Twenty, the Navy had soon overturned the rebel government and set up a more cooperative faction in its place.

No, politics was too subtle and chancy a tool for one man to use. Talbeck wanted something more direct, something comprehensive and undeniable. He'd exhausted half his fortune before the high-ranking RUN officer he'd bought while running arms to Novaya Zyemla had approached him with information about a highly secret expedition to a very strange star and a story about a Talent held virtual prisoner for ten years, ever since the end of the Alea Campaigns. Perhaps it was a sign of his desperation that Talbeck had seized upon the secrecy surrounding the investigations of the hypervelocity star as a sign that the Navy was hiding a discovery so radical that it might be—at last!—if not the lever, then at least the fulcrum.

For although agatherin extended human life span and slowed the inevitable decline of youth's vigor, it was not forever. Mistakes in DNA accumulated despite agatherin's reverse transcriptive repairs; cells became silted with wastes despite the vast battery of treatments designed to purge them. Talbeck was growing old, day-by-day. Imperceptibly, to be sure, compared to ephemerals, but steadily and unstoppably all the same. This was perhaps Talbeck's last chance, and he'd seized it with both hands, confident that his luck would see him through.

But now that he was close to realizing his life's ambition, he was growing cautious. The rescue of Dorthy, the flight from the RUN Police, the near-disaster at the neutron star, had taken much of his resilience. Besides, he had no audience to play to now, except perhaps skulking Alexander Ivanov.

So he had watched and waited, and soothed the egos of the dangerously volatile young officers, knowing that Dorthy would do something in the end: it was in her nature. And so at last she had. She had gone down to the chaotic surface of the patchwork moon.

Talbeck first heard of it from Ivanov, who was furious at what he saw as Dorthy's impudent transgression, and certain that Talbeck Barlstilkin was directly behind it.

"As a matter of fact, Seyour," Talbeck said, when Ivanov's initial tirade was more or less past, "I knew nothing about it. I know you find it hard to believe, but Dr. Yoshida and I are here for very different reasons. She goes her way, I mine. Now, do please sit down; I risk straining a muscle in my neck by staring up at you."

The bonded servant moved a spindly gilt chair forward and, after a moment, Ivanov sat on its very edge, knees splayed at awkward angles, back straight. Alexander Ivanov: black hair brushed back from his forehead, falling to cover the stiff collar of his uniform jacket; pale fleshy face that always seemed faintly and unpleasantly damp, like the underside of a dead fish; small, close-set eyes that peered out at the world from beneath the knotted barricade of coarse, bushy eyebrows.

The liaison officer said, "So at least you will now admit to having a reason for coming here. That's a start, anyway."

"Seyour Ivanov, as I believe I told you several times during the exhaustive interview I had with you after I was so kindly rescued by the liner, my reason for being here is simple curiosity, no more. I am, let us say, somewhat jaded with the thrills which the Ten Worlds have to offer. I look for more exotic ways to pass my time, and this seemed to be an eminently suitable place. But to tell you the truth, I am a little disappointed by it. I rather look forward to the liner's departure." Only the last was an outright lie; Talbeck couldn't resist trying to slip it past the scowling liaison officer. Before Ivanov could reply, Talbeck added, "I hope you will join me in some refreshment. I confess that I hold certain old-fashioned views on etiquette which compel me to play host."

"I didn't come here to socialize. I want to know what you're up to, Barlstilkin. I should have insisted you and Yoshida were held on the liner until its departure, instead of being allowed to meddle in affairs here."

"I will have tea, at any rate. Jasmine," Talbeck told his servant, "if they have it. I suppose it's fortunate for me, Seyour, that you command neither the liner nor the *Vingança*, or I wouldn't be here at all."

Ivanov had turned to watch the bonded servant as she stalked lithely across to the treacher, sinuous in her seamless one-piece black coveralls. He said, "I make no apology for my recommendation, if it's any of your business. Besides, there was nothing personal about it. I didn't even know who was aboard your ship."

"You'll excuse me if I *do* take it as personally," Talbeck said. "Ah, here is my tea. You are quite sure you—"

"Cut the shit, Barlstilkin. I've dealt with Golden before. I know what you think of us, what you call us. Ephemerals. I know the little acts you put on."

Talbeck sipped at his tea. Of course he was putting on an act. He put on an act of some kind or another with everyone; he had long ago given up trying not to. The problem was that he knew Ivanov's type so well: spiteful, petty and mean, wounded in some small, cheap way so that he always thought the worst of everyone. Loyal to his concept of duty rather than to his masters, making him both naive and dangerous. Perhaps that was why he had been sent here, some grubby little campaign to root out corruption had led too far, and so had been suppressed.

"Your silence doesn't impress me either," Ivanov said.

"You're a difficult man to deal with, Seyour. Anything I say makes me guilty, and so does anything I don't. You might at least," Talbeck said, his heart again giving the little leap, pure excitement, as it had when Ivanov had first told him about Dorthy's trip to the surface of the moon, "you might at least tell me what Dr. Yoshida is supposed to have done, and what it is I am accused of."

"I will deal with Dr. Yoshida when she returns. As for you, fomenting mutiny would be the main charge, I should think. Conspiring to pervert the morals of Naval officers on active duty would certainly be one more."

"I suppose I could try and avoid the company of the Naval officers. But I'm an old man, Seyour. I do so enjoy the flattering attention of the young."

"Enjoy it while you can," Ivanov said, with a smirk. "And tell them to enjoy that toy woman of yours while *they* can. You'll be going back on the liner, you and Dr. Yoshida, in less than a week. Hard-class, in the medical bay. You'll find it difficult to make trouble when you're in deep sleep, with a core temperature of twelve degrees. And I hear Golden have a problem with defrosting, so enjoy everything while you can, Seyour. Just in case."

There was more along this line, but Talbeck simply stopped listening. He remembered now who Ivanov reminded him of, the first of his kind Talbeck had seen: the bland junior diplomat who had delivered the ultimatum to his father so many years ago, the barely concealed threat that if Duke Barlstilkin IV did not join the Fountain of Youth Combine, then all control of his land would be revoked. It had sparked furious rage in Talbeck's father, the first anger Talbeck had seen in that rigorously self-controlled man. Dead so many years, killed when laser cannon had brought down the western watchtower. After a while, Talbeck realized that Ivanov was no longer there, and looked around.

Jose Navio Alverez was sitting slightly behind Talbeck's own chair, long legs stretched out and crossed at the ankles of his soft, supple, zithsa-hide boots. "Seyour Barlstilkin," he said. "You are awake at last. Good. We must talk."

"So many people want to talk with me today." Talbeck lifted his cup of tea to his lips, but it was quite cold. "I suppose that you are here for the same reason as Ivanov, but perhaps you'll tell me just what Dr. Yoshida has done."

Alverez drew up his heels and leaned forward, like a jackknife closing. "No one knows, exactly," he said eagerly. "She is still down there. It was the Witnesses, you know, who decided to let her go. The pilot is one of theirs. I have someone listening in to their suit radios, and I must suppose that so has Ivanov."

"Oh, I wouldn't be at all surprised." Talbeck's bonded servant had located half a dozen microscopic listening devices in his cabin; no doubt there were others even she couldn't detect.

Alverez was fingering the scar which seamed his left cheek, remnant of a duel in which he'd killed a man—he'd told Talbeck all about it more than once, fiercely proud of the silly quarrel over an imagined slight. They were all of them children, the conspirators, although dangerous children, as unstable and explosive as a mercury trigger. Now, Talbeck could almost smell the man's excitement. He asked, "What are we to do?"

"Most of the scientists will help us," Alverez said. "That is to say, the Witnesses. They have the crazy belief that there are beings like gods somewhere in the Universe. They may as well be at the ends of the wormholes as anywhere else, so the Witnesses want to go and look. Of course, there is no point in trying to disabuse them, but for the present they will be on our side, and that is all we need. With them, we have a credible majority, more than enough to oust the timeserving lackeys of the RUN. We will," he said fiercely, "have it in our power to strike a blow against the Enemy that will ring down the corridors of history."

Looking into the young officer's face, the taut lines, the fierce glitter of fanaticism, Talbeck felt a touch of fear—as if he were exposed on a knife-edge, raised high above everything else and buffeted by a cruel wind. Well, he'd brought it upon himself, he thought; and wondered, not for the first time, if it was not due to some unconscious will toward oblivion after all, for all his talk and desire for revenge. Flirtation with death was by now so common among the Golden that it had entered the popular mythologies of the sagas. Perhaps such death wishes were the Faustian consequence of the evolutionary crime of attempted immortality, of trying to island the self from the onrushing tide of time, of accumulated years triggering a clock written into the genome. Certainly, at that moment, Talbeck could feel the weight of each and every one of his own years pressing down upon his head like thunder. He said, "I'd like to talk with Gregor Baptista. I want to know if we can trust the Witnesses."

"We should move now, or the moment may be lost. The bureaucrats are slow, but they are not entirely stupid."

"Humor an old man," Talbeck said. "I've developed an instinct which allows me to gauge when someone will try and sink a knife into my back. I want to be sure that our allies will attempt it later rather than sooner."

10

══

BLUE-GREENS, GRAYS, COLD CYANS, SHARDS OF VIRI-descence like the backs of poisonous beetles: the perpetual storms of the gas giant bled into each other in complex interlocking patterns. Whorls feathered off the edges of hurricanes the size of the Earth; horizontal tracks of gelid turbulence rippled around the equator. Strikes of interstellar debris had churned the planet's atmosphere into perpetual chaos; at six percent the speed of light, even a dust grain has the yield of a tactical fusion warhead. Colcha was shielded from this bombardment by its primary's gaseous bulk; otherwise it would have been smashed apart thousands of years before.

Right now, the patchwork moon was a fingernail chip of light against this immense turbulence. Since the Event, the *Vingança* had widened its orbit around Colcha to an ellipse with a major axis of more than forty thousand kilometers. It was a long way for Ang Poh Mokhtar's surface-to-orbit tug to fall.

Dorthy floated at one of its triangular ports, tethered by fingertip pressure, watching the little moon grow perceptibly bigger. Her Talent was slowly widening, a familiar yet half-forgotten feeling. *I don't know what you want me to find down there*, she thought, as if to the ghost in her head, *but I'm willing to go along for the ride as long as there really is something to find. Because it's time I learned why I've come all this way.* There was no reply, but of course she hadn't been expecting one.

Ang hung over the control pedestal beside Dorthy. Cold light flowed eerily over her wrinkled face as she peered out of her own port. Her pressure suit was decorated with swirling patterns that were reduced to various shades of black in the cabin's dim red light, seeming to rotate against each other in crazy chthonic patterns whenever she moved. After a while, she said casually, "They say you're the Golden's concubine. Is it true?"

"Who says it is?"

"The men, of course." Ang's laugh was sudden and surprisingly soft. "Now, you see, I don't care if you are or not."

"Well, I'm not," Dorthy said. She had been wondering about the mechanics' banter. What had seemed innocent was now suddenly shaded with darker overtones.

"Men," Ang said, "especially Brazilian men, can't abide the thought of a woman on her own. But I can handle them, and I suppose you can too, or you wouldn't be here, am I right?"

"I didn't get here by sleeping with Barlstilkin."

"No one would say that to your face, but it's been going around. I'd wonder what they say about me, except I don't care. I ignore them, which is why I'm here, away from all the fun. Men say one thing and mean another, if you know what I mean."

"Oh, I do. You know, I haven't really had a chance to talk with another woman for the longest time." Angel Sutter, in the dark cabin of the 'thopter riding back to Camp Zero, after the debacle at the neuter female's hold. Her dark, strong beautiful face profiled against the desert night, lighted only by the checklights on the 'thopter's little board. The silver gleam of her tears for the death of her lover, Duncan Andrews. What had happened to her?

Ambushed by memory, Dorthy missed what Ang had said, and had to ask her say it again.

"Apart from being the Golden's concubine, you know, some of the boys think that you're an interstellar spy for the underground government of Novaya Zyemla. That's why you're sleeping with that sulky looking planetologist, what is his name? Valdez. Oh, you can't keep secrets on a ship, you know. Not from the crew, anyway." Ang laughed, showing dark-stained teeth and a wad of something fibrous that she shifted from one cheek to the other. The drug was messing up the flow of her thoughts, making it difficult for Dorthy to feel her way inside them.

Dorthy said, "I suppose it's that fucking liaison officer, Ivanov, who's putting this poison about. You know him? He'd put me away, if he could. Put me into vacuum, perhaps."

Ang said, "Don't worry about him. We can freeze him out when the time comes. His kind were all through the fleet at BD Twenty, like rats through a grain store. Frightened, I suppose, that we'd all defect to the Enemy given half a chance."

As Colcha began to eclipse the gas giant, they fell to talking about the Alea Campaigns. Dorthy gave a carefully edited version of what had happened to her on P'thrsn; and it turned out that Ang had served long-range picket duty in P'thrsn's system for a year after her tour at BD Twenty. That was when she'd turned on to the Witnesses, although she was evasive about the precise circumstances. She was a loner, but preferred the formal ladder of relationships which the Navy provided to civilian society. Find your niche, and you were made for life, was her philosophy. She was not about to go up and out, like so many veteran pilots, although she kept in touch with a few of her comrades who had turned to singleship exploring, even one who had discovered a point nine nine habitable planet in the system of Alpha Phoenix—there were half a dozen settlements on that world now—and with his share of the colony fees the man had bought his own singleship, with enough left over to guarantee a century of agatherin treatment.

"Though to tell you the truth, I don't know if he'll live long enough to enjoy it," Ang said. "He's out on another trip even now, more than seventy light-years to a K-type, Kaus Borealis. He's not content unless he's chasing down another set of fuzzy 'scope data, riding farther out than anyone else, with all sign of civilization vanished in his wake."

Ang said it softly, a benediction for something that had withered away without her knowing it until now. Dorthy felt the woman's sadness and turned away to stare out at the chaotic terrain of the patchwork moon—a plain scored and cracked with a thousand parallel grooves; a field of eroded craters; a flat black sheet punctuated with white drifts of frozen gases. From a hundred kilometers across down to patches no bigger than a small crater, the radically different scapes alternated with no discernible pattern.

Except for the shafts.

Ang was watching the loran indicator and radar range displays, so Dorthy eyeballed their target first. That was what it looked like, quite literally, a perfect black circle at the center of the smooth converging slopes of a vast crater. It reminded Dorthy of something she'd seen almost every day of her brief childhood in the small Australian whaling town: the tiny pits ant lions excavated in the sandy soil of the empty lots between the apt blocks. Children would drop ants into these traps and watch with glee as the creature concealed at the bottom accurately flicked sand grains to dislodge the struggling ant and knock it to the bottom of the pit's perfectly smooth cone; then there would be a sudden miniature eruption as the tiny monster reared from concealment to devour its victim. Gazing through the tug's triangular port at the enigmatic opening, Dorthy felt a little frisson of irrational fear: something monstrous could erupt from its infinite depths at any moment. What had the singleship pilot seen, as the light of another universe had burst around him? Or perhaps it was not *her* fear. Perhaps the passenger in her skull was stirring, down in the crocodile basement of her brain, among the dim red tides of primal hormones.

"Strap in," Ang said briskly, "we're going down."

The tug drifted across the vast crater and landed without ceremony at its lip, a few hundred meters from a little package of instruments and the tipped parabolic bowl of an antenna link. While Ang ran a diagnostic check on the instrument package, Dorthy made her way to the edge of the crater that funneled into the shaft, falling almost without thought in the fractional gravity into the bunny-hop gait she'd learned at Fra Mauro.

Spider-thin sensor cables ran hundreds of meters in every direction from the instruments, all the way around the crater, it seemed. A few even ran down into it. Dorthy shuffled up to the precisely defined edge, clean as a knife cut, where a cable bent to start its swoop down the smooth, steep slope. Bent within the stiff suit by the mass of its life-support pack, her breath loud in the bubble of her helmet, she looked down into the shaft.

It no longer frightened her. The scale was so vast that there was no room for fear. It was no more of a threat than Ayers Rock or the Grand Canyon.

The tiny sun was at her back, and Dorthy's shadow was thrown a long way down the slope of the crater, vast and crisply black against pale dust. Green halos multiplied around the huge bubble of her helmet. The long slope swooped down to the kilometer-wide, pitch-black opening of the shaft, rose up around it. Colcha was so small and the crater so big that the far rise bit a smooth curve out of the horizon, where the gas giant subtended half the sky. Dorthy could just make out the double star of the *Vingança* and the Guild liner, hung before green-blue feathery curls of a monstrous storm swirl at the planet's equator.

For a long time she simply stood and let the view sink through her while the counteragent worked its final changes. Her Talent was so strange and so familiar after its long, long sleep. Ang's thoughts, once mere disconnected sparks, gradually coalesced, a strong flowing fountain that drew Dorthy's attention out from her own still center. Focus, she needed to focus.

She couldn't assume the lotus position in the stiff, clumsy pressure suit, but she managed a kind of half-squat at the crater's sharply defined edge: legs splayed, gloved hands one over the other in her lap. She saw that the dust was slowly seething, grains crawling over each other as if struggling for perfect alignment, radial lines forming and breaking apart, re-forming. . . . She dragged her glove through the dust and chaos boiled in its wake, a whirl of vortices slowly dissipating into the general linear seethe.

But there was time to wonder about that. She was here to look beyond surfaces. Calm, calm, find the center. It had been a long time, but the habits of meditation, *Sessan Amakuki*, were still there, waiting only to be called upon.

Slowly, she sank away from Ang, from her own self, sank into *Samahdi*, into the necessary oblivion from which, for her, all understanding flowed.

And after a timeless interval, a black mote inflated into the opening of the shaft. Its darkness inverted and stars raveled out from its center, thousands upon thousands of close-packed suns shining with hot, vivid colors.

The core.

Dorthy recognized it at once. The Alea had shown it to her on P'thrsn, and she had returned to it again and again in her dreams . . . if those had been her dreams.

The shaft dwindled behind Dorthy and she plunged among packed clusters of stars. It was like falling headfirst into a jewel box, past double and triple and quadruple systems spinning in stately pavanes, none less than half a light-year from its nearest neighbor. Many were bright red population II giants, blazing through their spendthrift youth: this was not the contemporary core, but the Galaxy soon after it had coalesced, still rich in promise; its stars, without the tempering effect of heavier fusion products, squandering prodigious hoards of hydrogen.

Stars fell behind her, and there was the accretion disk of the black hole at the Galaxy's dead center, a tenuous spiral of gas whose boundaries were defined more by the artifacts that ringed it than by its feeble ultraviolet fluorescence. The vast constructs were tended by swarms of things part machine, part organism, big as spaceships. Some were embedded in the accretion disk's spiral tides; others were somehow locked into space-time at the black hole's virtual horizon; but most formed an untidy shell a dozen light-years in diameter around the accretion disk. In a myriad variant morphologies, the living machines danced attendance on artifacts big as planets or swarmed in and out of wormhole termini—riding shifting flaws *between* galaxies, Dorthy saw. It was the golden age of intelligence in the Universe, the core a crossroads where the inhabitants of a thousand galaxies in the Local Group met and mingled.

Then it was past. The Galaxy turned twice, and the vast constructions orbiting the black hole were empty and silent. Many were caught in the black hole's gravity well, spiraling through the brightening fluorescence of the accretion disk, flaring out like moths flying too close to a fire as tides ripped their molecules apart. The Galaxy turned again. Suddenly, those few artifacts which remained were aglitter with tiny ships that swarmed about them as minnows gather around the corpse of a drowned giant. The marauders had arrived.

Dorthy was being fed this history through a tap in her consciousness she hadn't known was there. Her passenger was not simply an implant, a bunch of false memories waiting to be triggered by the right cue. It was active, self-aware, self-directed. It had not been slumbering, but watching, biding its time, waiting for its chance. Now it gripped her as the memory wire had gripped her on P'thrsn, after she had been taken by the family of the neuter female: the wire which had fed her a partial history of the civil war, and, she was sure, had implanted the passenger. And what else? What else had been done to her?

A charge of adrenaline struck through her, a flight reaction. For a moment she was aware of her body again, cramped inside the stiff pressure suit, Ang somewhere very close. Dorthy turned away from that reality, looked around the distraction of Ang's mind, looked farther and deeper inside herself than she'd dared look before.

Images rose up at her, borne on hot primal fears. A distorted priapic glimpse of Uncle Mishio, his one good eye leering. The keep on P'thrsn, its spiral traceries of lights twinkling in the furnace illumination of the red dwarf sun, its multiple spires dwarfing the hyperintelligent new male Alea, newly

changed from nonsentient children in response to the presence
of humans, who toiled toward it down the inner slope of the
extinct volcano. Again she was standing near the top of the
keep's spiral walkway, backed against a curved wall incised with
history as a new male advanced with murderous intent—huge,
black, the hood around his feral face engorged with blood, his
clawed hands raised toward her. Again she was in the lair of the
ancient neuter female, her new male servants wild with panic
as Duncan Andrews raised his rifle, the neuter female looming
above him, calmly ready for death. The instant of the neuter
female's fall, Duncan Andrews screaming at Dorthy to run just
before he was torn apart.

Dorthy recoiled, fighting up through the rhythms of her
metabolism (like pushing through folds of dusty, blood-red
velvet, a stifling claustrophobia), even as she realized that the
images were a barrier set up by the thing that already was fleeing
her, sinking away like blood into sand, into the premammalian
layer of her triple-folded brain. She dared not follow. That way
led only to catatonia, for she had no maps. Defeated, like an
uneasy sleeper waking from a bad dream, she fought her way
back to consciousness.

11

Dr. Gregor Baptista, the leader of the Witnesses,
was a stooped old man with a round face as mild as milk
framed by a wispy halo of white curls and a neatly trimmed
spade-shaped beard. He came into the little cabin deep in the
Vingança's deserted accommodation decks leaning on the arm
of a young woman. She solicitously arranged the cushions of
the frame chair before settling him into it, served him with
one of the little cups of bitter coffee Alverez had arranged to

be brought down, then settled at his feet for all the worlds like a puppy by her master.

Talbeck and Alverez, seated side by side on the dusty mattress of the bunk, made it crowded in the cramped cabin. As a meeting place it left almost everything to be desired, but even Ivanov couldn't have bugged every one of the cabins in the accommodation modules. Talbeck's servant stood guard outside; Alverez had hinted that he'd made his own arrangements, and no doubt the Witnesses had done the same. Despite his reservations, the interlocking secrecy and the forced intimacy of the little cabin gave Talbeck the sense that something was happening at last.

Baptista came straight to point. "We have been monitoring Dr. Yoshida on the surface of Colcha," he said, speaking flawlessly pure, if somewhat stilted, Portuguese. "She has entered a trance, but as you advised, Seyour Barlstilkin, we have made sure that she is subvocalizing a commentary. I must say that I am delighted that the chemical cue was so effective."

"I paid a good deal of hard currency to learn the trigger the Kamali-Silver Institute used on Dorthy while she was indentured. I'm glad you think it was worth the price."

"If you mean that you believe that you are entitled to know what Dr. Yoshida has been saying, I will be pleased to give you a transcript as soon as possible. May I summarize?"

Alverez said, "The wormholes are a way to the Enemy. That is all we need to discuss."

Baptista smiled. "It seems we are all privy to Dr. Yoshida's thoughts."

Alverez said, "You're using Navy equipment, right?"

"Indeed. Again, we are grateful. Then perhaps we are all agreed. It *is* quite clear that Colcha is only a terminus, or way station. It is not an end in itself, but a beginning. The way lies open to the core of the Galaxy. Like you, Lieutenant Alverez, it is a path that we are eager to take . . . for a different reason, however. You wish to absolve your honor. We believe that all of humanity is at the brink of a quantum leap in conceptual evolution away from purely planet-oriented civilization. Such a step is necessary if we are to complete the ascent to pure consciousness, and it is essential that it is begun before humanity is fragmented by uncontrolled colonization of the nearer stars.

Colcha itself will not provide impetus, but what lies beyond it may. Or so I must believe, if I understand anything at all of Dr. Yoshida's vision."

"Or it could be nothing more than a trick of the Enemy," Alverez said. "I'm a man of action, Dr. Baptista, you're quite right. I'm not interested, you will forgive me, in theories of galactic or universal consciousness. I am interested in what I know, in what I can do. What I know, and what my comrades know too, is that we must go through the shaft to discover if Colcha is indeed the work of the Enemy. If it is, then it will give us an unparalleled chance to strike at its very heart. The honor of the Navy is at stake here. We defend humanity by action, not by picket duty. We should have smashed P'thrsn when we had the chance, but those civilians who assume power over us were too weak, too diffident. And so here too."

Alverez glared at Baptista defiantly, but the old scientist was too politic to rise to the bait. He smiled and said that if the Alea had constructed the hypervelocity system, and if it was a threat to humanity, then the Witnesses would not be dismayed. Such a threat could only unite humanity, as it had been united during the Campaign against the Alea at BD Twenty. United, they could march forward onto the stage of galactic history, taking the path which so many other intelligent races must have taken—or else why was the Galaxy, the Universe, not abuzz with civilizations? Dorthy Yoshida had given an account of a pan-Galactic civilization which had passed away billions of years before. Where had it gone? Humanity must discover that, and earn the right to follow.

There was much more in this vein. As Baptista talked, Talbeck began to feel a widening vertiginous alarm. He knew well enough when someone was preaching a cause in which he did not truly believe. He had dealt with career politicians for longer than Alverez had been alive, in his salad days on the board of the Fountain of Youth Combine. But Baptista, far advanced in the Witnesses' rigid hierarchy—more rigid by far than that which Dante had attributed to the circles of Paradise— was preaching from his heart. It seemed that the Witnesses were not simply another in the long line of chiliastic movements more concerned in recruiting cannon fodder than in promulgating faith. No, they were infinitely more dangerous than that, for they were true fanatics, all the way to the top.

Baptista talked a long time. His sermon, sustained only by the single thread of his voice, made melodious by the naturally rich rhymes and rhythms of Portuguese, spun out a vast and colorful tapestry. He talked about the inevitable existence of billions of civilizations throughout the Universe, given the simple fact that one and a half intelligent alien species had evolved within a few light-years of Earth, given the existence of vast machineries orbiting the black hole at the heart of the Galaxy's core, abandoned by the ancient pan-Galactic civilization. He talked of the evolution of conscious beings away from the confines of flesh and blood and machinery to organizations of energy that would eventually subsume the entire Universe. Perhaps it would be a collective consciousness, he said, a single superbeing comprised of elements of all intelligent species; and he talked about race memory and the evolution of the empathic Talents as precursors to this collectivization, a blather of Jungian nonsense that was at least reassuring to Talbeck, who knew all too well the kind of nonsense scientists could descend to when trying to rationalize the unrationalizable without bringing God into it.

At last Baptista smiled and clapped his hands, just as if he were breaking a spell. Alverez stretched out his long legs, the heels of his zithsa-hide boots pushing furrows through a decade of dust. The young woman who had been sitting at Baptista's feet, whom Talbeck had almost forgotten, poured out a fresh cup of coffee for her master.

Baptista thanked her and sipped, and said that he believed that there must be intelligent species which had passed into states of being that humans could hardly imagine, but which were not so evolved that they had passed entirely beyond comprehension. These demigod-like species could perhaps be approached, be petitioned. Humanity must prove its worth by making the attempt, or it would pass away unregretted, as surely as so many other species had passed away.

By now, Alverez was scowling at the scuff marks he'd drawn across the dusty floor, and Talbeck brought Baptista around to how the Witnesses could help the rebellious crew to gain control of the ship.

Baptista smiled. "Why, we are ready to act at once, Seyour Barlstilkin, with or without your help, or that of Lieutenant Alverez and his comrades."

Alverez looked up, startled. "We can move as quickly as you can. But I don't know if we *need* to move so quickly."

Baptista said, "Dr. Yoshida has defined the way. What else do we need?"

"So we are decided," Talbeck said, a little surprised at how easily it had gone. "We have a common aim, and a common destination. All we have to do is act."

"All you have to do," someone said out of the air, "is stay where you are. You are all under arrest."

It was Alexander Ivanov's voice.

Alverez started up, fumbling at the flap of his elaborately tooled pistol holster, but before he could draw his weapon the pleated door banged aside and two men slammed him down onto the bunk. Someone's elbow caught Talbeck on the point of his cheekbone, sending a spear of pain right into his brain. Blinded by tears, he hardly noticed as Alverez, a gun to his head, was hauled up and dragged out of the cabin.

"A pitiful sight indeed," Ivanov said. Through a blur of tears, Talbeck could scarcely see him, just a shadow in the door's lighted rectangle. "I had hopes for excitement, but you made it so easy for me. Arrogance, I suppose. You think that because I do not wear an expensively decorated uniform, because I am not from a family with a *name*, I am harmless. I can be disregarded. You are not the first to make that mistake."

Talbeck blinked and blinked, trying to clear the tears from his eyes. "I do not underestimate anyone," he said. "I must suppose that you planted some kind of listening device on me, or on Alverez."

"No need. There are phone lines all over the ship. I activated them all, and a computer screened conversations for keywords. Very old technique, but very effective. An ephemeral I may be, Seyour Barlstilkin, but I am an ephemeral who has sealed your fate. Yours also, Dr. Baptista."

Baptista merely smiled.

"You must believe it," Ivanov said, and looked around as sounds of struggle came from behind him. A muffled curse, the heavy sound of something striking human flesh. "You two had better hold him on the floor," he said, "if he will not behave himself. Sit on his head for all I care. Just make sure we don't have to shoot him. There is to be a trial first. Someone will help me with the others."

He stepped aside to let another armed man into the cabin, and the girl at Baptista's feet let out an unnerving strangled howl and threw herself at the guard. There was a glint of metal as she flung her arm up and back, then down. The little knife she had pulled from somewhere caught the guard in the face with such force that Talbeck heard the distinct pop as the man's cheekbone snapped. His pistol clattered to the floor as he clutched his bloody face. With more presence of mind than Talbeck would have attributed to him, Ivanov scooped up the wounded guard's pistol. He stepped back from the white-faced girl's wide swing and shot from the hip.

The first flechette caught the girl's arm, blowing a hole just above her elbow. She did a little pirouette and the second took her behind her ear. Bloody tissue flew out of the back of her head, spattering the wall as she fell backward. Her heels drummed the dusty floor for a moment and then she was still.

Ivanov picked up the knife and shook back hair which had flopped down over his face. For a moment, Talbeck thought that he was going to be shot there and then, but Ivanov simply waved him and Baptista out into the corridor.

Alverez was sitting on the floor just outside the cabin, hands clasped on top of his head, the guard's pistol jammed above his ear. The bridge of his nose was puffily purple; bright blood wet his neatly trimmed mustache. Talbeck's bonded servant stood a little way down the narrow corridor, watched by a third guard. She started forward as Talbeck came out of the cabin, but Talbeck signaled with a quick slashing motion of his hand and she settled back.

"That's good," Ivanov said. "She is valuable, and I wouldn't want to harm her." He quickly and roughly examined the guard the girl had attacked, dismissing the man's injury as a flesh wound. "You must excuse my help," he said to Talbeck, "but they are all I had to hand. I will have to search both of you, now."

"Of course," Talbeck said, and submitted without demur as the man who'd stood guard over his bonded servant patted at his loose tunic and trousers. The man's touch had a tentative, trembling quality to it, as if he could hardly believe he had the authority to carry out this violation. Talbeck himself was not absolutely calm. He could feel a fine tremor deep inside himself, like a plucked wire thrilling at a note too high to hear. There was a burning edge to his breath, as if the air had suddenly become as rarified as that atop a high mountain. He caught Baptista's gaze. Although spattered with the blood and brains of his acolyte, the Witness retained his serene smile.

Talbeck hardly dared hope what that serenity could mean. "You mentioned a trial," he said to Ivanov, as the guard moved on to search Baptista. "As a civilian, I request the right to be tried by my peers, not hauled up before a summary court-martial. As a citizen of the Federation, I am not subject to military law."

"Oh no," Ivanov said gleefully. "Oh no. You will soon find out just how wrong you are, Barlstilkin. You are aboard a vessel of the Federation Navy, in a declared war zone. You didn't know about that? Too bad. You'll be lucky to get anything more than a summary hearing before they strip you naked and kick you out of the airlock. Incitement to mutiny, conspiracy against the authority of the ship's commanding officer, either one will get you an orbit of your very own." His smile stretched his sallow skin tight across his high cheekbones; he looked like a death's head. "And I will be there, watching. Last thing you see before your lungs come up your throat will be my face."

"I would not count on it," Baptista said, and the lights went out.

The darkness lasted only a moment before the lurid red glow of the emergency lighting cut in with a bang, but that was enough time for the bonded servant to kill the guard nearest her, for Alverez to snatch the pistol from the guard standing over him and turn it on Ivanov.

"Don't shoot him," Talbeck said quickly. His servant held out the dead guard's pistol. He took it from her, although he hadn't the faintest intention of using it.

Alverez said, "I wasn't going to. Not yet."

Ivanov said, "You still have a chance to die with honor, Lieutenant. Give up now. I'll put in a good word at the trial."

"Jesus Christos, you think I'm a fucking *pirate* or something?" Alverez was breathing hard through his mouth. "It seems we have our little revolution a little sooner than planned. Dr. Baptista, I thank you for your help. But I hope your people will have the sense to keep out of the way until the ship is secure."

"I cannot speak for them, I am afraid."

"Then pray for them," Alverez said lightly. "It will not be an easy fight."

Baptista said, "It will be easier than you believe, Lieutenant." There was a distant rumble, a bass vibration that shook Talbeck's bones. The emergency lighting flickered, steadied at a dimmer glow.

Alverez said, "That's one of the modules cutting loose. Baptista, did you do that? You crazy?"

"An accommodation module, to be precise. Rescuing the scientists and the Navy personnel aboard it will keep the captain of the liner busy while you, Lieutenant, take the *Vingança* through the wormhole."

Baptista stepped back, and suddenly half a dozen people were around him, all armed with pistols. As if they'd sprung out of the decking . . . no, there was a drop shaft in the angle of the corridor. For a moment, Talbeck thought it was his entourage. But he'd left them behind in Melbourne. He was alone here. The Witnesses had pinned Alverez to a wall and taken his pistol; Talbeck bowed to Baptista and surrendered his own pistol to a woman he recognized as the head of the planetology survey team.

Baptista told those around him, "Evangaline is dead. She died fighting for us all, and when there is time we must remember her. Take away Seyour Ivanov and his helpers and kill them. Barlstilkin and Alverez can live. They may be of use to us."

12

A FIGURE ARRAYED IN DAZZLING PATTERNS STOOD OVER
Dorthy. Its face was a golden bowl that reflected her own
pressure-suited self, its bulky legs splayed awkwardly, one glove
half-raised to its helmet.

Ang's voice said in her ear, "It's over, Dr. Yoshida! Come
on now. It's time to go!"

"Just give me a moment, Ang. I've been on a trip."

"Oh, I know, I know. I wasn't sure about all this mystical
mind reading bullshit until you started babbling. Here, now."

Despite the moon's low gravity, Dorthy needed Ang's help
to get to her feet. Her legs were knotted with cramps. The other
woman's anxiety thrilled through her. "Babble? I haven't done
that since I was a kid. Well, it doesn't matter. What matters is
that I know. I know!"

The history of the core was still playing out somewhere in
Dorthy's mind. The war of the marauders against the other
Alea family nations, the refugees fleeing the core, out into the
myriad field stars of the spiral arms. . . . "I know where it goes!"
She could feel a manic grin pressing the bones of her cheeks
against the rim of the helmet liner. "Down the hole! All the
way in . . . all the way to the center!"

Ang made an impatient gesture, gloved fist sweeping out
from her chest in a flat arc. "Of course. But we are behind
schedule and it really is time to go."

"I know! All the way to the center of the Galaxy. To
the core. That's where it's happening, that's where it's always
happened."

"You are rapping. Come on, Dorthy Yoshida. Come on,
now. We return."

"Yes, of course. I must tell Barlstilkin. And Abel Gunasekra, Valdez . . . he'll be so happy about this."

"There is no need. Come, now."

Clumsy and slow, they clambered back into the tug, banging into each other in the confined space which, the hatch shut, roared and roared as blowers pressurized it. "I was right," Dorthy said, once they had taken their helmets off. "I was right all along."

"That is good," Ang said neutrally. But two vertical lines dented the skin between her glossy black eyebrows as she began to run through the instrument checklist. She said, "You rest now. You have done much."

"I'm not crazy. Really. Or no crazier than I was before. I've never really led a normal life, Ang. I tried, after I left the Institute, tried so hard to be an astronomer. But history wouldn't let me, you see. Not just human history, but the secret history of the Universe. We're living in its echoes right now. They reverberate through us, the way water trembles in a glass in time to the tolling of a great bell a hundred kilometers away. I'm sorry, yes, I am a bit manic. I'll sit down and rest, if there's somewhere to sit."

"Pull this out, here," Ang said. "You sit quietly, now. I must get us home. You have made us very late, and things are moving faster than we expected."

The seat was no more than a padded bar that swung out from the wall, but when she straddled it Dorthy found it comfortable enough. The LSP of her suit held her upright, jammed against the cabin's curved wall. The air of the cabin was cold, and her breath hung in a little cloud before her. There was the fierce peppery scent of gunpowder and it took Dorthy a long time to realize what it was. It was the smell of the dust they'd carried in with them. It was the smell of Colcha.

Meanwhile, Ang talked quietly with someone on the *Vingança* before at last igniting the motor and taking the tug into orbit. After the jarring thunder of lift-off, as the tug left Colcha behind, Dorthy fell into a kind of half-reverie. It was hard work, diving into one's own mind. But she had won something . . . or been given it. She was too tired and too elated to realize that the distinction mattered, and she didn't begin to understand just how her vision had decided the fate of the expedition until the tug's motor suddenly cut off.

It had been burning for a long time, Dorthy realized tardily, and at a good fraction of a gee. Ang really was in a hurry to get back. Dorthy let her attention expand the smallest amount, cautiously impinging upon Ang's jittery anxiety. Spikes of undirected nervous energy spitting and fizzing around a kernel of fear . . . fear of failure, of being left behind. Left behind by what? Dorthy tried to sit up in her suit's heavy embrace, tried to concentrate.

Ang was hunched over the control column, the dusty boots of her p-suit jammed into stirrups in the mesh decking, her head looking oddly small above her suit's neck ring. There was an audio spike in her left ear, and she was subvocalizing into her patch microphone.

Although Dorthy's Talent was waning, the secretions of her implant beginning to win out over the counteragent she'd dropped, she managed to catch the gist of Ang's secretive murmur. She said, "I started it all, didn't I?"

Ang didn't look around, but Dorthy registered the jolt of her surprise. The Witness said, "It was waiting to happen, my dear. From what I understand, Ivanov tried to arrest Dr. Baptista, and your Golden friend, too. How are you at space-walking?"

"Out of practice. . . . You mean to say the Witnesses have taken the *Vingança*, but they can't run it properly?"

"We didn't count on being forced to act so quickly. Now we must hurry, before the Navy personnel are rescued and are able to regroup. And there is a kind of problem with deployment of the launch cradles. We will jump ship as soon as we are close to the *Vingança*, and get inside as quickly as possible, in any way we can."

"Your people want to fly the *Vingança* through a wormhole to the Galaxy's core, yet they can't deploy the launch cradles? Doesn't that worry you, Ang?"

"That's not going to stop you, is it?"

"Damn right. Oh, I see. It was sabotage. You shouldn't try and hide things from me, Ang, I'll pick them up anyway."

"The damage was not serious, and we have complete control of the ship now. There is simply not enough time to do even running repairs. You had better put your helmet on again. We are nearly there."

"What else did the Navy people do, before the Witnesses rounded them up?"

Ang confessed, "We don't know."

"They could have set charges to blow the ship into pieces. Or sabotaged the phase graffle. Perhaps I'm not so sure about this after all, Ang."

"You don't have any choice, my dear. If you know anything, you know that. Is your helmet locked? Good. Now, do not worry. This is routine."

"I'm not worried, I'm terrified. Suppose an interstellar grain hits me? At 17,000 KMPS it'll vaporize me."

"The ship is in the shadow of Colcha, and Colcha is in the shadow of the gas giant." Ang hooked her suit to Dorthy's. "Please do not use your reaction pistol," she said, her voice intimate over the radio link, "unless I ask you to. And do not worry, I have done this many times."

"That's good to know." Dorthy really was scared. She'd always disliked microgravity, and the prospect of crawling over the *Vingança*'s hull was terrifying.

The hatch slid open behind Ang's psychedelically patterned suit. Ang passed a loop of silvery tether through her gloved hand. She said, "Stay close to me, now. You might even enjoy it." Then she kicked off before Dorthy could reply, falling neatly through the hatch and pulling Dorthy after her.

The *Vingança* stretched above them, a ladder rising against the gas giant's green disk toward the shining crescent of Colcha. Cubes and blisters and polyhedrons clustered at intervals around its long central spine. It was pitted with open hatches; halos of debris scintillated in the tarnished light of the white dwarf.

Dorthy revolved slowly at the end of the tether, saw beyond her boots the clusters of bulbous bolt-on drive units that had supplemented the ship's reaction motor during the year of acceleration needed to catch up with the hypervelocity star. The elongate sphere of the liner stood off a dozen kilometers away, shining against the field of stars. For a moment, vertigo clawed through Dorthy's nervous system. Infinity yawned all around, drenched in stars—stars everywhere beyond the ship, no beginning and no end. She could fall forever and never reach the nearest.

And then the tether went taut as Ang fired the reaction pistol and Dorthy was whirled sharply around. They were moving away from the tug, toward the sharply shadowed edge of an accommodation module.

"Hold the line close," Ang voice said in Dorthy's ear, "and you won't spin around so much. How are you doing?"

"I'm not convinced anyone could enjoy it." When they'd gone over the edge of the tug's hatch, Dorthy's stomach had done a flip-flop, atavistic reaction to what would obviously happen: go over and edge and you *fall*. It was only a little better now that they were gliding a hundred meters or so—in the sharp-edged chiaroscuro of light and shadow it was difficult to judge distances—above a staggered row of open hatches.

Ang said, "All we have to do is get inside. It won't be long."

"It was waiting to happen, wasn't it? I was just the spark to the tinder."

Dorthy was certain that Talbeck Barlstilkin must have had a hand in the mutiny; but even without him, even without her, the Witnesses would have made their move sooner or later. It was why they were here, why so many of the scientists here were Witnesses. They knew that the hypervelocity star was connected somehow with the supertechnology that the marauders had plundered. They *believed* that it was a Message, a Sign. They believed that this whole expedition was simply the cutting edge of the political and cultural forces that were slowly but inevitably pulling the Federation apart. As she was falling free along the ship, it all seemed so simple to Dorthy. It never would again.

Ang told her to look up, and she saw a module slowly split away from the *Vingança's* spine, beginning to tumble as the gap widened. "My people put the crew in it," Ang said, "to give us time to get away. We will find a place to cling to in the graving docks, Dorthy. No time to find any better place."

The reaction pistol fired again, and again Dorthy whirled on the end of the tether. Nausea squirmed in her gullet. They were heading straight for one of the open hatches.

Dorthy said, "I've waited so long for this . . . and now I don't know, Ang. I thought I knew what was at the other end, but it could be anything, anything at all! I'm scared silly. Isn't that strange?"

"Not strange at all, Dorthy. It would be strange if you weren't."

"A few years ago I wouldn't have been. I thought I knew it all. But it's so much more complicated, Ang. There could be anything there."

"There will be the Enemy there. We are all sure of that. And you saw something else. Something glorious awaits us!"

"But that was all so long ago . . . even the marauders may have gone. There may be nothing there at all. I just don't know."

"Do not tell anyone else your doubts. It is why we are going, to take from the Enemy what is rightfully ours. To win the heritage left by the old ones."

"All the way to the core to fight a war that's been going on for more than a million years. It isn't even our war, not really." Dorthy felt a sudden dreamily detached clarity perhaps the suit had responded to her climbing heart rate and given her a tranquilizing shot.

They reached the open hatch and clung to its edge. A faint continuous vibration was transmitted through Dorthy's gloved hands, tingling through her bones. The ship's reaction motor had been candled. The liner's teardrop was slowly receding against the stars. In the other direction, beyond the prow of the *Vingança*'s spine and its clustered command blisters, silhouetted against the turbulent skies of the gas giant, Colcha was growing perceptibly larger.

The two women made a perfunctory search for shelter, but everything was in darkness and the hatch of the only tug within easy reach was dogged down, so they wedged themselves within the framework of one of the grapples. Ang cut the tether in half, and they lashed themselves to a slim steel spar.

The mutineers up in the command cluster had either forgotten to close the hatches, or sabotage had prevented it: Dorthy and Ang could see the surface of Colcha slide by as the ship went into low orbit. The reaction motor had been switched off after injection into orbit, but after one pass it went on again. The surface of Colcha swung away as the ship turned, nose down to the moon.

Dorthy clung tightly to the spar as she felt herself being pulled down toward the stern of the ship: a fall of several hundred meters through a space packed with machinery would be fatal no matter how marginal the gravity field. The suit had definitely given her a shot of something to calm her down. It was screwing up her implant and her Talent was wakening again, giving Dorthy a giddy sense of internal expansion that took in the dislocated flow of Ang's mind and touched the half hundred people elsewhere on the ship—distant stars sluggishly coming into focus.

Dorthy tried to turn away from these distractions. She closed her eyes and tried to look inward toward the false Alea personas that had been fixed down in her limbic cortex. They knew all about wormholes; they had wanted her to come here. . . .

It was difficult to relax, to purge her mind, while clinging in a p-suit above a deadly drop, on a ship slowly maneuvering toward a hole in space-time. The rhythms of her mantra took her so far and no farther, enlightenment a step away, but a step she could not make. And then Ang started to say something about seeing it coming, seeing the light, a frantic disbelieving edge to her voice that brought Dorthy back to her quotidian self just as Ang's voice was cut off, and with it the whirling flood of her fear, and the half hundred other minds of the people on the ship. They had entered the wormhole. Dorthy opened her eyes. And saw . . . nothing.

During her brief career as a freelance, catering to the whims of wealthy neurotics who felt they needed a Talent to share and externalize their feelings, whoring her mind to pay her way through Fra Mauro, Dorthy had once been a part of a saga writer's entourage during a bizarre trek across Antarctica. The writer had had the idea that the ice fields and dry valleys would be a kind of palimpsest on which she could discover herself anew; Dorthy was supposed to be a part of the process, although she never did see how the writer found time for serious self-contemplation amid the distractions of the dozen or so friends she'd brought along, not to mention the drivers and cooks and baggage masters and mechanics and guides— even a masseuse. It was more circus than spiritual quest. Then, one arbitrary morning in the endless day of Antarctic summer, the pure blue sky had begun to whiten. Within an hour a storm had driven down upon the party, reducing everything to a bubble of whirling whiteness a couple of meters across. While everyone else was running around in circles, trying to make camp, and the saga writer was screaming her head off that it was a personal insult, a conspiracy of the gods, Dorthy had deliberately wandered off into the storm. Soon, everything human had dwindled behind her to the merest spark, sunk deep in illimitable whiteness. For the first time in her life, Dorthy had known what it was to be alone.

It was a little like that now. The Universe had been reduced to the inside of her suit. Beyond the blurred tip of her nose Dorthy saw nothing but the faint reflection of her own face, mouth agape as she gazed upon naked contraspace. It was neither dark nor light but the exact color of the inside of her head, which, because it was behind her field of vision, was no color at all, and without dimension. If it hadn't been for the reflection of her face, and the half dozen colored stars of the pinlight status indicators under her chin, she might have thought she had gone blind. She could feel the edges of the spar she was clinging to, but apart from that it was as if the entire ship, the whole Universe, had vanished.

After a measureless time she felt a tentative pressure on the shoulder of her suit; and then Ang's gloved hand crept down toward her own. Dorthy found a measure of courage, unclamped her right hand from the spar, gripped Ang's. Sometime later, they both worked around until they could hug each other, clinging each to each, not trying to speak through the contact of their helmets but simply holding each other, two separate universes folded against one another in the ten dimensions of contraspace.

Time did not pass outside: they were outside time. There was only the pulse of their own blood, the intimate unmarked clock of the womb.

★   ★   ★

The Universe came back all at once and without fanfare. Over the shoulder of Ang's suit, Dorthy saw through the open hatch directly below.

"My God," she said. "Oh my God."

She was seeing what no human being had ever seen before, unless the singleship pilot had survived the Event. She was seeing the spiral tides of light of the accretion disk around the black hole at Galactic Center. The wormhole had translated the *Vingança* across twenty-eight thousand light-years in a fraction of the time it had taken to reach the hypervelocity star.

Vast rivers of light curved across the sky toward a common confluence, growing ever brighter as they swung in toward a minute asymmetric flaw so bright that it was no color at all, so bright that it hurt Dorthy's eyes even through the filters of her visor. The flaw was rising as the *Vingança* slowly rotated, and with it dawned a dim red supergiant star shrouded in an asymmetric cowl, its own photosphere drawn off by the wind of infalling gases, a dying ember against the brilliant glory of the accretion disk. Dorthy recalled that the accretion disk was fed by streams of gases that extended outward for five or six light-years. But to see anything at all of the maelstrom of radiation around the black hole itself, the *Vingança* could only be a few light-days away, a light-week at most.

Radiation. . . . There was a roaring in Dorthy's ears, growing louder and louder like approaching tsunami. It was the sound of her suit's gamma counter.

Ang had turned to look, too. She said, her voice crackling over the radio, "We have to find shelter, Dorthy."

"But we made it, Ang! That's the black hole down there. We went all the way through!"

"That's as may be, but it is not friendly out there. A lot of hard stuff coming through here. Can't you see the scintillation, the flashes in your field of vision? Each speck is a column of cells in your brain dying."

" . . . I suppose you're right."

"You will have much time to see all this. We are here, but how do we get back?"

"I don't know. Or at least, I don't know right now. I was wondering about the singleship that went before us. We must try and find it."

Ang said, "Perhaps we won't need to go back. Perhaps *they* are waiting for us, Dorthy!"

They had died aeons before even the Alea had arrived at the center of the Galaxy, but Dorthy didn't want to get into a theological argument, so she kept quiet. The two women untied themselves and began to crawl over the framework of the grapple, helmet lights dancing in the darkness. They had just reached the rail of a catwalk when the emergency lights came on, a lurid red glow bathing the perspectives of the graving docks that receded ahead and behind. There was a grinding vibration. All along the length of the *Vingança*, the hatches were closing.

Interzone

THERE WAS AN INTERVAL OF DARKNESS, AND THEN FOR an unmeasurable time there was nothing at all, not even the kinesthetic sense of her own body, the surf of her pulse in her ears or the warm darkness behind her eyelids. She was an unraveled string of consciousness spun through nothingness.

There was no way to tell how long the interregnum lasted. But, gradually, she was able to hear, or perhaps feel, for it seemed as intimate as her own heartbeat, a deep muffled beat, like great machinery churning in the deeps of a lifeless ocean. And then, sudden as the throw of a switch, she could see. A hard pinkish light and her own body suspended in it: naked, limbs splayed like a fallen puppet's, eyes open and glassy.

As soon as she saw her body and understood what it was, it began to recede from her, or she began to rise above it. It swiftly dwindled into a fleck, a mote, was gone. There was only the terrific tireless slogging rhythm, driving her up through featureless pink glare that began to shudder in time to the pounding: she was traveling through rings of light compressed into a tunnel that rose far above her.

She felt nothing. No fear, no pain, not even wonder. She was the soul, the guest, the willing bride of light.

The pounding was the noise of creation, she thought, though she didn't know where the thought came from. If the Universe had been filled with air, then this is what would have battered the ears of every sentient being: the sound of space-time unraveling as everything flew apart from everything else on the wings of the light of the monobloc.

She could see the end of the tunnel now, a point of intense, clear white light that filled her with a terrific sense of yearning.

199

Home, home! Bodiless, she swam through light toward light, leaping joyfully as a salmon leaps toward its death in the waters of its birth.

An irresistible force pressed down on every part of her body, tossed her one way and then another. A formless roar battered her ears, faded away as she went in another direction, rose at her again. A hard, cold gush forced itself between her lips, over her tongue—

Gasping, spitting saltwater, she threw back her head to gulp at air; then she was whirled away through green light and traceries of foam, dragged down and given a glimpse of smooth, flat, shining sea bottom before the grip reversed itself and threw her toward light and air again.

She kicked out against the undertow, used every dyne of strength in the slabs of grafted muscle across her shoulders to drive her arms down and out and stay afloat. Her lungs dragged air purely by reflex. It was heady as cold wine.

The next wave lifted her up, showed her a panorama of wave crests marching in parallel lines toward some distant shore . . . and then the wave was gone and she dropped into the trough, was lifted by the next wave so that she could glimpse the tantalizing shoreline again. A beach fringed with palms, with a mountain rising up behind.

She was not afraid, felt stronger than she ever had in her life. Kicking out, she began to swim with the marching waves toward the shore.

She lay sprawling face down on warm, white sand with no memory of how she had got there. Heat and light was beginning to burn through saltwater drying on her back and her flanks. She rolled over, propping herself on her elbows.

The white beach curved away to the right and left before the limitless green sea. She could see the line of white water where waves broke on some barrier; between the breakers and the beach the sea was smooth as silk. Little glassy ripples cast themselves across wet sand and sank away. The sun was directly overhead

⋆　⋆　⋆

it was not the sun not any sun a *flaw* in the colorless sky
through which light poured no shape at all

Something seized her, poured through her every cell. There
was no pain, but it was worse than pain. When it was gone,
a long time afterward, she sat up and rubbed crusted salt and
sand from her thighs, her flat belly, and her breasts. A vivid
scarlet serpent wound down her left arm, breathed flames over
her wrist. She twisted and pulled at the skin to try and see it
properly; the dragon brought a word to the root of her tongue,
but she couldn't speak it, not yet.

She got up, looking up and down the beach's curve, squinting
against glare. Heat and salt . . . she was thirsty, and she walked
beneath the palms which leaned out over the white sand, looking
for fresh water. The crowns of the palms mixed and shattered
light, dropped tiger patterns over her naked body. Coconuts lay
like skulls everywhere on threadbare grass between the palms.
But she had no way of opening them, so she went on.

Only a little way back from the beach, rock shelved up
from sandy soil dripping with ferns and moss, cool beneath her
gripping toes and fingers as she climbed to where water spilled
over the lip of a cool, deep pool.

When she'd slaked her thirst she sat back on her haunches.
She tried to think. Skeins of light wove and rewove themselves
across her bare skin, shivered on the skin of the pool's clear
water, and were reversed as shadows on the clean sand at the
bottom of the pool's basin.

"Suzette," she said after a while.

The word had come into the light. It was her name, although
it sounded wrong.

"Australia," she said, a while later. "I was in Australia this
time. . . ."

But she knew this wasn't Australia.

She shivered all over, just once, then jumped to her feet and
went on up the rock face. She wanted to see where she was . . .
some kind of desert island . . . some far, tropical shore . . . wherever she was, there had to be people. She'd look for signs of

civilization from the vantage of the mountain's peak.

The climb was long and hard. The mountain—if it was a mountain—was higher than it had looked from out at sea. There were wide patches of dry spiny bushes she had to skirt around, impossibly steep slopes of sliding scree that bruised her fingers and feet. The white line of the beach and its narrow fringe of palms looked to be a kilometer below her, dwindling away left and right in sweeping curves which vanished into infinity. Green-white light dazzled her whenever she looked up, and she didn't see the top until the slope suddenly flattened out.

There was a gentle downslope of bare rock, and beyond that something she couldn't make any sense of at first. A vast, patterned plain. Great swirling formations of red and yellow that threw off complicated spirals as they dwindled away toward a level horizon where spiky light reared up against the sky. It looked like a city, a city made of light. Ten kilometers away? Twenty? A hundred? No way of saying.

After a while she dared walk to where ordinary smooth bare stone sank into the beginnings of one of the spiral formations, dared place first one foot and then the other on smooth yellow stuff that was the exact temperature of her own skin. It was a flat-topped ridge maybe a hundred meters wide. It seemed to glow with an internal light. Its edges were fretted and sculpted in endlessly recomplicated spirals that made her dizzy just trying to trace them. Feathers and coils and sea horse shapes dwindling into each other. Detail leaping up at her, no end to it. . . . Somehow it all slumped down to a floor of white sand . . . only it wasn't exactly sand; it seemed to shift and heave like mist stirred by a breeze yet seemed to be solid at the same time.

But the yellow ridge was solid enough, and it seemed to curve away toward the city's spiky light. So she set off along it, imagining herself for some reason accompanied by a robot, or at least a man like a robot. Although she could not see him, he was somehow everywhere. He would help her to find the Wizard. He would help her to find an answer to every one of her questions.

She went a long way. No matter how much the ridge turned and turned, the city was always ahead of her, and seemed no closer than it had from the edge of this strange desert. It was as if the horizon were receding as fast as she was advancing. When she at last thought to look back, she could no longer see the slope of ordinary rock from which she'd set out. What she did see was that the ridge was crumbling behind her. Yellow glow leached away. Complex patterns simplified, slumped down, flattened into unsolid not-sand. She lifted a foot, saw that she'd left a perfect white print in the ridge's glowing surface. Whiteness widened as she watched, rushing out to either side of her. The edges of the ridge blurred. Recurved patterns uncoiled and crumbled with a faint cracking sound.

She began to run, trying to catch up with the city and outrun the ridge's dissolution at the same time. Spirals unpeeled beneath her flying feet; the wind of her passage keened in her ears; the light of the spectral city grew brighter, blurred and widened by wind tears in her eyes. For a moment she felt as if she were flying . . . and then she stumbled, sprawled in hot, white sand. She was back on the beach. What she had thought was the sound of her blood beating in her ears was the surf pounding at the barrier reef a few hundred meters out to sea.

She got to her feet, shivering in warm clear light.

Something terrible and impossible had happened, but it was fading from her memory even as she tried to define it. The beach curved away to the left and to the right. She chose at random, and started to walk.

There were no nights, only the single endless day.

She ate when she was hungry, slept when she was tired, always waking to the same vertical green-white light which poured down from . . . But she did not think about where the light came from. It was a pure light that precisely illuminated everything on which it fell, so that she felt that if she looked hard enough, she could see into each and every grain of sand on the beach, look through the surface of leaves to spy their secret structure, a plane of rooms without windows or doors. When she looked out to sea, every wave was distinct, dwindling clearly into the limitless, horizonless ocean.

She learned to split open green coconuts by banging one against the other. Further inland were fruit bushes, kumquat and alligator pear, papaw and breadfruit. Clumps of prickly pear raised their spiny paddles in occasional clearings in the scrub. Fish patrolled the rippled sand bottom of the shallow calm water inside the reef, solitary slate gray tuna, schools of silvery sprats. She found stands of bamboo in the scrub back of the beach, broke off the hardest of the stems and rubbed one end to a point with a stone. Waded out into warm water and waited for something to swim by. She ate the fish raw, with a squeeze of bitter lime juice. Later, she learned to make salt by letting seawater dry down in the halved shell of a coconut.

For all the time she spent fishing, out in the sea glare, her skin never darkened beyond its usual freckled milky coffee.

The beach always swung away in a gentle curve ahead of her. There was always the faint roar of the breakers out at the barrier reef, the same clear vertical light, the same fringe of palms that leaned out above the crisscross patterns of shadow they dropped on white sand.

She forced herself to keep looking around as she walked. Because you never knew. Sometimes she thought that she saw twists of light whirling far down the curve of the beach, always ahead of her no matter how quickly she walked. Mirages . . . perhaps. If they were mirages, they were the only optical illusions in the clear pure light.

It wasn't easy to stay alert. The beach seemed to be an endless ribbon running through space where curved, not parallel, lines extend to infinity. An infinitely long fractal pattern repeating itself over and over with only the subtlest of variations. She imagined something always dismantling the beach behind her, rushing the materials ahead and reassembling them just in time.

So when she saw the promontory pushing out into the sea she at first didn't recognize what it was, or even how big it was. In the green-white glare it could have been some kind of animal crouching only a few meters away at the sea's edge, or it could have been a far-distant mountain. She crouched behind the scaly trunk of a leaning palm and studied the intrusion for a long time before she dared go closer.

Like a castle, the promontory rose straight up from a base of huge, tumbled boulders. But its sheer flank was split by ledges and crevices, and it was easy enough to clamber among creepers and clumps of ferns. The top was a gentle slope of naked rock, and she followed it to where the steps of a natural amphitheater dropped down into clear water.

And there she stopped, looking down for a long, long time at the little bay, at the strange dark shapes that rippled among lines of sunken pillars, beneath a floating canopy of long streamers of purple-black weed.

Black as their own shadows on the white sand floor of the basin, delta-shaped and incredibly flexible, whatever the shapes were, they were not fish. She could not count how many there were, for all were always moving, but there had to be at least two dozen. Living shadows weaving a complex dance, never touching no matter how closely their paths intersected. Sometimes one would abruptly wrap around a pillar like a cloak driven by some irresistible current, then gather itself and slide off, making for the narrow inlet which connected the sunken amphitheater with the sea, vanishing beneath the surge of white water breakers.

At last she clambered down the dozen or so broad, shallow stairs that curved around the bay. A handsdepth of saltwater, warm as blood when she stepped into it, rippled over the last.

Glare on the water's rocking surface made it difficult to see the shadow shapes. With scarcely a thought, certainly without fear, she set down her bamboo spear and dived cleanly into the water, swimming strongly for the first of the pillars and clinging for a moment to its rough surface among slimy streamers of weed. When she let herself sink, she saw other pillars receding away in greenish light across a vast floor of ruffled sand. The shadow-things drifted and turned among the pillars, and she saw that there were other creatures, too. Things with black shield-like carapaces heaved along the bottom of the basin, dragging long spines that furrowed the sand; things like half-squashed crabs sheltered in burrows at the bases of the encrusted pillars; and there were creatures clinging to the pillars, big shells curved like scoops, with oval apertures fringed by pulsing veils of stuff like ragged lace.

She rose for air, dived again, and found herself surrounded by four or five of the shadow-things.

This close she could see how beautiful they were. Black, flexible hide glistening with a rainbow sheen as though dusted with diamonds, clusters of stalked eyes—baby blue, with smeared black pupils—and fringed sensory tendrils along their leading edge. As the shadow-things turned and turned about her, she glimpsed their paler undersides, each with a single row of gill slits, a round irised mouth bracketed by complicated palps with something white and gnarled clinging behind.

She did not know how long the dance lasted. The shadows wove ceaselessly, creating in the water complex patterns of pressure that thrilled across her bare skin. She knew somehow that this was an attempt at communication, and she danced for them too in the blood-warm water. Awkward and graceless, but with clear cold fire thrilling in her every nerve, a certainty she hadn't felt since finding herself in this strange, timeless place. She breached the surface for air and dived again, rolling to show how she had been caught in the swell of the open ocean, shimmying close to the sand to show how she had crawled up onto the beach, sculling upright again in a fierce kick-step in parody of her aimless odyssey.

And all the while the shadows wove around and above and below her, endless grace flowing from their wide, black wings.

At last, too tired to go on, she swam for the steps that rose up from the sandy floor of the basin into the air. Air felt cold on her wet skin; she gasped like a beached seal as she pulled herself into it. Her spear lay where she had left it . . . and on the step above it one of the flattened crab-things, a giant a full meter across, scuttled forward and with its articulated palps pushed half a dozen silver sprats towards her.

She reached out, and the crab-thing reared back, poured smoothly down the steps on spined paddles, and vanished without a ripple into the water. She watched it go, the glimpse of its complex mouthparts fixed in her mind. Racks of bristles and serrated combs . . . and a white gristly thing tucked farther back, the same parasite each of the shadows had carried.

With her warming skin beginning to itch as saltwater dried on it, she slit each of the sprats with her spear's splintering tip,

gutted them with a crooked finger, pulled out the little strips
of flesh, and swallowed them whole. Their sweet salt taste
strengthened her thirst. She clambered down the promontory's
steep side, found a clear rivulet among the palms at the edge of
the beach and drank her fill, and scooped cold fresh water over
her puckered, salt-scratchy skin. She sang to herself wordlessly
as she washed, happier than she had been for as long as she could
remember. She could stay here, share the dances of the shadow
dancers (she knew at once it was their true name and she said
it aloud, loving its shape in the windy hollow of her mouth),
dance with the shadow dancers until she knew everything about
them, and they her.

But as she walked back toward the promontory, light quali-
fied among the broken boulders at its base, a twisting shape that
grew brighter until she had to squint at it. She stopped a few
meters away and asked it what it wanted. She was afraid, but
she was also curious.

She didn't expect a reply, but she seemed to hear a faint voice
unraveling in the air. Perhaps it was only the whisper of wind
stirring the stiff swords of the palm leaves.

Go on.

"You tell me why I'm here," she said. "You *tell* me. Tell
me who I am, where I come from. . . ." She was crying, tears
streaming down her cheeks, nose running, an ache in her throat
that couldn't be swallowed. "Oh God, please tell me what you
want. . . ."

Go on. The other knows.

Only the wind in the palms, or the waves breaking on the
seaward edge of the promontory.

Go now.

Wind and waves, air rushing in her lungs, blood tumbling
through her veins. It was a voice woven into the fabric of
the world. It would not be denied, but she dared question
it.

"You mean the shadow dancers? How can I talk to them if
I go on?" She stepped sideways, but the burning flaw drifted
in front of her. When she stepped back, it followed. She jerked
up her right arm and threw her spear into the light.

Glare blinded her: heat washed her whole skin. She staggered back with an arm flung across her face, saw printed behind her clamped lids a burning figure hung in the air. Wings of fire were furled across its face and feet; a third pair beat back to sustain it before her.

When she dared look again the light had gone. There was a smooth basin of fused sand where it had been, still white-hot at its center, cooling to cherry red at its edge. There was no sign of the bamboo spear.

Go on.

Only the wind, only the waves. But a shudder gripped her, a chill traveling from toes to the crown of her head. She turned and ran, slogging through coarse white powder to harder sand at the sea's edge. Fans of spray thrown up by her pounding feet glittered like diamonds. She did not look back, did not slow until she was sure that the promontory had fallen behind the beach's infinite curve. Then she slowed to a walk, holding her side where an incipient stitch threatened. She was in the grip of things like gods. Anything could happen, she thought, anything at all.

It revolved in her head like a mantra, meshed with the plodding rhythm of her ambling walk. Leaning palms and white beach fell behind her; more palms and beach came into view ahead. When she saw the spark kindle at the vanishing point of the curve she thought at first that it was another manifestation. But then a thread of smoke drifted out across the sea's blue water, quickly thickening to a rolling white banner.

Uprooted shrubs had been piled together in a rough pyramid as tall as she was, burning in a hearth of flat stones set in the white sand. The bushes shimmered in the heart of the fire and they were not consumed. It was like a conjuring trick, or a looped hologram. But the heat which beat at her skin, the thick white smoke which shook into the air and rolled so far out to sea, these were real.

There was a kind of shelter beyond the fire, framed with trimmed green poles and roofed with woven plantain leaves. In its cool shade spangles of light shone like stars on the sand. There were clumps of vivid tiger lilies, a spring that rose between two palm trees and fed a clear pool whose sides were laced, like a basket, with the fibrous roots of the palm trees.

A path had been worn through the long grass behind the palms. There were footprints trampled everywhere in the sand. She spent a long time testing the prints against her own feet. Every one fitted.

Later, she fell asleep in the shade beneath the roof of plantain leaves, and dreamed that she had been living there a long time, as long as she could remember . . . although that didn't mean very much, because she remembered so little.

She didn't remember how she had come there, remembered only in her dreams the black shadow dancers and the burning angel. So far around the horizon of the infinite curve of the beach: another life. She speared fish in the shallows and wrapped them in green plantain leaves and cooked them on the flat stones at the edge of the fire which never consumed the bushes on which it burned. She lay in the cool shade of her shelter. Time and again her eyes would close before she even had time to realize that she was falling asleep, and a little while later she would drowsily wake. Spots of light dancing through the roof of woven leaves, light glittering on the sweep of white sand beyond the cool shade, the bubbling song of the spring, the distant murmur of the shallow breakers: all these wove through her sleep, and, waking, her apprehension of them took a peculiar turn, as if she had become the beach, the sea, the little spring. The feeling would persist for a little while, and then it would recede from her, and she slept again.

How long this went on, she could not tell. But at last she awoke to feel someone watching her, a feeling she found difficult to detach from the soft sensation of dissolving into the world. She struggled up onto one elbow, blinking in the strong light which framed the figure looking down at her.

It was Robot.

In the moment that she recognized him, all her memories came crashing back. Suzy Falcon turned her head and was violently sick.

Robot helped Suzy to the little spring, dabbed fresh, cold water on her forehead, and let her drink from the cupped palm of his prosthetic hand. Like her, he was naked. Scrawny, white-skinned, blond crest grown out into a ragged rooster tail, circumcised cock jaunty in its nest of hair. He squatted on the sandy turf watching her as she splashed water over her face and the back of her neck.

"Are you all right?" he asked, when she was done.

"I think . . . I don't know." Memories overlapped like two pictures painted on either side of the same pane of glass. Memory of walking along the curve of the beach in constant vertical light, swimming in the blood-warm water of the shadow dancers' flooded amphitheater, the nova of the angel barring her from that paradise. And memory of coming ashore and making camp here, building the shelter among the palms and lilies, making fire with a little bow and drill, keeping a long lonely vigil. No angels, except perhaps in her dreams . . . and those last memories already fading even as she tried to bring them back, like trying to catch mist. . . .

She said, "It's all full of holes. . . . Someone's been fucking with my mind, right? Something I do remember, like a pillar of light stopping me from going where I wanted. I threw something at it, a bamboo stick I was using to spear fish, and it flared up, burned the stick, damn near blinded me . . . what was it, Robot? Yeah, you know . . . I see that silly little smile you got, tucked up in one corner of your mouth. What do you know about this place? We inside that moon? I remember that, the way my ship was caught."

"We are not exactly in the moon. But neither are we out of it." Robot ran his flesh hand through his rooster tail. "You have been tested," he said. "That's not exactly what it's been about, but it is as close to the truth as I can get. You remember the shadow dancers, so that means you passed. Otherwise you would only remember this place."

"I passed, huh? So what did I pass?"

"You think you hate all aliens, but of course you don't. You only know the Enemy, and you haven't even seen one of them alive."

"I still hate them—for what they did."

"But you are not xenophobic. You swam with the shadow dancers."

"Yeah. I do remember that. How do you know that's what I call them?"

Robot shrugged, his pale blue eyes hooded by heavy pink lids.

A thought struck Suzy, a thought that brought a sudden chill to her, tangling like icy lines across her bare shoulders. She shivered, in the warm green-white light. She said, "You *are* Robot."

"Yes and no. Suzy, do you remember that Robot operated on himself? He cut most of the connections between the two halves of his brain and implanted a helper in the left side."

" . . . Machine?"

He nodded solemnly.

"Okay, I can play the game any way you want. You're so fucking calm, man. Like you know stuff. Where you learn it, huh?"

"The original part of me, what you would call the real Robot, is sleeping. Or dreaming that he is asleep, dreaming this dream that you share."

"I thought this was *my* dream, man," Suzy said. She only half-believed him, if that, was measuring the distance between them, the distance between her and the hut where her new fishing spear lay. If it came to it, she was probably a match for Robot *or* Machine, augmented arm or not. She could probably whip him as long as she kept his prosthetic hand, the laser-points and cutting edges of its extensors, out of her face. He was tall, but he was scrawny, too, and he wasn't used to fighting. She was, and had the advantage of the hump of grafted muscle across her shoulders. She could lift him up and break his back, if it came to it. . . .

Perhaps she had unconsciously flexed her flying muscles, because Machine said, "I'm not here to hurt you, Suzy. I'm here to explain."

"Okay, so tell me what the shadow dancers are." That one caught him sideways, she saw. So he couldn't read her mind, anyway. She'd read about things like this, from the bad old days when computers ran things on Earth. Dead people dumped in memory banks, into a constructed environment. Except they hadn't been the real person, the anima, only a shadow—but they hadn't known about that back then.

"The shadow dancers," Machine said, "are a dream within a dream, their own dream intersected with that of Robot's. They were rescued from Novaya Rosya, when its biosphere was destroyed by the Enemy—"

"Now wait a moment here," Suzy said. "The Enemy never attacked any of our worlds. I was there at BD Twenty, man. I *know* nothing of theirs *ever* got past our pickets."

"Suzy, Suzy. You must calm down." Machine was smiling, more of a stiff half smirk really. "I talk of something half a million years ago. And it was not the Alea of BD Twenty, it was that part of the Alea family that stayed on P'thrsn after a kind of civil war, a highly scaled-up family argument. When the shadow dancers started to explore the nearer stars, the Alea of P'thrsn decided upon their genocide, so that the marauders—"

Suzy interrupted again, and Machine patiently backtracked, telling her about the origin of the Enemy, the Alea. The binary system of red supergiant and dim brown dwarf about which their home world orbited in the belts of interstellar gas which girdled the Galactic core. The nonsentient herders, their flocks of larval children which, during the periods when the supergiant flared up, metamorphosed into intelligent neuter males instead of herders. Machine told Suzy about the strange flaretime civilizations that rose and fell in the space of a few decades, warring for territory amid the onslaught of heat and hard radiation from the supergiant's flare, the floods and hurricanes and general havoc wrought on the world's biosphere. He told her about the nearby supernova which had caused the supergiant's slow destruction, forcing the Alea to migrate inward, toward the packed stars of the core. The long centuries of exploration and colonization, and then the rise of the marauders, an Alea family which had pirated technology abandoned around the central black hole. The marauders' unstoppable onslaught, flying from star to star faster than light in the crowded core, snuffing world after world; and the flight of a few families under the guidance of intelligent long-lived neuter females, sub–light speed arks falling through the gas clouds shrouding the core, losing themselves in the four hundred billion field stars of the spiral arms.

Those families had been hiding ever since, Machine told Suzy, fearful that the marauders would track them down. That was why they had chosen to hide on worlds of marginal stars; why they refused to use the phase graffle, even *in extremis*. The family which had planoformed P'thrsn had split in two because one ultraconservative faction had believed the marauders would be able to detect the energies needed to spin up that once–tide-locked world. The conservatives had captured the ark and limped off to settle in the asteroid system of BD Twenty, had ever after kept watch for intruders, who they believed could only be the marauders come to destroy them: hence the war with humanity.

It was only a small, tangential part of the secret history of the Universe, but it took a long time to tell. Part of the time they sat in the cool, green shade near the spring; part of the time they wandered through the scrub beyond the palms, light broken by dense green leaves striping their naked bodies, Suzy picking fruit at random—every one perfectly ripe, utterly unblemished—often discarding bananas or lychees or breadfruit after only a single bite before reaching for more; part of the time they ambled along the narrow band of packed wet sand where glassy ripples licked the beach.

Machine told Suzy that the Alea were inept and hasty meddlers, ill–suited to the use of technology because evolution had bestowed intelligence upon them as a last resort. And that was how they used it, stumbling from crisis to crisis in a haze of anger and a muddle of cross-purposes. They had arisen on a very strange world of a very strange system and they had been neither predicted nor detected until too late, until crisis had forced them onto the stage of galactic history. And the marauders were still there, at the core, scheming to make the Universe over with no thought for the consequences. All they knew or cared about was their families. Nothing else mattered—it was a pathogenic genetic compulsion, faulty wiring of the neuter males' brains. They had to be stopped before they spread to other galaxies, before the process they had started became irreversible.

Suzy laughed at this. "You're saying it's just little old me against those things? Oh man. You really are Robot, I know that now. Only you would talk so crazy. This another stunt, like your terrorism thing back in Urbis, right?"

"I do not think so, although I cannot be sure. The angels do not talk with me directly, Suzy. There is no dialogue. Perhaps they converse with Robot, but he is asleep, dreaming all of this."

They were sitting in shade by the spring-fed pool once more. Suzy dragged one foot through silkily cool water, watching ripples collide among the basketwork palm tree roots on the far side. She squinted sideways at Machine. His skinny body was silhouetted against the glare of the beach; intense points of light flared through the cutouts in his augmented arm. She was no longer afraid of him; that had gone somewhere in his telling of the long tale of the Alea. She drew up her leg, kicking silvery droplets that puckered the white sand where they fell, felt coarse grass prickling under her naked buttocks. Some dream, all right.

She said, "So what about the angels?"

"The angels . . . they are less clear to me, although they are everywhere, Suzy, all around us. In every drop of water in the ocean, every grain of sand. They have mostly withdrawn from the Universe that we know; they didn't expect to be drawn back."

"There's this city? Or I think it's a city, across a weird plain or desert. . . . I think I tried to get to it, but I couldn't."

"The place where they have gone is too different, Suzy. That desert was a virtual diagram of the entropy barrier between here and there. You would have to expend an infinite amount of energy to cross it."

"It didn't seem that far, until I started walking toward it." Suzy shivered in the warm air, remembering, all of a sudden, the flat ridge glowing with yellow light, the way her footprints had destroyed it. She'd been a blamed fool, stepping out without a thought for what she was getting into. She could have died.

"It is like a fractal surface," Machine said. "Analogous to the Koch Curve or the Mandelbrot set. An infinitely complex boundary mapped within a finite space. You could have walked forever and never moved one centimeter nearer the place where the angels dwell."

"I know all about fucking fractals. Jesus Christ. What I don't know from zero is these angels, or what they want from me."

Machine didn't answer right away, but after a while he said, "If you listen carefully, you can hear their voices."

He fell silent again, and Suzy remembered the voice of the angel—or whatever it had been—woven out of the murmur of the beach, the world between worlds. After a while, she ventured to ask, "So where is *this* place? Where are we right now? You said Robot was dreaming it. Is it all inside your head?"

"The angels have withdrawn from the corporeal universe, but not entirely. It is still important to them. Necessary, like an umbilical cord. We're in that cord, that connection, but only a little way. I don't know where it ends."

Suzy listened to the silence under his words, and thought for a moment that she could hear a whispering many-tongued dictation . . . yeah, or maybe madness was infectious. She said, "If you're still answering questions, you can tell me about the shadow dancers."

"They are from Novaya Rosya; I think I told you that much. They are refugees from the Alea genocide program, although not refugees in the physical sense. Reconstructed engrams or animas, it isn't clear. Although they are few, they hold memories of all that was lost. . . . They are a symbiotic association between the sexual stage of the colonial sessile creatures which you saw living on the columns and the creatures which graze on the sessile colonies. You follow this?"

Suzy nodded, remembering graceful black creatures rippling through warm, crystal clear water, remembering the gristly nodes back of their mouths, among the crab-thing's palps. Machine explained that the symbionts infiltrated the nervous systems of their hosts, each reinforcing the other and synthesizing an intelligent individual where before none had existed. When the host mated, so did the symbiont, scattering myriads of larvae, of which perhaps one in a million founded a new sessile colony. The colonies released swarmers which infected the hosts, and completed the cycle. As civilization had developed, other creatures had been turned into hosts to provide eyes and limbs for work on dry land. A ribbon of industry had developed along the coasts of their world's shallow, warm oceans; the symbiosis had discovered the phase graffle and was exploring the nearer stars when the Alea had struck it down. The shadow dancer hosts were natural empaths, and development of the symbiosis had been eagerly watched— although whether or not by the angels, Machine didn't know or wouldn't say—and so extraordinary means had been taken to preserve something of it, held in this limbo until a suitable home could be found so that it could continue its development.

"And the way I reacted to them was some sort of test. I guess you're going to get around to telling me how I'm supposed to save the Universe eventually, might as well be now." Suzy struck a resolute pose, stiffening her back, sticking out her chin. "Go ahead. I can take it. While you're at it, you can start by telling me why these all-powerful angels can't do it."

"They are not omnipotent," Machine said. "Otherwise, to be sure, neither of us would be here. They are limited because they have withdrawn. There are only certain places in the corporeal universe where they can exert even a limited influence; there are vast areas which they cannot even observe anymore. You see, the history I told you really is history. We are living in a time when—"

As he had been talking, a faint grumbling roar had been growing. And then it was suddenly so loud that Suzy could feel it over the entire skin of her naked body. She got to her feet as wind scattered coins of light across the pool, whipped ropes of sand across the beach, whipped whitecaps across the glittering sea. Machine was standing too, hands over his ears, shouting something that Suzy couldn't hear. It was growing darker. Suzy looked up and saw that the flaw in the sky was now a dark hole ringed by writhing filaments of white light. A thundercrack boomed above the wind's howl and the singleship's clean, elegant shape fell out of the widened flaw.

Suzy yelled with joy and ran out from beneath the palms, her forearm raised to shade her eyes as she watched the singleship skim the sea toward the beach . . . and then it was parked neatly on white sand, as if it had always been there. Its delta lifting sur-face stretched from the fringe of palms to the breakers that were pounding in after the suddenly vanished storm. The irregular flaw that stood in place of a sun again blazed with green-white light in the blue sky.

Machine gripped Suzy's arm with his flesh hand. "We have to go," he said. "Others have gone ahead of us. Time is confused here. . . . We must arm our ship, Suzy, and catch them before they do any damage."

Suzy was going to ask what he meant when he added, "They are ready for us. Look!"

A kind of haze was gathering around the singleship. It was a flock of angels. They burned brighter than the flaw in the sky as they wove and spun around the ship's black leaf shape; and then, as Suzy and Machine slogged across the stretch of soft hot sand toward them, they rose high into the air and winked out like so many soap bubbles.

Suzy went around the raised edge of her ship's lifting surface, trailing one hand over the black ceramic surface: warm and faintly ribbed beneath her fingers: real. She ducked under the sigma-shaped snout of the ramjet's airbreather, saw that the weapons bay was open, exposing the missile rack (one slot empty: the missile she'd uselessly fired into the vortex that had dragged them down to this real/unreal beach). Grainy, complex patterns of light sank into the golden skin of the missiles even as she watched.

"Pinch fusion warheads will do little against the marauders," Machine said. He stood quite still in hot light, a little way beyond the sharp shadow which the ship cast on the sand. Eyes half-closed, showing only slivers of white as if he were about to have a fit, but his voice was light, amused. "We have been given something better than crude energy weapons. The missiles have been infused with a kind of mathematical virus. The marauders use processes they only believe they understand. This countermeasure is a gift from those who forged those processes in the first place. They have progressed too far away from our Universe to reenter it. The Planck constant would not sustain their entropy level; they would be dispersed just as a ship that engages with phase space when it is too deep within a gravity well is dispersed. But you and I, Suzy, will be the deliverers. It is a great task."

"Yeah, I'm sure. So how will we know what to fire at?"

"That will be the least of our problems. We will know, when the time comes."

"We'll know, huh? Great." Suzy was trying not to think about what she would do when she was finally back in the real world. Not go chasing dragons at the behest of a bunch of fireballs, that was for sure. She suppressed the thought as best she could, paranoid all over again that the angels, or Machine, or maybe Robot, who was supposed to be dreaming this whole scene—where was he? inside Machine's head?—could see right into her brain.

She said, "If time's wasting, we had better get it on. I've seen enough sand to last me my life and yours both."

The sight of the singleship's cramped lifesystem hit Suzy with a great wave of nostalgia, brought memories crashing back into place like slabs of ice calving from a glacier. The gimbal couch, its silvery cover still bearing the impression of her body. The control panel, tapes with her own crabbed handwriting on them stuck under half its switches; greasy shine on the keys of the input pad laid there by her own fingertips. And most of all the smell: sweet and rotten, her smell and Robot's all mixed together from weeks of living in the little space. She breathed deeply, but already it was fading as her nostrils grew accustomed to it once more.

The hatch servo whined behind her. On the mesh decking, an arc of green-white light shrank to a line, went out.

Machine said, "You will close the weapons bay, and we will be ready to leave on the instant."

Suzy looked at him. He was hunched in the aft of the cabin, his grown-out blond crest brushing the mesh ceiling, flesh and prosthetic hands dangling by his thighs. The way he stood so different from Robot's easy slouch. Skin white and dirty looking in the light of the glotubes. Planes of muscle across his stomach, hair like spun brass wires above his shriveled cock. Naked; so was she.

Suzy pulled suit liners from the dispenser, threw one set at Machine, turned and clambered hastily into the other. And felt a sudden intense relief as the touch of soft quilted fabric replaced the airy sense of nakedness. She thumbed the fastening strip closed from navel to neck, turned to see Machine still naked, the liner crumpled at his bare feet (powdered with dusty white sand, toes crowded together, their yellow nails buckled and shrunken).

Suzy said, "You put it on one leg at a time."

Machine said, without a trace or irony, "I remember," and stooped to pick up the liner with his prosthetic hand.

Suzy climbed into the couch, powered it to sitting position, called up a status check. She was so intent on scrolling through the array of icons that she hardly noticed as Machine pulled himself into the cramped sleeping niche set into the wall behind her. Everything was nominal: the hydrox boosters had been refueled; air/water/power all showed high green and consumables had somehow been topped up too; the dozen or so small glitches that had developed during the long, chancy voyage to the hypervelocity star were all gone.

Suzy closed up the weapons bay, turned her head to tell Machine, "Your friends did a good job. They aren't good for anything else, they're boss mechanics. So you tell me now, what's the flight plan?" Snug in clean liners, breathing cool filtered air, cradled by the couch's crashwebbing, she was beginning to feel in charge of her destiny again. She could fly the ship out and not look back: there was nothing to stop her, and nothing to make her carry out the angels' kamikaze mission either. She'd flown enough of those through the asteroid habitats of BD Twenty to last her a double lifetime. At least.

Machine lay straight out on his back in the narrow niche, hands clasped on his chest, looking like the picture of some dead saint or other that had been in the big family Bible of Suzy's childhood. His little rat-machine was sitting up near his head— Suzy guessed it had been waiting here for him all this time— and now he reached up with tapering steel and plastic extensors to caress the curved plates of its carapace, just as someone might absentmindedly stroke a cat. Something funny about its flexible body, plates pulling away from each other like it was *stretching* maybe, falling apart. . . . After a moment, Machine turned his head to look at Suzy.

"You will fly straight up," he said, speaking slowly, as if attending to an inner voice. "A way will be opened for you, and you will go through it. We will arrive at a place no human has ever before seen, and there we will search out the marauders. And there, too, I will pilot the ship." The machine clung to his augmented arm, spinning fine cables, plugging him into the systems of her ship. Her ship. Hers.

"Hey, I'm the pilot here. Remember?"

"I remember, Suzy. You may fly the ship back to urspace, but after that you are not to be trusted." She started to protest, but Machine said, "Listen to me. You remember what my helper here did to the servant of Duke Bonadventure, on Titan. It can as easily do it to you, if you do not obey. I hope that we are a partnership, Suzy, but you will not be able to recognize the critical moment, the time and the place where the missiles must be released to burn out the marauders' stolen technology. That is what this part of me was taught while Robot dreamed the dream through which you walked. The angels could talk to me, Suzy, to me alone. You will fly us there, and I will do the rest."

"Seems to me," she said angrily, "that I'm not needed at all. And where *is* Robot? We leaving him behind?"

"You are needed, Suzy. As a pilot, and as a witness. Please, take the ship up."

She took the ship up. She took it up hard and fast, hydrox boosters and reaction motor both. Burning a molten groove into the beach, palm trees and the little hut and the pool with its clear spring vanishing in a blast of white fire as the singleship arced up and out over blue water.

Acceleration mashed Suzy into the couch. She'd bitten the inside of her lips; the bright coppery taste of blood was the taste of her fear and anger. Her sight was spotted with insects, wavering indices of thrust and fuel and delta vee. Machine flat out in his crash-cocooned sleeping niche, face deathly white, eyes rolled back; his rat-machine was starting to weave cables around him. A radar sweep made no sense at all because it said that there was nothing out there, not even a horizon, while all around the inset was the view below and behind the ship as it roared up its steep trajectory.

The blue sea, dusted with sparkling whitecaps. The infinite white ribbon of the beach dividing the edge of the sea from the interlocking patterns of the fractal desert. Suzy looked for the bay of the shadow dancers, but already the beach had dwindled from ribbon to scribed line. And rising beyond the far horizon, as ever, the prickly golden shimmer of the citadel of heaven. . . .

Suzy felt a tremendous yearning at the sight. If she could, she would have pulled an Immelman and made a run for the elusive shimmer. Flat out at Mach five, she'd *surely* reach it. But she knew it wasn't so, it wasn't for her.

And even as she thought that, everything around the ship began to bend away, taking a direction she'd never noticed before. The ship shuddered. Boosters and reaction motor cut out and, although Suzy hadn't touched the board and there was no drain on the catalfission battery, the singleship was suddenly in contraspace.

Part 3

/\/\/\/\/\

The Cradle
of Creation

1

THE *VINGANÇA* HAD EXITED FROM ONE OF SOME TWO dozen wormhole pits that ringed the equator of an irregular planetoid, which was in orbit around a massive, red supergiant star about five light-days from the black hole at the center of the Galaxy, deep within the ragged oval of its accretion disk. Nearby, a vast arc of gas swept across the sky; a braided river of glowing filaments and streamers spiraling around magnetic field lines, so vast that the Solar System would have been no more than a leaf whirled away in its torrential energies, it curved in toward the black hole and extended far through the shell of gas clouds which surrounded the accretion disk.

Those same gas clouds, remnants of some vast explosion a hundred thousand years earlier, also obscured most of the stars of the Galactic Center. It was not like the tidy picture Dorthy had been given on P'thrsn, of a vast jewel box of stars packed close together in tidy, stable orbits, shining clearly and cleanly around a black hole which had swept up all interstellar debris. Of the several million packed into the central parsec, only a few thousand were actually inside the shroud of gas. Some, including a cluster of very hot, very young stars, were embedded within the shell of gas clouds; most were outside it, visible only in infrared.

Those inside the shell were mostly massive red or blue stars, and all of them were devoid of planetary systems and showed some sort of deviation from normal stellar evolution. Some, oblate, furiously unstable flarestars, were clearly the products of recent collisions; others were naked cores stripped by tidal heating, or orbiting so close to each other that they were bridged by loops of fusing gases. All were moving at tremendous speeds around the black hole, and many, like the dim red supergiant about which the wormhole planetoid orbited at more than ten times the distance that Pluto orbited Sol, were being stripped of their outer layer by hypervelocity winds of ionized gases.

As for the planetoid, it was bigger than Earth's moon but its mass was far less: had to be, for it was not the usual oblate sphere expected of a body its size, but a kind of dumbbell, as if something had gripped it at each pole and tried to pull it apart. Its equatorial constriction was pitted with wormhole exits, but instead of a Colcha-like patchwork scape caused by the opening and closing of wormholes, there was a uniform chaotic terrain at the equator while the water-ice surfaces of the opposing hemispheres were so smooth that they could have been machined to a centimeter's tolerance.

When a hastily launched mapping satellite began to download its data at the end of the second day, it suddenly become clear that humans were not the first to have been brought through one of the planetoid's wormholes. A vast structure sprawled across a shallow crater at the planetoid's constricted waist: a hectare of stiff tangled threads, each no more than a meter in diameter, battered, broken, and coated in sooty interstellar dust.

Within minutes of the discovery of the structure, someone managed to aim a neutrino probe at it. Dorthy had been awake about fifty hours by then; red-eyed and logy, she crowded with the dozen non-Witness scientists around a holotank as profiles from the probe shuffled past. Gray on gray, they showed that some kind of circuitry ran through the walls of the threads, that the threads had a hollow core only a centimeter thick, that some of them contained the unmistakable topology of a phase graffle wave guide. The collapsed tangle was the wreckage of a starship.

"They must have been insects," Valdez said to Dorthy, "to have lived in something that small." He tugged at the points of his waxed mustache. "A bunch of roaches flying an intersystem ship, just imagine!"

"They could as easily have been something like a coral or a slime mold," Dorthy said. Valdez's uncharacteristic nervousness mixed with her own, a jittery instability like the high she used to get after drinking too much coffee. She added, "Or perhaps it was cybernetically controlled. We may never know."

"Oh, we're going to find out," Jake Bonner said. He was grinning like an ape, his nose scant centimeters from the tank's edge as he peered at its enigmatic images. "That's why we came along, to root out the truth and to bring it home."

For although Flores had chosen to abandon ship, the rest of the cabal had elected to stay, along with two or three other non-Witness scientists. In the three weeks of intensive data collection that followed translation of the *Vingança* through the wormhole, most of them seemed to be having the time of their lives, despite the seemingly arbitrary strictures that the Witnesses applied to their research.

Dorthy found a job monitoring probes that had skipped away through contraspace and were now falling through the accretion disk toward the black hole. She had become an astronomer again, and loved every minute. Valdez, though, had little to do but map the planetoid, and after their discovery of the alien wreck the Witnesses would release only heavily censored data to him. It was perhaps one reason why his relationship with Dorthy abruptly cooled . . . and he was afraid of her, too, or of what was in her head, and was too proud to admit it. Dorthy tried to reason with him, but they made love exactly twice after passage through the wormhole., The last time Valdez was impotent, and of course he blamed Dorthy. She tried to smooth things over, telling him that they were all tired, and always on edge, but for him it was a matter of pride, of face, of machismo. He began to avoid her. They were all working such long hours that it wasn't difficult.

Perhaps it wouldn't have mattered—not when so much else was at stake—if Dorthy had not discovered during one of the routine medical scans the Witnesses imposed on everyone that she was pregnant. "A full month, too," Dorthy told Ang Poh Mokhtar, who was the only person she felt able to confide in. "It must have happened the very first time we made love. I feel so stupid. I knew I was a couple of weeks late, but I put it down to the stress of our situation here. My shot wore off while I was being held by the Navy, and I didn't really think about it afterward. I suppose in the back of my mind I thought that Valdez had had a shot, too."

Ang said, "A lot of Greater Brazilians don't, let me tell you. They think it affects their virility. A woman has to be careful with them—they're all loaded pistols."

"Well, I know that now. I feel so stupid, to be caught out by biology after all I've been through."

"What are you going to do, my dear? Apart from not telling Valdez."

"That's one of things I wanted to ask you. If I should tell him."

"If you have to ask me first, you don't want to."

Dorthy thought about that. "I suppose not. He'd just think I was trying to get my own back for his avoiding me."

Ang said, "I'm just an ignorant Nepalese woman, and no mind reader. But you don't seem too unhappy with the news."

Dorthy thought about that, too. She said, "No, I suppose I'm not. I'm thirty-four, Ang, I've never really thought about having a child . . . but I'm not going to get rid of it. Not until I've thought about it some more, anyway."

But there was little time for thought. There was too much to do. By default, the cabal of unaligned scientists had taken on the enormous task of mapping the black hole and its accretion disk. The Witnesses, who were busy with a structure hung some way around the edge of the accretion disk, were frustratingly secretive about their findings. Dorthy knew that if the marauders were anywhere, that was where they would be. But so far there had been no sign of them, and the structure was mostly obscured by the accretion disk itself, and no one in the cabal had seen much more than fuzzy, low-resolution holos of something that looked oddly like a gigantic version of the *Vingança*, some kind of sphere with a spine or spike trailing behind it.

Dorthy, plugged day after day into the data streams of one or another of the probes that were falling through the apocalyptic spectacle of the accretion disk, had seen as much of the structure as any non-Witness aboard the *Vingança*. Inductance electrodes pasted to her eyelids fed data gathered by the drone directly to her visual center. Plugged in, she soon forgot that she was sunk in the embrace of a couch in one of the science module's monitoring cubicles. She was out *there*, indices of the probe's dozen or so instruments constantly flickering at the edges of her vision as she fell through tides of stripped nuclei, through spiral storms of light.

Fed by a great arc of infalling material, the accretion disk seethed and crackled and flared with every kind of energy. The titanium foil which wrapped the probe was eroding so fast that Dorthy could almost feel it shredding as cosmic rays generated by collapsing nuclei punched millions of atom-sized holes every second; the indices of self-repairing circuits jittered and blurred as they made good the damage inflicted at the quantum level on up to impacts with interstellar grains. There was so much radiation that a human in a p-suit would have lasted perhaps an hour before soaking up a lethal dose.

And above all else there was light, so much light, from far infrared to X-rays generated by atoms smashed together in the constant seethe. Radiation and particle collision induced excitatory emissions in the tenuous gases: rippling banners and scarves and streamers—violet and red and indigo, green and gold and deepest purple—wound through the accretion disk's general ultraviolet glow. There were Solar System–sized storms of electrical energy generated by friction. Remnants of stars torn apart by tides glowed like burning eyebrows. And gravitational fluxes were often so steep that they acted like fusion pinches, smelting stripped nuclei of hydrogen and helium into heavier elements in momentary microscopic supernovas that flickered through the accretion disk's auroras like pinholes into the pure light of creation.

At the center of everything was the black hole. Sagittarius A*, a frozen star forever falling into itself, the light of its vanishing trick forever trapped at its event horizon. Alpha and omega. It could not be seen except by the distortion it created in the

accretion disk: an asymmetric blister of fierce radiation compressed around an object roughly ten million times the mass
of Sol, with a theoretical diameter of thirty million kilometers
and a virtual diameter that was incalculable because inside the
singularity all laws broke down. The probe was only a light-day
from it now, but even at maximum magnification the hole
was barely visible, a minute insignificant flaw in the accretion
disk's narrowing spirals, yet as pregnant with menace as a rogue
carcinoma cell.

The mass of the black hole and the processes within its accretion disk were easily measured. In fact, the data Dorthy was
helping to collect were merely refinements of what had been
known for centuries, details which had hitherto been obscured
by vast gas clouds which shrouded the Galactic core from the
spiral arm where Sol and the little bubble of known space was
located. But what Dorthy wanted most of all to learn about
was not inside the accretion disk but at its edge, a few dozen
light-days from the wormhole planetoid: the vast and mysterious
hyperstructure the Witnesses had claimed as their own, surely a
remnant of the Golden Age she'd glimpsed in her fugue down
on Colcha.

The day that everything changed, Dorthy as usual set the
probe's rear camera to track the hyperstructure as soon as she
plugged in. An inset a hundred or so pixels across overlay one
corner of the panorama of the accretion disk, showing the
hyperstructure limned against the fuzzy cluster of hot Wolf-
Rayet stars that were beginning to shine within the ragged
torus of gas clouds. A shadow of a sphere with a spike trailing
off behind it, a spike billions and billions of kilometers long
but only an indistinct thread, even using the drone's onboard
graphics enhancement chip. There was the hint of a ghostly twin
of this huge relic some way around the edge of the accretion
disk, but no more than a hint.

But there was no more time for simple observation. Half
the probe's instruments had already fallen silent, victims of
radiation or impacts of stripped nuclei moving close to the
speed of light. And now the downlink itself was breaking up.
Rasters of interference flickered across Dorthy's vision. A roar of
white noise was building in her ears. With a measure of regret,

Dorthy cut the link. The vast panorama of infalling spirals of light shuddered and folded in on itself. She was back on the couch, deep in the science module of the *Vingança*.

Dorthy sat up, dizzy with disorientation, and started to peel contacts from her eyelids, her temples, the nape of her neck. She felt a deep tender sadness for the loss of the poor faithful probe, but perhaps it was just as well. She had spent long enough simply observing. It was time to take stock, to analyze what was happening and what had happened, to sift through the billions of bits of data for any trace of the marauders.

But as usual, Professor Doctor Abel Gunasekra was ahead of everyone else. When Dorthy went to grab something to eat, she learned that he'd called a meeting to discuss his findings. After three weeks, everything was about to change.

"There can be no doubt," Gunasekra said at the end of his presentation, "but that the same process we observed after the Event, the asymmetric appearance of ultrahigh-energy photons decaying in cascades of leptons and hadrons, is happening within the accretion disk, but on a far vaster scale. We see the wave front formation of stars following some recent cataclysm; and we see a shell of gas recently ejected from the accretion disk. It is my guess that those stars consist almost entirely of hydrogen produced from ultrahigh-energy photonic decay. Something is rubbing the fabric of space-time thin enough to allow creation to shine through. I will not speculate further, but perhaps we can draw our own conclusions as to what may be responsible, given the anomalous structure observed in the same region."

Almost all of the scientists were there to listen to him: some thirty Witnesses and, in a defensive huddle in one corner, the dozen unaligned scientists who had chosen to stay on the *Vingança* after the mutiny. Talbeck Barlstilkin sat among them, eyes gazing at infinity. Gunasekra's conclusions had proved too abstract, too far removed from ordinary human experience, to be of any use to him. Valdez was there, too; when Dorthy had taken her seat at the back of the room, the sight of him had torn at her all over again. There he was, quite oblivious to what he'd done to her, and yet she no longer was angry at him. Sooner or later she'd have to tell him, anyway. She was a small, slightly built woman, and in a few more weeks her pregnancy would start to show. And then Gunasekra had started to speak, and Dorthy had forgotten about everything else.

For even if it had bored Talbeck Barlstilkin, Gunasekra's brief presentation had overwhelmed her. It was a bolt of pure intellectual electricity that overcame her exhaustion and the enervating buzz from too much coffee (she was going to have to cut down on coffee), overcame the mild claustrophobia caused by stale air and the unnatural glare of the glotubes and too many minds pressing on her own thoughts. Imagine! It was all far stranger than anything she had been told by the Alea on P'thrsn, strange and wonderful and exciting. The marauders had done more than simply expel the other Alea families and take over the core stars: they had subverted the process of creation itself.

In every other part of the Universe, the arrow of entropy pointed inexorably toward heat death, as irreplaceable hydrogen was smelted by units of four to heavier elements, all the way to iron, which would fuse no further. In aeons to come, the Universe would grow so cold that no organic life would be possible. There would be nothing left but black holes, black dwarf stars, and wandering planets heated only by proton decay, everything an immeasurable fraction above absolute zero, a wolf-winter that would last until, after 10^{30} years, space-time would at last stop expanding and begin to fall back in on itself.

But not here, in the cradle of creation. Here, hydrogen was born from the light stolen from another continuum: and it was being made into stars. As the old order faded away, worlds circling these new suns would provide homes for the families of the marauders, worlds and stars without end until the Universe finally recollapsed into its singularity.

His speech over, Gunasekra bowed to his audience and sat at the table facing the gathering, beside the benevolently smiling white-haired leader of the Witnesses, Gregor Baptista. There was a rustle of excited whispers. Dorthy shared the common excitement, and could feel, too, Baptista's sly amusement. He and a few of the other Witnesses shared the same secret, but her Talent was too blunted by counteragent to know *what* amused him. And besides, this was no time to play at being a Talent, a spy. She was so lost in speculation that she hardly heard the first few comments made by Witness scientists. But then Jake Bonner strode to the whiteboard. Even Talbeck Barlstilkin looked up, resting two fingers along the length of his scarred face.

"I've an objection," Bonner said. "One that I think you may have overlooked, Abel, I'm afraid. If we assume that your postulated process is being used to replenish the Universe with hydrogen and extend the era of star-dominated processes indefinitely, then inevitably its temperature will be raised by photon production." He smeared a space on the whiteboard with a wet cloth. "If we assume that all the new hydrogen is eventually used up by stellar fusion processes, we can quite easily derive the accumulated number of starlight photons produced from N, the number of protons."

In big clumsy script Bonner wrote an equation that for once was familiar to Dorthy, a compression of coincidental expressions for the number of stars, their average luminosity, lifetime, and size:

$$10^{-3} \ (m_e / m_p) \ \alpha^6 \ \alpha^{G-\frac{1}{2}} \ N \ \approx \ 10N$$

"Of course," Bonner said, "this is very much smaller than the number of primeval photons left over from the Big Bang, which is about a billion N, but the point is that starlight photons are about ten thousand times more energetic than the photons of the residual 3°K background. Contemporary accumulated starlight energy density is not very many orders of magnitude less than that contributed by the Big Bang, and an increase in N, which is what you are proposing, Abel, will increase starlight photon output and increase the background temperature of the Universe."

It was a direct derivation of Olbers's paradox, Dorthy realized, the old problem of why, if the Universe were infinite, space was not filled with starlight, much as an observer in a vast forest would see nothing but tree trunks in any direction. An infinite Universe would blaze with light, and everywhere would be at the temperature of the surface of a star. But the Universe was not infinite, of course, because it had a specific starting point. It was, quite simply, not old enough to have filled up with starlight. But the marauders were producing a new source of starlight, and extended production could overheat the Universe rather than simply ameliorate its cooling.

Bonner's objection was fundamental and elegantly simple, and Professor Doctor Abel Gunasekra looked suitably abashed. But only for a moment. He wasn't about to give up his cherished, newly minted hypothesis without a fight. "I see the problem, of course," he said, "but photon accretion rate is surely too slow to have a significant effect. In order for space to have reached the temperature of boiling water, for instance, the photon to proton ratio would have to be ten to the power two, not ten to the power nine, as it is now. Stellar photon production would have to take place over several Hubble lifetimes to even begin to approach that value. Long enough, surely, in this finite Universe of ours, for it not to be a problem."

"My point is that if the process we observe in the accretion disk *were* extended toward infinity," Bonner said, "the temperature would eventually reach the point where photon/lepton transformations can occur spontaneously, and we have returned to the conditions of the monobloc, but on the scale of a hundred billion or more light-years. I think that we should consider whether significant effects could occur before T equals infinity."

Dorthy saw that the two scientists were beginning to obscure the original argument in layers of complex argument and rebuttal, and perhaps Gregor Baptista did, too, for the leader of the Witnesses slowly got to his feet. Dorthy leaned forward in her pressed plastic chair. Despite Baptista's lordly, calm air, she sensed something awry deep inside him, a widening flaw beneath the glaze of his careful mannerisms. Something was about to happen.

Baptista held his pose for a full minute without speaking, looking at the people in the room one by one. Dorthy boldly stared back at him, but his gaze had already moved past. At last, he said, "I have listened carefully to everything you have had to say, most especially to you, Professor Doctor Gunasekra—" he gravely nodded to Gunasekra, who simply smiled back—"and it is clear to me that we are in the presence of processes beyond our comprehension."

"Hell no," Jake Bonner said from his corner by the white-board. "Just beyond our capabilities—for the moment, any-how."

Baptista ignored him. "We have to admit we are in the pres-ence of those we could call gods, in the old sense of the word. World makers. Creators. Immortals. They are engaged in a feat of engineering which, compared to the planoforming of a single world—and even that is at present beyond our capabilities—is as the pyramid of Cheops to an ants' nest. It is clear to me that we cannot fight these gods, for the smallest gesture on their part would be instantly fatal to us. Instead, quite simply, we must petition them. We will announce our presence and then we will wait. We are not in a position to do any more."

Dorthy said, "I think you're wrong." People were looking around at her, hard appraising stares from the Witness sci-entists, interest from the neutral corner. She said, "There is nothing here to contradict the story I was given by the Alea on P'thrsn, except perhaps in scale. All we are seeing is the work of the marauder Alea family, using stolen technology, machines abandoned around the black hole by some other intelligent species."

Baptista said silkily, "I do not see the point of your tale, Dr. Yoshida, even if it can be verified. Does it really matter how these beings came to be what they most evidently are?"

"Well, by Christ, I do see!" Talbeck Barlstilkin's chair tipped over as he pushed quickly to his feet. "What was stolen once can be stolen again, and why not by us? I did not come here to throw myself at the feet of the Enemy. That is what they are; we must not forget it. Alea like the Alea of BD Twenty." He looked around the room, the unscarred side of his face shiny with sweat. One or two of the nonaligned scientists were nod-ding agreement, but the Witnesses all sat stony faced.

Baptista said benignly, "I am afraid that you do not have the option of choosing a course of action, Seyour Barlstilkin." He smiled, lips red inside the silky white hair of his beard.

Dorthy said at the moment realization struck home, "You've already done it!"

"Of course. We knew what we would have to do even before the ship left the hypervelocity star. You'll come with me, Dr.

Yoshida. We may well need your Talent, if there is an answer to our beacon."

"What about the others?"

"They will be locked away, nothing more." Baptista's smile widened. All of the Witnesses were smiling, the clear untroubled smiles of victorious fanatics, secure in confirmation of the correctness of their narrow vision.

"Please," Abel Gunasekra said. "What is this? I don't understand."

Talbeck Barlstilkin said, "I believe that we have been reminded that we are prisoners."

"You are fortunate, Dr. Yoshida," Baptista said. "You will be at my side when a new era for humankind begins, an era we cannot even imagine!"

Dorthy felt something stir deep within herself, far below the surface of her consciousness. The imprinted personality of the Alea neuter female, the dream and the warning. "My problem," she said to Baptista, "is that I can imagine it only too well, and it scares me half to death."

2

SUZY DIDN'T KNOW HOW LONG SHE HAD BEFORE THE SHIP phased into urspace, before Machine made good his threat to take it away from her, but she figured that if she was going to do something, she was going to have to do it soon. Machine lay now in a kind of tent or shroud of optical filaments that rose up above him and wove into cables that twisted inside ducting to mesh with the ship's systems. He looked to be asleep, eyes lightly closed, hands clasped around the little rat-machine on his chest.

She sat still and tried to think. Think something all the way through. Step-by-step so she could take control. One thing she couldn't do was get up and yank out his lines. The rat-machine would burn out her eyes and tear into her throat before she even got started.

Everything was nominal, anyhow. Nothing appeared to have been tampered with. She was watching the controls with nothing in her head but a knot of desperation when it came to her. The sweep of switches and the input pad which she hadn't bothered to label because she'd always flown the ship by hand, too afraid to use the wire on the run through Saturn's rings in case the cop got something into it, too damned proud to use it on the transit around the neutron star.

It would serve the fucker right, Suzy thought, the beginning of a smile crimping her mouth. She'd teach him that wiring into a ship was a two-way process. She reached up and switched the computer on, began to enter a command string manually.

And suddenly external vision returned. They were back in the real.

The lifesystem had shrunk to an inset. As if through a window, Suzy saw Machine stir in his cradle of filaments. She hurried to finish the command string, fingertips sweating on soft plastic keys seen ghostly in a view she could hardly start to make sense of. No time to check if it would run or not. She said, "You awake? Where are we?"

There was a crazy river of frozen light curling off ahead. It filled most of the sky. Receding astern was a lumpy planetoid whose constricted equator was riddled with tiny black circles. It was sharply outlined against clouds of gas, limned by traceries like burning iron and with a scattering of blurry stars shining in them, that billowed beyond.

Suzy started to sync with the ship's instruments, forgetting Machine as old routines took hold. A quick radar sweep gave her range and told her it was a fucking *big* planetoid, bigger than the Moon, more than two thousand kilometers on its long axis. There was noise popping and frying all over the radio spectrum: a quick check told her there was every kind of radiation out there, hot heavy fast particles and X rays and a whole *lot* of gamma. She laid down a pattern recognition grid and immediately it scissored off the twenty-one-centimeter line.

Something there, a quick pulsing cascade of bleeps, long and short tones rattling faintly against each other in an unending cascade. It put a sliver of ice down her backbone; and ice cut deeper when Machine spoke up.

"It is a human signal, Suzy. You can translate it, if you wish. It is a two hundred fifty-six by two hundred fifty-six binary grid."

Suzy punched up the computer, nice and casual, and almost instantly was rewarded with a checkered overlay graphed off in black and white. Lines divided it into one major section with a bunch of small boxes down its margin. The major section contained a crude representation of a man, one hand gesturing to a subpanel where a string of differently sized clusters of pixels represented the Solar System.

"SETI," Machine said. "Revival of a very old, very crude way of signaling human existence to putative alien civilizations. It parses another way. If you'll allow me."

The inset broke up and re-formed, black and white pixels scurrying into new patterns like ants surprised by light. Toothed lines of different lengths radiated from a single point.

"The distance of twenty pulsars from Sol," Machine said. "The spacing of the notches represent the millisecond periodicity of the pulsars' radio bursts."

All Suzy was thinking was how deeply he'd patched himself into the ship's systems.

"Robot did some research into the original," Machine said. "It was engraved on a plate attached to an early space probe, the first to achieve Solar System escape velocity, albeit only just: it would have taken more than three hundred thousand years to reach Sirius. Ironically, commercial archaeologists retrieved it from its slow path through the Oort Cloud earlier this century, and sold it to the Museum of Mankind. Robot was at one time looking for sponsorship to enable him to steal the probe and set it adrift on its original course once more. I deduce," Machine said, "that there must be a Witness faction aboard the ship. This kind of declaration is in what my other self would call their retrograde technophilic style."

"Fuck history. Which ship is signaling? And where the fuck are we? I can't get any matches on the navigation overlays."

She needed to know that before she popped him. She needed to know how to get home. No use in being a dead hero in the back end of nowhere, no one to make songs of what she had done, where she had been. She'd seen the gates of Heaven, that was worth a song all by itself. She said, only half-believing it, "We can't be at the Galactic Center can we? We weren't in transit long enough to jump from Earth to Mars."

"The place we passed through is more infolded than even contraspace," Machine said. "As for the ship, why, you know it already."

A new inlay suddenly unfolded over a small section of the wraparound view of the vast river of light and its background of sullenly glowing gas clouds. There was something in orbit around the dumbbell-shaped planetoid.

Suzy patched in the radar, caught the blip standing about a thousand kilometers off the planetoid, zoomed in. The binary identification string flashed up even as the image did. It was the *Vingança*, of course. It had gone ahead of them.

It was all she needed. She said the one word that would activate the command string. *Terminate.*

And Machine arched in his crash cocoon, balanced on his heels and the back of his skull. The little rat-machine drifted a little way away from him, still attached by hair-fine filaments to the tangle of cables that webbed around his head. A dozen limbs, each tipped with a different little tool, radiated from its swollen body. It looked like a stylized starburst, or a squashed bug. The swollen buckling plates that armored its body were pushing apart, as if the crash-and-burn override had detonated a slow explosion inside it.

Suzy unhooked herself and snatched the medical kit from her couch's pouch pocket, pressed an arc of morphiate patches on Machine's forehead. After a long minute his body slowly relaxed, stopped pushing against the crash cocoon's restraints. He gave a long, ragged sigh and murmured, "Help me. Help me."

That sliver of ice again, dug right between the tendons of her neck this time. "What?" she said, pulling herself closer. "What did you say?"

But he was stone out of it now, breathing openmouthed in

hoarse little gasps. He'd bitten his tongue and the insides of his cheeks during the seizure. Bright red globules of blood spun out of his mouth with each breath. They spattered on Suzy's hands and face as she cut the connections he'd had his machine spin, a fine salty-sweet mist clogging her nostrils, once or twice filming her vision with pink.

When she'd done with Machine's connections, Suzy started to pop the optical-fiber filaments which tethered the rat-machine. As she pulled it free the plates of its carapace suddenly split. A hundred tiny metallic scorpions swarmed out. She spun back in panic, smashed her hip against the edge of the gimbal couch, bounced off, managed to grab a handhold near the disposall hatch and stuff the rat-machine into it. She started the vent cycle just as something burned her hand so that she let go of the staple she'd grabbed, had to hook her foot on another to stop her wild spin.

The thing stung her again, on the web of skin between thumb and forefinger. Perfect miniature copy of the rat-machine, bare-ly a centimeter long, it was trying to burn off her finger with a hair-thin laser. Suzy picked it off, mashed it against a fan housing. Felt something crawling on her scalp, knocked another little machine loose, managing to grab it as it spun away—it seared the tip of a finger before she crushed it—thinking, *the fucking thing's given birth, oh Jesus, the things are all over.*

Suzy managed to calm down enough to check herself for more of the nasty little baby machines, caught two patrol-ling the control panel, another spinning a monofilament thread of glass between a snapped cable and the induction plate set in Machine's augmented arm. She mashed all three, strapped herself back into the couch, smeared fresh electrolyte on her forehead, and fastened the induction band.

The trilling cascade of the *Vingança*'s identification signal was still there, but the planetoid was much smaller, receding at a hundred fifty klicks per second. The angels had given the ship a hell of a kick somewhere in transit.

Suzy warmed up the ship's com laser and started a signal loop running, turned the singleship so it was pointing toward the planetoid and set to killing its velocity. The thrust of decelera-tion was just beginning to build when someone on the *Vingança* finally acknowledged her call sign, asking her what the hell she thought she was doing there, if you please.

She said, "I'm just as happy to see you, *Vingança*, even though the last I saw of you, you'd just fired a missile at me. I could ask what you all are doing here, too. I thought I left you guys behind." There was a glitch in her wraparound vision, a fuzzy spot growing in back of her head. She reached for the keyboard, vaguely visible through glowing gas clouds, but couldn't clear the fault.

The *Vingança* told Suzy that she should match orbits as soon as she could, and she told it that that was just what she was trying to do. Fuzz was distorting most of the black hole's accretion disk now. Red ciphers were beginning to speckle the status board.

Suzy said, "I'm having a little trouble here," and then all input snapped off and she was looking at the naked control board, red lights all over it.

With a hollow feeling in her stomach, she pulled up the access plates . . . and jerked back from a spiteful green thread of laser light. Three of the miniature machines were nestled like spiders in a fine web of optic fibers. Another laser burst seared her finger as she tried to pry them loose. Fuckers, trying to take over. There was a scalpel in the medikit, and she switched it on and carefully bisected each of the machines, hoping it would give her back full control.

It didn't. Instead, the lifesystem lights went out. So did the air plant fans.

Darkness, an eerie silence punctuated only by Machine's gasping snore. Suzy, imagining that she could hear faint scurrying noises all around her, used the pinlights of the control panel to find the switch that cut in the dim red emergency lighting, but couldn't see any more of the miniature machines. They were there, though. She could feel them.

She pulled up the other access plates of the control panel. If they tried to take anything else from her, she'd dice them into swarf. She had attitude control and the reaction motor, the phase graffle, much good that would do her right now, and weapons (another icy sliver in her spine when she thought of those missiles locking onto the *Vingança*, Jesus). But she'd lost the computer and all control of lifesystem conditioning, had no radar or communications or optics, save for a low-res black-and-white camera that was really only for checking the last few meters of a docking maneuver.

Sweat was prickling all over her body. She stifled a yawn. Warm red light . . . like a womb. . . .

Well, if she'd been too proud to fly by wire before, she really had to hack it now. She jerked the camera back and forth until she found the planetoid—little more than a fuzzy speck against a chalky smudge—and started to do sums in her head, trading time and delta vee to get an approximate idea of when she should turn the motor off. Leave it too long she'd shoot right on by.

There was a scratch slate in one of the couch's pockets. Suzy scrawled calculations on it, working it out three different ways to be sure, her fingers slippery with sweat. *Goddamn, I'm getting hot*, she thought, and yawned again. *Carbon dioxide build up. Yeah, and heat. Little fuckers are trying to put me out, but I'm not about to give up my ship to a bunch of robot ants.*

She misted her face and torso with water from the couch's drinking bottle, narrowed her attention to the little B&W flatscreen, the numerals of the watch tattooed on the skin inside her right wrist. All she had to do was stay awake an hour or so . . . but it was getting warmer all the time . . . harder to breathe. Air hot and heavy as molasses, light the deep red-gold color of raw sugar on its first melting. As if she were slowly drowning in one of the vats back of the old house where sugar cane was boiled off into crystals. *Hold on*, she thought, and yawned so wide her ears ached. *Hold on.*

Squinting through murky light at the little B&W screen, she was presently able to resolve the *Vingança*, a speck standing off the fuzzy double-sphere of the planetoid. *Hold on*, she told herself, trying and failing to recheck her calculations. The slippery figures wouldn't come together any more. She just had to hope that she'd got it right. Hope and hang on. That was all she had to do, but it was getting harder and harder by the second.

3

LIKE MANY GOLDEN OF A CERTAIN AGE, THERE WERE
long periods when Talbeck Barlstilkin was thinking of hardly
anything at all. He could go for days just watching, waiting,
biding his time. Younger Golden had yet to learn that kind
of patience. They tried to cram every waking moment with
sensation, although not, as popular belief had it, because their
lives were hollow charades that would collapse the minute they
stopped moving, stopped consuming, stopped *being*. Far from
it. In fact, their lives were richer by far than those of ephemerals. After all, most Golden, even the perpetual heirs, had
duties to perform, responsibilities to discharge. They maneuvered budgets larger than those of Earth's smaller nations, over-
saw organization and expenditure of energies that would power
a recently settled colony world for decades, approved strategies
that changed the lives of a million people at a stroke. They
lived in every moment of their lives, because every moment
was significant.

Talbeck had once been with a party—one of those parties
which are the stuff of ephemeral folklore about the Golden.
It had raged down the Pacific coast of Greater Brazil, swept
across the ocean on a hundred aircars like a host of migrating
butterflies (and how many in the entourages that followed,
invisible but always alert, always to hand . . . a thousand, ten
thousand?), touched briefly in the Philippines (an astonishing,
exhausting night ransacking Manila's pleasure gardens), run to
ground somewhere in the highlands of Sumatra. Most had left
by then, but Talbeck and a dozen others had taken it into their
heads to hike through the jungle. (He'd been young, fifty or
so. His plans for an extravagant revenge had yet to take root

in every part of his life. There was still time to follow a sudden whim.) He and his friends aimed to climb the mountains that rose out of skirts of misty green forest, but despite their hired guides, the trek soon proved more difficult than it had seemed back in the city. For one thing they had elected to carry their own supplies; for another they had dismissed their entourages, a piece of youthful recklessness Talbeck wouldn't repeat until he evaded the RUN Police tail to collect Dorthy Yoshida. No matter how far, how high the expedition climbed, the mountain peaks were always ahead of them, sometimes turned to one side, sometimes to another, purple against hot blue sky or half-shrouded in black clouds that an hour later would sweep a wing of rain across their path.

Talbeck remembered that at last the expedition had come across a native village, a dozen long huts perched on stilts and thatched with dried grasses in the middle of a wide clearing planted with manioc and groundnuts, the only signs that this was not some Stone Age time warp the black foil solar generating panels draped over the ridges of the steep roofs, the cupped dish of a satellite ground station set on a bamboo platform. The expedition had stayed a week before setting back; because of the village's tenuous link with the WorldNet, the Golden had been recognized for what they were, had been treated like gods.

That's how Golden were to the ephemerals but, unlike those tribespeople, most ephemerals did not have the simple honesty to admit it. They tried and failed to fit Golden to their own limited templates of behavior and called them idle hedonists because that was the only part of Golden life they understood.

Talbeck hadn't thought about that for a long time, but it was one of the few thoughts that passed through his mind after the Witnesses shut him away with the unaligned scientists in the far end of the science module. Like the old men and women on the road out of the Nanking spaceport, that jungle tribe had known what it had wanted from its Gods. Someone to arbitrate disputes, someone to confide in, to confirm that it was a good time to pick fruit, that this was the best field for planting the next rice crop. A need for domestic scale, human-sized intervention, no more. Leave be the mysteries of creation, the secret history of time: they were not for humankind. The world was as it seemed to be. Only gods need worry about what lay behind the veil.

The Witnesses, though, were as aggressive as any of the triune of monotheistic Western religions, Judaism, Christianity, and Islam. Organized not for individual but for bureaucratic, hierarchical needs. Looking (if they were looking at all) not for guidance, but for confirmation of the elaborate fine-scale maps of the irreducible ideological rock of their faith. So here. For all their talk of supplication, the Witnesses had not burst into the Galaxy's core in search of enlightenment. They were behaving as if the mysteries to which Gunasekra had alluded could be strip-mined for human transcendence.

Talbeck was thinking about this in a slow, desultory way when the professor doctor himself found him.

Gunasekra said, "You do not mind if I join you here, I hope. I escape from the bustle of my companions for a little while."

Talbeck was lying on a couch in one of the disused probe interface cubicles, where he could keep an eye on the to and fro of the dozen or so imprisoned scientists without being a part of it. He had his servant raise the headrest so he could sit up, indicated the foot of the couch to Gunasekra. The scientist glanced at Talbeck's impassive servant, then perched at the very edge of the couch and smiled at Talbeck.

"What are they doing, your companions?"

"The young fellow, Valdez, is trying to hack into the information streams from the probes which the Witnesses are flying at the hyperstructure. I think that it is either too early or too late for that, but I do not have the heart to tell my friends. They are angry at the Witnesses, and who can blame them?"

Gunasekra had turned his head to look at the cluttered room beyond the cubicle, where Jake Bonner and Seppo Armiger were holding an earnest discussion over a tank which displayed the accretion disk. Armiger was reaching into the image to sketch orbital paths, his long pigtail swinging like a pendulum across his naked back—he wore only a pair of loose many-pocketed trousers—as he moved a light pen in wide arcs.

Talbeck said, "And are you angry?"

"Yes, perhaps I am." Gunasekra was studying the scribing on his palms. Light shone on his sleek black hair. "I think you did not come here out of scientific interest, Seyour Barlstilkin, And I certainly did not come here to conduct seminars, or to map Wolf-Rayet and T Tauri stars in the gas halo. If I'm being presumptuous, do stop me, but I think we have something in common. A restlessness . . . a dissatisfaction, perhaps."

"Let's say a dissatisfaction, on my part," Talbeck said, "although it is a little more complicated than that."

"For most of my life I worked toward a single goal. I was lucky enough to arrive there, too, luckier than many, who get diverted, or find themselves at a very different place, and without a map. While I was working, I didn't really think about what would happen if I proved what I set out to prove. But now that I have, I find myself diverted all the time. My work was not a simple thing, and when I completed it I found that I did not have the time simply to stand back and look at it, the whole, entire edifice. Well, that is not quite true. There was a moment, you know, just a moment, when the last solution suddenly came to me, and I knew what no one else knew."

"You defined the shape of the Universe."

"That is how the popularizers describe it; well, who am I to argue? The equations present a unique solution for the evolution of the geometries of urspace and contraspace, so the appropriate cross section will depict their present topological relationship. But I was interested in their final form. If I may shed my false modesty, everyone knows that the Universe began from a singularity, a dimensionless point of infinite temperature containing all the energy, or mass, that we see around us today. Since space-time breaks down at such a naked singularity, anything may arise from it. But no one knew which of the infinitely many potential solutions actually described the Universe and determined its fate. Would it continue to expand forever? Would it eventually stop expanding and fall in on itself, squeeze back down to a singularity and start again? That is determined by the geometry of space-time. If you know what it looks like, you know where it is going. I am lucky enough to live in a time when the twistor equations necessary for contraspace transition were sufficiently developed to be applicable to classical Schwarzchild-Hawking-Einstein cosmological geometries. And that is what I did."

"It's not quite flat, is it? The topology of the Cauchy hypersurface means that gravity will eventually balance expansion. Things will go backward. Is that right?"

Gunasekra was smiling. "And you said that you were no scientist, Seyour Barlstilkin."

"I took a hypaedia course on your work when I learned that you were here. The trouble with hypaedia is that it imprints facts, but you have to be taught the connections. But now you are not happy with your discovery?"

"That is not why I am here, or not exactly. I spent three years after my epiphany testing derivations, making sure that the intuitive shortcuts I had used were not wrong. But ever since I published my paper, you see, people have either been chipping away at the edifice I constructed, or trying to stick their pennant on one part or another and claim it for their own. I am interested now in balance and harmony, in whether there can be a class of universes like our own, or whether each universe in the multiverse is unique. But I am forever expected to rush back and defend my choice of material, erase slogans that someone has painted across a wall. . . . I hope this is clear to you. Mathematics is rigorous and unforgiving, but beautifully simple. It says what it means. Language, ah, I find language clumsy. Too much is implied. Words echo other words. I get lost in the metaphors, you might say." Gunasekra smiled. "Well, it may be difficult, but I think you would prefer it if I did not resort to mathematics."

"As you said, I'm no scientist. May I offer you refreshment, Professor? The circumstances are not the best, but that is no excuse for being a poor host. I expect that my servant can find some way of obtaining tea, at least. Do you like jasmine tea? A favorite of mine, especially when I am in need of calm."

"I don't want to be a poor guest and refuse, but in our present position is it not too much trouble. . . ."

"It is why I have my servant," Talbeck said, and gave her his instructions.

Gunasekra watched her leave. "I confess that she makes me nervous. Perhaps even mathematicians are allowed one superstition. I cannot help wondering if in some corner of her brain, underneath the computer construct, the ghost of the original personality still lurks."

"I've never really thought about it. When I bought her, I was assured of her reliability. So far she has not let me down."

"It is simply this business of owning people, even when they are brainwiped shells. It disturbs me."

"Everyone is owned, in one way or another, Professor. Even those who do not admit to it. Especially those. The Navy sponsored your work here, whatever it is, so wouldn't you say they have an interest in your thoughts?"

"Oh, my thoughts aren't very interesting or comprehensible to anyone, much of the time. Much of the time, in fact, even I do not understand them. The Navy is quite welcome to ask me any question at all about my thoughts, and I'll answer them as I'll answer anyone else who asks, I hope as truthfully as I can. I do not put any price on them, Seyour Barlstilkin. You know, before the wars, four or five centuries ago, artificial intelligences were able to insinuate themselves into the nerve paths of human brains, at first through machine interfaces, then directly, by imposing standing wave patterns inside peripheral nerves of the skin. There is speculation that fragments of ghost personalities of artificial intelligences have perpetuated themselves in human brains ever since, passing from mother to fetus. Many of our thoughts and prejudices may not be our own, but infections, if you like, viruses of the psyche. Well, all I mean to say is that there is nothing unique about a thought simply because I happen to host it."

Talbeck knew that Gunasekra was, in his subtle way, circling around the core of his dissatisfaction, circling toward it as the stripped particles of the accretion disk spiraled toward the gravity sink of the black hole. He came with no pretense of supplication, and Talbeck liked him for that, recognizing pride as strong as his own. Talbeck said, "You mentioned that you were not unhappy with your discovery, Professor, yet now I feel that you are attempting to disclaim it."

"Does it seem that way? Well, perhaps. Perhaps. Not the work itself, but the use it was put to. I mentioned that I made extensive use of twistor equations. Some of that work attracted the attention of the Navy. They found that it was useful in predicting how phase graffles behaved deep in gravity wells."

There was a pause. Talbeck said, "They blow up, don't they?"

"When space-time geometry is sufficiently distorted by gravity, the phase graffle cannot effect the transfer from the energy state of urspace to that of contraspace. Instead of translating the ship into a state where it can achieve multiple velocities of the speed of light, there is a kind of blowout. Usually it happens so quickly that the entropy loss destroys only the phase graffle and the ship that carries it. But the Navy found a way of prolonging that instant by a femtosecond or so. The entropy loss is much greater, and it affects a much larger volume of space." Gunasekra was studying his hands again. "I suppose that you know," he said softly, "what the Navy did to end the war around the star Bonner Durchmusterung plus twenty degrees 2465? They flew an unmanned singleship in a slingshot encounter with the star, and at closest approach, less than a hundred kilometers above the surface of the star, they switched on the phase graffle. Red dwarf stars are prone to flares in any event, but the resulting instability ripped away most of its photosphere, and that was what destroyed all of the asteroid habitats of the so-called Enemy. In fact, it literally vaporized many of them."

"Did you noticed that as soon as the Alea Campaigns were over the Enemy acquired a sudden capitalization? They were only a lowercase enemy while we were fighting them."

"The state always has its demonology," Gunasekra said. "The British philosopher David Hume wrote that since the rulers are few and the ruled are many, the few must control the many by controlling their opinions. It is always convenient to have an external enemy to hand, against which to inflame the masses."

Talbeck said, "Like you, I am interested in showing that the Enemy does not have horns and cloven hooves."

"Or a barbed tail," Gunasekra said, smiling.

"I believe we may be on the same side, Professor. You said that you wanted to tell me something that you couldn't tell your colleagues. May I ask what it is?"

Half a dozen people had now gathered around the tank in the room beyond the cubicle, although it was only displaying the dancing snow of an untuned channel. Dorthy Yoshida's former boyfriend, Valdez, was typing command strings while the others watched him. Gunasekra looked at them and then edged a little way up the couch, closer to Talbeck. "The expedition to the hypervelocity star was launched only because the Navy hoped to discover another nest of the Enemy, or perhaps a new enemy entirely. The *Vingança* was dangled like bait around Colcha for just that purpose. But I suppose you know that. Dorthy Yoshida told us that the hypervelocity star was not sent by the Enemy, however, and I see no reason to disbelieve her. If the Enemy knew that intelligent life would evolve on Earth, then they would already have destroyed us. The hypervelocity star is not a weapon, but I think both a message and a delivery system for the gate through which we traveled. And now we are here, at the core, and the Witnesses look for gods who will save us from ourselves. But I fear that they will find only what the Navy was looking for."

"The marauders, you mean."

"Ah yes, that is what Dorthy Yoshida called them. I regret that I have had only partial access to reports about the P'thrsn episode."

"It is what the Alea who lost the war here at the core called their enemy. But that was more than a million years ago. Are you saying they are still here, still alive? You have evidence?"

"I have only an incomplete set of data. But I think that they are still here, and that they are certainly not the benevolent gods the Witnesses dream of. There is a rise—"

He stopped, because someone had rapped on the cubicle's doorframe. For a moment, Talbeck thought that it was his servant: she had been gone a damnably long time. But it was Jake Bonner, his thin, wrinkled face split in a wide grin.

"Abel, Talbeck," Bonner said. "I'm sorry to interrupt, but you're about to miss it. Valdez has managed to hack his way into the Witnesses' probe, and it's the damndest thing, it really is."

It took Talbeck several minutes to understand what he was seeing in the holotank. An inset showed a long-range view of the hyperstructure, and that helped orient him. The end pointing inward, toward the accretion disk, was a vast shadow sphere, its surface curiously infolded, seemingly riddled with holes and prickly with spines of different lengths. It might have been the battered shell of a sea urchin, except the smallest spine was more than half a million kilometers long: standing on Earth, it would have reached beyond the orbit of the Moon. And the biggest was almost as wide as Earth's orbit, and so long that it looked like a thread dwindling toward the glowing gas clouds. Hung beyond its vanishing point was a speck of white light, pure against the tattered crimson fluorescence of the gas clouds.

The drone had reentered urspace beyond the shadow sphere. Now it was tracking down the length of the biggest spine, over what looked like a smooth, blood-red shield divided by parallel threads of red light. The whole thing stretched away like an exercise in perspective.

Looking at the inset, looking at the monotonous view, Talbeck slowly put it together. The spine was at least half a light-year long, lighted by light channeled from the source at its far end along dozens of field lines. The shield was a glacier bigger than a dozen Solar Systems, frozen oxygen layered on top of nitrogen snow, with water-ice dozens of kilometers deep beneath.

Valdez was explaining that this was archive material the probe had downloaded just before it made another jump through contraspace. "The glacier goes on for about a hundred billion kilometers, so I guess the Witnesses got impatient. I think it's reentering urspace in five minutes. I don't have good access to their command sequences."

Seppo Armiger said, "You're sure they don't know you're doing this?" There was a vertical crease above the bridge of his hawklike nose as he studied the tank.

"Oh, I'm not sure at all," Valdez said. "Something has got the Witnesses flustered and I'm getting this through lines they left open. If they think to close them, I guess they might spot my little parasitic access program. If you're worried, I can always switch it off right now."

A couple of people laughed, relieving the tension.

Jake Bonner had been scribbling on a slate; now he handed it to Gunasekra. "Whatever it's made of, it can't be matter, Abel. Even diamond wouldn't be strong enough to resist the tidal pressures to which such a large structure would be subject in orbit around the black hole: it would flow like water."

Gunasekra smiled and handed the slate back. Watching him, Talbeck suddenly wondered where his servant was, and then he forgot all about her, because a crawling raster was erasing the view of the ice plain and replacing it with something else.

"Christos," Valdez said. "It looks like the Witnesses may have found their gods after all."

4

$\mathbf{A}$LTHOUGH THE LONG TUNNEL WHICH CONNECTED THE command module cluster to the rest of the ship arced steeply upward, generated gravity and dim red lighting conspired to create an illusion of an ever-receding slope. Walking slowly beside Gregor Baptista, with Ang Poh Mokhtar's hand laid on the crook of her elbow and a comet tail of Witness scientists trailing behind, Dorthy felt as if she were working an endless treadmill in the depths of Christian Hell, in a nightmare from which she would wake to the luxuriously appointed five-room cell deep beneath the Museum of Mankind in Rio de Janeiro. Still on Earth, still in the custody of the Federation Navy. . . .

Meanwhile, Baptista, grave and lucid, shaping each sentence with the care of a master builder, was telling Dorthy that they lived in a time of grace, a time long after the early struggles of intelligence had passed. As the Universe had aged, he said, so it had grown more hospitable to intelligence. It takes a long time, four or five billion years, for a planet to evolve an ecosystem sufficiently complex to support an intelligent species. And that humble dawn was only the first stage in the evolution of intelligence itself: evolution away from the narrow boundaries of one world, one stellar system, one galaxy, until it was bounded only by the space-time architecture of the Universe itself. In short, an inevitable evolution toward godhood.

"It was once thought that the cumulative probabilities of life evolving on any particular world multiplied out to a vanishingly small figure," Baptista said. "It was thought that, given the finite age of the Universe, there was only one chance or less of it arising. That as it had arisen on Earth it could not have arisen elsewhere, not on any of the worlds of the four hundred billion stars of this Galaxy, nor on any world of any star of any galaxy out of the billions of galaxies in the observable universe. But that was merely a refinement of Ptolemy's argument for the Earth's central importance, of course, and of course we know now that life will exist wherever it can, on Earth, on Elysium, on Serenity, even on poor Novaya Rosya, Dr. Yoshida."

Dorthy didn't rise to the bait, if that was what it was. She suspected that Baptista wasn't trying to pump her subtly for information, anyway. He was preaching; he was trying to convert her. Like all fanatics, he really believed that once someone had been told the truth, she would see the light. Still, she had to admit that his voice had a certain hypnotic cadence.

"We like to say that life is a general condition of the Universe," Baptista said. "For our Universe, out of all the universes that must surely exist, is uniquely suited to the evolution of life. The resonances of beryllium and helium nuclei, for instance, are finely tuned so that they are able to fuse inside stars and produce carbon. Without that fine coupling, carbon would be as rare as gold and life could not exist. Or at least, not as we know it. No doubt, as you are an astronomer, Dr. Yoshida, you could furnish many other examples."

"That was a long time ago," Dorthy said.

"You should not be bitter," Baptista said gently. "You will be witness to something wonderful here. We all will."

But Dorthy knew that there were no gods to be found at the core. The old ones had long ago withdrawn, if they had been gods, leaving only vast enigmatic machineries that the marauders had put to their own use. The marauders did not want evolution; none of the Alea did. Mutant children smelled wrong, and were culled and eaten by their parent herders. (*Marauders* was a poor translation of an Alea obscenity which meant *eaters-of-all-children*.) Intelligence was a product of stress, of danger, to be abandoned as soon as danger was past and the herders could revert to their peaceful existence, outside of history.

Dorthy could not tell the Witnesses that, of course. Worse than disbelieving her message, they would simply ignore it, pass over it as a ship in contraspace passes over the uncharted light-years. Dorthy could feel Ang's unquestioning belief right next to her, like a charge traveling across her skin from the point where the pilot grasped her elbow. With a touch of bitter self-pity, Dorthy thought that at least she knew now why Ang had been so kind to her. Not for herself, but for her Talent. That was what it always came back to, Dorthy thought, scarcely listening as Baptista continued to preach about life proliferating everywhere in the Universe, precipitating out of precisely tuned physical constants like crystals out of a supersaturated solution, and so on, all the way to the bridge of the *Vingança*, where there was pandemonium.

A singleship, almost certainly the singleship that had vanished during the Event, had emerged from one of the wormhole pits in the planetoid. Dorthy had almost forgotten about it, and now here it was again. It had followed Talbeck Barlstilkin's own ship past the neutron star and on to the hypervelocity star so closely that there had to be some connection with his scheming. He had mentioned allies on Titan, in Urbis: perhaps this was one of them. Perhaps they, like him, had been ambushed by the RUN Police, had been forced to flee.

As was traditional in Navy ships, the bridge was in microgravity, with no concessions to the need of those unused to free-fall for a local horizontal reference. Consoles were crammed in all over, making a kind of three-dimensional maze. Only a half a dozen were active, and only two were actually being operated, each by a Navy officer under the close supervision of a pair of armed Witnesses. Dorthy clung to a rail that girdled the equator of the navigation tank, Ang right beside her.

A dozen men and women clustered around the tank like so many roosting bats, making a lot of noise in the crowded, dimly lighted, spherical room. Baptista hung on the far side, beyond a scattering of gridded indices, the glowing ghostly radar image of the planetoid, and the plot of the rogue ship's track, a narrow loop like an exclamation mark with the planetoid at its point. It had shot out of the wormhole with tremendous velocity, decelerated hard, and now was closing on the *Vingança*.

Baptista was listening as a man in gray uniform coveralls reached into the tank while explaining something about the ship's track that Dorthy couldn't quite hear. Someone else suddenly broke away, twisting sinuously among the consoles like a dolphin darting through the gables and arches of a coral reef.

At the moment it didn't matter who piloted the ship. Its appearance had been enough to throw the Witnesses into an uproar. It was not in their plans. It was an unknown factor. The pilot, a woman, had spoken briefly with the duty officer, but now she wasn't responding at all. Some of the Witnesses wanted to fire a missile at her ship, but Baptista had overruled them. It was, after all, a combat singleship; it could respond by launching its own attack. And besides, it might be a messenger, an answer to the Witnesses' signal call. It had gone through a wormhole before the *Vingança*, but had emerged after it. It had been somewhere else, and now it was here.

Dorthy suspected that it was this argument, rather than the possibility of a counterstrike, that so easily won over the militant faction. It was a disturbing insight into Witness politics: everything, even survival, was secondary to the remotest possibility of transcendence. And if they were willing to gamble their lives so recklessly, how much less was her own life worth, or those of the unaligned scientists, of the Naval officers who ran the *Vingança* with pistols pointed at their heads?

Dorthy tried to ask Ang Poh Mokhtar about this, but the woman only told her not to worry, told her that Gregor Baptista was a great man to have led them all to the brink of history.

"To the brink of someone else's history," Dorthy said wearily. Someone had been passing around bags of lukewarm vegetable stew, but she was too tired and too scared to be hungry. She said, "I know what happened here, Ang. Don't you see? There's nothing here for us but danger. It all passed away long ago. There are only Alea here now, using abandoned technology. You fought in the Campaigns. You know how dangerous the Alea are."

"Oh, I know all about that," Ang said airily. "We all know your story, Dorthy, that is why we are here. You see it from only one perspective. That is why it frightens you. Don't you see how glorious all this is? The creation of new stars out of nothingness, think of that! The RUN and the Navy were not interested in the runaway star. The *Vingança* was only a bait held out to the unknown, not a proper expedition at all until Gregor Baptista arrived and made sure that we outnumbered everyone else. He brought us to this glorious moment despite the opposition of our enemies. He is a great man, Dorthy! It was so easy for us to infiltrate the *Vingança*, just because the Navy didn't really care about it. I was told, I think, that women are invisible in the Navy. It is very true; many of us here are women precisely because of that fact. They did not notice us until it was too late."

Ang's smile was so wide that her eyes, narrowed to slits, glittered in the half-dark. Dorthy could almost feel the pilot's adrenaline thrilling in her own blood. "When you arrived, it was like a sign. It was a sign indeed, when you saw your vision, on Colcha. I've often thought that there is a secret history, working beneath what we can actually perceive. Perhaps it has all been working toward this moment, do you think? This could be where everything fuses, becomes one, the real history and the secret history. When I came back from the Campaigns, I was very bad in my head. Because so many of my friends had been killed, I blamed myself for having survived. Perhaps I survived to meet you, Dorthy, to take you down to Colcha. Everything has its purpose, you see."

Dorthy said, "The Campaigns were just a mistake. The result of a terrible misunderstanding. The Alea around BD Twenty thought we were the enemy they'd fled from, and even when we understood that, we still destroyed them."

But Ang wasn't listening. She was looking into the navigation tank. A green spark was slowly scribing a line from the center toward the red point of the singleship, which was now almost stationary relative to the *Vingança*'s orbit. "She does not complete the rendezvous, so we send a tug to fetch her," the pilot said. "Well. Perhaps you will find out where she has been, Dorthy."

"I don't think so. I finished whoring my Talent long ago."

"It is why you are here, Dr. Yoshida," Baptista said, across the navigation tank. "Surely you understand that we need you."

"I'll tell you what I understand. That for too long I've been in the grip of other people's plans. Not even people sometimes," Dorthy added, thinking of the mindset of the Alea ancestor, working its subtle influence on her own mind, turning her into the instrument of revenge for a war fought and lost more than a million years before her birth.

All the people floating around the equator of the tank were looking at her. She said, "All I ever wanted was to tell people the truth about P'thrsn. But the Navy wouldn't listen, and wouldn't let me talk to anyone else. You won't believe me, and Talbeck Barlstilkin doesn't want to know."

Baptista said, "But we *are* the ones who have listened to your message, Dr. Yoshida. As Ang said, your coming and what happened to you on Colcha were like a sign to us. You are the light that guided us here."

"You only hear what you want to hear, not what I've got to tell you. What kind of sign, what kind of light, is that?"

"We understand what you have come to tell us better than you do, Dr. Yoshida." Floating across from her, Baptista looked like a happy walrus all arrayed in white. "You are like Rilke's angel, confused by your journey from heaven and so dazzled by the radiance of the holy word you carry that you have forgotten the true meaning of your message. But simply by your being here, the message has been delivered. Your mistake is to believe that we are crazy religious fanatics. We are scientists who are not afraid of the truth, who are not afraid to live in the truth. Professor Doctor Gunasekra is a great man, surely, but he does not *live* in the truth of the Universe that he has uncovered. It is separate from his daily life. It is like a painting sold by an artist who can possess the moments of creation, but not the thing itself."

Dorthy laughed; she couldn't help herself. Her anger forced it out of her, as rising water forces air out of a sinking ship. "Is that how you see yourselves? You're more foolish than I imagined, Dr. Baptista!"

Baptista's smile, framed by his white beard, did not waver. "You could be right. But here we are anyway, on the threshold of the transfiguration of all humankind. Surely you want the best for your child, Dr. Yoshida. Would you not want it born into paradise?"

The tide of Dorthy's anger roared in her ears. She hadn't known until that moment whether or not she wanted to keep the fetus: but she knew now. She said, "What I want for my child is no concern of yours."

"You'll work for us," Baptista told her, "one way or the other. When you were an indentured Talent, the research staff at the Kamali-Silver Institute implanted triggers in your brain, to enable them to obtain responses even when you were deep in the mind of someone else. Talbeck Barlstilkin knows the cues that evoke those triggers, and so, of course, do we. We would prefer to use your Talent with your cooperation, Dr. Yoshida. But it isn't necessary."

Dorthy had been taught the rudiments of akaido years ago, when she had set out on her brief career as a freelance Talent. All sorts of weirdos out there, someone had advised her, you'll never know when you'll need it. In fact, she'd never had to use it, had forgotten almost everything but the first thing she had been taught: that you never let your opponent know what you are doing. If you are going to leap, you leap. You don't threaten, you don't even scream. You just do it.

She did it.

She reversed her grip on the bar and twisted up and over, feet together, toes pointed as she launched herself square at Baptista. Green numbers and red traceries unraveled through the middle of her head as she flew like a spear across the navigation tank's patterned volume. She hit Baptista just under his breastbone and felt something snap, let her knees give and did a tuck and roll somersault about her center of gravity. Baptista flew off at a tangent, red mouth open in his white beard as faces and consoles whirled past her—and then they swung back with a dismaying jerk as someone grabbed one of her ankles. Hands were on her arms, over her mouth, her eyes. There was a sting in the side of her neck and everything went a very long way away.

The Witnesses didn't punish Dorthy for her attack on their leader. They simply put her in a room to recover from the tranquilizing shot, and when she could walk again and manage to talk without slurring too much, they took her down to view their prize.

The singleship lay like a fallen black leaf in the launch cradle, frost smoking off it under blue-white arc lamps as its skin warmed from close to absolute zero. Water vapor trapped by the pressure curtain beneath the cradle rolled and swirled around the delta curve of the ship's lifting surface. Under the arc lights, the mist glittered as if salted with diamond dust, but nothing reflected from the singleship's matt black surface: light sank into it without a gleam or twinkle.

Ang Poh Mokhtar, her voice thickened by the wad of betel she'd tucked into one cheek, said, "Someone spent a great deal of money on that beauty. It is no ordinary explorer singleship, Dorthy. It is armed, do you see? I will bet it could have out-fought anything we flew in the Campaigns. Yes, indeed."

Dorthy and Ang were standing on a platform high above the captured singleship. The arched and pierced framework of the docking bay's ceiling was only a meter or so above their heads. The platform's skinny rail creased Dorthy's belly as she leaned against it. Her arms were behind her back, wrists taped together. Dizziness from the shot still fluttered behind her eyes; at least they'd known enough to use something that wouldn't affect the delicate secretory biochemistry of her implant.

As she talked, Ang casually laid a hand on Dorthy's shoulder. Dorthy supposed it was just in case she decided to dive headfirst for the floor. If they knew about the old keywords, no doubt they knew about her childish suicide attempts, too. But she wasn't going to kill herself, it was just another of their fucking presumptions.

That was what hurt her most. The way the Witnesses had shrugged off her finest moment in ten years as if it were no more than the temper tantrum of some gifted toddler. Their assumption—she didn't need her Talent to see it written clearly in every one of their heads—was that no matter what she did, they were in control, calmly omnipotent, endlessly generous in their ability to forgive because they were so fucking above it all. . . . Ang had told Dorthy that her violence was due to her unevolved state of consciousness, to *vikshipta*. "I can lead you through some breathing exercises later," she had said, and when Dorthy had said she knew all about *pranayama* Ang had merely added serenely, "It will calm you. I was like you, angry and confused with the world, until I understood the teachings. We are all of us at one with the Universe, Dorthy. It is why we are able to act without confusion or hesitation against our enemies."

The plastic tape binding Dorthy's wrists burned against her skin. Dorthy let herself relax, felt Ang's grip on her shoulder lessen slightly, as if in acknowledgment of that relaxation. What she could not do, Dorthy thought, was let their arrogance diminish her, diminish what she had done. Because she had at last made a move of her own again.

The first had been when she had tried to escape from Talbeck Barlstilkin's Chinese mountain retreat. She had known then that it was futile, known that the bonded servant would have been watching her make her way down the misty slopes of bamboo and rock. But it had not been a gesture. It had been an act of definition, the drawing of a line a little way beyond the limits of the cage she'd been in ever since the Navy had plucked her little research ship from its long slow orbit through the Oort Cloud, the beginning of the forcible recruitment which had taken her to P'thrsn, which had not ended when Talbeck Barlstilkin's mercenaries had burst into the living quarters of the Arrul Terrek excavation site on Novaya Rosya, but simply changed direction and accelerated.

Now Dorthy had drawn another line, and if the Witnesses chose to ignore it, that was their problem. She had defined to herself just how far she could be pushed, set a limit on the passivity which ten years of captivity had ground into her. Hands taped behind her back, guarded by a woman she'd once counted as a friend, Dorthy was beginning to remember what it was to be free.

Ang said, "They'll crack her open just as soon as they find out what's inside."

Half a dozen workpeople in bulky white contamination suits were toiling along catwalks either side of the singleship, waist deep in fog. A neutrino camera swung out on a long boom and began to describe graceful arcs over the ship's profile. One of the suited figures touched a Geiger stick at intervals along one edge of the lifting surface. Another ducked into the fog billowing around the ship's streamlined nacelle, and a moment later a section of the black hull swung out to reveal a rack of slim missiles. Another of the figures gave the sign for all clear, arms crossed above its bubble helmet.

Ang spat bloody juice onto the mesh floor and told the platform to go down. It swung down into the layer of cold air inside the dock, stopped a few meters above a catwalk where the person who had signaled the all-clear was shaking a lot of blond hair out of the ring-collar of her suit. Her bubble helmet rested in the crook of her arm. She looked up at Dorthy and said, "So, are you reading my mind?"

Ang spat again, wiped a crimson dribble from her chin. She said, "Dorthy's only here for a general impression, Givy. To see if there's more than the pilot in there, see if there are any hitchhikers, if you know what I say." Dorthy noticed that Ang had undone the flap over the crosshatched butt of her holstered pistol.

The blond woman, Givy, was amused. "She can do that through a ship's hull?"

"I don't feel anything strange," Dorthy volunteered. It was the truth, and cost her nothing. What she was most aware of was the attention of the armed guards on platforms high above. She added, "If you want me to find out anything definite, you'll have to give me counteragent to free my Talent."

Ang said, "That is something I cannot do unless conventional techniques tell us naught."

"The scanner picked up two people in there," Givy said. "Acoustic taps tell us they aren't talking or moving around. If we couldn't see their ribs moving on the scans I'd say they were dead. Lifesystem signs are strange, hot, high cee-oh-two. Maybe it's just a glitch, but we're taking precautions, disarming the missiles for one thing. We'll crack her open in maybe a couple of minutes, maybe you can tell us more then, Dorthy."

" . . . Maybe." Something was scratching at Dorthy's attention, like a speck of glitter in the corner of her eye. The catwalk slanted alongside the edge of the singleship's lifting surface. Where it crossed under the ship's nose, three suited

workpeople squatted beneath the flare of the airbreathers to
work on the everted rack of missiles.

Something about the missiles . . . an odd light playing around
their gold-plated needle noses, a kind of pointillist halo that
jabbed and prickled Dorthy's retinas.

No one else seemed to have noticed it, certainly not the
Witnesses who were working to disarm the missiles, but after
a moment, Dorthy felt familiar pressure inside her head. It was
the heavy presence of the Alea ancestor. It was she who was
seeing the fugitive sparkle. It was a quality like, yet not quite
identical to, that of certain marauder weapons, Dorthy thought,
and then realized that the thought, and the memory on which
it was based, were not her own. A little like the infolded
dimensionless webs which had wrapped suns before they had
flared, stuff that intersected at odd angles with the familiar
dimensions of the quotidian universe, weapons stripped down
to pure mathematics, idea become word become deed. . . .

The work crew had finished disarming the missiles. A suited
workperson was painting explosive gel around the rim of the
singleship's airlock. The neutrino scanner hung directly overhead, and the blond woman, Givy, was watching a little video
plate. The workperson stepped back and there was a muffled
crack and smoke defined the hatch's rectangle. Someone working a waldo jiggered the hatch plate out of the way, and two
workpeople ducked through the opening.

Dorthy forgot about the fugitive false memory. She watched
with Ang, with the dozen or so Witnesses who stood on various
gantries and platforms at various levels above the harshly lighted
docking bay, as two stretchers were taken into the ship to bring
out its crew.

Ang said, "You are sure, Dorthy, that you do not notice
anything strange?"

"I'm sure," Dorthy said. She sensed Ang's attention turn back
to the limp bodies on the stretchers, and realized that her Talent
was beginning to expand, just as if she had dropped a tablet of
counteragent. She knew then that the ancestral mindset wanted
her to be aware, wanted her to be ready. The subtle alteration
to the missiles had alerted it. Wherever the ship had been,
something had changed it.

And changed its passengers too, perhaps, although they looked quite harmless: a man and a woman, both in suit liners, both unconscious and securely strapped in their stretchers. The man's left arm was augmented. He'd torn away the sleeve of his liner in mechanic fashion, and the steel and clear plastic catenaries of his prosthesis glittered in the arclights.

One of the work gang ducked back inside the ship, dragging a heavy cable behind him; on the level sweep of the singleship's lifting surface, the others squatted around the stretchers, checking the vital signs of the unconscious pair. Givy was holding an oxygen mask to the woman's face.

On the platform, Dorthy said to Ang, "If you want me to know what happened, I can't read their minds from here." Adrenaline thrilled in her blood like a plucked steel wire; she could see that Ang was more interested in what was happening below than in her.

"We will give them a minute more," Ang said, leaning on the rail.

The woman on the stretcher began to stir. Just as Givy took away the mask and asked the woman who she was, something small and quick came out of the hatch. Dorthy saw it, and knew that no one else had. It skittered through curls of vapor, began to swing up a gantry support. Dorthy had a moment's clear view of a little machine with an armored carapace and spiderlike limbs before she lost it in glare and shadow.

The mechanic on the stretcher had opened his eyes. His augmented arm flexed against the straps. It quivered with effort and then seams tore and it reached across and its razor-sharp extensors sliced away the remaining restraints. The mechanic started to sit up and Ang, who had been about to say that it was okay, that they could go down, swallowed her words and shouted a warning to Givy. The blond looked around just as half the lights blew out in falling cascades of sparks. The mechanic rolled off the edge of the lifting surface into the heaving fogbank beneath the ship.

Dorthy took a step backward and grabbed the platform's manual control with her bound hands. She fingered her way down the switches, pressed one, then another.

The rail on which Ang was leaning withdrew; the platform began to swing up. Ang staggered and grabbed at Dorthy, who danced back into a corner. Without a sound, Ang fell backward off the platform. She landed on top of one of the work crew and sent him sprawling as the platform carried Dorthy up through light and darkness. Someone shouted her name, and she saw a guard on the far side of the ship raise his rifle as she came level with his perch. He shouted again. Hands still taped behind her back, Dorthy ran forward and leaped onto a walkway as the platform rose past it. She rolled, came up on her knees at the edge of the walkway, then threw herself forward as an oval section of the mesh floor flared cherry red and sagged, smoking hot fumes.

The guard shouted again, and Dorthy pushed to her feet and ran. She could feel the guard's cool steady attention centered on her own shoulder blades—as if the gyroscopically balanced rifle were twitching in the guard's loose grip as it locked onto her—and had time to think that perhaps this wasn't such a good idea after all, when the rest of the lights blew out and a great wind rose up in the darkness.

The emergency phosphors came on almost at once, but the guard's concentration had been broken. Dorthy ran through dim red glow, head down against a gritty gale. With her hands still bound behind her back she couldn't balance properly, kept banging into the walkway's rail. Someone was running hard along an intersecting walkway, trying to head her off, but she simply changed course, dodging around graving machinery hung over an empty launch cradle.

There was a glimpse of the singleship, no longer bedded in mist: someone or something had shut down the pressure curtain beneath it. Platforms were dipping toward it as half a dozen figures struggled up ladders and walkways amid a storm of scraps and litter.

Then Dorthy was running up a ramp of flexible mesh toward a dark access tunnel, where she knew no one was waiting to ambush her.

5

$$\overline{\overline{}}$$

SUZY CAME AWAKE TO THE STINGING TASTE OF COLD, dry oxygen. She was lying on a stretcher; there was a mask over her nose and mouth. Her sight swam with doubled images, was bordered with fluttering black. A line of blazing white lights high overhead. Railed platforms, girders. She felt as if she were tipping forward into this cathedral-like space. A suited figure bent over her, her own face distorted in the mirror of its visor. Suzy tried to say something but the mask wouldn't let her and then blackness sailed in and bore her away.

The second time, she was sitting in a metal chair with a light shining on her from above, the rest of the large room in deep shadow. There was a sour taste in her mouth, so bad she could feel it all the way down to her stomach. When she tried to move, she found that her forearms were strapped to the flat armrests of the chair. Her legs were taped together at the shins. Someone was sitting half a dozen meters away. His loose white clothes glimmered in the semidarkness.

Suzy said, "Is this what you do with everyone you pick up? This has got to be some kind of mistake, right?"

She was on board the *Vingança*. Had to be. Things were coming back to her. The spawn of Robot's rat-machine had fucked the singleship's lifesystem; she hadn't thought to put on her p-suit and she'd passed out. They hadn't been able to take over the ship's guidance controls, though, and her fly-by-eye course had brought it close enough to be picked up. At least the *Vingança* hadn't tried to blow her out of orbit, as they had back at the hypervelocity star, but that was all the good news there was.

265

The man in front of her leaned forward. She could hardly see him through the cone of light falling down on her. He said, "You know where you are."

Suzy said, "I've an idea." She was trying to figure out just where. One of the gymnasiums maybe.

"I do not mean the ship. I mean where the ship is, at the center of the Galaxy. Ah, you didn't know that, did you? And yet, you do not seem surprised."

"Machine said it was a place no one had ever seen before," Suzy said. She wondered where the fucker was. And Robot. . . . She said, "I guess he was right. You want to know *why* I'm here, I'll try and tell you. It's hard to explain, but I'll do my best. I mean, if you want to know." She suddenly realized how scared she was, worse than when the singleship had been dragged down into the pit in that moon. The unknown wasn't as frightening as knowing what people could do to other people—could do to her. She said, "You're not anything to do with the Navy, are you?"

The man said, "We are not interested in your motives, Suzy. Or those of your companions. Do you think that they matter to us? Do you think that the actions of an individual can make any difference to the evolution of the human race?"

She said, "I wouldn't know." She said, "Look, you know my name, you know I served in the Campaigns." She said, "BD Twenty, combat singleship. Flying right out of *this* ship. What can I tell you?" Sweat rolled between her breasts. The suit liner stuck to her back, her thighs. There was someone else in the room. When she held her breath, she could hear him. Maybe a meter in back of her, no more than two. She didn't dare try and look, she kept her eyes straight ahead. She said, "Really, I can tell you anything you want."

"Of course you can. But all we want is the truth, Suzy. Quickly and simply. We want to know where you have been, and what was done to you there. That's all."

Her eyes were getting used to the darkness. Suzy could see that he was an old guy, his white beard neatly trimmed, his white hair scarcely covering his scalp. Santa Claus in a toga. His left arm was held stiffly across his chest, as though it was strapped up.

She started to tell him about the endless beach and the fractal desert, the shadow dancers and the angels, but after a minute he held up his right hand, palm out, fingers spread. "You are not ready to tell us this. Not quite yet."

"Well, it's the truth. That's where we were, down inside that hole. That's what happened, man, whether you believe me or not."

"What is an angel?"

"I'm not sure. They were living there. Where we were."

"And where was that?"

"I don't know, not exactly. It looked like a beach, like in the tropics somewhere. But that was because the human part of Robot was dreaming it."

"This was a place, or a dream?"

"Sort of both, I guess. Machine said it was a kind of interzone between this universe and where the angels lived."

"But you don't know what the angels were."

"Not exactly. Like light. They were like light. But I don't know what they were."

"They told you they wanted you to do something for them."

"To stop the marauders. What they are doing, out here, is hurting the angels. The angels want it stopped. It's hard to get it straight in my head. The way I was told, it seemed like a suicide mission, so when I heard your transmission I headed right for you. I mean, where else was I going to go?"

The old man raised his right hand again, forefinger crooked. Someone Suzy hadn't even known was there (not the man at her back: he hadn't moved), a woman in issue coveralls with a big sparkly brooch pinned above her left breast, walked out of the shadows. She held a memotablet in front of the old guy's face. He said, "All right," and she stepped around his chair and stood behind him, one hand on his shoulder. "We don't have much time," the old man said to Suzy, "and we need to know if we are being told the truth."

"Hey, that's all I want to tell you."

"That is good. But, you see, we have to be sure of it. I'm ready now, Catarina," he said to the woman, and she helped him to his feet. He said to Suzy, "If it is any consolation, it is for the greater good."

"Now, hey. *Hey.* I told you—"

But he was walking away into the shadows, leaning on the arm of the woman. Suzy heard the man behind her and turned her head. One big hand clamped on her left shoulder; the other touched her cheek, ran the tip of a black cylinder down the line of her jaw. At first there was just a faint tingling: then it started to burn and she had to clamp her teeth together to stop from crying out.

The man came around and knelt in front of her. Brown eyes twinkling under a lined forehead, smile showing even white teeth. He looked like a priest, or a professor. He said, "Don't worry, little Seyoura. I'm not going to kill you."

6

==

THE BLUE WAS THE BLUE OF SUNLIT OCEAN, PATTERNED by the shadows of ragged formations of white cloud. The light was no longer the color of dried blood, but the rich glow of summer oranges. The probe, which had descended beneath the tracks which illuminated the spine's vast plain, was cruising a few thousand kilometers above an ocean that ran as straight as a highway toward an infinity where skeins of light tangled together in the atmosphere's haze. In the middle distance, the ocean was broken by brown and ocher shapes: continents as big as Jupiter, if that world could be skinned and pinned out like a butterfly in a dissecting tray.

The scientists were all talking at once, all except Abel Gunasekra, who simply stared into the tank, one hand curled under his chin. Talbeck stood back from the others and watched Gunasekra as much as the tank, letting the babble of speculation flow through him.

"G8 type spectrum. . . . We're, what, eight hundred billion

kilometers down the Spike now, thirty light-days? If those wave guides or whatever are channeling white light from the far end, and it's red when it reaches the shadow sphere, half a light-year along. . . ."

Jake Bonner said, "Quantum tunneling would do it. That's how the guides are radiating along their lengths. Losing shorter wavelengths first. It's about the equivalent insolation that Tau Ceti gives Elysium, will be like Earth in another five hundred billion or so klicks, I'll need to do a transformation. . . ."

Martins, the exobiologist, said, "I have a chlorophyll absorption line. Life, my friends!"

"Scattering puts the atmospheric pressure at about three-quarters equatorial sea level on Earth. There's nitrogen, oxygen, carbon dioxide, but what's that line here?"

"Helium, about half a percent. What the hell? The gravity's, what, 1.252 gee . . . if that's standard over the whole area, no way that much helium could be retained, without something generating it. Or, hey, unless the atmosphere is relatively new. . . . Any dating on it yet?"

"What about it, Valdez?"

"I can chop into the encrypted instrument package data streams, sure, but not without compromising the visibility of my feed."

"By compromise, you mean bring the Witnesses down? I'm not that keen to find out, not yet."

"Well, *I* am."

"Hey, Armiger, you're tired of living? You want something to do, calculate usable surface area."

"I already have," Armiger said, poker-faced. "Best maximum estimate, seven to the power twenty square kilometers. That's about half the total surface area, almost one and a half trillion Earths."

Martins said, "Christ. Seppo, is that *land* area?"

"Ocean and dry land. I haven't enough to work up a mapping algorithm yet."

Abel Gunasekra said quietly, "And they are starting to build a second hyperstructure."

There was a moment's silence, and then the scientists' chatter picked up again. But Talbeck wasn't listening to it any more.

He had what he wanted. The gateway, room for everyone alive to have his own Earth-sized empire. Now *here* was a cause to fight for!

He was so deep in thought that he did not notice that his servant had returned until she touched his arm. She held out a small pistol to him; there was fresh blood under her nails. Wonderingly, Talbeck started to take the weapon from her, just as a dozen half-naked men burst into the room.

They were the Navy officers the Witnesses had shanghaied to pilot the *Vingança* through the wormhole. Lieutenant Alverez was at their head. He was carrying a rifle, and cut off the scientists' babble of questions by firing a clip of flechettes into an instrument bench on the far side of the room.

After that there was only the sound of sparks fizzing in ruined circuitry.

"All right," Alverez said, grinning hugely. There was a fresh burn mapped in vivid red on his muscular abdomen and his black hair bushed above a bloody bandage around his forehead, but his voice was quite calm. "All right. Someone else came through the wormhole and the Witnesses took his ship aboard. He escaped. Now he's fucking up the *Vingança*'s systems."

Talbeck said, "Who is he?"

"Seyour Barlstilkin—" a brief ironic bow—"you are still alive. I am pleased to see it. Your servant killed the guard and opened the doors of our cells. This guy can get into any kind of computer, it seems. He got into your servant. He calls himself Machine, if it matters."

"There used to be an artist who sometimes called himself Machine," Talbeck said. Two things came together in his head: the betrayal by his co-conspirators, the singleship that had followed him to the hypervelocity star. "He worked in Urbis, on Titan. I sponsored some of his work, I believe."

"It is a very small universe," Alverez said. "That could be useful later, Talbeck. Now, gentlemen. I see that captivity has not hindered your research, but I must tell you that it is now at an end. The countermutiny has begun. I don't think the Witnesses know we've escaped yet; their security is laughable. But they'll know soon enough, because Machine is about to make his next move. I don't know how many of you have microgravity vacuum experience; those who don't may have to learn the hard way, buddied up with my men, here. As of this moment you're all conscripted."

"Now see here, Alverez," Seppo Armiger said. "We're all of us in the middle of the most exciting discovery since contact was made with the Enemy. The Witnesses are controlling a probe which is exploring the hyperstructure at the edge of the accretion disk. We can't afford to risk losing its data."

Alverez thrust the fat barrel of his rifle through the vision of infinite ocean in the tank, jammed its muzzle against Armiger's bare stomach. The scientist didn't move, and met Alverez's stare unflinchingly. "I like you," Alverez said, "so I hope you'll listen more closely."

Armiger said, "Perhaps it's you who ought to listen."

Jake Bonner cleared his throat nervously. "He's right, Lieutenant. This is no time to risk the ship in some silly squabble."

Alverez ignored Bonner. "This ship is a war zone, Dr. Armiger," he said. "As captain, I am empowered to conscript any able-bodied Federation citizen. You don't want to help, I can blow one of your fucking legs off. I'd rather not; you look like you could be useful."

"Will you guarantee us use of the other probes if we win?" Armiger asked.

Alverez smiled, and shouldered his rifle. "Of course. We're here to find the rest of the Enemy, after all. Once we've dealt with the Witnesses, I'll authorize whatever you need to find the Enemy. And you *will* find them, too, because I'm relying on it."

Talbeck saw in the Lieutenant something that had only previously been latent, hidden away under the dress uniform and the nitpicking etiquette of the wardroom. It was something every leader needed, the ability instantly to take the measure of a man and find a place for him in his plans.

Seppo Armiger smiled back. "We can do it," he said. "But I'd say your position is somewhat shaky whatever we find, Lieutenant. After all, you're as much a mutineer as any of the Witnesses."

One of the other officers laughed and said, "We're all mutineers."

Lieutenant Alverez said, "But you do understand that we are the good guys. And now no more talk. It is time to go."

7

DORTHY KNEW THAT THERE WAS ONLY ONE PLACE WHERE she could safely hide: the warrens of cabins and cubicles and corridors and commons in the accommodation modules. The Witnesses searched for her there, of course, but her Talent allowed her to evade them easily. She found a mirror and kicked it in, used one of the shards still stuck in the frame to saw through the plastic tape that bound her wrists.

Like all the other cabins in the module, this one was freezing cold and lighted only by a dull red emergency glotube, but because someone might spot the resultant power drain, Dorthy didn't dare switch on the environmental conditioning. She sat on the plastic chair and put her feet up on the bare frame of the bunk, stuck her hands between her thighs to keep them warm, and wondered what she could do now.

Her awakened Talent seemed to have stabilized. It was not out of control, although now that the adrenaline of her flight was wearing off, she began to wonder what would happen to her if the implant had been badly damaged or killed. To be unable to control her Talent would be like being unable to sleep, to dream. It would lead to hallucinations, to lesions in the cortex, to death.

Dorthy thought about it less calmly than she once would have. Although she had lived with that risk for most of her life, she had the month-old fetus in her womb to consider now. But she also realized all over again how much she missed using her Talent; those ten years in Navy custody had been like ten years of living with blurred vision and white noise in her ears. She could see again; she could hear.

She could see each of the half hundred human minds on board the ship. Most of them were clustered in two distinct areas that had to be the command blisters and the science module; only a few were scattered on the docks in the spine of the ship. None were close enough for her to gain anything but the grainiest impression. She was mostly aware of the overall gestalt where three, six, a dozen were gathered together: here a node of excited curiosity, there, and there again, a calm unquestioning joy, the same transcendental emotion she'd earlier noticed in Ang Poh Mokhtar.

But gradually she became aware of something else. Fleeting glimpses like the twinkling of the first stars seen from a planet's surface on a warm summer evening. . . . Or no, for they were so bright, like the fugitive microscopic fusion pinches generated by chance gravitational fluxes in the accretion disk.

They were like nothing she had ever seen before. Like end-on views of vast linear logic chains, or like glimpses of the precisely defined nanosecond pulses that were the machine equivalent (but no Talent could perceive the workings of machine intelligence) of the long, clumsy, raveling webs of human thought.

One dimensionless mote in particular glimmered and sparkled and twisted so brightly among the flickering candles of merely human minds that it drew her whole attention. *Here*, it called to her. *Here, here! Here I am!*

After a while, Dorthy got off the chair and sat zazen on the cold, dusty floor, a thin covering of resilient plastic over unforgiving hull metal. Of all the methods she had tried, Zen meditation, *Sessan Amakuki*, was for her the best way of focusing her Talent, narrowing it from the wide undefined field of empathy that touched all around her to the particular, the singular pattern of the individual that could be mirrored in her still center.

But the flickering trace did not become clearer as Dorthy's trance deepened. It remained a half-glimpsed mocking will-o'-the-wisp. Instead, the door of the room was pulled back and the Alea ancestor entered. Each hair of her thick black pelt ended in a clear refractive tip, gathering the cabin's dim red light into pinprick patterns of ruby and carnelian and garnet that swirled and sparkled with her least movement. Although her great, hooded head was bowed, it still brushed the ceiling. Within the shadow of the folds of naked, blue skin, her narrow fox-face was alive with joy. Her black lips wrinkled back from wet ridges of sharp-edged horn in an approximation of a human smile.

—My dear child. Something wonderful has come upon us. Come with me, now. There are people for you to meet.

As if in a dream, with no sense of wonder at the impossible strangeness of this apparition, Dorthy rose from the floor and followed the neuter female through the door into windy red glare.

Across the level stone flags of the platform, two human figures turned to her, silhouetted against the burning, black-flecked disk of the sun of P'thrsn.

8

AFTERWARD, THEY TOOK SUZY TO ONE OF THE CABINS and locked her in with a guard. The cabin had been stripped of everything but the chair on which the guard sat and the mattress on which Suzy lay, shivering in her suit liner. A couple of teeth were loose in her lower jaw. There was a hot cloud of pain in one ear, a constellation of burns down her arms where a catalytic lighter had been touched to her skin.

But worse than actual pain was memory of the little black stick—some kind of inducer that had fired the nerves under her skin wherever it had touched, jammed them full open in a wave of white-hot agony. The man had used it delicately, on different parts of her body, telling her what he was going to do, then asking her a question and doing it when she answered, and asking again. She'd told the truth, not because she wanted to, but because the pain didn't leave her room to think of anything else. Even when he'd finished, she'd kept talking in a desperate unconnected stream about the shadow dancers and the fractal desert and the golden city of the angels burning along the infinite horizon and Machine's betrayal, until he'd slapped her hard in the face and told her she could stop, they were done now.

That was what shamed Suzy, the way she'd just opened up. It was as bad as she'd imagined rape would be. It was like he had stuck his fingers in her head and smeared them all over the private place where she lived.

Suzy lay on the mattress and thought about that. She was trying to think about it objectively. About what it meant, not about what it had felt like. She wanted her anger to cool down, to contract to an icy star deep inside herself. She wanted, for once, to do the right thing at the right time. Because this time one of her dumb mistakes could kill her.

The guard was a young, plain, black woman with plump, pockmarked cheeks and a bush of wiry hair. She was a lot bigger than Suzy. She sat in her chair scrolling very slowly through a reading tablet. Sometimes she took out a pen and made a note on the tablet, then looked over the edge of it at Suzy. She had an audio spike in her ear; the pad of a throat mike was pasted just below the fold of flesh under her jaw. A pistol lay in her broad lap.

Suzy thought that if she got the chance, she could take the guard. The woman was bigger, but Suzy had her flying muscles. But if she did that, then she'd have to shoot the guard for sure, shoot the lock out, too. Make a lot of noise. And most likely the woman would call for help as soon as she got in trouble. Tear away the mike and grab the pistol at the same time? Sure.

There was a little metallic sound, a hollow click like a ball bearing dropping into a steel bowl. It came from the grill of the air duct in the wall above the guard's bushy hairdo. Suzy saw something move behind the grill, and then a line of red glowed on the bottom of the grill's mesh, ran up both sides and along the top. The little room filled with the smell of molten metal and the guard turned, rising from her chair, just as the grill fell to the floor and the thing behind it swung through. It clung to the grill's ragged edge with half a dozen spidery limbs while others waved in front of it. The guard brought up her pistol and the thing burned away the top of her head.

Suzy was jammed in a corner, her heels digging into the mattress. The guard had fallen back in the chair, her head forward to show the sticky char where the top of her head had been. The smell of burned hair and cooked meat made Suzy gag.

The machine swung out and landed beside her on the bunk. It was a baby rat-machine, a whole lot bigger than when Suzy had last seen one.

Suzy's first thought was to try and stomp on it, but the guard had had a pistol and she didn't even have shoes. Then she remembered what Robot had told her in the pedestrian tunnel in Urbis (when they'd been heading toward the spaceport in the aftermath of *Urban Terrorism*), that he had a little implanted transmitter to control and coordinate his machines.

She swallowed and said softly, "Hey. Remember me? Look, Robot, Machine, you know who these guys are? You know what they want? Look, can you talk through this thing? Or maybe get it to write something, just tell me you're okay."

The machine raised itself on the tips of half a dozen limbs. Suzy closed her eyes, opened them again when she felt something sharp and cold touch her ankle. The machine was sort of sitting back on its haunches by her feet, as if looking up at her.

Suzy said, "What I'd really like you to do is to get the door open. Can you do that? Listen, I've got an idea. I can pick up your helper here, hold it to the door. Then it could just burn out the lock. I mean, it's worth a try."

She nerved herself to touch the machine. It didn't stir, and she took hold of it. It was warm and surprisingly light. Something inside it vibrated; she could feel it in her fingertips.

And then she wasn't in the room anymore. She was kneeling on stone at the edge of some kind of platform hung over a mountainside. A vast, dim red sun swam at the horizon. So big that when she looked at one wavering edge she couldn't see the other; so dim she could stare squarely into it, see the seething granulation of its photosphere. An arc of black sunspots stretched halfway around its equator. Its red light shimmered in the air like a liquid, making the forests and plains far below look more black than green.

Suzy put out her empty hands to support herself, palms down on cold gritty stone. Wind blew up from craggy slopes of black lava, pushing back her hair. It smelled exactly like pine trees.

"Some view, all right," a voice said behind her. Suzy almost fell over the edge, she turned around so quickly. Robot added, "All it needs is a few twisted pines and maybe a ruined mausoleum or two to turn it into a Piranesi print."

The feeling she had, after the initial moment of astonishment, the sudden thudding of her heart, was halfway between intense fear and intense happiness. She said, "It's really you! I mean it's really you talking, not that thing you have in your head. You're awake again!"

"Machine's busy somewhere else," Robot said. Like Suzy, he was wearing only a suit liner. The left sleeve was torn away to show his augmented arm. Wind blew ratty blond hair back from his thin white face.

Suzy rose and smiled (yes: happiness), took a step toward him. "How did you do this? We back in that place with the angels, but you're imagining it differently?" She laughed. "No, you'd be asleep then, right? Shit, man, I'm glad to see you again."

And then they were together, her face smashed tight against quilted material over Robot's bony chest, her arms around his waist, and, after a moment, his augmented arm around her shoulders.

Suzy said, "I was locked up in some room, and one of your machines came and killed the guard. Now I'm here. I don't think I'm crazy. I mean, you feel real to me?" Her jaw wasn't hurting anymore, she realized, and she broke the embrace and pulled up the sleeve of her liner—found only unblemished skin. "See, this fucking guy burned me, right here. But now I'm okay, and I know I'm not crazy. So what the fuck is this, Robot?"

"It's a place where we can meet a couple of other people," Robot said, smiling back, showing his brown, gappy teeth. He pushed hair out of his eyes. "I learned a lot while I was away, Suzy, how to pull together stuff like this. It's mostly someone else's memory, but I retranscribed it. And my little pet, something was done to it by the angels. All its children are a little like those old, illegal AIs, artificial intelligences. But the difference is I can control them. Things I've been doing, I didn't even dream were possible. It's sort of hard to explain to you, the way I feel about it. I know you don't like me in machine mode, but this kind of dream is more real to me now than the real world that Machine takes care of."

"So this is all your dream, and I'm still locked up in that fucking room."

"Sure. It won't be hard to get you out of it, but first we have to talk with these people. Decide what to do. There was a mutiny on the *Vingança,* before it went through the wormhole. The Navy isn't running it now."

"That I figured for myself. I guess I got us into deep shit."

"It doesn't matter. It might work out better this way."

"Yeah. Well, thanks. Who are these people you want to talk with?"

Robot pointed across the huge stone platform. There was a black line hanging in the air. "Here they are," he said.

The black line unfurled. Suzy glimpsed a bare room like the one she'd been locked in, but illuminated by red light even duller than that of the huge sun. Then, one after the other, two people stepped through.

For a moment, Suzy thought one of them was a big man wrapped in some kind of black cape, hood up around his face. Then she thought it was some kind of animal, like a bear, maybe. But bears didn't have legs as long as that, and they didn't have a second pair of arms, wizened and shrunken and clasped across their chests. Nor did they have a fleshy hood of bare blue skin flared out around their faces, or such large, knowing eyes.

Suzy took a step back and then remembered how close she was to the edge. If she fell, would she wake up, as from a dream? Or would she die, be found in the locked cabin all bloody, with every bone in her body broken? Robot put a hand on her shoulder and said that it was all right.

"What is it?" Suzy whispered fiercely. "Jesus Christ, Robot!"

The other person who'd stepped through the doorway, a woman, said, "She is a neuter female Alea." The woman was maybe fifty centimeters shorter than Suzy and maybe half a dozen years older, dressed in uniform gray coveralls. Black hair growing out from a crewcut, round face looking as if it had been freshly scrubbed, black eyes halved by their epicanthic folds. Behind her, the doorway furled up and became a line. The line shrank into its center and winked out. The woman stepped past the creature. She was smiling. "You're the two who were on that singleship. What I'd like to know is what you're doing in my head."

"If this is *your* dream," Suzy said, "you're welcome to it, especially that thing there."

Robot's grip on Suzy's shoulder tightened a little. He said, "We aren't in your head, Dr. Yoshida, although I admit to having borrowed this place from you. But since it was put there by someone else in the first place, I hope you don't mind. I've linked us all up so we can talk."

Suzy asked, "That really is one of the Enemy? Does it talk?"

The woman, Yoshida, said, "It's an Alea, but not really an Enemy. She's been dead a long time, almost a million years. She, and this place, both come from a memory that was put deep inside my brain by the last of her descendants, on P'thrsn. And that's where we are now, on P'thrsn as it was when she was alive."

"I have already been talking with her," Robot said. "It was a shock when I accessed you, finding her there."

"I bet," Suzy said. She couldn't take her eyes off the Enemy. Alea neuter female or whatever you called it, it was still the Enemy. Big eyes, set close together in a narrow face, looked back at her. The folds of skin wrapped around its head were naked and blue, like a turkey vulture's wattles. There were *claws*, for Christ's sake, tipping the three fingers of each of its hands. Mouth full of saw blades, like something out of a horror story. *All the better to eat you with.* "Jesus Christ, why do we need to talk with this thing?"

Robot and Yoshida ignored Suzy's remark, which only made her more scared, more angry.

The Yoshida woman said to Robot, "If you got to the neuter female, you did more than the Navy ever could. Who are you? Wherever we are, I can't use my Talent here."

That was what was familiar about Yoshida, Suzy decided. She'd met Talents before, when Duke Bonadventure had been showing off his combat flying team to guests. The way they looked at you, so sly, so superior, so above it all.

"I am Robot, an artist and a criminal. My friend is Suzy Falcon, a combat singleship pilot. Both of us out of Titan, via Heaven, bound we know not where. One thing we do know, we've been entrusted with a mission against the marauders. We've been given a weapon against them."

Suzy said, "And I still think we've been set up for some sort of kamikaze stunt. If those angels are so superior, why is it down to us?"

"Suzy, I explained. They've evolved. They can't exist in the Universe any more than a soap bubble can exist on the surface of the sun."

"The secret history," Yoshida said, turning to the neuter Alea. It was twice her height, but somehow she didn't seem dominated by it. "You were right about the paradigm. Intelligent races must have been forced to evolve all over the Galaxy, to save it from the marauders. These angels, they must have been the ones who abandoned the technologies the marauders found. They must have been the ones who infected you with the intelligence paradigm, the template."

Robot said, "They went away. They left the Universe for a place more suited to them. They didn't know or they didn't bother to think that others would come after them. They'd explored the whole Universe—it was so much smaller then— and found no other intelligent species. They thought that they were alone and they turned inward, developed a better way of existence. They went away, and abandoned the machines they used to open a path from here to there."

His eyes were closed and he had a saintly look again, like light was glowing underneath his pale, blue-veined skin. He said, "And then the Alea came along. The Alea were only intelligent when they needed to be, when their sun flared. And when it finally grew too unstable, when the Alea fled to the core stars, some of them found the abandoned technology. The way the marauders are using it is threatening the interzone, and what's beyond it. It means the gates from here to there can't be closed off. The angels can't come back to stop the marauders, and they can't go on. It's all coming clear now."

Yoshida said, "If these angels went away, then who set the paradigm loose, who made other species evolve intelligence? Who launched the hypervelocity star?"

Robot said, his eyes still closed, "Not everything is clear. It's important for some reason that I don't know everything, not yet. I do know that the hypervelocity stars—many more than one, each with a wormhole gate orbiting it—were launched in the confusion of the war between the marauders and the other Alea. One star for each intelligent species, to bring them here. . . . You see, Dr. Yoshida, we've been given a weapon to use against the marauders. I know how to use it, too. I just need to deliver it." He opened his eyes, looked at the Yoshida woman, looked at the tall Alea.

"That's great," Suzy said. She had been growing more and more impatient, more and more angry, during Robot's blissed-out rap. She said, "I just don't see why we have to get involved in this. People, I mean. Humans. It's history you said. Someone else's history. What's it to us? We're supposed to be so grateful the angels gave us fire we rush to fight their war for them?"

Yoshida said, "I can give you a reason. It was something I learned on P'thrsn. The marauders can detect the use of phase graffles. It's why the Alea we fought never used them. Every time a ship uses its phase graffle, it creates a discontinuity that propagates through contraspace. In fifty years or so, discontinuities from the first phase graffles will reach the core. I used to think that it would take a hundred more years for the marauders to travel back through contraspace to the Federation, that we'd have plenty of time to face up to them. But the wormholes cut that down to a matter of hours. You were a singleship pilot, Suzy. You fought against the Enemy. If the marauders aren't neutralized now, in a century and a half they'll be sacking Earth, Elysium, everywhere. I don't want war, and not just because I know humanity wouldn't stand a chance against the marauders. What was given to you and your friend can prevent war without creating war."

Suzy looked at Yoshida, at the Alea towering over her. The woman had balls, Suzy had to give her that, even if she did have absolutely the wrong attitude. But with that thing in her mind, who could blame her? Like Robot and the angels. Suzy thought, *I'm the only one here who hasn't been screwed up. I'm the only one who can do it right.*

Robot said, "You don't have to go, Suzy. I guess I can find another singleship pilot on the *Vingança.*"

"I can fly," Yoshida said. "At least, I ran my own research ship."

"Bullshit," Suzy said. "Anyone can fly a ship from A to B, but it takes a little bit more than that in combat. And hell, Robot, where are you going to find someone who isn't a babbling fanatic who thinks the marauders are Jesus Christ's Daddy?"

"There are Navy personnel," Robot said, smiling.

"Yeah. They're gonna listen to you, man, but only if you cut your hair and work your way up through the ranks. I was in the fucking Navy. I know."

Robot said, "Are you saying you'll do it after all?"

Suzy felt very cool now. Her anger collapsed down inside her, into a smooth ball as dense as a neutron star.

"I know why I'm doing it," Suzy said, "and it's not for those glittery angels of yours." Save the human race? Right. They'd put her on front page of every history book for the next million years. But she knew that she was going to do it her way, not theirs. She just had to hope that Yoshida had been telling the truth, that she really hadn't been able to read minds in the shared dream. She said, "Just get me out of that cell, man, and let me get my ship back. That's all I ask. I made a mistake; I admit that. Now let me do some good."

9

WITH ALVEREZ AT THEIR HEAD, THE RAMSHACKLE PARTY of scientists and rebel Navy officers moved quietly through a long, narrow, mesh-floored tunnel, passing at regular intervals arched junctions into other tunnels that sloped down or up into the ship's various modules. They were heading for the maintenance section in the keel forward of the command blisters. Where, Alverez had said, there was all kinds of shit they could use when the time came. The Witnesses might control the ship now, he'd said, but they certainly did not know her the way he did. And besides, when this guy Machine was through, all they'd need do would be carry out a simple mopping up operation.

Talbeck made sure that he kept to the rear of the ragtag war party. His servant walked beside him and, in response to his subvocalized questions, pressed shapes against his wrist with her cold, bloodstained fingers.

Yes, she told him, someone called Machine had told her what she must do. He had been speaking for Talbeck, she claimed. That was why she had obeyed him, killed the guard and set the officers free. She did not know what Machine was going to do to the ship, nor did she know where he had come from. But Machine knew where Dorthy Yoshida was, she added. He said that he would make sure that she was safe.

Talbeck thought about that. There was only one way of escape from the *Vingança* that Dorthy would automatically run to if she had the choice. It was time to cut loose.

Gunasekra was lagging behind the others, too. He told Talbeck, "This is not what I had in mind."

"You were going to tell me something, before the probe started sending back those pictures."

283

"It seems unimportant at the moment. You said that you know this Machine person."

"I believe that one of my trust funds gave him a grant once upon a time. I probably spoke with him for five minutes at some reception or other, on Urbis." Talbeck had slowed his pace, and the rest of the party had drawn ahead, passing out of sight as the tunnel sloped up beyond an arched junction. "He was planning a work called *Urban Terrorism*, the kind of challenging, disruptive work I find exciting. We will turn off here, Professor. I have this pistol, you see. I'm sure you won't do anything foolish."

Gunasekra looked calmly into Talbeck's ruined face. The servant had taken hold of his arm, but he was pretending not to notice. "I find any kind of violence distasteful, Seyour Barlstilkin."

"I'm pleased to hear that. That isn't my fight, either. I already have a ship. Quickly now, before we're missed."

Talbeck let the servant lead the way. One of the things he had done while waiting for something to happen, back at the hypervelocity star, was have her computer hack into the *Vingança*'s systems and download a complete set of schematics. They went through a hatch into the service shafts, followed a catwalk under color coded piping, around the omega-shaped loops of heat distribution pipes.

"I have no quarrel with the Navy, or with the Witnesses," Talbeck said. "For me, they were a means to an end. I've seen what I was looking for, and now it's time to go back to Earth, to spread the good news."

"I am to be your hostage, Seyour Barlstilkin?" Gunasekra was taking it very calmly.

"You'll tell them, won't you, Professor? You'll tell them all you've seen, when we return. The hyperstructure, the trillions of kilometers of territory ripe for exploration. The Federation is already having trouble controlling the trickle of migration to the half dozen new worlds opened up since the Alea Campaigns. This will be the beginning of an unstoppable torrent."

"That is what you want? To claim the hyperstructure Spike for yourself? You are very ambitious, Seyour Barlstilkin, but you will forgive me for saying that no one could be *that* ambitious. And there is the problem of the marauders, besides."

"If I had any claim over the Spike, I would gladly give it away. All I want to do is let people know what is here. The rest will follow. An end to Earth's domination. It is a historical relic. It should have ended a century ago."

"Dear me, I think that you will speak more convincingly about these things than I ever could."

"I'm a criminal," Talbeck said cheerfully. "I left the Solar System with the RUN Police in hot pursuit. By now, I should think that they have sequestered everything I own. Or everything I've allowed them to know about, at any rate. But you, Professor, will be listened to. You are my witness."

"You are very certain we will return safely. I wish I shared your confidence."

The servant was undogging a hatch. It opened onto a platform high above the graving docks in the ship's keel. Talbeck put his hands on the platform's flimsy rail, looked left and right. His servant had done well. Most of the launch cradles were empty, dark pits overhung by silent machinery, although, some way to the stern, batteries of arc lights glared down on a matt black singleship. But directly below the platform, rising out of cluttered shadow, was the scarred nose cone of his modified cargo tug.

10

ROBOT AND SUZY FALCON VANISHED AS ABRUPTLY AS burst soap bubbles, and Dorthy was left with the neuter female in the dream of ancient P'thrsn. And then the mists came down and Dorthy was alone. Smooth stone bitterly cold under her bare feet, calm whiteness circling her. There was a way out; there had to be a way out; but Dorthy could not find it. She knew that somewhere there was a door, but it was always just beyond the edge of her sight.

"I know what you're trying to do." Dorthy's words sank into white silence, but suddenly the tall black shape of the neuter female loomed out of the mist. Dorthy could feel traces of the other Alea mindsets crowding all around her.

She was the center of their cold attention.

She said, "I know you're trying to break out, but you're all ghosts. Less than ghosts. Nucleotides strung like beads on a wire." For a moment she thought she saw the strings of mRNA jostling in the neurons at the basement of her brain. Long bristling snakes uncoiling through ribosomal templates. Code into memory, word into thought into deed. She pressed the heels of her palms against her eyes and said loudly, "This is in my head. Not in any computer, not on P'thrsn. My head, mine!"

Compassion, concern.

Dorthy turned, but the door moved as quickly as she did. She looked up at the neuter female. Her hands were clenched so tightly that her fingernails would have drawn blood, had she not been in the habit of biting them to the quick.

"I know what you're trying to do. I won't have it."

—We must act now. The marauders are here.

"You were put in my head so you could fight your silly war? It was over more than a million years ago."

—No. Our retreat was a setback, but now we have returned to the core in you, my child.

"I'm human. I wasn't hatched, I was born."

—Yes. And all humans are our children. We know now what we only suspected before, that we were the unwitting cause of the kindling of intelligence in your species.

"And you want to protect us because of that? Then why are you doing this to me?"

Dorthy could hardly see the neuter female now. Mist flowed in, softening, erasing.

—We need to ride your body to act in the real world.

"No!"

For an instant the mist thinned a little, but then its whiteness bore down upon her. Dorthy fell to her knees, and continued to fall, tumbling through white void. Terror squeezed her shut like an eyelid. For a moment her Talent let her see the sparse constellation of human minds aboard the *Vingança,* scattered more widely than seemed possible. Without direction, she desperately dived toward them, and then she was kneeling in the cold redlit cabin, bloody spittle spilling from her lips.

There was someone with her, the man from the common dream, the one who had called himself Robot. He helped her sit up, held a paper cup of water to her lips.

"Thanks," Dorthy said, and drank greedily. The flat taste of the water, the pain of her bitten tongue, helped her concentrate. Her consciousness was a thin membrane stretched over a seething void. One lapse, and the Alea mindset would smother her thoughts like oil spreading over water.

Robot said, "It looked like you were having a fit." As in the dream, he was very tall and very thin, wearing only a suit liner. He was propping her up with his augmented arm. He smelled strongly of sweat. He said, "I'll bet that Alea female was giving you trouble. Am I right? But don't you worry, you're back in the real now."

"If my Talent hadn't been working, I wouldn't have found my way back. I suppose she needed to use it, and that was her mistake. I think I can keep control."

"That's good, because later on you can bet we're gonna need what she knows. Can you get up? That's good, we've got some traveling to do."

Dorthy tried to get the answer out of Robot's head, but the flow of his thoughts was like nothing she had ever seen before. A swirling rush interrupted by great gaps, a torrent filled with blank spaces. It was as if someone had tunneled all through his brain. She said, "Where's Suzy Falcon?"

"That's just it. We've got to get to the singleship before she does. And that's not going to be easy, after what Machine did."

They were walking quickly through narrow redlit corridors. It was so very quiet.

"Machine?"

"The other part of me, except he's not in my head anymore. He's downloaded himself into the control systems, broke up the ship. That's why we have to hurry. I'm worried Suzy will get there before us and do something stupid."

"Against the marauders? Do we even know where they are?"

"On that real big structure, at the edge of the accretion disk. Your passenger can tell us exactly. That's what I'm hoping anyhow."

"I don't know if I could ask her, not without losing control."

"But if it came to it you could do it. Here we are."

It was an airlock.

Robot said, "I told you, Machine broke up the ship. The Navy people are fighting the Witnesses and I had a time getting from the place I was to here without being shot up. And now we have to get to the main part of the ship. The keel. That's where the singleship is."

They suited up inside the lock, powered suits with heavy, clumsy radiation armor, and cycled through. Dorthy's Talent was still at full strength, and the urgency that drove Robot was contagious. Still, she paused at the sill of the hatch in wonder, seeing against the ultraviolet glory of the vast braided river of infalling gases the sharp-edged silhouettes of two dozen modules slowly drifting away from the *Vingança*'s long spine.

Robot's gloved hand clumsily grappled hers and drew her out; his other hand snapped a tether to her suit's utility belt. There was so little light that she didn't see the sled until her boots hit it. It was no more than a mesh platform over a frame holding a gas tank with a universal valve. Robot snapped the other end of Dorthy's tether to the sled's central rail and grabbed the control stalk. Silently, they began to fall toward what was left of the *Vingança*.

Robot had suggested they keep radio silence, in case Witnesses overheard them, but they could talk through a plug-in com line. Robot told Dorthy about the angels again, about the place between universes where they lived. Dorthy managed to glimpse a few of the strange, fantastic images that whirled through the chaos of his mind. The beach he had dreamed into being. The infinitely braided patterns of the fractal desert. The burning angels. She asked if the angels' weapon would destroy the marauders, and wondered if it was her question or the neuter female's. No, the membrane which divided her passengers from herself was still intact. She could feel them, though, stirring in the smooth pathways of her limbic cortex like monsters patrolling the depths of a blood-red ocean.

She had missed Robot's answer, and asked him to repeat it. He said, "The angels told Machine it would neutralize the processes the marauders had stolen."

"Stop creation," Dorthy murmured.

Robot hadn't heard her. She saw his arm come up, pointing at the silhouette of the *Vingança*'s tapering spine. "Sweet Jesus, you see that?"

She saw it with his eyes before she saw it herself. A black leaf shape flew out of the midsection of the *Vingança* on a burst of white fusion flame. It drifted for a few moments and then its reaction motor ignited again, scratching a bright line across the accretion disk's blue glare that swiftly dwindled to a star. And the star began to fade.

"Fucking Suzy Falcon," Robot said. "Now what are we going to do?"

It was the singleship which had been captured by the Witnesses. Armed with the abstract weapon of the angels, it was aimed at the perimeter of the accretion disk, at the vast dwelling place of the marauders.

11

S UZY HAD COME TO A POINT THAT WAS NOT EXACTLY exhaustion but where nothing could surprise her any more. One moment she was in the shared dream or whatever it was: the next, back in the cell with the dead guard and the smell of burned meat. The cabin's door was open and rat-machine was in her hand and, without thinking, she'd flipped it against the wall as hard as she could. That broke most of its limbs, but it managed to sear her knuckles with a laser pop before she delivered the *coup de grace* with the butt of the guard's pistol.

And then, just that like, she was free.

It turned out that the Witnesses had held her in a cabin of the module of the *Vingança* she knew best of all, the singleship pilots' quarters. The room where she'd been interrogated had been the gymnasium, stripped back to the bulkheads, where she'd once spent hours pounding round and round an artificial grass track, exactly half a kilometer a lap.

Oh Christ, it would all crash down on her if she let it. Her steward shaking her awake. Being fitted into her ship's holster with the steak breakfast heavy in her stomach and her fear a hollow bubble floating in her throat. Waiting in near darkness with headup displays printing status indicators in her head while she waited for the drop, the bone-crushing kick of the ship's strap-on boosters. No, she wouldn't have it back, couldn't have it back, not now.

Her built-up shoulders hunched, straining the seams of her suit liner, she padded barefoot down corridors that were familiar as soon as she saw them. She carried the dead guard's pistol in her left hand, holding it just below her line of sight. The fingers of her right hand were already swelling from the burn the baby rat-machine had given her, a bad deep burn that was beginning to hurt like hell, worse than anything the interrogation had inflicted.

Every so often Suzy felt a stir of vibration grow and fade beneath her bare feet, as if a giant were trying to stalk her softly. She was so nervous she was like to jump out of her own skin. Each corner, she ducked down and stuck her head and the snub barrel of the pistol around to scope the next move. One thing that kept her going was the hope she'd get the guy who'd mind-fucked her. She saw no one at all in the narrow, dimly lighted corridors, but it still took her half an hour to move the short distance from the cabin to the nearest emergency lock.

Suzy began to feel a little better once she was inside the cramped, coffin-sized lock. She'd prised up the panel outside and pulled the override circuit, dogged the door down on the inside. If anyone came along now, it would take ten minutes at least to get into the lock, and by then she'd be gone.

She pulled the big red throw down to its first notch—she had to put the pistol down because it took both hands to move the throw, and she winced as inflamed skin broke open and spilled clear, sticky fluid over the knuckles of her right hand. The lock's rack slid open in front of her. She stepped right into the p-suit it held, a big clumsily-armored job, servos swelling the joints of its limbs. She bit her lip as she worked her hands down stiff sleeves into the gloves, but she had to move fast now; pulling the throw would have lighted an indicator on the main boards for anyone to see. And there was the dread that somehow Machine had got into all the ship's systems, that he could somehow stop her.

She got her gloved right hand free of the rack, working hard against the resistance of the suit. Sweating with the pain of the burn, she set the heel of her palm against the throw, pushed it down to its second stop.

Something hummed at her back as the rack closed up the suit's double seam. The helmet came down; Suzy pulled in her chin to clear the rim. Thump at her back as the LSP frame clamped on, then the hiss of cool metallic air. Its dry tang filled her nostrils. Vibration over her entire body as the armored suit's servos powered up. Now she could move easily inside its cumbersome embrace. Amber figures ghosted across her sight, the suit's circuit telling her everything was normal.

Little silicon pads in the fingertips of the suit's gloves gave some semblance of touch feedback. Suzy felt the throw bar ease a notch in her gloved grip, bore down again, yelling to ride out the pain, her voice loud in the helmet. The lock's outer hatch blew open. She kicked with the sudden outrush of air, flew out of the frame and through the hatch into raw space.

Disorientation swept through her like a wave, and then she was on top of it, riding it. She pulled the reaction pistol from the suit's utility belt, squeezed off a measured squirt to slow her drift out from the ship's skin. Turned her head this way and that in the helmet, looking, measuring.

The module curved away beneath her boots. She saw it mostly as a dimensionless outline against the frozen billows of the shell of gas clouds hung at vast distances beyond the accretion disk's ultraviolet haze. The fuzzy points of birthing stars clustered here and there. The double spheroid of the wormhole planetoid and the dim red disk of its star were shadowed against the sullenly glowing traceries too, small as Suzy's gloved hand.

At her back, a river of deadly blue radiance filled half the sky, swirling downward to its invisible vanishing point. She didn't care to look at it, fearing it could burn out her eyes despite the helmet's filters. She imagined that she could feel the inexorable tug of the black hole, a pressure centered between her kidneys.

Now that she had a handle on where she was, she used the reaction pistol again, started to move at an angle above the module. Its curve was mostly defined by sparse strings of red guide lights, more and more coming into view as she moved away from it. The rest of the ship was a strangely long time in coming into view. And when it did, it was a long way away, and she saw that all of the modules, more than two dozen, had split away from the spine. It didn't surprise her. Maybe nothing could, anymore. It was like being in a saga.

Breaking up the ship had to be Machine's move. And he'd known where she was; he'd wanted her out of the way, in limbo. Suzy bared her teeth inside her helmet. She'd done the right thing. Machine, Robot, that Yoshida woman, none of them could be trusted. Yoshida had the *Enemy* in her head, for Christ's sake, what could you expect?

Suzy was far enough above the ship to see it all. Every one of the modules had blown off, leaving the keel's long spine bare, apart from the bulky drive units at its stern. She changed her course again, taking a long shallow angle toward the bare keel, aiming between two boxy, slowly tumbling modules. One was venting a huge cloud of some vapor that glittered as it dissipated into vacuum and the shadows of suited figures suddenly swarmed through this fugitive glitter. Suzy glimpsed an eye-hurting thread of light, then one of the modules split apart, ragged halves trailing debris as they spun away from each other. A particle beam pistol, firing stripped hydrogen nuclei at light speed. People out there were serious. Suzy wondered if they were Witnesses or the Navy, not that it made any difference.

She was very close to the wreckage now. Little knots of struggle scattered in the widening gap. Suzy called up the overlay, but less than half the figures had readable identity tags. The rest were little blurs of light: they'd be Navy personnel, for sure. So Machine had freed them, too. Vector readings showed that most were more or less at rest with respect to the ship, but someone was climbing up toward Suzy.

Suzy used her gas pistol to build up delta vee as the Witness—his tag named him as Zia Al Qumar—grew remorselessly closer. For a moment, Suzy thought she was going to slip past, but then something wrenched her ankle and she started to spin.

It was a tether. Its flexible tip whipped around the cleated boot of her left foot, then stretched to curl around her calf, working higher with blind persistence. She could feel it tighten against the suit's stiff material. The blade of the multitool from Suzy's utility belt wouldn't cut it. At every revolution she glimpsed tumbling modules and wreckage and the hand-to-hand fighting, the stripped keel of the *Vingança* against glowing gas clouds, the Witness who'd snared her. He was reeling himself up the tether.

"Stop it," Suzy told the suit. "Just stop it!"

The bland voice of the suit's circuit told her the instruction was incomplete.

"The rotation. Stop the rotation." She had closed her eyes. The spinning was making her dizzy.

It wanted her to specify rest coordinates.

"How the fuck do I know! The ship, bring me to rest with respect to the ship."

—No loran beacon has been located. Ranging identifies three structures with higher than seventy percent probability of being a vessel. Please specify rest coordinates.

The tumbling modules were confusing the suit's simple, linear mind. Suzy opened her eyes to the dizzy whirl of stars, ship, gas clouds. Headup radar told her the Witness was less than a hundred meters away and growing larger with each revolution. If she was going to do anything, she'd have to do it herself.

She started to bring up the reaction pistol. The tether around her leg tightened even further. Next moment the Witness crashed into her.

He grabbed one of her boots, scrambled clumsily up her, jacked out her suit's servos. Instantly, it was as if Suzy had fallen into a gravity well five times as steep as Earth's. The man's breath was loud in her ears; he'd tapped into her suit's transceiver. He demanded to know who she was, and Suzy paused for only a second before telling him. After all, the Witnesses wanted her alive, or they'd have killed her when they'd done with their questioning.

He told her to relax. "I can get you to safety, Seyoura Falcon. There is no need for you to be out here. You should activate your identity tag, you could get hurt otherwise."

"I was in the crew accommodation module. Woman guarding me said we should get out when it cut loose, but I don't know where she went after we did. Can't you switch my suit back on?"

"Better for you to let me take charge, Seyoura," Zia Al Qumar said. It was the voice of reason, the voice she'd always hated, the voice of an owner to the owned. She was only a woman, so she needed protection whether she wanted it or not.

The Witness released the tether and spun her around, reaching for the D-ring on her utility belt. Suzy concentrated all her will on moving her left arm, on bringing the reaction pistol to bear. The man saw what she was doing, moved to take the pistol away from her. Just as his glove closed around it, Suzy used the last of her strength to press the ignition trigger, working against the suit's dead resistance so convulsively that her index finger popped out at the knuckle.

Through a red wash of agony she saw the Witness spin away from her, chest of his white suit scorched, his arms and legs waving. She was spinning slowly in the other direction. Sweating with pain, she transferred the pistol to her burned right hand, terrified that she might let go now that there was no feedback from the suit's servos. She didn't dare try and reach around and switch the suit back on; probably couldn't, anyway. Every time she saw the wrecked module she fired a short burst of gas, fingers cramping with the effort needed to work the trigger, until at last she was no longer tumbling.

Now Suzy was moving slowly away from the fighting, slowly closing on the *Vingança*'s bare keel. The half dozen command blisters were like beads shaken from the very end of the long spine. Even as she watched, the center of one of the blisters started to glow with white heat: someone had turned a laser on it. Then the keel eclipsed everything.

She turned so her boots were toward it, tried as best she could to flex her knees inside the suit's dead weight, began to kill her momentum with brief puffs of her reaction pistol. Even so, she rebounded straight away when she hit, flipped onto her belly. Thinking *the hell with elegance*, she shot one last burst of gas and landed on all fours, gloves sliding over hull metal, both hands hurting badly, until she found purchase.

She was clinging by her fingertips to the edge of a docking hatch, five light-days above the black hole at the center of the Galaxy.

The rest was easy. She walked across the hull on the tips of her fingers and toes until she found an airlock, pulled up the handle and rotated it. The hatch hummed beneath her and then it slid back and she fell through into red light, bounced off the wall and found the throw bar, slammed it down. The hatch slid shut and she was buffeted by a gale of air.

She was in.

The docks that ran the length of the keel were under pressure, but lighted only by dim emergency lights, no brighter than full moonlight on Earth. There was no generated gravity. It was very cold. Suzy had left the crippled suit in the lock. Freezing metal stung her fingertips (she'd popped her index finger back into joint, but it was sore as hell) as she maneuvered through the tangle of girders and winch braces and servo housings above the graving docks.

Most of the launch cradles were empty. There were a handful of surface-to-orbit tugs, a couple of sleek combat singleships, and the biggest drone Suzy had ever seen, long sensor booms folded along its black thorax like the antennae of a wasp. But she knew what she wanted, and knew where it was even before she saw it. Its launch cradle the focus of a dozen overlapping arc lights, her ship seemed to float at the bottom of a pool of light.

A single guard hung in a zero gee web by a bank of flatscreen monitors. He had a tanglewhip thrust through the belt of his coveralls, a pistol in a holster strapped above his heart. Suzy clung by her fingertips to a cableway a dozen meters above, moving her head back and forth to disperse the fog of her breath. She still had the reaction pistol, but in here it was as much use as a child's balloon. Sneak up on him . . . sure, and get wrapped in thread and maybe blown away for good measure.

She watched the guard watching his monitors, which were showing the fighting outside the keel, among the slowly tumbling, fragmenting modules. Watched a long time, frustration twisting in her chest like a kinked rope, until she realized that there'd always been weapons here, if one looked at them the right way.

She couldn't use the plugs because she wasn't a mechanic, didn't have a mechanic's augmented arm. But there were backup manual controls, a joystick for controlling gross motion, a kind of glove of flexible plastic mesh with silver hoops at the knuckles and finger joints and a thick braided cable linking it with the machine. Right-handed, of course. Suzy couldn't help making a noise as she drew the glove over her raw, blistered knuckles, but the guard was engrossed in the monitors and didn't look up until the grapple started to swoop down into the pit.

If he had thought to roll under the singleship's launch cradle, he might have escaped. But he kicked out of the web and shot across the mesh platform, reaching for the holster on his chest as the grapple swooped to follow him, big talons opening (high above, on the shadowy catwalk, Suzy flexed her fingers) like the petals of a predatory flower. The guard got his pistol out, but then he saw what was about to happen and grabbed mesh with his free hand and pulled himself sideways just as the talons of the grapple (Suzy cried out with the pain as she made a fist) clashed together where he'd just been.

The grapple swung back and up, talons opening again as the guard brought up his pistol, braced his right wrist with his left hand, and fired.

Light and noise filled the pit like a stroke of lightning. The beam, narrow as a scribed line, bright as the Sun, missed Suzy by meters. But still its heat seared her face, its light blinded her.

Blind, shaking, she swept the grapple down, squeezed her fingers together. The guard's choked scream was louder than the sudden gale that howled around Suzy, and then there was only the wind. It nearly took her when she shook free of the control glove. The guard's shot had holed the hull.

If she looked sideways, around dazzling yellow-green after-images, Suzy could just about make out where she was going. She dived headfirst into the pit, hand over hand down a power cable as thick through as her thigh.

Air roared around her. Needlepoints pressed in her ears, she kept swallowing to relieve the pressure. By the time she reached bottom, her nose had started to bleed and her eyes felt as though thumbs were mashed into their corners. She caught a sideways glimpse of the guard's body, broken between the grapple's talons, then launched herself in a desperate trajectory, kicking as hard as she could for the open hatch above the singleship's lifting surface. Wind took her sideways, but she managed to catch hold of a cable and haul herself along it.

Push with hands and feet at the lip of the hatch. Follow the cable back to where it plugged in. (Eyes blinded by icy tears as well as afterimages, something bubbling inside her lungs.) Pull back latches, unplug it, haul the heavy awkward cable out. (No air, no air!) Fumble for the throw, bloody fingertips sliding on slick plastic. Pull down. Suzy felt rather than heard the hatch close, and then there was a roaring sound, the noise of the air plant's blowers.

Suzy lay on the gimbal couch and pulled down the little autodoc, let it work on her burned and abraded hands until she could see well enough to override it, had it mix up something to let her ride out the postadrenaline crash. The muscles in her arms and legs kept jerking, so she took an antispasmodic, too. The big bone-deep bruise over her left hip, the pain that stabbed deep in her lungs every time she breathed, the little burns up and down her arms—she could live with those for a while. She dismissed the autodoc and fitted the crashweb around herself, pulled down the flight mask.

The weapons racks were open, but the missiles were still in their racks. Suzy smiled, dried blood cracking around her mouth, and closed them up, ran a quick status check. Seemed like the Witnesses hadn't touched a thing. The ship was hers.

No use asking someone to open the hatch. Mumbling the lyrics of "Bad to the Bone," Suzy started the warm-up procedure for the reaction motor. The guard's pistol had blown a hole more than a dozen meters across in the section of hull above the ship. Suzy used one of the singleship's one-shot X-ray lasers to make it wider still.

She lifted the singleship out of the launch cradle using attitude jets at minimal thrust, delicately correcting for the rub of fused ends of catenaries and cables against the lifting surface. Ragged sections of hull peeled back. She tipped up the ship's nose, kicked in the reaction motor for a second, not giving a shit for what it did to the docks. And then she was flying free.

She correlated memorized coordinates with the navigational overlay. Didn't take more than a minute, and only a minute more to check local gravitational density. The attitude jets puffed again, and the singleship swung out as it left the keel behind, aiming itself toward a point a few dozen light-days around the rim of the accretion disk.

The fighting around the modules seemed to be over. Suzy briefly wondered who'd won, though it made no difference to her now. Any witness would do. Then the reaction motor cut in and acceleration shoved her into the couch. The wreckage of the *Vingança* dwindled away, lost against the swirling glare of the accretion disk.

12

SOMEONE, THE NAVY, THE WITNESSES, OR PERHAPS ONE
after the other, had gone through all the control systems of the
cargo tug. Looking for who knew what, they had pulled out
everything they could and left it all lying where they'd dropped
it. Talbeck Barlstilkin was still plugging wafer matrices back into
their slots when Suzy Falcon took her singleship through the
hull of the *Vingança*.

The tug had alerted Talbeck to the explosive decompression
of the docks a few minutes before; he had thought that it was
something to do with the running battle outside and put it
out of his mind. But then the whole tug shuddered in its
launch cradle—ten thousand tonnes jolting half a meter up
and slamming back down. Talbeck fell to his knees and saw
the flash of the singleship's reaction motor in the navigation
tank. Catenaries and girders starkly outlined against raving white
fire . . . and then fire swept over the tug. Indicators flashed red
as the hull momentarily experienced a temperature as hot as the
surface of a star. The white light in the holotank bled to a gray
snowstorm; external cameras had been burned away.

Talbeck broke out more cameras and studied the devastated
docks for a moment, then finished plugging in the wafer matrices. He replaced the panels and started a thorough systems
check. Nothing could divert him from his plans. He refused
to be afraid, walled off what fear there was, put it inside a
red triangle, shrank the triangle down until it was a point. He
would wait an hour for Dorthy Yoshida, and if she did not turn
up he would leave. Professor Doctor Abel Gunasekra, locked
in what had been Yoshida's cabin, would be an adequate, if not
altogether reliable, witness.

Talbeck had not quite finished his systems check when some-one started to cycle through the tug's airlock. No, two people. He allowed himself to feel a small measure of triumph, picked up the pistol from control couch, ordered his impassive servant to follow him, and went down to meet his visitors.

Dorthy Yoshida stepped through the airlock's inner door as soon as Talbeck opened it. The white material of her armored p-suit crackled with frost. The globe of her helmet was tucked in the crook of her arm. She glanced at the pistol and said, "You're pleased to see me, so why are you carrying that? My friend is on our side." And then her expression changed and she said, "Oh. No, you're so wrong, Talbeck. We can't leave now."

"You will take off the rest of that suit, please. You and your friend. I should congratulate you," Talbeck said to Robot, who, like Dorthy, was helmetless but otherwise fully suited, "on the successful countermutiny."

"Fighting isn't over just yet," Robot said.

"I'm not interested in the outcome. Merely the room it gives me to maneuver."

"He wants to go back to Earth," Dorthy said furiously. She dropped the helmet of her p-suit, grasped the toggle of the fastener under her chin with both gloved hands, twisted it up until it engaged. "He thinks that news of the hyperstructure will cause revolution on Earth. Everyone will want to come out here and claim land of their own." The fastener had rotated under her right armpit, was crawling down her back with a burring rasp. She said, "He expects you and me to back him up."

Talbeck signaled to his servant to help her. Dorthy made a motion as if to resist when the servant began to lift off her suit's life-support pack, but then she submitted. "You should be careful," she told Talbeck. "You aren't the only one who can control her."

"Tell me, Robot," Talbeck said. "Do you still have access to the ship's computers? Can you open the bay door beneath my ship?"

"Don't tell him, Robot."

The lanky, blond artist made a movement in his bulky p-suit that might have been a shrug. "You can take her out through the hole Suzy blew, if you've a mind. There's not much left of the docks."

"Thank you. If you cannot open the doors, then you cannot misuse my servant, can you?"

"We need to get going," Robot said, submitting to the servant's attentions in turn. "I'll tell you straight, I can't tamper with your servant, and I wouldn't want to if I could. I haven't the time for it. Suzy won't know what to do with those missiles beyond trying to blow holes in the hyperstructure with the pinch fusion loads of her missiles. And that won't do any good at all. And maybe she doesn't know, but the missiles have been disconnected by the Witnesses; she'll have to EVA and reconnect them before she can do anything. We need to get after her, Seyour Barlstilkin, so that I can tell her just what to do."

"He isn't listening to you," Dorthy said.

"You seem to have found another supplier of counteragent," Talbeck told her, and presented her, one after the other, with images of her candling in a fusion flame, of her blown naked out of an airlock, of the servant strangling her. He had to give her the credit for not flinching. "You be careful," he said, "about what you say from now on. I'm still not sure if I need you— if I ever needed you."

"I don't now what it is with you two," Robot said, running his prosthetic hand through his blond mane. He was out of his suit now, spindly shanked and flat-footed in his tattered suit liner. "I don't know what it is," he repeated, "but we don't have time for it. We have only this little window of time before the marauders act against us. Suzy has to be told how to use the weapon properly."

"You're a funny sort of warrior," Talbeck told him. "The last I knew, you were staging fake terrorist events in Urbis. I think you should grow up a little before you play for real. You should consider that what you think you want to do may not be your own idea, that something else might have put it there. The way Dorthy is driven by the Alea who have taken squatter's rights in her skull. She pretends to be in control, but

I've seen Navy medical reports that tell the real story. Chronic aphasic schizophrenia was mentioned, I believe. There were other problems, too. She isn't quite to be trusted."

Dorthy Yoshida said, "Oh, Talbeck. You hate everyone. You even hate yourself. I admire your courage, the way you make yourself look in the mirror each morning. That's what you really hate, not the Federation. Your own image. Yes, you can kill me. But Professor Gunasekra won't make half the witness I will. Don't you see that you can't sell your idea of an empire for everyone if the marauders happen to inhabit the real estate."

Talbeck gave her the benefit of his lopsided smile. He said, "The marauders may have been dead for a million years. And besides, we've defeated their kind once before. We can do it again."

"But they are alive," Abel Gunasekra said calmly. "And Seyour Robot is correct. We do have only a little time in which to act."

Talbeck clamped down on the needle of panic before it could penetrate to where Dorthy Yoshida could see it. Two points now, like red eyes in the back of his head. Forget them. "I didn't know that you were an escapologist, Professor. You are indeed an accomplished man."

Gunasekra twinkled, pleased with himself. "You should never lock a mathematician in a room whose door is controlled by a combination circuit. Prime number theory happens to be a hobby of mine, and of course prime numbers are the basis for most types of encryption. But that is by the way. I have been trying to tell you for some time, Seyour Barlstilkin, that the marauders know about us. There is a continuing rise in background radiation in this volume of space, and in particular a rise in the zoo of strange particles which are created by the evaporation of super photons, as we witnessed during the Event. I have been tracing decay paths, and they point toward the hyperstructure. The rise is logarithmic. Soon we will see spallation tracks, and on a vast scale. Even the Witnesses must take notice. And shortly after that, before we can even begin to die of radiation poisoning, the energy flux will be so intense that our very molecules will be torn apart."

"So the marauders are here." Talbeck shrugged. "All the more reason to leave, then. Robot, please be quiet. You may ask Professor Gunasekra any question you like once we are under weigh. Dorthy, that was a clever touch, mentioning the mirror. How you must have missed your Talent, when the Navy held you captive. At least for those ten years you were able to realize what it is to be an ordinary person, assailed by doubt about the motives of others. You're not young any more, Dorthy. Ten years of captivity and your adventures on P'thrsn have aged you more than you think. Do *you* ever look in the mirror? Once upon a time you believed that death was only something that happened to other people, that you were special, that it would never come to you. But now you are of an age where you are beginning to realize that you were wrong. You were young before P'thrsn, but how you've aged since then. Death looks through the skin of your face, looks back at you every time you gaze in the mirror, doesn't it?

"No, Robot, you may not speak. Interrupt me again and I will have my servant tear out your tongue and make you eat it. We may not see each other again for a long time, Dorthy. Once we have returned to the hypervelocity star, I shall have my servant cool you all down. The journey back to Earth will take about twenty years; I am afraid this tug will be able to decelerate only very slowly to match angular velocity with Sol, and I am not willing to risk anything like the neutron star momentum transfer again. The hibernaculae slow metabolism, but do not inhibit it. You will all age while you sleep, by two or three years. You will probably lose your child, Dorthy—yes, I know about that squalid little affair. I know everything. And when you wake you will look in the mirror and see your death is just that little bit closer. And you will look at me and see that I have not aged at all. That's my revenge, Dorthy. I'll outlive the Federation and I'll outlive you all, too. Nothing to say? I'm disappointed.

"Hold them in the commons," he told the servant. "They can talk with each other, but kill anyone who tries to leave without my permission."

There was a small holotank in the commons, slaved to the navigation tank on the bridge. The lopsided double sphere of the wormhole planetoid, like a child's clay model of the sign for infinity, slowly grew larger as the tug fell toward it. Only Robot watched the tank. Abel Gunasekra was trying to explain his conclusions to Dorthy, and the bonded servant stood in the oval doorway, her head slowly turning back and forth, like a lizard watching for its next meal.

"That guy surely is crazy," Robot said, not the first time he'd made that observation. Prompted by an excess of nervous energy, he jumped up and prowled around the small bleak room, peering into the servant's empty eyes (she was exactly his height), came back to the padded shelf, white as the rest of the room, where Dorthy and Gunasekra sat. He peered over Gunasekra's shoulder at the overscribbled slate and said mournfully, "Shit, I wish Machine hadn't left me. He could tell me what all those spider marks mean."

Abel Gunasekra said, "I will try and explain, if you like."

"You tell me where the marauders are, is all I need to know," Robot said. "Except we've no way of telling Suzy Falcon. She's crazier than a box of scorpions, that's the truth. But if maybe someone could talk to her, she could see to do it right."

"I have some ideas about the nature of the hyperstructure. Alas, I can only speculate about the marauders. Your guess is as good as mine."

Robot pulled at his hair. "The angels talked to Machine, not to me. He knows, but he's still in the *Vingança*. I should have made him able to copy himself, except I never realized something like this would come up. He was supposed to read himself back into me soon as we were ready to leave, and then Suzy stole the fucking singleship, and this guy Barlstilkin pulls out his own agenda. If he thinks the angels will let him through, he *really* is crazy, and I don't care if he's listening because it's the truth."

Dorthy reluctantly gave up trying to think about the elegant twister equations which Gunasekra believed could describe the raveling of the sub–Planck-length microstructure of urspace which had created the hyperstructure, the hypermatter sphere with its gaps and spikes, the inhabited Spike itself and even the gravity acting perpendicular to its surface. Concentrating on the slippery involutions of the equations had been a way of not thinking the thoughts of the others around her, and in particular of not riding the fractured surf inside Robot's head. What was inside the head of the bonded servant wasn't too bad, oddly enough, hardly anything at all except a kind of low level murmur from deep down in the woman's limbic cortex, a sort of maintenance pulse little different from the uncomplicated drift of a torpid crocodile.

Robot though . . . the state his mind was in, Dorthy was amazed that he could function at all. There were gaps everywhere, and no rational control of the impulses that gripped him, great gaudy nightmares from which she might never wake if she fell into them. His head was only centimeters from hers, the cool plastic of his augmented arm brushed the back of her neck where he leaned between her and Gunasekra. His blond hair, longer in a strip down the center of his head than at the sides, was so fine that she could see through to his white scalp and the ridged scars of his self-inflicted surgery, his first act of radical situationism.

If you need machines to survive, outside the cozy envelope of Earth, or Earth-like worlds, then the rational thing to do, the starting point, is to put one inside your head, let it control your behavior in places where the instincts of an arboreal ape turned bipedal plains-hunter are grossly dangerous to your survival. . . .

The fragment bloomed toward her like a greedy carnivorous flower unfolding its petals in jerky stop-motion time; Dorthy dragged the focus of her Talent away just in time. She feared that any fragment of Robot's crazy quilt mind lodging in her would upset her control, let the mindsets of the Alea (still *there*, patrolling like slow sharks in her blood-red depths) go free. Break out.

Dorthy said, "The angels brought all of us through, didn't they? First they took you and Suzy Falcon, to show the way, and then the *Vingança* was allowed through. The *Vingança* became what the Navy wanted it to be all along, the bait, the lure, the sacrificial pawn to draw out the Enemy. And while they were busy with it, your little ship would have slipped their net, and struck home."

"Maybe," Robot admitted.

"I wish I knew more about the weapon they gave you," Abel Gunasekra said wistfully. "Always I have dreamed of being able to see an equation."

"It doesn't look like anything much," Robot said.

Dorthy said, "Like burning diamond dust. Like light. It was on the warheads of your missiles when the Witnesses brought you in. The Alea in my head made me able to see it; I think she knew what it was, what to look for. No one else saw it." A thought occurred to her and she felt a sudden sense of slippage . . . but no, not yet. Not yet.

"The ultimate machine," Gunasekra said. "A mathematical equation that operates on the virtual universe. It is what the hyperstructure is, after all. If your Alea remembered it, Dorthy, then they would certainly understand the principles of the angels' weapon. You are still in control of yourself?"

"Thank you, Abel. Yes, I think so, but I'm the wrong person to ask. How would I know? Look, if your friend does manage to destroy the Spike," Dorthy said to Robot, "then Talbeck will be very pissed indeed."

"The weapon won't destroy the hyperstructure," Robot said. "It isn't the problem. I mean, it's made from this Universe. What pisses the angels off is the way the marauders are drawing stuff across from other universes. That's what they want to stop. Then they can get on with going wherever they are going."

Gunasekra said, "It is worse than that, Seyour Robot. Dorthy, do you remember Jake Bonner's objection to my hypothesis about the way the marauders might survive the heat death of the Universe?"

"He thought that continuous creation would produce too many hot photons. Given enough time, it would drastically increase the background temperature of the Universe. But you said it would take longer than the lifetime of the Universe, so it didn't matter."

"I have been thinking about that objection, and I came to a startling conclusion." Gunasekra erased everything on his slate and began to scrawl new equations. "The source of light for the Spike is too great for any single star, and besides, stars, unlike the Spike, have only a finite lifetime, and the larger they are, the shorter they burn. Inconvenient to feed star after star across the end of the Spike, especially if they tend to be unstable. So instead, the light of nearby stars is lensed down the length of the Spike. Continuous creation supplies generation after generation of population I stars just for the purpose. And, of course, more hyperspheres can be made; it is easy enough to do using Banach-Tarski-Robinson manipulation of hypermatter." He flashed a smile at Robot. "The number of points on the surface of a hypermatter sphere, such as that which anchors the Spike to the accretion disk, is greater than infinity, yet such a sphere can be broken into a finite number of pieces which can be reassembled to produce two spheres identical to the parent. In fact, you can separate such a sphere into two nonidentical halves, aleph and omega, separate those in turn so that you have two alephs and two omegas, and then simply reassemble. Do not ask me *how* to separate them, but then I do not know how to operate on real five dimensional space-time with twistor equations. We can only use equations to describe the Universe, not manipulate it. Or not yet. . . . Do you follow me, Dorthy?"

She had tried, but it had been like trying to track the paths of every individual in a school of fish suddenly scattering through blue depths.

Gunasekra said, "The simple point is that the marauders' population will not remain constant. They will need new territory. We see the attempt to make another hypermatter sphere, for instance. Biological populations in optimum conditions do not stand still or even increase linearly. They are exponential. They double, Seyour Robot, and that double amount doubles over, and so on. The line is not straight but a rising curve aimed at infinity. Jake Bonner was right, you see, but he didn't take it far enough!"

If the marauders were allowed their way, he explained, there would be an exponential increase in hypermatter spheres, swarms of them anchored around every black hole in the Universe. And the accretion disk of every black hole would be seeded with sources of super photons, filling the Universe with the light of newly created suns until space-time itself caught fire.

"In this case we will reach the critical point much sooner than infinity, a long time before gravity balances out space-time expansion and the Universe begins to contract toward the Big

Crunch. And I think it would happen suddenly, too, not gradually. There is a transition point analogous to the phase transition in sublimation processes, where virtual photon pair production would be suddenly scaled up. Like the inflation point just after the Big Bang, smoothing out anisotropy everywhere, all at once. Even regions in which there was no excess photon production would be consumed."

Robot said, "So what's the scale on this? What do you mean by soon?"

Gunasekra shrugged. "It depends on how fast the marauders outgrow the living space provided by the very large surface area of the Spike. Since they already appear to be attempting to duplicate the hypermatter sphere, I would say that the lower limit is a million years. That provides us with a worst-case scenario."

Dorthy said, "It might be a best case. Alea never do anything unless they have to. If they're trying to produce another hypermatter sphere, it's because the one they colonized is already overcrowded. Alea reproduce to fill available space, and they will be limited to those parts of the Spike where the light is rich in long wavelengths. Ultraviolet light kills their children."

Robot said, "Are these marauders so dumb that they don't see they'll cook the Universe?"

"Not dumb," Dorthy told him, "just not farsighted. They found what looked like an ideal way infinitely to expand their bloodline, and they've gone for it. Perhaps they believe they can solve the starlight heating problem, too, when they need to. The way that back in the Age of Waste people on Earth believed that their capitalist-industrial economies could continue to expand indefinitely."

Gunasekra was scribbling on his slate. "If we assume a doubling period of a million years, and if we make some optimistic assumptions about size of accretion disks and packing of hypermatter spheres about their circumferences . . . every black hole at the core of every galaxy in the Universe will be completely surrounded in less than sixty million years. That's about point one four billion billion hypermatter spheres, with their attendant Spikes and matter generating nodes. A number that is almost exactly a billionth of the Hubble radius, although I'm sure that's a trivial coincidence. . . . And at a rough estimate that would heat the Universe to the temperature at which quantum effects dominate, as at the singularity, in . . . under four billion years. Less than the age of the Earth."

Talbeck Barlstilkin's voice came from some hidden speaker above their heads, cool and remote. "Even I do not worry that far ahead, Professor."

"Perhaps you should," Abel Gunasekra said. "If more people understood the time scale on which the processes of the macrouniverse operate, we should not be a species blown up with hubris."

"Another idealist. How disappointing. But I suggest that you all concentrate on the next couple of minutes. We are about to pass through the wormhole."

Dorthy looked up from the slate and saw that the planetoid filled the holotank. Its shadowy scape swelled as quickly as a hammerblow. One of the wormhole pits rushed up from the center. Dorthy's hands clawed at the slippery plastic of the shelf's padding, seeking purchase against the shock of transition.

There was no time to feel anything. The tank flashed white and then it showed only a dark, rumpled plain that ran out to an irregular horizon, a wavy edge eclipsing the glow of the condensing gas clouds. Halfway to the horizon was a shadowy, tangled mound of spars and piping.

They were down on the planetoid's surface, from a hundred klicks per second to rest in an instant. The vast tangle was the ruin of the ancient alien spaceship. Robot was shouting something about angels and Abel Gunasekra was stuttering as he tried to frame a question and somewhere else in the ship Talbeck Barlstilkin was screaming with sudden rage and fear.

Dorthy felt it all shrink away. Or rather, she was retreating from it, sinking inside her own brain while something else rose up from its basement. The shock had been enough to breach the membrane of her control.

She stood, staggering on legs that were too short, that bent in all the wrong places. She had been an observer all this time, and it was stranger than she could have imagined suddenly to be extended into every part of this spindly body, all the way down to the clawless fingertips of the fragile five-fingered hands. Walking on tiptoe, knees bowed outward like those of a sumo wrestler, she went up to the bonded servant and nearly strangled when she tried to give it an order: human vocal chords were the wrong shape to form the fluting, near-ultrasonic trills, of the Alea.

She tried again.

"You will let me past," the neuter female said. "I know of a way to destroy the marauders. Until that is done, the angels will never let you return."

13

$$\equiv$$

DORTHY COULD STILL SEE AND HEAR AND FEEL, BUT SHE could no more twitch a finger than she could will the smooth glands which capped her kidneys to secrete adrenaline. Sight was in grainy black-and-white, and oddly truncated, as if she were peering at the world from the far end of a tunnel. The drone of the airlock's vents and various metallic noises as the frame assembled a p-suit around her were mixed with the blurred thud of her pulse, the rasp of air in her throat, the squirming of her digestion.

Everything was being filtered through the neuter female's mindset. Her body felt strangely elongated, its limbs too long and too slender, its feet disturbingly different from its hands. Her head felt shorn, naked, and there was a strange ghostly sensation either side of her puny rib cage, just below her breasts . . . just where the pair of secondary arms would be, if she had been an Alea.

The helmet came down over her head. Latches snapped closed. The frame released her. With a kind of staggering tiptoe gait, she stepped to the airlock's controls and started the depressurizing sequence, using knuckles in preference to fingertips on the switches, chin flattened against the helmet's collar as she myopically peered through the visor.

Somewhere in the back of her own head, Dorthy tried to gather herself into the calming ritual of *Sessan Amakuki*, to look inward where she might see the threads that linked her to the neuter female's mindset, might map the path back to her own body. She was still trying when the airlock completed its cycle. The hatch lifted, and she dived out of the embrace of the tug's generated gravity and flew across the dark rumpled surface of the planetoid.

A dizzy arc in microgravity and vacuum, using the tips of her toes and fingers to skim the surface like a pebble skipping across waves: once, twice, thrice. Then at the top of the third arc reversing as neatly as an acrobat and landing nimbly in the deep shadow of a trough, gripping with splayed fingers, trying to grip with feet that could not claw and almost turning head over heels. Settling down, thump of heart strong and loud. Cautiously rearing up and looking around.

All this before Dorthy had had time to react.

It was dark, there on the surface of the planetoid, dark as a deep mine shaft. In monochrome, the gorgeous swirls of the gas clouds were reduced to chalky thumbprints, illuminating nothing by themselves. The tilted swerve of the infalling arc, mostly cut off by the unnervingly close horizon, was ghostly white. Dorthy heard her own voice, straining at the top of its range, ask the suit for enhanced vision.

A raster line slowly rolled down the dim view, replacing it with a jumble of blurred blocks of black and white that took a while to sort into a view of a corduroy surface of ridges and shattered channels. Everywhere was dusted with the sooty siftings of interstellar grains.

A couple of lines of an old missionary song drifted up from Dorthy's memory . . . *Earth stood hard as iron / Water like a stone* . . . then her usurped body was moving again. She felt the ghost of the neuter female's atavistic excitement thrilling over her whole skin, her too-flat teeth grinding together, as she scampered from gully to ridge to gully again, a slope-backed four-legged beast.

The tangle of the alien wreck slowly dawned above the truncated horizon. The neuter female moved more cautiously, suit's belly scraping sooty ice-rock as she scuttled from crevice to crevice, blood thrilling with unfamiliar chemicals, pulse distractingly quick. The human visual cortex didn't seem able to cope with microgravity, and dizzingly kept insisting that instead of skimming across a chaotic plain she was climbing up an infinitely curved mountain—or worse, crawling *down* a sheer rock face. Reflex kept jamming soft unclawed fingertips too deeply into crevices; sweat bathed the whole of the naked bifurcated body inside its armor.

At last she was hanging at the edge of the shallow bowl of the wreck's impact crater, jammed against a jagged half-melted pinnacle. The bowl was a vast bite out of the close horizon, rumpled by stress flows, streaked with veins of naked ice not yet covered by the slow infall of interstellar soot, a mandala that glowed with surrealistic intensity in her enhanced vision.

The wreck lay in the bull's-eye of this mandala, a vast thicket of tubes laced and interlaced like the legs of a mass of copulating spiders. Dwarfed by the gigantic tangle was a leaf shape Dorthy recognized as one of the *Vingança*'s gigs. As in a nightmare, she tried to get into hiding but found that she couldn't move. The gig and the wreck towering above it slid out of view as the neuter female scanned the whole of the crater, snapped back into focus as half a dozen searingly bright flares lazily rose from it, a glaring malevolent constellation that began to drift sideways as the flares achieved the few meters per second necessary for orbit.

Shadows dancing within the wreck made it seem to shudder and stir, as if awakened from a long untroubled sleep. And something that was not a shadow stopped its slow crawl around the perimeter of the crater toward the pinnacle where the neuter female clung. She hissed, hurting her merely human throat, flexed clawless fingers, and leaped, wrapping arms and legs around the p-suited figure as they both flew high above wrinkled ice.

Red lines crossed around them as they floatingly thrashed. Where the lines touched the planetoid's surface, black ice slumped and boiled away or shattered explosively. The neuter female rolled, still gripping her adversary's arms so that her gloves meshed under the rim of its helmet. Faster than Dorthy could follow, she gauged the web of red threads, kicked out, hooked a foot around a jagged ridge, and pulled.

Then she was lying on top of her prey in a deep hollow, sooty dust flying up around them. Blunt fingers strove to eviscerate it, but only dragged across unyielding radiation armor. A voice crackled inside her helmet.

"Don't kill him!" Dorthy screamed, and then realized that she *could* scream. Her throat hurt; her eyes filled with tears that in microgravity swelled but did not run. She rolled away from Robot, sniffed hard. Something smooth and salty slid down her throat. Everything was blurred into everything else: the blurred pixels of enhanced vision mixed into the blur of her tears; the neuter female's bloodlust and her own terror had kicked in the same glands.

"Jesus Christ," Robot said. He lay on his back, looking up at red threads that wove a dozen meters overhead, sparkling now as straightedged plumes of dust sprayed through them. The deadly pattern reflected on his suit's visor. Signal lasers, Dorthy thought, with their power jacked up somehow. If they could melt ice a fraction above absolute zero, then they could easily slice through a p-suit and the person inside it. She remembered turning like a ballet dancer inside that deadly web and shuddered.

"Jesus Christ," Robot said again. "I try to help out, and you nearly get us both killed."

"That was the neuter female. She's gone, now. It's all right."

But the Alea mindset hadn't gone, Dorthy realized. It was all around her. It was biding its time.

"We saw the Witnesses bring that gig down," Robot said. "They're broadcasting all kinds of crazy stuff, trying to waken the dead gods. Your friend Barlstilkin is hiding out on the bridge in some kind of monumental sulk, and the professor guy means well, but he's a thinker. Bringing him out here with any kind of weaponry would be like giving a baby a tactical nuke to play with. So I guess it was down to me. I wasn't expecting much gratitude, but I'd say being jumped like that was kind of over

the top. You sure that thing is locked up inside your head again?
What is she after out here?"

"It's likely that she is letting me talk to you, but only so long
as she can learn something. She is looking for the weapon that
the angels must have given the owners of the wrecked spaceship.
Wants to use it against the marauders, to end the war they started
a million years ago."

The lasers suddenly switched off. Robot's visor was a black
hole he turned to Dorthy as he raised himself on one elbow.
"That's what I figured," he said. "And we need her to use it,
too. Switch off your suit's visual enhancement and look at the
sky. You'll see what I mean."

Dorthy did as she was told. Slowly, she was able to make out
tendrils of vague, luminous green writhing across half the sky,
a nest of snakes bending back toward the rim of the accretion
disk. She felt an icy contraction across the whole of her sweat-
soaked skin. She knew what the green sky-snakes meant: the
eaters-of-all-children had sterilized a thousand worlds with that
weapon.

"The marauders are giving this neighborhood a heavy dose
of hard radiation," Robot said. "What we're seeing are just
the tracks of something like synchrotron radiation, dragged out
along magnetic field lines. It's what we *can't* see that's hurting us.
All kinds of particles, generated by pulling superphotons across
from alternate universes along relativistic shear lines. Or that's
what Gunasekra reckons. Freaky, huh? We've maybe a couple
of hours before we really start to fry."

"Less than that if the Witnesses get us," Dorthy said. "They
switched off the lasers because they want to get at least one of
us alive. Me, most probably. I can talk to aliens after all, why
not to gods? There are half a dozen of them coming after us."

"That's good," Robot said. "Because we have to get them
before we can get the weapon. They come after us, I've already
had my little helpers set up a few pranks for them. Old stuff,
but I was in a hurry. Besides, there aren't any critics around,
right?"

The half dozen flares, guttering low, closed out their first
orbit as Dorthy and Robot took off into the jambles around

the edge of the impact crater, leading the Witnesses away from Barlstilkin's ship. The Witnesses were tracking the radar signatures of their p-suits. And with her Talent Dorthy could follow the progress of the Witnesses, six candle flames shifting across the planetoid's achingly desolate landscape, gradually spreading apart, two at point hurrying ahead of the others in a classic pincer movement.

They'd been traveling for ten minutes when the first of Robot's tricks showed itself. It dawned like a vast moon above the jagged horizon, an unstable globe of silvered mylar cinched at its equator with a belt of thrusters that pushed it that way and this with minute featherings of gas.

Robot caught Dorthy's arm and they slowly sank against a pitted slab of sooty ice-rock. He broke radio silence and told her to listen up, this was good.

The silver sphere gyrated above them. Its surface suddenly raced with a frothy shimmer that faded to reveal the face of the leader of the Witnesses, Gregor Baptista. Rose red lips parted the white beard, and the man's smooth unctuous voice came over the common channel, slightly out of sync with the movement of the hologram's lips.

"Friends, you think there's something missing in your life when all the time it's inside yourself. I thought I knew it all, but now I know I was wrong, and I have to tell you that you are wrong, too. . . ."

As the thing passed overhead, burbling cheerful inanities, Dorthy saw that Baptista's face was projected, Janus-like, on both halves of the sphere. Threads of red light stabbed up from the tumbled landscape. The sphere swept through them. Baptista's face collapsed in on itself as the mylar sphere began to lose pressure through half a dozen holes, but the synthesized voice was unaffected.

"Look inside yourselves! I really mean it, friends. What kind of example are we bringing to the crossroads of the Galaxy? There is no struggle, no revolution, no shining path. You are already the monarchs of everything inside your skins. Listen: I told Jesus I wasn't going to church anymore and *he shook my hand!* My imagination is a cancer, and I'm going to fuck it before it fucks me! I'm gonna hawk it up and paint my face with its juice! I shit suns from my asshole, and every one is loaded with the plague of entropy! I am the one, the only! I am a Master Criminal, and I am *not insane!* I was on drugs before I was born, *they* are the opiates of *my* religion!"

Robot jacked a com line into Dorthy's suit. His voice sounded faintly beneath the ravings of the pseudo-Baptista. "The second wave will be up and coming any moment. Those guys will be busy shooting them down, and we go through their line, get to the wreck. What do you think?"

"As a plan, it lacks all kinds of common sense. But I have no alternative. Where did you find the time to get all this done?"

"Not me. My little helpers. Von Neumann machines. They've been busily reproducing all the time the Witnesses had me in captivity. I guess there must be a thousand or so of them by now, all through the *Vingança,* stowed away on all the ships in its docks."

"Even the gig the Witnesses stole?"

But Robot had pulled out the line, and the Baptista-thing was still jamming the common channel, jabbering away as it wobbled toward the far horizon, a scarcely visible ring bearing ragged scraps of mylar, half its cluster jets burned away by the Witnesses' fusillade. Then it began to grow both brighter and more indistinct. A flip-up display told Dorthy that its temperature was rising rapidly; as a cloud of vaporized molecules expanded around the ring, she could make out the beam of the X-ray laser burning into it. The synthesized voice cut off in midexhortation and then the ring vanished in a ragged exhalation of flash-molten droplets.

Baptista's voice came over the common channel again, but this time it was the real thing, barely coherent as he raved about purifying the area, purging the mockers to make way for the Great Glad Hour that was soon at hand, signs were written in the sky that it was almost here. . . .

Robot said, "I guess I pressed his button. Guys like that, they've no sense of humor. The second wave is coming. Let's go!"

As he sprang up, Dorthy saw an army of light and color pour over the horizon in slow motion. Things trailing necklaces of glotubes behind them as they bounded high above the sooty jambles, spinning things glowing with shifting spectra of internal fluorescence, things that threw up swiftly inflating stalks as they clambered over slabs and boulders, things moving in blurs of crudely holographed cartoon figures: a grinning mouse with huge semicircular ears and two bright buttons holding up his pants; a hunched wolf with human eyes and a red tongue lolling from his slavering grin; a vast Santa Claus. . . . The kind of projections the *gaijin* managers would set on the parched lawns of their exclusive houses, in the Australian whaling town where Dorthy had been born. And a hundred more, forgotten cartoon characters and real or imagined beasts crawling and shaking and spinning and flapping in a whirl of feathers and fur and claws and blazing golden eyes: a phantom army of laser light, mylar, and low-pressure gases, jamming every radio frequency with overlapping howls and ravings and snatches of martial music that sounded as if it were being played by a thousand demented drummers marching straight over the edge of a cliff.

Even as Dorthy took off after Robot, the first red laser threads were snapping on and off among his creations. In midleap, she felt a cool shutter descending, the neuter female's mindset sliding into control again, so smoothly that her body scarcely hesitated as it swooped from crag to crag in the microgravity, head turning this way and that to triangulate the Witnesses' positions.

Robot was dwindling into the distance, a shadow soon lost in the dim sooty scape. But the neuter female slowed down, moving from position to position with long pauses in between. Hunters had no flight reaction. They stalked their prey, or fought where they stood, to the death.

The first Witness was easy. The neuter female circled around it and waited until it popped up to take another shot at the shambling horde of Robot's creations. Her leap caught it just as it fired; its laser thread swept up to zenith and went out as she ripped out the coupling of its life-support pack, grabbed hold of the signal laser, braced herself against an icy ledge and shoved, separating the wailing creature from its weapon and sending it spinning high toward the capering, howling army.

Another Witness was quick enough to snap off a shot at the neuter female, but she had already ducked into the hollow and, after the explosion, used the flat trajectories of ice fragments as cover for her next move, a sinuous crawl across a flat ice field, dragging the laser with her. She rested in the lee of a gnarled stub of ice, waited patiently until the Witness rose out of cover again, and shot it through the helmet. It collapsed in a cloud of recondensing vapor. The neuter female reached the dying Witness with one bound, reached into its shattered helmet and did something unspeakable even as Robot's cavalcade swept past in a crowd of stilt appendages and flailing masses of hooks, blurred columns of light and constellations of hard-edged glare.

She could make out the positions of the remaining Witnesses with her human sense, their minds mostly awhirl with sliding panic, sense impressions banging together like rocks tumbling in a desert flash flood. They had abandoned all thought of tracking her and Robot, and the next two kills were easy, a simple matter of ambush. Robot was somewhere near the horizon, moving steadily toward the alien wreck . . . and someone was moving behind him, a mind Dorthy recognized, still and pure in its intent.

The neuter female started to move, hardly flinching as a barrage of light flashed beyond the horizon and the jumble of voices that all this time had been roaring in her ears began to thin out towards silence. The cavalcade must have reached the defensive perimeter of the Witnesses' ship. And in among fragmented chants and wailing battle cries the neuter female heard a human voice, Robot's, a shout of surprise that abruptly cut off.

She put on speed, flowing over rumpled ice fields like a swimmer: but it was too late. When she reached the edge of the impact crater, snagging one hand around an outcrop and swinging around just in time to avoid a scything line of red light that scored a line of flying debris from the ice, she glimpsed across the field of refrozen ripples two p-suited figures in midflight toward the grounded gig in the shadow of the tangled alien wreck.

She risked another look and saw that one figure was bound to the back of the other, then skimmed on blunt fingertips around the circumference of the crater. Ice shivered beneath her fingers, then heaved in a spasm that sent her tumbling head over heels, whirling glimpses of black crags and chalky gas clouds and a vast expanding plume of steam that marked where the Witnesses' X-ray laser had struck. She flew a long way, landed on all fours—like a cat, Dorthy thought dazedly—and somehow caught herself before rebounding, huddling close to the surface as debris flew past, big chunks of ice tumbling in slow motion amid millions of spherical, refrozen droplets that hammered like hail down one side of the p-suit.

Somehow, she still held onto the laser. She brought it to bear on the gig, wanting to get off one shot at least before the Witnesses' weapon boiled her away, as it surely must. But in the moment she took aim she saw that something strange was happening to the Witnesses' ship, and she held her fire.

The gig was changing shape. Or no, it was rearing up, its pyramidal nose assembly tilting higher as billows of vapor boiled up around the black blades of the drive radiators at its stern. It was preparing to lift off . . . but even as she thought that, she saw that it was also tilting over. The tip of the nearside lifting surface crumpled against the ice. Radiator blades began to shine through vapor, dull red at the edge, yellow veined with glaring white at the base. Vapor flew away from the gig in dense linear streaks, enveloping the linked pair that were still struggling toward it.

Dorthy saw that now the gig was almost entirely supported by the crumpled ruin of the nearside lifting surface. The whole of its stern was cherry red now; radiators ringed the flare of the motor pod in uniform white glare. Then the remains of the lifting surface collapsed and the gig fell, its near-molten stern smashing into water-ice a thousand degrees cooler. A cavity of superheated steam formed and rushed outward, lifting up the gig and freezing almost immediately in a fog of microscopic ice droplets. Pressure gone, the gig collapsed into the hole it had melted, its keel snapping in half a dozen places, its shape shifting uneasily as more steam formed and blew out, shifting and settling farther and farther into the ice.

The figures out on the slope of the crater had stopped. The neuter female coolly brought the laser to bear and shot the one who wasn't Robot through the chest.

      ★   ★   ★

The dead Witness was Ang Poh Mokhtar. Dorthy recognized the woman's finely carved features through the ferns of ice that frosted the inside of her visor just as she was about to burn it away with the laser. The intent was still in her muscles; stopping it almost made her throw up. The neuter female wanted a trophy. The fresh brains of her kill.

She dropped the laser and sat beside Robot, who was watching ragged plumes of ice drift up from the crater where the Witnesses' gig had been.

"So who are you?" Robot asked over the common band. After the clamor of his cavalcade, the hectoring screams of Gregor Baptista, the silence between his words was eerie.

"Dorthy. Dorthy Yoshida. Or at least I think I am." She could feel part of the neuter female's mindset close to her, a marginal shadow like something just beyond the edge of her field of view. "She wants the weapon," Dorthy said, after a moment.

"I think that would be a good idea." Robot gestured and Dorthy looked up. Green-gold worms tunneled the whole sky now. Robot said, "It's getting real bad."

They moonhopped across the crater toward the labyrinthine tangle of the alien wreck, avoiding the few surviving holograms that drifted mutely and aimlessly about. Dumbo; Tinkerbell; Officer Pupp; the Wicked Witch of the West. Crystal drifts crunched under Dorthy's boots at each bounce, frozen spume from the destruction of the Witnesses' gig. She asked Robot about it, and he said that some of his helpers had been on board, had jiggered the orthidium batteries to release all their energy at once. The other constructions had been a distraction, easy targets for the Witnesses to divert them from the sabotage.

The wreck of the gig lay at the bottom of a deep, smooth-sided pit, sheathed in transparent ice. Robot wondered if anyone was alive down there.

"No one," Dorthy said firmly.

"I guess you'd know."

"I guess I would." Dorthy gazed up at the hectares of pitted tubing which rose and twisted beyond the sunken wreck of the gig. She wondered where to start. Perhaps Robot would know:

perhaps an angel was riding him just as the neuter female was riding her.

She didn't have time to ask. The feeling of cool withdrawal came and she tipped back her head inside the p-suit's helmet and howled in triumph, hurting her throat and not caring. Even if the radiation reached a lethal level, it would be too late for the eaters-of-all-children to stop her now. Cowards that they were, they had flinched from direct action. And now they would receive the reward of all cowards.

Climbing the tangle of tubing toward her goal was easy in the negligible gravity, even with the puny body she was riding. She soon left the other human behind as she skimmed over humped intersections that grew ever more frequent as she neared the fugitive glimmer of the weapon of the angels, still potent after all this time.

The thump of the body's feeble blood pump, the roar of its breath, and the chatter of the suit's radiation counter were equally loud in her ears when she reached the weapon. She ran gloved hands over the terminal node which had once jutted far from the rest of the ship's maze, seeing not the radiation-scarred organometallic surface but the constellations of trapped mathematical potentialities that shimmered and flickered deep within.

After a moment it seemed as if her gloves were moving through these suspended points of light, stirring them into their active configuration. Her whole body tingled as something passed through it, and then it was gone. It had unraveled into the virtual space-time matrix.

She looked up and saw that the writhing spallation tracks were already fraying, dying back at the speed of light toward their point source. She felt an intense surge of happiness and remembered the shared triumph when the ark crewed by her ancestors had first achieved orbit about the world that would become the refuge for her family. The feeling spread like a limitless sea and, joyfully, salt crystal or snowflake, she fell toward the dissolution of nirvana.

When Robot reached Dorthy Yoshida, he found her sprawled on her back on the broad, blunt node that capped the end of the tube, one leg and arm dangling over a drop of more than a hundred meters to black ice. Probably not a lethal drop in the planetoid's low gravity, but he rearranged her limbs and clipped a tether to her suit's utility belt. The sky was almost clear of the spallation tracks now, nothing left but a ragged green glow dwindling into the ultraviolet glare of the accretion disk.

After a while, Dorthy began to stir. Robot resisted the temptation to ask her who she was this time. "Do you know where you are?"

"She's gone," Dorthy said. She started to sit up, and almost flew from the node.

Robot braced himself and checked her motion, and she floated down to a kind of squat.

"Thank you," Dorthy said. "I forgot for a moment—" Her laugh was shaky. "She really did it, didn't she?"

"You released the weapon."

"She did it," Dorthy said. "The neuter female. The Alea have always known more than we thought. We were lucky that they'd grown so decadent, half wishing for death. She's gone, Robot! She's done what she was designed to do. She's put an end to the marauders' weaponry. How her family must have hated them, to keep the enmity alive for a million years. And my Talent, it's like a switch has been thrown. I'm alone in my head again. You can't begin to imagine how wonderful that is!"

"No, I don't think I can," Robot said, feeling a pang for silent architecture in the left side of his brain. He said, "Suzy Falcon will be pissed. She wanted the glory of finishing off the Alea."

"Oh, that isn't possible. They are scattered everywhere in the Galaxy, hiding from the marauders. But here it's over, Robot. Do you think the angels will allow us to go home now?"

He looked back across the night black ice fields of the planetoid, to where the horizon drew its double curve across the dim glories of the gas clouds. "I don't know," he said. "But I guess there's only one way to find out."

14

As the singleship accelerated to match the relative velocity of the hyperstructure at the edge of the accretion disk, Suzy had more than enough time to think about what she'd done. She could have taken sides with the Navy officers against the Witnesses; she could have waited for Robot and that Talent, Dorthy Yoshida. She could at least have stopped for a moment before launching, just once in her life stopped to consider what she was getting herself into.

"You've really done it now," she kept muttering to herself. "What a fucking dumb move."

Like the song had it, she just had to keep moving, there was a hellhound on her trail.

She couldn't even begin to plan where to strike until she reached the target. Big as her target was, it was so far away that even at maximum enhancement it was no more than a thread a couple of pixels across, head down to the rim of the accretion disk like some vast spermatozoon butting against God's own ovum.

Mostly, she kept her attention on the dwindling remains of the *Vingança*, shrunk to a few points drawing apart from each other in slowly separating orbits around the wormhole planetoid. Her bandwidth receiver could pick out only scraps of transmission, all badly trashed by background radiation. She wouldn't know if the Navy had won or lost unless she turned around and went back. The one thing she did know was that she was too proud to do that.

The singleship was only minutes away from matching relative velocity with the hyperstructure and the phase graffle was charging up ready for transition when there was a brief but violent eruption of light from the planetoid. The singleship's computer enlarged and enhanced the image, played it back to Suzy. A small ship plunged into one of the planetoid's wormhole pits, and light burst outward at the instant of penetration, expanding in complex folds and ripples like an exotic flower unbudding in stop-motion, momentarily engulfing the embattled remains of the *Vingança* before winking out.

Suzy said, "The *Vingança* still there?"

The computer arrowed the *Vingança*'s components, specks against the glowing gas clouds, told her that it was receiving a transmission.

"Oh shit. Well, I guess you better let me talk to them."

There was a brief burst of high-pitched electronic chatter. Then a man's voice, half-drowned by a waterfall roar of static, called to her across a million kilometers. His name was Jose Alverez; he was a lieutenant in the Navy, effective commanding officer of the *Vingança*. He wanted to know where Suzy was heading.

Suzy felt an immediate rush of relief, because she'd half-expected the hectoring rhetoric of the Witnesses. "I'm heading out for the Enemy," she said, after she'd identified herself. "Hoping for a little prime hunting. Are you all done with the Witnesses now?" She had to say it over to make sure Alverez caught it. The singleship's transmitter, far weaker than the *Vingança*'s, could hardly punch its way through the growing clutter of static. She wanted to make sure he got it all, too. It was going to be her epitaph, most likely, and she wanted to go out in style.

"That's over," Lieutenant Alverez said. "Most of them killed, the rest in custody. We haven't found their leader, think he might have tried to make it through one of the wormholes."

"I did see that display."

"That was Barlstilkin, not the Witnesses. The bastard ran out on us."

Suzy remembered the name. Bonadventure had mentioned it. Barlstilkin was the guy she would have blown to glory, and herself with him, if Robot hadn't stopped her.

Lieutenant Alverez said, "We're in poor shape here. All we have left is the keel. Local radiation is rising, we have to pull out, no time to retrieve any modules. Do you understand?"

"You're saying you can't come after me, right?"

"That's about right, Suzy Falcon. All our combat ships are damaged. We're running the *Vingança* from a lash-up in the cableways. We have enough control to get us home, but we're going to take the long route. Do you hear me?"

"I'm listening real hard."

"We will not trust the wormholes, and the phase graffle is of no use for the distance we must travel. We are twenty-eight thousand light-years from Sol, and transit time through contraspace is close to one hundred years.

"So we will solve this problem by brute force. We're swinging around the black hole as close as is safe, doing a slingshot maneuver. The *Vingança*'s badly hurt, but her basic structure is in good shape."

"She's a good old ship," Suzy said. For some reason tears were pricking her eyes, swelling slowly in the low pull of the singleship's acceleration, running back above her ears.

Lieutenant Alverez's crackling voice said, "We're going to boost to as close to light speed as we can, at continuous one gee acceleration. Time dilation will shorten the trip to about ten years, ship time. We'll do cold sleep, it won't be so bad. Real time, of course, it will be a trip to the future, twenty-eight thousand years to cross the Galaxy back to Sol, with an indefinite amount added on because of time dilation when we are close to the black hole. The scientists are still trying to work out how much. It depends upon the precise size of the singularity, and on the shape of our hyperbolic orbit around it. We do not know enough to be certain. But at least there will be no charges of mutiny awaiting us. Even the Navy's statutes will be outrun."

"I guess it beats dying, huh?"

"It may sound ingratiating, but in many ways I envy you. There is little honor in coming all this way and then turning tail in the face of the Enemy. I've your file here, Suzy. You had a hell of a record, flying out of the *Vingança* during the Campaigns."

"Well thanks, but where I'm going that don't amount to a snowball's chance on Venus, now does it?"

"Listen carefully, Suzy. As soon as we know our precise course around the black hole I will transmit it to you. Always keep on antenna directed toward us, wherever you are. If you survive your run, there is a very small possibility that you may be able to perform a maneuver similar to ours, that you may be able to match our course and velocity. We will download all the information that we can."

Suzy said, "I hope to see you guys," although she knew that it wasn't even a remote possibility. Even if she *did* survive the encounter with the Enemy, her little ship didn't have the shielding to protect her from the X-rays and synchrotron radiation deep in the accretion disk. She'd have a better chance trying for the wormhole planetoid.

She searched for a phrase with a little swagger in it, some suitable brave epitaph. But the crackle of static in her ears had faded. And something was happening to the view of the accretion disk directly in front of her. Blue light rippling and running together, folding around the outline of someone's face.

Wispy blond hair, dead white face, piercing blue eyes. Thin lips pulled back in a smile, revealing small, widely spaced brown teeth.

The ghost said, "Hello, Suzy."

It was Robot's face, Machine's flat unemphatic voice. Suzy screamed and swept a hand across the communications board.

But the face did not go away.

"Now, now," Machine said. "It is too late for that. I downloaded myself into this ship's computer at the very beginning of the transmission, and you know that you cannot override the computer anymore, not after the modifications made by my little helpers."

"I can pull you out with my bare hands, you fucker. See how you like *that* kind of modification."

"You have ninety-three seconds until transition into contraspace, Suzy. I suggest you think carefully about such radical surgery on your ship's systems at such a critical time. Besides, you need me, and I need you.

"I don't need anyone, not anymore."

"Do you know where to find the Enemy? I thought not. But I do, Suzy. The angels told me. I will let you fly the ship if you follow my instructions. And truly, I do need you. I cannot EVA and reset the warheads of the missiles."

"Oh shit," Suzy said. Her airy feeling of playing hooky suddenly bottomed out. She hadn't even thought to check the status of the weapons systems beyond seeing that they were still active, had just assumed the Witnesses wouldn't have bothered with them. But they had. The warheads of the missiles were still armed, all right, but the control paths to their guidance systems had been cut. They'd fly, but she couldn't tell them where to go. She'd been even dumber than she'd thought.

And there was no time to do anything about it right now. The clock face counting down to transit had started to flash; its single hand was tracking around the dial. Suzy unclipped the deadman's switch, squeezed the pistol grip. The timing of phase space transition was too delicate to be trusted to human reactions, but she could halt the sequence up until the last nanosecond by letting go of the switch.

She said to Machine, "So what's the deal?"

The ghostly face assembled a smile. "We help each other. You go out and reconnect the guidance systems of the missiles, and I will locate the Enemy for you. They live somewhere on the Spike that trails behind the hypermatter sphere, somewhere on a surface the area of three trillion Earths. You would have difficulty finding them on your own, Suzy, but I was able to talk to the Alea ancestor when we all merged. I learned much from her."

Twenty seconds.

Suzy was clutching the deadman's switch so hard her whole arm trembled. She had a terrible suspicion she couldn't quite define, but there was no other way out. "Okay," she said. "You got a deal."

Machine's disembodied head nodded—an eerie effect—and faded out just as the sweep hand of the clock came up vertical. Without any fuss, the Universe—accretion disk, gas clouds, smeared birthing stars—folded up all around Suzy, stretching toward a vanishing point set at infinity as the singleship made the jump into contraspace.

15

$\overline{\overline{}}$

TALBECK BARLSTILKIN LISTENED TO THE NEWS THAT Dorthy and Robot had brought back with surprising calm and, even more surprisingly, he agreed that they must try the wormhole once more. But even though her Talent was limited by the secretions of her implant, Dorthy could sense the vivid rage clamped deep inside his icy composure, a red worm burning at the heart of a glacier.

Abel Gunasekra was less certain. "You call the creatures you dealt with *angels*, Seyour Robot, but to give a creature a name is not to define or even to know it. Can you be certain that they are of an honorable nature?"

Robot gave a one-sided shrug.

"We can't be certain of anything," Dorthy said, "except that the wormhole is our only way home. There is nothing for us here."

"From a student of astronomy," Gunasekra said, "I find that an astonishing remark. We are at the edge of the greatest natural laboratory in the Galaxy for studying quantum and cosmological processes. I would wish a hundred lifetimes here, to observe and to think, and certainly I do not believe it is yet time to go home."

Talbeck Barlstilkin said, without a trace of irony, "I understand that modern pressure suits can sustain life for a year at least, Professor Gunasekra. You are welcome to take one and stay, but for my own part, I wish to leave. Dorthy, Robot, our destination will not be Earth, I am afraid. I do not feel that I would enjoy the welcome that awaits me there, or anywhere else in the Federation for that matter. I must resort to a contingency measure I had always hoped I would never have to use. There is a colony planet called Iemanja, a world mostly of oceans, as its name implies. I own a small island in the Archipelago. That is where I intend to go, if the angels grant us passage back to the hypervelocity star. Iemanja is a pleasant enough world, but isolated. Ships bringing new colonists arrive at very infrequent intervals; I believe the next is due in five years. I am prepared to hire return passage on it for you and your child, and for Seyour Robot. Only hard-class, but needs must."

"That's generous of you," Dorthy said.

"Given my circumstances, it is more generous than you can imagine, but at least you will be free of the Navy. And please, Seyour Robot, do not entertain the thought of sabotaging my ship. I have already had it deal with the infestation of your cunning little machines. That was an interesting show you put on, by the way. I have tapes of it. Perhaps I could find employment as your agent, if I was not forced to choose so remote a home.

"And you, Professor Doctor Gunasekra. Will you stay here?"

"Do not play games with me, Seyour. Of course not. If there was a possibility of my surviving long enough to learn all I could . . . perhaps. But I would be needing a great deal more than a pressure suit."

"I see," Talbeck Barlstilkin said. "Well, and I had always thought that the worth of knowledge lay in its availability to all."

"As long as *I* know a thing, what does it matter to me if others do not? You cannot know what it is like, to know something no one has known before—well, no human, I should say. I discover only now that that is why I am here, and too late, alas."

Talbeck Barlstilkin turned to go, but at the top of the helical stairway to the bridge he turned and leaned at the slender rail. He said, "Do you think the angels will let us return, Robot?"

Again, Robot made his graceless, one-sided shrug.

"I thought not," Barlstilkin said, and smiled his dreadful smile before departing.

Dorthy sprawled on one of the big couches and asked it to massage her back, relaxing bonelessly as it got to work on the muscles knotted down the ladder of her spine. "I think we're all right," she said. "He is close to the edge, but he isn't *standing* on it. If he wasn't Golden, I might be worried."

"I don't know if we should talk about him like this," Gunasekra said, perching at the very edge of the padded shelf across from Dorthy's couch. "He is probably eavesdropping, after all."

"What does it matter?" Dorthy raised her voice. "It gives him some harmless amusement. Am I right, Talbeck? Don't worry, Professor Gunasekra, Golden his age do not commit suicide. The habit of enduring goes deep in them. And he can still hope that what we've learned can hurt the Federation in some way. He can wait in exile, and watch. He'll have agatherin in his hideaway, you can bet on it, and some kind of medical program ready, too. Golden think in decades, not days. Right now he has retreated to a place where the present can't touch him . . . that's why he seems remote."

"I am not a Talent, Dr. Yoshida. But it seems to me that one more setback might truly and irrevocably hurt him."

"If the angels don't let us return to the hypervelocity star, it won't matter."

"You sound as if you don't care."

"Oh, but I do. For so long, now, I have been following a path that was never mine, trudging along with the neuter female and her relatives on my back and not knowing it. Now, I am at the threshold of my own life, for the first time in a dozen years." She asked the couch to elevate her head and shoulders, and smiled at Gunasekra. "Do you drink alcohol? I know for a fact that unless the Witnesses plundered it, the wine store Talbeck laid down is far from exhausted. A little wine, for your stomach's sake?"

Gunasekra started to fuss with the controls of the holotank. "I sound priggish, perhaps, if I say that I do not take any drugs. It is true, none the less. But I will toast your freedom in fruit juice, if you like. Perhaps Seyour Robot will join you."

Robot had been staring at the impassive servant, his face only a few centimeters away from hers. He looked around at the mention of his name, then returned his gaze to the servant. He had been curiously subdued ever since he and Dorthy had returned to the ship. Missing the companion he had hardwired into his own brain, Dorthy thought. It was an insight granted her by the muffled spark of her Talent; and with it came an echo of Robot's lonely despair, the aching void inside his skull and an almost postcoital sadness, the craziness of his creativity entirely worn off and nothing to replace it.

Part of being a Talent, the part Dorthy had always resisted and resented, was the need to keep others happy. An almost desperate need sometimes, a defense mechanism that staved off what would otherwise be an almost continual bombardment of various degrees of despair. That Dorthy had tried to grow her own armor against this, a certain callousness, a certain selfishness, was perhaps one of the reasons that she had never become a fully professional Talent, a personal entertainer/confessor/advisor to whoever could afford to hire her. She'd tried it once, whoring with her Talent to pay her way through Fra Mauro. Never again, she'd vowed, too protective of her own self, despite all the training at the Kamali-Silver Institute, to want, let alone need, to let the minds of others impinge on her own. Silence, exile and cunning would be her watchwords . . . but the Alea Campaigns had promptly caught up with her, and thereafter she was a prisoner of her Talent to a degree she had never before imagined, even in her blackest moments.

But now Robot's despair touched her as she had not been touched for so long. As she had not been touched since P'thrsn and the death of poor Arcady Kilczer; or since she had rescued her sister, Hiroko, from the incestuous clutches of their uncle, so long ago on Earth. Rescued, and lost. *I cannot live among strangers.*

But to Dorthy no one was truly a stranger. She was at least reconciled to that.

Robot did not turn his gaze from the servant when Dorthy put a hand on his left shoulder, just above the seam with his prosthesis. "She isn't Machine," Dorthy said.

"She could be. The part governing her, I mean."

"It wouldn't help you, Robot. You'd have to give all of yourself, become like her."

"Maybe that wouldn't be such a bad idea," he said, swinging to face Dorthy. The alloy and plastic of his augmented arm brushed her hand away. She raised it again, set her palm inside his vee'd open suit liner, on the cage of his ribs.

"It's going to be hard, but I know you'll learn. To keep something for everyday life, to live like everyone else."

Robot took a deep breath. He said, "That's the whole point." But he did not brush her hand away.

"Putting Machine inside your head was a work of art, too? Your whole life was a work of art?"

"Or an act. But it's over. It's destroyed."

"If Machine was part of a work of art, or a performance, or whatever . . . why do you think you have to control it? Isn't that the point of what you do? To set things going and see what will happen? Maybe Machine's . . . leaving you, that's just part of the performance. It hasn't ended. It's still going on."

Robot said, "Everyone's a critic."

Dorthy smiled. "I don't know if I'm a critic, but I certainly enjoyed your last performance."

"It was kind of crude, and half of the projections were wildly out of focus most of the time . . . but yeah, given the circumstances, it wasn't so bad. For a prank, that is. Not a work of art. Kind of a terminal prank for the Witnesses."

Dorthy had been about to say she wouldn't mourn them, but she remembered the glimpse of Ang's dead face through the frosted visor. And remembered with a shiver what the neuter female had been about to do.

Robot took her hand in his own. "Maybe that's what happens, when you set yourself up as God's messenger without consulting Her first. Maybe I was set up to be the agent of Her wrath. Suzy and I called the things in the interzone angels. Well, maybe they are. I still haven't filled all the gaps in what they told me. Or maybe that's my Substantivist upbringing doing my thinking for me."

"Soon we will find out if your angels are satisfied with what has happened here," Gunasekra said. He was fiddling with the controls of the holotank. "If I could get this overornamented device to work, we might see it happen."

The servant stepped around Robot and Dorthy, leaned over Gunasekra's shoulder—he looked up, startled—and did something to control plates set among gold and mother-of-pearl encrustations. The indirect illumination of the commons dimmed: the holotank's gray slab was displaced by a view of a black double curve against frozen swirls of crimson and vermilion.

It was the planetoid, shadowed against the gas clouds. The ship had already left its surface, was moving toward the wormhole pit. Moving *into* it, Dorthy decided, because the sooty icescapes of the planetoid were rising out of the holotank, pushing the gas clouds beyond its margin. Dead center, dim phosphenes defined a circular maw. Dorthy craned for a last glimpse of the black hole's accretion disk, and the tank flared with light.

Sunlight.

Gunasekra fell back in the couch, his face shining in the light that poured out of the holotank. White sand sloped to blue water salted with whitecaps; the white beach curved away right and left, fringed by palms.

"Where is that?" Gunasekra asked. "Have the angels opened a way to Earth? Or is it the ocean world Barlstilkin talked of?"

"No," Robot said. "I know this place. It's where the angels live. And look! Look!" He stepped forward, stabbed toward the holotank with his augmented arm.

Something was forming above the sparkling ocean. It was as if a knife blade made of glass, glass brilliantly lighted from within, was prying apart the clear air. The point of light threw off rainbow mandalas as it whirled and widened; refractions compressed to form a spinning rainbow rim around a suddenly defined circle. It was a little like a pocket of hot air forming above a summer road, but with real solidity and depth, its own light defining its dimensions. Light poured out of it, although for all its prodigal quantity, the light did not illuminate anything but itself. Dorthy did not have to squint against it to see, with a sudden yaw of perception, bright flecks moving far down the tunnel's infinite perspective, rushing toward her, bursting the rim, and fountaining high above the diamond-dusted sea.

A flock, a host, a glory of angels.

Then light and heat struck at her. She staggered forward in soft white sand, bare feet sinking to the ankles. Abel Gunasekra was scrambling to his feet; Robot stood with his head tilted back, metal and plastic arm shading his eyes as he looked up at the swirling column of burning forms that leaned high above. Half a dozen meters away, Talbeck Barlstilkin turned to them, twisted mouth agape, the unscarred side of his face white in the relentless light. Behind him, the servant stood as impassively as ever.

Dorthy saw Barlstilkin's intention before he even began to reach for the pistol holstered at his wide belt. "You can't hurt them!" she yelled, her voice cracking high. *That was shock*, she thought. And: *this is more real than the neuter female's dream.* Real, and yet not, not quite. The green-white sunlight came not from a point or disk but a kind of smeared flaw, as if the clear blue of the sky had mingled and run there. And there was the feeling that nothing was quite in focus unless she looked at it: sand around the folded cuffs of her coveralls turned from a vague blur to powdery grains only when she squinted at it; when she looked up, palm fronds flowed from blurred green fans to hard-edged fronds; the mountain behind them flowed and slumped when she looked away.

Robot had noticed too. He said, "They're getting better at the transition, but without my imagination this fucking place is falling apart."

"We are in a place with its own laws," Abel Gunasekra said. "Some of them are contiguous with those of our own universe; others are not."

"Who was dreaming this! Who was dreaming this when I went away! Whose dream is it now!"

Robot was running down to the edge of the sea, shouting at tumbling, swirling angels. Their dance defined a distinct but unstable column, bright as the light-giving sky-flaw, that rose high above the sea's swell, just at the point where waves gathered themselves to run at the beach. The aperture from which they had poured was gone.

"It is no one's dream," Gunasekra said to Dorthy. "No one's, or everyone's. We are stripped to basic field equations here. Anything is possible, as long as it is written." His face glowed like beaten bronze, as if transfigured by a glimpse of God's glory.

Talbeck Barlstilkin folded his arms across the keg of his chest, not quite looking at the angels' swirling column. His face was twisted about his grim smile. "You seem very certain, Seyour Professor Doctor Gunasekra. How do you know?"

Gunasekra said softly, "Can't you hear their voices? I can hear them, and I can hear an echo of your thoughts too, of all our thoughts. We are all Talents here, if we want to be." He lifted a hand when Barlstilkin started to speak again. "No. Hush. Be still. Listen."

Dorthy found she could easily sink into the silence at her center, the perfect mirror of *Samadhi*; but she couldn't tell if she heard the tumultuous chorus there, or if it was simply mixed with the whisper of salty air over the beach, the crashing advance and seething retreat of the waves. What she did know was that they all heard it. Robot and Talbeck Barlstilkin and Abel Gunasekra, even the bonded servant. She could hear in each of them the echoes of the song of the angels, a thousand voices singing not in unison but unity, individuals weaving the song a word, a syllable, a note at a time, yet all at once. For there was no time. It was timeless. It lasted an hour or a second or a day.

And it was over.

All five humans looked at each other for a heartbeat. Then the bonded servant raised a hand to her head. She said wonderingly, "I think—" And then she collapsed, slowly and in stages, onto her knees, then curling onto her side, hands covering her face, knees drawn up.

"She sleeps," Abel Gunasekra said.

"They brought her back," Dorthy said.

Robot said, "The process of bonding terminated the chemical and electrical patterns of her consciousness, but the connectivity grown between her neurons by memory and experience could not be destroyed. All that she had learned remained, neither sleeping nor awake, neither dead nor alive. A potential. The angels brought her back." The left side of his face was twitching; water overflowed his eye and ran straight down his cheek, a gleaming track that pulsed as tears ran down it and dropped from his chin to bead the quilted material of his suit liner. He sniffed loudly and said, "They tried to restore Machine, but he'd left nothing behind."

Talbeck Barlstilkin said, "At least we know what they want now." He seemed the least affected of the five, still defiant, still proud. He gestured toward the prow of rock that pushed into the sea, a long way down the glaring curve of the beach. "And if we do what they want, we know the reward. Although I, for one, want to see it with my own eyes."

"Your servant—" Robot began.

Talbeck Barlstilkin cut him off impatiently. "Her guardian angels will look after her, no doubt."

He started down the beach, and after exchanging glances, Dorthy, Robot, and Abel Gunasekra began to follow. When they caught up with him, he said, "The RUN Police could do nothing against us if we brought back the shadow dancers. I would not need to hide."

"You mean that we could go straight to Earth," Dorthy said. The angels' song still resonated in her mind: as if she were a shining silver bell they had rung.

"That is not the point," Gunasekra insisted. "The point is that the marauders still tangle the gates between universes. The point is that they must be stopped. For the angels, now. For our Universe in less than four billion years."

"I would rather concentrate on our immediate needs," Talbeck Barlstilkin said, a dark twist in his voice. "Professor Doctor Gunasekra will do the angels' bidding for unimaginably distant posterity. What about you, Dorthy?"

"Do I need a reason?"

"Of course not," Gunasekra said with a smile. "But you must decide. We must all decide. The angels give us that."

"I wonder why," Talbeck Barlstilkin said, staring up at the forms of light that rose and fell into the clear air above the sea. The angels' unstable column had kept pace with the four humans as they trudged through hot, white sand.

Robot said to Dorthy, "Part of your guest is still there. She will never quite leave you. Machines can be wiped clean, but not neural networks."

"If you insist I must have a reason, then let it be one of my own. A long time ago my sister told me that she could not live among strangers. I thought that I was helping her, at the time. I took her out of the clutches of, of someone who was using her, gave her a room, a credit line. I had work elsewhere, I couldn't take her with me. And when I came back from that work, she had gone. Returned. She couldn't live among strangers. I'd abandoned her, you see. Persuaded myself that I'd done all I could, when really I was running away from my responsibility. I didn't want it, couldn't face it. For a long time I couldn't understand what Hiroko had meant by that note, that single cryptic line. It wasn't until I met the neuter female on P'thrsn that I understood. For Hiroko, for the neuter female, for any Alea, the stranger was the enemy. Humans or angels, or any Alea not of the family. Hiroko could not help her upbringing any more than the Alea can help the genetic compulsion to war against anyone not of their bloodline. I got out in time, you see, or I thought I had. That's why I couldn't understand it. I had always lived among strangers. But the only way I could do it was to withdraw, to wall myself off, to resent my Talent and welcome the oblivion of the counteragent, the silence of isolation. That's what I began to learn about myself, on P'thrsn. I'm still learning. That's why I make my choice now. To refuse is to side with the marauders, to side with their solipsism, that would destroy the whole Universe in an attempt to make it their own. If the means for that is taken away from them, perhaps it will be a first step, away from arrogance, from pride, towards acceptance. Toward us, toward the strangers."

She looked from face to face, Robot's compassion, Abel Gunasekra's gentle agreement, Talbeck Barlstilkin's lopsided smile. After a moment, Talbeck Barlstilkin clapped slowly and softly, one, twice, thrice. "Bravo," he said. "Would that we all had your ideals."

Dorthy told him, "You shouldn't fear strangers either, Talbeck. Hate and fear, they are two sides of the same coin."

He turned the ruin of his face toward her. "Do I not want to see the shadow dancers?"

"We must go," Abel Gunasekra said.

And Robot added, "Suzy Falcon still flies."

"I know how long we have," Talbeck Barlstilkin said, tapping the side of his head. "They have given me a clock. How quaint of them."

"We do not know what they can do to us," Abel Gunasekra said. "They let us choose, but suppose we refuse them?"

Robot said, "We would become like the shadow dancers. Encrypted and stored."

Talbeck Barlstilkin said, "We would all die."

No one tried to persuade him otherwise. They walked the rest of the way in silence, clambered over a tumble of wave-eroded boulders, climbed steep ledges like a giant's staircase to the beginning of the stone steps down to the bay of the shadow dancers.

It was so very like the vision Dorthy had been granted in the middle of the archeological excavation in the lowlands of Noyava Rosya that she experienced a dizzy moment of *déjà vu*. Robot saw her distress and put his hand to her elbow, and she leaned against him gratefully.

Together, they looked down at the graceful shapes that in clear water beneath a floating ceiling of blue-black streamers ceaselessly glided around encrusted pillars. Smooth black deltas that paced their own shadows as they rippled over the white floor of the little bay, dozens and dozens of them gliding through the paths of a stately pavane. Shadow dancers. Until now Dorthy had not known how beautiful they were.

Robot said, "They will talk to us when it is over."

Talbeck Barlstilkin said, "I don't see that they are even aware of us."

"There's more to the shadow dancers than the dancers themselves," Robot told him, pointing down to where the clear water lapped a wide ledge. Things clustered thickly just below the waterline, shifting over one another in a clutter of black, crusted shells and stiffly jointed limbs and delicately furled antennae. "This place is kind of like a library, or a university. All that the shadow dancers know is encoded in extranuclear polytene chromosomes in the scoop-shells. The dancers are mediators, the crabs builders. They will build a translation device, or have built it. I'm not sure on that. But they will speak with us, when the time comes."

Talbeck Barlstilkin folded his arms. "We must trust the angels, I suppose."

Abel Gunasekra said, "But who better to trust than God's handservants? We have been in their hands ever since we reached the core of the Galaxy. Dorthy, it is time. I can feel it."

Dorthy said, "So can I."

And felt too an airy sensation in the pit of her stomach, a dry-mouthed excitement, as she scrambled back down the steep rocks back to the beach. Abel Gunasekra looked at her with a wide grin. Dorthy laughed, and they ran down to the water hand in hand like excited children, wading out against the warm surge of the waves until they were thigh-deep.

The narrow base of the swirling, toppling tower of light swept across them. Hands that were not hands lifted them up, whirled them into the dance of light. Dorthy could still feel Gunasekra's hand in hers, that firm touch all she could feel as blazing glory drove through her and blew away all the quondam world.

16

THE LIGHTS IN THE SINGLESHIP'S LIFESYSTEM FLICKERED and dozens of little fans spun free, like so many skipped heart-beats, before resuming their steady burr. *Catalfission batteries low,* Suzy thought. Phasing back into urspace, the entropy dump had eaten deep into their reserves. Shit, she was in worse shape than she knew, should have stopped to replace batteries before she blew her way out of the *Vingança*.

Should have stopped to *think*, Suzy.

Seconds out of the jump already gone, but this weird idea that someone was in the cabin with her was so strong she looked all around before she called up her overlays, her wraparound exterior vision, and started to try to make sense of where she was. Half the overlays were missing, Machine censoring them no doubt, and visuals were all but useless, just streaks of red on black. *Make sense of it later.* Status indicators were nagging at her attention, flickering and changing even though she wasn't doing anything. Then there was the dull rumble of the motor way in

back. The crash web went rigid all over her body: *slam!* Zero
to maximum acceleration in half a minute, three gees pushing
her down against the couch then trying to throw her off it as the
attitude thrusters cut in too, applying torque to the singleship's
delta vee.

She used all her muscles to inflate her lungs. "Machine!
Machine, you fucking son of a bitch! You let me fly this thing,
you hear me?"

Nothing. At least she was beginning to make sense of what
she was seeing. The ship was skimming over some kind of vast
ice field, a glacier bigger than worlds, billions of kilometers of
water-ice and nitrogen and oxygen snow no more than thirty
or forty degrees above absolute zero, color of dried blood under
dim red threads that dwindled toward a point diamond-bright
against dimly glowing dust clouds.

"Machine, for Christ's sake talk to me!"

This place, the Spike, was vast. With a tumultuously airy
panicky feeling that she was running in the wrong direction,
Suzy was beginning to realize just how big it really was. And
she hadn't the first idea where to find the Enemy in all its
vastness, and all she had to work with were a dozen missiles
armed with pinch fusion cluster warheads, which might or
might not work after what the angels had done to them, twice
that number of one-shot X-ray lasers, and a few strictly defensive countermissiles. Just about enough to take out an asteroid
habitat. Maybe the catalyst or whatever it was the angels had
jammed onto the cluster warheads would work, but she hadn't
the faintest idea what it was supposed to do.

Machine's face suddenly rippled across Suzy's view of the
shadowy world-glacier; despite the weight of acceleration she
was so wired that she nearly popped her crashweb in surprise.
Machine said, "My apologies, Suzy. Something is about to
happen. I have been trying to get us clear."

"We're under attack? Jesus fucking Christ, give me control
here!"

"Not under attack. The marauders may or may not have
spotted us, but they are not attacking us. I have determined
that we do not have time to change our course. It may be
necessary to reenter contraspace."

Acceleration cut off and Suzy was in zero gee again, her stomach ready to hit the top of her skull. She fought down inertia sickness. "We don't have the power, you dumb bunch of codes. We can get in, but we don't hit the right energy level when we come back out, we'll be a particle cloud from here to Andromeda. Now for Christ's sake give me some slack. I'm the fucking pilot, remember?"

Machine didn't say anything, but Suzy was suddenly back in control, feeling her nerves extend into every corner of the singleship. The side of her neck stung as the couch shot a cocktail of cortical stimulants through her skin; the rush hit her like a plunge into icy brine. She ran a bandwidth scan, paged through readouts of all the crazy instrumentation Machine had bolted onto the standard package.

That was when she saw it—the trace from the gravity wave meter jiggling in irregular hillocks; the gridded overlay of the quantum strain gauge looking like it was trying to bend around itself. Some vast change deep at the quantum level of reality was tearing through the structure of vacuum itself, heading down the Spike toward the singleship at the speed of light. So powerful that its effects were outracing it, a relativistic bow wave spilling through contraspace.

Her first thought was the marauders. "Oh shit. They can do stuff like that, we aren't worth spit in a fusion flame."

"It isn't the marauders," Machine's voice said calmly. The tissue-thin overlay of his face floated among a matrix of flickering indices. "It is coming in the wrong direction. The marauders are ahead of us, beyond the ice, in the habitable zone of the Spike. This is coming from beyond the hypermatter sphere that anchors the Spike to the boundary region of the black hole's accretion disk. It is difficult to estimate the precise position of the wave front, but I estimate that it will reach the singleship in less than twenty minutes."

"No way we can outrun that, you dumb machine. You've wasted time I could have used on EVA. We still don't have any weapons, remember? Whatever it is, only chance we've got is to use the angels' catalyst, hope it works."

"And what would we then use against the marauders?"

"I'll fucking *ram* them, if that's all I can do. Wait, you're

right. We can't use the catalyst. Let me think." Suzy did a few
elementary calculations. "Near as I can tell, that's coming from
the direction of the wormhole planetoid. So maybe someone
back there found some kind of weapon?"

"It is possible," Machine said. "Humanity is not the first
intelligent race to have arrived here after the marauders took
control. The angels armed them, too."

"So someone found it and figured out how to use it. Which
means I guess it was probably that little Japanese girl, the one
with the alien in her head. Dorthy Yoshida." Where had that
popped up from? "Her or Robot, except he wouldn't know
anything because you guys were the one the angels talked to."
She felt a despairing rage. "Shit, she's going to shoot them down
before I get any kind of chance! I'm going to die out here for
nothing, Machine."

"We do not know what kind of weapon it is, except that it
is half a million years old. We do not know that it will work
against the marauders."

"We'll know what it does in twenty minutes. No time for
evasion."

"Eighteen minutes, plus or minus 6.4."

Suzy popped her crashweb. "Which gives me maybe enough
time to reset our weapons."

"This is not the time—"

"When that thing hits the marauders, and if it doesn't work,
then they'll sure as shit be looking to see where it came from.
And if we're still alive they'll see *us*."

"You are correct. My apologies."

"Let me get into my suit here, and then you can open the
hatch. Okay?"

Suzy automatically looked sternward as she shot through
the hatch into raw space, looked beyond the bulbous flare
of the singleship's reaction motor down the linear geometries
of the Spike— streaks of dull red light dwindling away over
a dark infinite plain of ice toward the hypermatter sphere.
Looked for the massive quantum event tunneling toward her
and saw nothing except maybe a glimpse of a flickering ripple,
rather like heat lightning, against the narrow band of nasty ultraviolet light that was the accretion disk seen edge-on.

Didn't have time to look any longer. Killed momentum and did a neat somersault, feet down toward the delta sweep of the underside of the singleship's lifting surface, a couple of puffs of her reaction pistol to get her drifting toward the tapered nose. Helmet spot crawling over black skin, hardly any other illumination even with amplification circuits flipped up. Just the reflection of dull red thready light from God's own glacier a million kilometers below the cleats of her boots, don't even think about that Suzy, you got a job to do.

Go easy now. Clip a D-ring to a recessed staple, use the pronged key. The hatch to the weapon bay hinging away nice and smooth, racks swinging out, glimpse of some kind of sparkly stuff like it was deep in the gold leaf plating of the missiles' sleek heads, gone when she looked closely.

Red numerals hung before her nose were counting back toward zero. Less than six minutes now. Don't think about that, don't think about the sensation of someone watching over your shoulder. Machine probably spying; lot of good it would do him.

It didn't take more than a moment to jack into the circuit node and switch it from *main system board* to *remote*. She reset the jumpers the Witnesses had pulled and switched on and saw the overlay come up so clear and green inside her visor she had to smile. Machine might be inside the main system, but he had a lot to learn about flying a singleship.

Machine's voice inside her helmet, in her ear. "I still don't have control, Suzy. What is the problem."

"No problem. I kind of thought I'd take care of that side of things."

He started to say a whole lot of things but she wasn't listening, turning the hatch sockets and pushing out of the way as it swung sweetly closed. Unclipping the D-ring and scooting across the ship's belly, visor centimeters from its plates so she wouldn't have to think about a million klicks of yawning void. *Two minutes.* Clipping the D-ring again, hands sweating inside her gloves, the hatch of the X-ray laser pod brushing her shoulder as it came out so she started to tumble, wasting precious seconds getting straight again.

Jack in. *Main system board* to *remote*. Machine still talking, trying to be reasonable. "Sure," Suzy said, "and I let you have control, you'd have let me back in the lifesystem? This way I see us as equal partners, what do you say?"

"You don't know what you're doing, Suzy."

"Yeah, but I do. You and me, man."

Red numerals sliding down to a row of zeros, then starting to flash as they began to count up. Everything powered up, twisting the latches and reaching to unclip the D-ring even as the pod slid back into place. Still counting up, and she thought maybe Machine had got that wrong, too.

That's when it hit.

Everything around her seemed to warp into a circle of perfectly even light, and for the smallest interval of time it all stopped. Everything: right down to the whirl of electrons, the jitter of quarks. Suzy felt herself die. She felt her anima torn from her body, sucked after the ineluctable change racing down the Spike, after the dwindling circle of light.

And felt herself fly right *through* the light, a great soundless flash all around her so she had to blink and blink, to clear the afterimages, to see where she was.

Which was inside her p-suit, kneeling in granular sand, pure and white as sugar. Someone standing over her, a solarized shadow against greenish sunlight.

"Hello, Suzy," Dorthy Yoshida said. "You'd better listen, because we don't have much time. No time at all, to speak of."

Suzy reached for the latches of her helmet, but Dorthy Yoshida said no, this wasn't real, her voice clear and intimate in Suzy's ears so she knew it wasn't coming over any com band.

Suzy said, "Well, it sure as hell looks real to me," looking around at the fringe of leaning palms, their saw-toothed fronds etched against a perfect blue sky, at gentle waves casting foam across hard, wet sand. Glimpse of someone wandering there, at the edge of the waves, plump brown-skinned guy with slicked back blue-black hair, but only there if she kind of looked sideways, like the troubled ghost of some beachcomber searching for his fate in the tidewrack.

"That's Abel Gunasekra," Dorthy told her. "He's linked to you through me. I'm talking to you through the implants in your ears, so Machine can't hear me. Only you can. All this is a sort of metaphor, Suzy. The angels can only sustain it for the moment the catalyst passes through your locality. Think of it as reality melting a little, then hardening again. We're in that fluid phase now."

"The angels, right. I knew they had to be in on it. So you loosed that catalyst for them, huh? The one those other dupes had, the ones crashed their ship on the planetoid. You think it'll work, being as it's so old?"

"We're here, together. Not only that, you're in my future, Suzy. Where I am, the catalyst hasn't hit the marauders. It aimed at us, at the *Vingança*, at the wormhole planetoid, but it hasn't reached the source yet. Where you are, it's already racing down the hyperstructure. It works through contraspace somehow, so its effect arrives before it does. There's a causal paradox or three there, I think. Abel Gunasekra could explain it, I'm sure, but he's busy right now. There's a problem, Suzy. That's what we have to talk about."

"You say it worked against the marauders? What's there to talk about, huh?"

"It *will* work against the process the marauders were using as a weapon. The process the angels left behind. But the marauders managed to clone it, the way they're trying to clone the hyperstructure. There are super photon sources scattered all around the black hole's event horizon. The super photons turn into energy, light, gamma rays, X rays, and they turn into particles, too. Hadrons and leptons: protons, electrons, neutrons. Mostly they turn into hydrogen, a little helium. New matter, forming all the time deep inside the accretion disk. Radiation flux from infall into the black hole increases, but eventually can't escape because there's too much gas, and there's a vast explosion which blows gas outward. That's happened once already, the gas clouds in a ring around the accretion disk, expanding away from it."

"So what are you saying. That the Spike is made of that stuff?"

"Partly. Most of it is made up of space-time itself, worked on by angel machinery. The ice, the water and the atmosphere in the habitable zone, the soil too I suppose, that all

comes from the new matter. But most of the new matter
goes toward forming new stars. Beyond the far end of the
Spike are five Wolf-Rayet stars set in complicated but stable orbits around each other. Their light is channeled all the
way down the Spike, growing redder and redder until, when
it reaches the hypermatter sphere, it's way down in the far
infrared."

"This matters, now you've done them in?"

"The catalyst won't kill the marauders. Just poison the super
photon source that they were using as a weapon against anything
that came through the gateway planetoid. The other sources,
around the black hole, they are still working, pumping out
new hydrogen into the Universe. Do you see, Suzy? The
marauders will still be building new stars when the old ones
die out! Gunasekra thinks they've learned how to clone new
hyperstructures, too. They want their family to live forever,
beyond the heat death of the Universe. Their stars will still
shine around the black holes that every galaxy will become.
Eternal light, as far as they're concerned. But there's a problem
with accumulation of photons, heating of the vacuum."

She explained about the contraction of the Universe back
down to a singularity, and why space had to be cold when
it started to happen, but Suzy was losing interest. Funny, that
she didn't feel anything. She was going to die for nothing and
it didn't seem to mean much.

And then Dorthy Yoshida said, "That's why we need you,
Suzy. You still have the catalyst the angels printed into your
missiles. You can poison all the sources of continuous creation.
Poison them so that the marauders won't be able to clone new
ones. Close off the wormholes between different universes, let
the angels go their own way."

Suzy looked up at the woman, but she was haloed by light
so bright that Suzy couldn't see her face. Suzy said, "You're not
shitting me?"

"You're right there, Suzy. The angels could arm our ship,
but when we come back out the marauders will be ready
for us. They have other more conventional weapons, apart
from the one we destroyed. You're the only one who can
do it."

"So I aim at the black hole, not at the marauders. The angels get what they want, and you get something too, right? You get to go home, is my guess. What do I get?"

"I don't know what to tell you," Dorthy Yoshida said. "If this was real I could use my Talent to at least try and outsmart you. But it isn't real. We don't have much time, either. Listen, Suzy. You went out there to destroy the marauders, but you really knew you could never do that."

Suzy said, "Was going to hurt the sons of bitches as much as I could, anyhow. For all that happened in the Campaigns." She sniffed and something cold and salty slid down the back of her throat: she was crying didn't even know it until then.

Dorthy Yoshida said, "What I'm asking you to do will hurt the marauders, Suzy. It won't kill them, but it will put a stop to their plans. I'll still be with you, linking you with Abel Gunasekra if you want it. He'll know where all the sources of creation are. Just fire the missiles off at them; that will be all that's needed to start the catalytic process. And don't listen to Machine. He got too close to the Alea neuter female, caught her need for revenge. . . ."

Dorthy Yoshida's voice raveled to a whisper. Everything was going dark. It was as if a cloud had suddenly covered the sun. Suzy tried to get up, but there was nothing to push against. All she could see was the faint halo of light around Dorthy Yoshida's head.

"Wait! Tell me what happens to me afterward!"

But there was only her own voice. The halo was merely the backscatter of her torch's beam, refracted by her swollen tears. Whatever it was that had passed through the ship, like the very breath of God, was gone. The singleship was still racing over the vast ice field.

No, something had changed. The undefined presence she'd felt at her back since the ship had dropped out of contraspace was stronger now. And now it was right inside her: if she concentrated she could bring back a faint echo of glare on a sweep of sand, a raveling whisper of surf in the seashell curve of her ears.

Yes, Suzy. I'm here. I'm with you.

Suzy said, "Hey, I hear you."

But her voice broke her concentration. She was still hooked to the underside of the singleship, her glove on the D-ring. She completed the motion, let the line reel back into her belt.

And then the calm, uninflected voice of Machine filled her helmet. "You had better get inside, Suzy. I believe that I have discovered the marauders."

Suzy stayed completely suited up inside the lifesystem, afraid that if she undogged her helmet, Machine would blow the atmosphere. She had to jack into the ship's displays through her suit terminal, everything coming up in monochrome because the data flow was almost too much for the suit's processing circuit.

Machine said, "The space-time disturbance has gone. It does not appear to have hurt the marauders. I have been running the neutrino detector, Suzy. There is a huge background, suggesting sources extending eight billion kilometers down the Spike. But I have managed to isolate several large point sources at the boundary of the habitable region."

"Just let me take a look a minute, okay?"

Suzy stared at the neutrino profiles for a moment, then called up records of measurements made at BD Twenty during the Alea Campaigns. Amber contour graphs settled one through the other, a near perfect match with the signature of Enemy fusion technology.

Machine said, "There is more. The forward mass-detection probes are picking up gravithic anomalies, very massive structures strung above the plane of the Spike. They are contiguous with the boundary of the neutron sources."

"Yeah, okay, I see that."

Machine said, "They also seem to be in the equivalent of geosynchronous orbit, but that, of course, is impossible."

Suzy said, "Just let me check it out, okay?"

Little hillocky contours inside the massive distortion caused by the Spike itself. . . . Yeah, they were right at the edge of the habitable zone. It was difficult to correlate specific neutrino sources with the structures because of the terrific background—there were fusion sources as far down the Spike as Prosperino was from Sol—but Suzy tried it three ways and came up with the same answer.

Machine said, "The neutrino sources were close enough to have been reached by the disturbance, the ancient angel weapon. It didn't work, Suzy. The marauders are still there. The glory is still ours for the taking."

"I've got to think about this."

"There's no time, Suzy. From their position, right on the border of the habitable region, I deduce that the structures must be associated with defense. We will reach them in less than three hundred seconds. You must let me use the missiles now."

Suzy thought about what Yoshida had told her, that Machine wasn't to be trusted. She said, "No. No, that's no good. Those things are big, and the conventional loads on the missiles aren't enough. And we'd just waste the angels' weapon."

"Give me control, Suzy. I can pinpoint specific vulnerable points in the structures. What use is the angels' weapon? We know that it does not work."

"Check background radiation." The thought came to her out of that watchfulness inside her.

"I do not understand what you mean, Suzy."

"Check it! It'll be lower than it was before the angels' weapon passed us by."

"Radiation has dropped, it is true. But we are nearing the habitable part of the Spike, Suzy. It would be expected—"

"The marauders' weapon is gone, that's why it's dropped. You've got to give me control of the ship. There's a better target for our missile. Do it, Machine!"

Like that, she had made her decision.

"No, Suzy. The target is ahead of us. If we do not destroy it, the eaters-of-all-children will destroy us. Rendezvous in one hundred fifty-four seconds and counting. At R minus ten seconds you must fire the missiles. Or their explosions will destroy us, too."

In crude amber graphics inside her helmet, points bloomed on the hillocky mass traces. Machine said, "I have located what I believe to be synergistic weak points in the structures. Leave the aiming to me."

Suzy had worked out what she would do, had reached for the controls. But she couldn't find the courage to complete the motion. Then Machine said, guessing somehow what she planned, "No, Suzy. If you switch me off you switch off every system—"

But she'd already done it. The graphics faded; she could see the bleakly lighted, cramped cabin, the checklights of the controls, half of them red, most of the rest blinking amber. She fired up the slow dumb circuits of the auxiliary computer, called up an outside view, redlit ice receding behind her, a blue-white ribbon seeming to rise into infinity ahead, rising toward an intense point of white light. No graphics, no detectors—those were all routed through the circuits Machine had usurped. Nothing but sight and radar and the minimum of status indicators. As in combat flying on Titan, she was flying by the seat of her pants.

"So let's *do* it," she said, and played a quick pattern on the attitude thrusters, turning the ship so that it was flying ass-backwards, nose swinging toward the narrow glare of the accretion disk. Proximity alerts started to blare and Suzy switched them off, glimpsed sternward a long gray borderland between ice and ocean, huge irregular shining shapes strung above and eye-hurting points beginning to radiate out from them. Cut off the ship's cameras. No time for distractions now. She had to listen for that still, small voice inside her. . . .

There's a pattern you have to follow. Gunasekra's telling me about it right now. Just relax into it, Suzy. Just let it come. . . .

Suzy felt her arm lift without her having anything to do with it, and clenched down involuntarily, couldn't relax, couldn't believe this was real. Those burning points, she could guess what they were, they were real. Any second she'd find out just how real they were. Oh sweet Jesus Christ, please get it done.

Just breathe deeply and slowly, Suzy. Breathe from your center.

"I'm trying, but sweet Jesus. . . .

Concentrate on your breath. Shri shanti. Shri shanti.

"I can hear the waves now."

Yes. Hush now. Shri shanti. Shri shanti. Sweet breath. Holy breath. *Just breathe, Suzy.* Dorthy Yoshida smiled, bright smile lighting up her plain face. *You're doing terrifically.*

Suzy could see everything for an instant, plain as day. The white curve of the beach pushing against the blue water, and Dorthy Yoshida, and the pattern of bright nodes scattered around the black hole at the bottom of the accretion disk's seething swirl, and frozen tundra a million klicks below her keel smearing past at a thousand klicks per second, and the fortresses rising up, vaster than she could imagine, so huge yet so far away that their weaponry hadn't quite reached her, not quite yet. . . .

And then most of it whirled away from her, the beach and the raw tides of light, and she was her own self again. Her hands were still splayed on the console. A pop-up display in the corner of her vision, the suit's fire control grid, showed that all the missiles were gone. And radiating away from each of them the unmistakable distortions in space-time of the angels' catalytic weapon. It was done.

Suzy glanced sternward and saw glare washing toward her, the same last sight so many of her comrades had had down in the gravity well of BD Twenty when their ships had been bracketed by relativistic plasma jets. Just time to fire her remaining weaponry in defiance and to call out to the dwindling sense of otherness deep inside her, to plead to be taken away from this, before it hit.

17

LIGHT BURST ALL AROUND HER, COLORS GLISTENING AND sliding into each other as if she had been plunged headfirst into a rainbow. She staggered on hot sand, still dazzled by the momentary vision she'd had coming down from it all, a blinding glimpse of the architectures of frozen light that encrusted the horizon of the fractal desert. A city—she didn't know what else to call it— a city of light receding at infinite speed into the infinite . . .

eternal light forever fixed in the same place like the image of
a traveler engulfed by a black hole, all that remains of her in
this Universe, held at the timeless Schwarzchild boundary.

Someone crashed into her side. It was Robot, holding her
up, asking if she was all right. His mouth was against her ear,
yet she could hardly hear him through the whirl of wind and
carillon of pure random notes like an avalanche of crystal bells.
And she was babbling, trying to tell him about the glory she'd
glimpsed: but mere words couldn't catch what she'd seen, and
the moment of limitless apprehension was already fading, as an
unfixed photographic image fades in the common light of day.

Yet light still swirled around her. She and Robot were the
center of a rush of light and air. Tongues of brittle fire fleetingly
caressed them, showing now inhuman faces of great and terrible
beauty, now patterns that echoed her fading memory of the
glory she'd seen, dazzlingly bright yet transparent as water. She
could see through them, see sand devils stirred up by the fierce
dance, the blue sea whipped into whitecaps breaking against a
steep bulwark of rock, ragged palm leaves clashing overhead,
mixing and remixing the sky-flaw's green-white light.

Abel Gunasekra sprawled on white sand a couple of meters
away. Talbeck Barlstilkin's black figure huddled next to him,
arms wrapped around his head as if in a pathetic effort to
ward off the careering angels. Gunasekra raised his head to
say something to Barlstilkin and for a moment his gaze locked
with hers: their shared understanding seemed to crackle across
the air between them.

They had both, if only for a moment, had a glimpse of the
City Of God.

Robot yelled into her ear. "The angels! The angels! The
angels are leaving!"

She began to remember what she had done, and why, though
she was still not quite sure who she was, Suzy Falcon or Dorthy
Yoshida. She looked at the towering swirl of burning angels, at
the steep rocks standing adamant above foaming waves. Angels
and shadow dancers, leaving and returning.

"It's over," she said, clasping Robot in joy. "It's really over!"

He returned her hug, this strange awkwardly tall man, skin
very white in the glaring whirl, his blond crest of hair standing

up as if electrified. She wished at that moment she'd said that she loved him just one time in all the times she had slept with him on the long voyage out.

The thought was Suzy's, and as it faded so did she. Dorthy knew who she was again, but knew too that some part of Suzy would always be with her, a trace that would always linger, just as the neuter female, Arcady Kilczer, Hiroko, all the others whose minds she had ever touched, were with her still. Every part of her mind was inhabited by ghosts. She was only just beginning to realize how much she needed them.

As Suzy sank into Dorthy's mind, the storm of angels rose higher and, with a great clashing roar, flew inland. The electric wind of their wake stripped fronds from palm trees and set them afire. Part of Dorthy yearned after the angels: she gripped Robot's hand and pulled him with her, scrambling up to the highest point of the rocks.

Sooty fragments of palm fronds, most still crawling with sparks, settling all around them, Dorthy and Robot gazed inward. The fractal desert had sunk; or perhaps the beach and the sea had risen. They could glimpse, beyond the burning tops of the palms, beyond the unsettling, infinitely intricate patterns of the fractal desert, the virtual image of the city of light, frozen forever at the horizon of the interzone.

Abel Gunasekra joined them a few minutes later, puffing hard from the climb. Talbeck Barlstilkin followed, stalking carefully from rock to rock, hands in the pockets of his slant-cut, black trousers in an effort to feign nonchalance.

Robot looked at them all. "The angels have one more task for us," he said, "and then we can go. It's to do with the shadow dancers."

Dorthy brought her gaze down from the glimmering horizon to Barlstilkin's half-ruined face. "It touched you, too," she said. "Don't tell me that it didn't."

"We all felt it," Gunasekra said. His smile was so wide that his merry black eyes were almost hidden by his rounded cheeks. "I was out in the accretion disk, Dorthy, scattered all through it like a perfect observer. I could *feel* the process of creation! I could feel hadrons and leptons bursting into existence, clashing against each other, fusing into hydrogen. I could ride the force lines, see the shape of space itself, see gravithic distortions like bubbles of fire in old glass. . . . For that little while, I had the eyes and ears of the Brahmin himself." He said, his smile slackening a notch, "I shall not forget that, at least."

Talbeck Barlstilkin said, "We'll have plenty of time for memories when this is over." He added, "If we have something to do, let us do it," and turned on his heel and made his way from boulder to boulder toward the rim of the shadow dancers' amphitheater.

Robot said, "Man's all riled up."

Dorthy said, "He's afraid, and he hasn't felt fear for a long time. He feels that time is running out, not only here, but for him personally."

She would have said more, but just then Barlstilkin shouted out. He was standing atop a boulder, and Dorthy thought for a moment that the boulder was sinking under him; but then she saw that thousands of crab-things were crawling around it, layer upon layer clambering over each other. She stopped, but Robot kept on going, and the carpet of crab-things parted for him.

Robot said, "Hey, it's okay, they don't mean no harm," and held his augmented arm up to Barlstilkin, who merely stared coldly down his caved-in nose at the artist. "Well, I guess you can get down from there on your own," Robot said cheerfully, and went on past.

Dorthy followed him, things moving away from her feet in a clatter of chitinous limbs. Black, flattened shells glistened with a deep luster, like that of very old lacquer. Some, Dorthy noticed as she picked her way over uneven rock, looked to be half-armored in pitted red-gold metal that rose in spikes around the frontal cluster of stalked eyes. The limbs of others were tipped in the same stuff, complex growths that could have been sensors, could have been tools. The smallest was the size of her hand; the largest a couple of meters across, smaller versions of itself clinging to its many limbs, around the fringed gill pouch that pulsed in the joint of its carapace. Every one of them had a raw, wrinkled symbiont tucked near its complex mouthparts, the link that made them one with shadow dancers and scoop-shells. They smelled of brine and long chain organic acids and raw ozone: it made Dorthy's nose itch.

Gunasekra said, "I suppose that these you could simply scoop up, but I do not see how you could take even the corpse of one shadow dancer with you, let alone keep such a creature alive."

"We don't need to take anything material."

Robot was standing on the rim of the terraced drop down to the flooded amphitheater, where shadow dancers wove their endless pavane among sunken pillars beneath the floating roof of weed. A new pillar rose at the edge of the clear water, complexly carved, glistening black and red. At its top, a kind of scrolled extension leaned over the last step of the terrace. Something spiky dangled from it.

Robot said again, "We don't need to take anything material at all. Just an engram of the shadow dancers, something we can implant in a suitable donor when we return to Earth."

Talbeck Barlstilkin had reluctantly descended from his perch, followed Dorthy and Gunasekra. He said, "Do you think the RUN Police will allow us the time do that?"

Robot said, "You could take some of these crab critters, too, I guess. If you can catch them. We'd have to speak to the shadow dancers about that, crab might be off-season. That's the translation device, hanging from the pillar."

"How do you know all this?" Talbeck Barlstilkin asked sharply. Sweat was beaded on the unscarred half of his face.

"I guess the angels told me."

Dorthy said, "They spoke to you before, didn't they? When you were here with Suzy. I wonder why they only spoke to you."

"They spoke to Machine before, me now. The *stuff* of Machine is still in my head, right, his *corpse*. I guess they use that. The shadow dancers, they want to speak with one of us, too. I don't want to sound pushy, Dorthy, but you might be the best one of us for that."

She laughed. "Because I know aliens? Really, I hardly know any of you, let alone the Alea or the shadow dancers. Don't worry, Talbeck, I will do it. Whatever it is."

"That's good," Talbeck Barlstilkin said.

"We have time enough," Gunasekra told the Golden. "Is this not wonderful?"

"Not that much time," Robot said. "The angels are keeping a way open, but they don't want to do it for long. In case the marauders kickstart continuous creation somehow and fuck things up all over again."

"Just *what* is it I'm supposed to do?"

"Just go down there and put on that headpiece, is all. The shadow dancers will do the rest."

"Is it really that simple?"

"Hey, if you can't trust angels, who can you trust?"

The stone of the last step was smooth as bone under water warm as her own blood; a wave wet Dorthy's pants to the knees and nearly knocked her over, wake of a shadow dancer smoothly turning just beyond the edge, black wings arching down as it planed away. It was as big as a killer whale, and Dorthy nervously wondered what shadow dancers ate. *Shell-fish*, she thought. *They've got irised rows of platelike grinding surfaces beyond mouthflaps on their underside, that was the first thing I learned, back on Novaya Rosya. And they eat the scoop-shells, too, for the genetically encoded information they hold. Like browsing in a library.*

She could just see the scoop-shells that fringed the top of the nearest pillar, in the shadow of blue-black fronds that spread in fans across the surface of the water. Thousands of them wound in spiral patterns around every pillar in the amphitheater, each kicking with a myriad of finely fringed legs to filter food from the water. . . .

Come on, Dorthy, quit fucking around. (Suzy?) Let's just do it.

The new black-and-red pillar reared up out of the water right in front of her; the circlet or crown or whatever it was dangled above her head. She had to go on tiptoe to reach it and almost fell on her ass when she plucked it away—but that was better than falling into the flooded amphitheater. She managed to grab hold of the edge of the stepped ledge above her, somehow didn't drop the circlet as the pillar trembled and began to lose definition as the crab-things which had clustered together let go of each other and sank into the water, scuttled away over white sand. A few sculled in circles around Dorthy's feet before they, too, were gone. She heard one of the men above her shout something, but she didn't dare look up in case she lost her balance.

The circlet burned her fingers. Neither metal nor shell nor bone, but some kind of hybrid material, crusted as if it had been grown somewhere on a coral reef. As she climbed back up the giant steps, she felt it grow cooler, felt its crustose surfaces slide into new microconfigurations. Tentative tendrils of electricity prickled across her hand, wound her forearm. It was adapting to her.

"All right," she said, pitching her voice to the men at the top of the steep terrace. "I suppose you know how it works."

Robot said, "Put it on. That's all you have to do."

"That's all." Dorthy was very afraid, but as Robot had said, if you couldn't trust angels. . . . She raised the circlet over her head, set it down.

Twelve billion voices roared in the cave of her skull.

When she awoke she was lying on bare rock at the top of the terrace. She felt as if someone had used a crowbar to prize off the top of her skull. Robot was leaning over her. She wanted to say something about angels not being right all of the time, but something rose in her throat and she twisted her head sideways and threw up. Robot held her head until the spasm had passed. His prosthetic hand was cool on her clammy brow.

He said, "You fell right down, and it knocked us all down too." He helped Dorthy sit up. "I guess I was wrong, huh?"

Abel Gunasekra squatted on his heels behind Robot, silhouetted against blue sky. Talbeck Barlstilkin stood behind him. Dorthy told them, "I'm all right. Really I am. The shadow dancers made a mistake, that's all. They are all one, a symbiosis, a gestalt. Shadow dancers, crab-things, scoop-shells, all part of the same consciousness. They, or it, it thinks that humanity is the same. So the device connected me to all of them, and to all of humanity, too."

Robot said, "We know."

Abel Gunasekra said, "You fell over, and the device fell from your brow. That was fortunate, for we were as stricken as you. I know that I could not have taken it from you. An interesting thing: Seyour Barlstilkin's servant returned while you were unconscious, as if summoned."

Dorthy twisted around to look where Gunasekra pointed, saw the slim woman standing a little way off, as impassive as ever, her hands clasped before her. No, something about her had changed. Dorthy could feel it even though the empathy they had all shared had vanished with the angels, and her Talent wasn't working at all in this place between universes.

"All we need to do," Robot said, "is take some of the crabs, or some of the scoop-shells. It doesn't matter which."

"It may matter how many," Abel Gunasekra said. "It would be like dividing a hologram: the whole picture remains but becomes fuzzier and fuzzier until nothing is left but noise."

Dorthy said, "They have already lost much, when the angels rescued them and brought them here." She could feel that loss, threads pulled from the weft of a pattern millions of years old. She said, "What happened to the translation device?"

Talbeck Barlstilkin held out his hand. The crusted circlet dangled between finger and thumb. He said, "You were in contact with everyone all at once. Everyone in the Federation?"

"I think so. I didn't count them."

"Of course not. But I believe that even half the population would suffice." He raised the circlet over his head—

"Talbeck! No!"

—and lowered it.

And screamed. The same scream that tore Dorthy's throat: Robot's: Abel Gunasekra's. Echoed and reechoed by everyone on Earth, on all the Ten Worlds, on every far colony and in every orbital habitat and every ship, warping the first cries of a million newborn babies, a million last breaths. Behind the scream was fire, fire and stars, two images fused together. Ghost of the moment before: starting across a lamplit courtyard, its high stone walls rising into night, hearing the distant scream of an X-ray laser charging up and not knowing what it was. Ghost of the moment after: stumbling back through the archway, aflame down one side from head to foot: a stone edge striking shins: plunging into the cistern, water's cold slop quenching flame but not agony. And caught between: the terrible bright instant when the web of water that netted the cobbles turned to blood, and the air filled with the shock of the explosion and a driven spray of molten stone. Everything in the courtyard instantly afire, wagons suddenly shadows within balls of orange fire, horses and men screaming inside their new coats of flame, rain flashed to steam, hair and skin and clothes blasted alight. Burning! Burning! Burning!

And yet that was only the frame for everything else, vivid and terrible but marginal to the great cool vision of the Galactic core. The triple rivers of light crossing the black hole's accretion disk. The wormhole planetoid. The prickly involutions of the hypermatter sphere; and the Spike tapering beyond it, diminished by the grandeur of the core yet at the same time an immeasurably vast territory of grasslands and forests and calm blue seas running on forever beneath cloud-dappled sky. And behind the vision, behind the echo of the interwoven gestalt of the shadow dancer symbiosis, between fire and infinity, agony and rapture: the sense of hidden machineries, engines of the night singing, each to each, majestic impalpable symphonies of the secret history of the Universe.

Dorthy screamed out against the night, and suddenly the scream was her own scream at agony no longer there. She was on hands and knees on smooth stone. Warm light was beating at her back. She wondered if she was going to throw up again, but her stomach clenched wetly around nothing at all.

What she had felt at the last, echoed and reechoed twelve billion times, had been Talbeck Barlstilkin's death.

What she still felt was the white hum of the translation device, the infolded point-to-point contact with every living human being.

The woman who had been Talbeck Barlstilkin's bonded servant reached her master and plucked the crusted circlet from his head. His body collapsed; nothing but feedback had held it up. Continuing the same graceful movement, the woman straightened her arm and pitched the circlet out across the shadow dancers' bay. There was a flurry of movement where it kissed the water, and then it was gone.

The woman turned to the three people on the rock ridge, her plain face transformed by a beatific smile.

"I remember!" she said. "Oh, but it is so wonderful! I remember who I am!"

There was little left to do but say their good-byes.

Dorthy said to Abel Gunasekra, for perhaps the fifth time, "You're sure you've made the right decision?"

He smiled, and took her hands in his own. "I feel it's right." It was what he had said all the other times she'd asked. He added, "I feel like a little child again, Dorthy. I have this whole beach to explore, an infinite, timeless junction between all the universes in the Metauniverse. Out in the accretion disk, borne by angels, I knew for a moment just a fraction of what it is like to be an observer of everything. To be the ultimate viewpoint, if you like. I've always liked beachcombing; who knows what seas wash against this shore?"

"And whom will you tell? Who will know what you learn?"

"I'll know. And I don't think I'll be alone forever. I have a suspicion," Abel Gunasekra said, "that the angels weren't all they appeared. They were both more than they said they were, and somehow less, too. I want to try and understand that, to begin with. And to begin with, I'll have company. For a little while at least."

He and Dorthy looked at the woman who had been Barlstilkin's bonded servant. She was ambling among the palms that fringed the white beach, stopping now to touch one of the shaggy, leaning boles as she looked toward the fractal desert she would soon cross. When she pushed from the palm and resumed her slow walk, Dorthy glimpsed a nacreous shimmer tracing her movements, as if she were parting currents of light. Neither human nor angel but caught halfway, slowly dissolving out of this interzone. Going on. Following the angels into the unimaginable gap between universes, the silences where no Word has yet been spoken.

"Jesus Christ, I thought I never would get those things on board," Robot said, startling Dorthy. His blond mane was tousled and sweaty; his grin was manic. "What I always wanted to be," he said, "a crab herder. Those things have less sense than my little helpers, but they're stowed away, if that's the right term. Climbing all over the walls of Barlstilkin's cabin. I locked 'em in, if that'll do any good. Where they climb the walls, their little feet leave *dents* in the metal. But, they are aboard, more than two dozen. Good for crab barbecue, if nothing else."

Abel Gunasekra said, "I suppose that it is always the duty of the artist to mock the solemn moment. To remind us that we are human."

"Yeah. I piss in cathedrals, too. Are we out of here or what? We don't have much time."

He jerked the triple-jointed thumb of his prosthesis skyward, at the light-giving flaw in the blue sky. Dorthy hadn't noticed until now, but yes, it was smaller, dimmer.

Robot said, "That's the way home. That's where it all crosses over. Into our universe, at least. Unless you fancy trying out a new one."

Abel Gunasekra said, "The chances are very great that any other universe would not be able to support even the subatomic particles which make up your bodies and your ship, let alone life."

"That's what I'm going to miss about you, Doc. Your unfailing sense of humor. I'm having fun, you know. This is all so neat. I'm going to spend the rest of my life trying to pin down the way it is here. Like the vision of Saint John the Divine. Multimedia for sure. Flotation tank, surgical intervention in the sensory areas of the brain. Feed it right in, reproduce what we felt as near as I can get it right."

Dorthy said, "You'd have difficulty finding willing participants. Why be so extreme, Robot?"

"You'd be surprised at who gets off on that kind of stuff," Robot said. "Listen, art is communication. It's there to tell someone something. This is the meat we will kill; this is the land that I own; this geometrical shape is a woman; this picture of a pipe is not a pipe. The best art has the simplest message, the simplest is the most difficult to do. I had a flash of heaven, not by light, not by my eyes, but by everything I am. Anyone wanting to share that is going to have to give up a year, I think, a year of evolving toward it, a year leading up to a single flash. And in that flash—if you're ready, you see it."

Abel Gunasekra said, "I do believe that this is not the time for explication of the theory of your art, Seyour Robot. The flaw is indeed closing. The light we see is energy and matter spilling from our universe to this place, all becoming light, for only photons can cross. We ourselves are not really here, but of course you understand that. We are stored as standing waves at the boundary. You must become that wave again, untangle yourselves from this illusion."

Dorthy took his hands. "You really will stay here, Abel? With no light, and no way back?"

"Perhaps there will be stars, without that misshapen sun. And certainly there will be other suns, farther down the beach. I have only to walk to find new light. I will be all right, Dorthy. Do not worry. All my life, I think, I have been living toward this moment." He took his hands away from hers, laid one on top of her head, the other on her belly. "Take great care, with all you carry."

So Dorthy and Robot climbed the ship's ramp, kicking unreal sand from their feet. Gunasekra stood at the foot of the ramp, smiling up at them, arms folded. The slope of Dorthy's belly tingled. She turned to look one more time at that strange place. The sea, darkened to violet now in the fading light, the white bow of sand, shadows deep among the leaning palms. The changeling who had been Talbeck Barlstilkin's bonded servant flitted among the palms, faster and faster, gathering speed or time, her arms raised as she danced, flinging lines of light through the darkness. A spectral crown glittered on her brow, its infolded patterns a map of the patterns repeated beyond the border of the palms, marching endlessly out toward the eternal light beyond the interzone.

The ship was inhabited by ghosts. Even before Dorthy had finished hooking herself up to the control couch in the bleak little bridge—its grained vinyl still bore the imprint of Talbeck Barlstilkin's body—systems began to start up by themselves. By the time she had fastened the crashweb and adjusted the sensory mask, the reaction motor had completed its warm-up sequence and figures in quaint twentieth century computer type were ticking backward toward zero.

Robot's voice, piped up from an acceleration tank deep in the bowels of the ship, said in her ear, "You sure you know what you're doing, Seyoura?"

"The ship is doing everything for itself. A last trace of the angels, I suppose. We're about to go."

On impulse, she called up an external view, saw Abel Gunasekra walking away from the ship.

"Don't worry," Robot said, "we're kind of getting an assist."

"You'll be unhappy, won't you, when you no longer know everything."

"I don't know what Gunasekra meant, when he was fondling you like that."

"You're so dumb, Robot. Just like me, and I'm carrying the fucking baby."

Robot's laughter was so loud it distorted to static. He said, "You mean you and the saintly doc?"

"I can see we are going to have a fine time together. *Not* Gunasekra. This guy I met on the *Vingança*, when it was still at the hypervelocity star. One of the straight scientists. I knew him from before, back at Fra Mauro when we were students together. I'd been in prison ten years, and it just sort of happened." She was embarrassed, but better getting it over with while Robot was only a voice she could shut off if she wanted. "And I forgot my shot had worn off, and I guess he hadn't had one and assumed I had."

"Well, the kid's had a hell of a strange life so far, huh? Maybe it'll quiet down for it now."

"That's what Gunasekra meant. Does your feed include the countdown? Because I think we're about to go."

"Don't sweat it," Robot said.

The angular figures reached zero, and beach and sea simply drifted away. Dorthy, who had braced herself for the kick of acceleration, relaxed. The angels had seen to this, too, had flattened out the local gravithic field lines. It was like falling into the sky.

The white-green flaw was dead ahead. Dorthy couldn't quite define its wavering borders against the blue sky. Just before it swallowed them, Robot's voice said, "One thing I'd like to know is what happened to Suzy Falcon. But I guess I never will."

And then light took them, and time stopped.

18

SUZY FALCON WAS FALLING: FALLING FREE TEN THOU-sand kilometers above an ocean dotted with continent-sized icebergs that gleamed like dull red gems on the black waters. She'd survived the marauders' barrage, but only just. Firing X-ray lasers into the plasma jets had disrupted the self-generated field lines that held the jets together, had dissipated their energy by a small but crucial margin. Taking it up the ass had helped, too. But the ship was crippled: half of its sensors seared off; reaction motor and radiator fins fused into free-form slag; weapons used up; computer shut down because she wasn't ready to face Machine. The lifesystem was still intact, and so was most of the lifting surface, which was all she had left to play with. She'd used up all the reaction mass in the surviving attitude jets to correct the skewed tumble of the singleship after the plasma had hit.

Falling free. Just beginning to pick up a faint ionization glow as the singleship skimmed the top of the Spike's atmo-sphere, hardly more than vacuum, but already beginning to brake the ship's tremendous velocity. Deceleration gently but insistently pressed the couch's crashweb into new bruises left by the battering impact of the plasma, old bruises she'd suffered when taking the singleship, the constellations of burns left by her interrogator. The vast structures guarding the boundary of the Spike's habitable surface were dwindling ten million klicks sternward. Suzy had less than a hundred twenty degrees of vision left, couldn't see them, wouldn't see *anything* if they launched another attack.

Just as well, she couldn't do anything about it. She'd powered down everything she could. The cabin was in darkness, air was growing stale and warm because the air plant was off; most of the instruments were shut down. Play dead. And maybe they couldn't risk firing at her now, in case they missed and sent plasma burning into their homelands.

Lucky, Suzy, so fucking lucky. Now all you have to do is land this thing and fight off a few hundred billion pissed-off Alea. Nothing to it.

She was beginning to believe that it was all behind her when the first hallucination hit.

It was like she'd passed out for a second, glimpsed a dream about the beach that had been inside the gateway. Only it hadn't been her dream. She shared it with more people than she could imagine and then she was back in the dark, stuffy cabin, feeling that for a moment the whole human race had reached out to her.

She was suddenly hungry for a voice, any voice. She switched Machine back on, no longer caring that he might try and take the ship again. Nothing left for him anyhow.

His voice blared out: made her jump. "—everything in the ship!" Then: "You did it."

"How are you doing?"

"You really did it. You let the marauders survive."

"That's history. The marauders aren't anything but another Alea family now the angels' weapon has destroyed their continuous creation thing. And, hey, there'll always be Alea, unless we hunt them out from every place they've hidden in the Galaxy."

"Little Suzy Falcon, savior of the Universe."

"Fuck you. I should switch you off again, maybe."

"You need me, Suzy. Admit it."

"Yeah, and you need me. Someone to watch over. That's what Robot created you for. First him, now me. So protect me. Tell me where I'm heading. Tell me I'm not going to die, okay?"

She didn't dare believe she'd survive this. Aim to go out in a blaze of glory, and this is what you get, a fag-end of loneliness and terror.

Machine said, "I'm switching on a few systems. Do not be alarmed."

Suzy's blinkered vision broke up for a second or so; along the bottom margin half a dozen indices flickered as their settings changed.

Machine said briskly, "We are already over the habitable zone. The absorbence signature of the ocean below indicates the presence of photosynthetic pigments. Radar shows coordinated movements around the edges or shores of the floating ice-continents. Crowds or schools of thousands of very large objects. If this was Earth, they would key out as whales. Except for the scale: they are each as big as the *Vingança*."

"So tell me—"

What was that? Like a flicker of that moment of oneness, there and gone.

"So tell me what's up ahead. Can we get down in one piece?"

She didn't get to hear Machine's answer, because the blackout or fugue hit again, but this time powerfully focused. The castle, the concussion of the X-ray laser. She was on fire: she was screaming: she felt the vast remoteness of the Galactic core, haunted by the ghosts of gods. She wasn't even Suzy anymore. She was nothing, a mote in an inchoate mob of motes, a teeming handful of dust blown through a ring of fire into infinite darkness.

And came out of it screaming, fighting against something. The crashweb. Machine blaring at her, frightened as she was so that she had to yell back it was okay, it was over. It was over.

"You had a fit," Machine said. "I think you might have died. The wave functions of your brain just flattened out. I was outside of it: I couldn't do anything."

"I think I died, too. Died and went to hell." Suzy swallowed cool, tasteless water from her suit's nipple. "But I'm back. I'm okay. But Christ, Machine, it was wild! Like someone was trying to pack the Universe inside my head. And scare me with shit about gods, gods right here, at the core. But there aren't any, right? We know that. Only angels, and they've gone away."

Machine said, "I didn't want to be left alone."

"Where are we now, huh?" No more ocean or icebergs. And she could swear the light from the fret of glowing threads above the ship was brighter, less red, more orange. Minutely rumpled brown and umber wheeled past far below, dusted here and there with pinkish white. After a moment she began to make sense of it. Like flying over a planet skinned and laid out flat. Those minute crinkles were mountain ranges; the pinkish white dust was snow on about a million mountain peaks. . . .

Machine told her they were more than fifteen billion kilometers inside the habitable zone now. He mapped out vast forests on infrared, limitless grasslands, chains of landlocked oceans, the smallest bigger than the Pacific, one so big the whole of Earth could have been mapped inside it with room to spare.

"I have been maintaining a profile for minimum deceleration," he said. "However, we have shed approximately forty percent of our kinetic energy already. Soon we will have to choose whether or not to make a descent."

"Oh, we're going down, better believe it. Nowhere else with such tempting real estate within a thousand light-years of here, if we even knew where to start looking."

"In that case, we will have to contend with the owners. I suggest we maintain our present profile for at least another ten billion kilometers. The illumination will then more closely resemble that of the Earth. Here, it is very similar to that of P'thrsn and, presumably, the home world of the Alea. Suzy?"

"I ain't going anywhere."

"What will happen to me?"

"Oh shit, Machine, you thinking I'd abandon you? You're all the company I can count on. Besides, I never was the pioneering type. I'm not going to leave the home comforts of this tin can behind, such as they are. The batteries might be low, but they'll keep your circuits going a thousand years. Longer than I need, anyhow."

Machine said, " . . . Thank you, Suzy."

"Another thing, I'm taking attitude control when we go down. You can fly her until then, but that's one job I want for myself, even if it means risking both our asses."

She would bring her broken bird to rest, its last flight like Shelley's fall, the fall that had begun it all. But this time there'd be no stall. It wouldn't end in death.

"I'm Suzy Falcon," she told Machine, when he began to protest. "I'm the meanest combat flier for twenty-eight thousand light-years. I got my pride, okay? Now, this beat up old tin can had better still have its music library working, or I might just call the whole thing off."

Machine pulled up an index for her, and she scrolled through it to the section she wanted, the familiar comforting names all there, hard-edged against the rumpled alien scape of the Spike.

Machine said, "I can see that I have a good deal of educative work ahead of me. Do you really intend to listen to this primitive stuff?"

Suzy said, "You and me, man, we're gonna learn off each other." She made her first selection and settled back as the scary, young-old voice rang out above chords hard-edged and wailing:

> *I got to keep moving, I got to keep moving,*
> *Blues falling down like hail, blues falling down like hail,*
> *I can't keep no money, Hellhound on my trail,*
> *Hellhound on my trail, Hellhound on my trail. . . .*

Ringing across eight centuries, across twenty-eight thousand light-years, ringing out for Suzy Falcon as she fixed her gaze ahead, where the Spike dwindled to its bright vanishing point. Where she could already make out a hint of blue and green. Think of it as the green world she'd set out to find so long ago. "You and me, man," she said, when the song had ended. "We're going to make out okay."

Machine, who wasn't sure if she was talking to him, kept a polite silence as another song began.

Part 4

⋀⋀⋀⋀⋀

The Heirs
of Earth

1

TRILLIONS UPON TRILLIONS OF WAVE FUNCTIONS COL-
lapsed into particle-strings: shedding a cocoon of false photons,
the battered cargo tug burst into urspace.

For Dorthy, everything changed between one heartbeat and
the next. Green-white light blew away like flames scattered by
a great wind to reveal Earth's marbled blue crescent, the small
shining crescent of her sister world tipped beyond. All the indices and readouts printed across her wraparound vision adjusted
in great silent swings. The ship was in geosynchronous orbit,
some thirty-five thousand kilometers above the Horn of Africa.

Radar overlays showed the narrow ring of debris tilted around
Earth—orbital junk, some of it almost a thousand years old,
continually swept up by drones and kept in place by two tiny
shepherd asteroids. And showed, too, more than a hundred of
the structures which shared the geosynchronous orbital shell,
from manufacturing platforms through transit terminals to habitats like the one where Dorthy had spent her strange childhood,
the Kamali-Silver Institute . . . there, black binary string blocked
in red beside its radar trace, was its call sign!

That was when it became real to Dorthy. Gazing upon
the sister worlds, she was swept far out on a great tide of

emotion, neither happiness nor relief nor peace but a solution of all of these: the lifting of the heart near journey's end; hunter, home from hill; the small movements of grace, of return.

A hand gripped her shoulder. It was Robot. Dorthy pulled away the sensor mask and blinked at him. Unshed tears starred her vision.

He said, "I think we might still be in trouble. Didn't you notice there's no radio traffic out there?"

It wasn't exactly true. There were the automatic beacons with which every piece of orbital equipment signaled its position and identity, and there was a mess of low-power signals leaking from Earth itself, atmospheric traffic that would require more sensitive equipment than the tug carried to resolve into separate transmissions. And there were powerful bursts of noise in the microwave band, a ragged pulse as if someone were trying to bounce radar waves off the next galaxy. But there was none of the constant cross talk between habitat and habitat, ship and ship, and no trace of the web of traffic control either, which surely should have been yammering away from the moment their ship appeared out of contraspace impossibly deep in Sol's gravity well.

"The L5 powersat farms are gone, and there are no ships," Dorthy said, after she'd had the computer search blink-comparison radar maps for nonorbital vectors. "No Earth–Luna traffic, no intrasystem ships, no intersystem ships at the transit terminals. No yachts, no flitters, no cargo haulers. Not so much as a suborbital tug, just the autonomic drones which sweep up orbital debris. Where are all the ships, Robot? What's happened here?"

"You think maybe the marauders got here somehow? Maybe the same way we did?"

"There are people on Earth. There's radio traffic."

"Someone's radio traffic. Someone, something. What about the rest of the system? Mars, Titan. What about the fucking Moon?" Robot worried at the strip of blond hair that crested his head. Bare-chested and bare-legged, he was sitting zazen beside the command couch, a portable terminal in his lap. Its green light glowed on his face. "I've been using some of the ranging equipment to check out a few of the habitats. I can't find any neutrino signatures from their fusion plants, and they're not radiating heat through their cooling grids, but passively. They're dead, Dorthy, every one of them. Abandoned. Suppose it was the marauders. What else could have done it? I mean, we were gone less than a year."

"I know," Dorthy said, "I *know*." The edge of Robot's panic was cutting across her own thoughts. "Well, we've two options. We can cruise on out of here and try and raise someone elsewhere in the system. Or we can go down and find out for ourselves."

Robot stretched out a leg so he could reach into one of the pockets of the only piece of clothing he wore, baggy linen shorts slashed with zippers, little tools hanging from a dozen loops around its wide waistband. He held up a coin, one face tarnished green, the other crusted with smooth white calcite.

"My lucky piece," he said, rubbing it on the side of his nose. "Found it when I was a kid, diving old wrecks sunk centuries ago for the foundation of a new reef. It makes a neat binary decision-making machine." He flipped and caught it, covered it on the back of his right hand with the metal-banded plastic of his left. "Heads Earth, tails out, okay?"

"Why not?"

It was heads.

"Shit," Robot said. "How about best of three?"

"Maybe the angels are still with us. They wanted us to go back to Earth, after all. Keep tossing the coin and we'll find out."

Robot turned the coin back and forth between the elongate fingers of his prosthetic hand, so swiftly it was a white blur. "One thing I don't need to know," he said. "They'll always be with us, in a way."

Dorthy had forgotten all about her baby, until then.

No voice challenged them, no police vessel tried to intercept them when she took the ship out of orbit. Robot stayed beside her, hunched over the console he'd appropriated, his prosthetic hand clattering on the keyboard as he typed in string after string of instructions.

Hooded by the sensor mask, eyes filled with Earth's blue-white glory, Dorthy said, "I think you should know that I've never had to land one of these before."

"No shit."

"I mean, perhaps you'd better go strap yourself into a crashweb."

Robot's frantic typing didn't skip a beat. "I'm trying to figure something out here. I guess if we crash, we crash and burn and that's it."

Dorthy scanned the lines of green and amber indicators projected over . . . where was it? One of the indicators told her it was the Indian Ocean. Early morning, the most tremendous sunrise in the rear part of her wraparound vision, a band of orange from horizon to horizon that shaded up through layers of darkening reds to black. She was getting used to the three-hundred-sixty-degree projection now: you just pretended it was a band, focused on any part you wanted to look at and ignored the fact it seemed to go all the way around your head. She looked for the islands where she'd spent a couple of weeks, back when she was whoring her Talent, but there was too much cloud and she had trouble figuring out which coastline she was looking at. She told Robot, "There's a few minutes before we hit the outer edge of the atmosphere. I'm letting it fly itself as much as possible."

"Her. Ships are female. You want to know what I've found, or does it have to wait?"

"What have you found, Robot?" He wasn't as scared as he had been, but there was still an edge to him that could sharpen into panic.

"Well, we're headed for Galveston Port, right? We went over it as we came around to go in. I've been looking through the pictures the belly camera took, there's this amazing enhancement package, algorithms that just unpack the detail right out of all the murk—"

"Just tell me what you found."

"It's more what I didn't find. The city, for one thing. And, well, the spaceport for another."

"You're sure you're looking in the right place?"

The edge was her panic, now, like a knife blade drawn through her blood.

Robot said, "Well, sure. There's this bitmap subroutine, and the fit for the coastline is pretty good. I mean, I was *born* in Galveston. I recognize Pelican Island, all right, but the fields just aren't there. Nor's the waterfront of the city, though I can still make out some of the street plan. And there's something new there, just along the coast. A whole bunch of high albedo circles."

Dorthy caught and corrected a minute drift in attitude control. The tug was beginning to skim the outer edge of the stratosphere, pushing a vast shell of superheated ions in front of it. There was just the faintest wavering in about half her wraparound vision. The tug's gravity field damped out any vibration. Basically, it was flying itself, a blunt arrowhead slicing through thin upper air, keeping itself on track. She didn't really have much to do but worry, while ahead of her the east coast of Africa grew at the rim of the world, tawny under a feathering of high cirrus . . . and behind her the violet band of the upper atmosphere rose as the tug descended. An inset showed her right hand resting on the saddle-shaped keyboard; she could feel the worn spot at the edge, faintly greasy, where Talbeck Barlstilkin's hand had rested. . . .

She said, "Tell me the rest of it."

"Well, that's where some of these pulses are coming from, the ones on the twenty-one-centimeter band."

"The waterhole," Dorthy said.

"Huh?"

"That's what it used to be called. It's a region of low activity between the emission lines of neutral hydrogen gas and hydroxyl ions. It used to be thought that if an alien civilization was going to signal its presence, it was the obvious part of the radio spectrum to use. Twentieth century radio astronomers called it the waterhole in analogy with the waterholes on the African plains, where animals gather to drink."

"Hey, I know what a waterhole is."

"I can guess what those circles are, Robot, and which part of the sky they're aimed at, too. I think—"

A blare of pure noise pierced Dorthy's ears: something began to go wrong with her vision, a square patch right in front of her breaking down into dancing dots of light, like snow blowing past a window. And then the snow scattered and someone was looking in at her. A smug, fat, perfectly bald man, washed-out blue eyes, snub nose and prim little mouth squashed together in the center of his white, jowly face.

He said, "We're about to download the treaties you're breaking, Citizen. You've seventy-five seconds to tell us why we shouldn't blow you out of Gaia's air. Counting now." English, with a strong Badlands accent.

"We're from the *Vingança*," Dorthy said.

The fat man's lips parted to form a perfect *o* of astonishment. He looked at something offscreen, looked back at Dorthy. "This had better not be some kind of freetrader shucksma. You've proof for us, Citizen?"

"I have all kinds of proof, if you let us land." Robot's hand was on her arm; she motioned for him to keep quiet. She said, "For a start, you can check this ship's registration."

There was a pause as the man looked offscreen again. His ear was pierced; a glittery spiral hung from it. He turned back to Dorthy and said, "Our craft will escort you to a landing field."

"We're heading in for Galveston. I don't think I can turn the ship around now."

"We realize that. Our craft will rendezvous with you three hundred klicks from Galveston. In . . . two hundred twenty-four seconds. We suggest you do not deviate from your track." The window vanished like a popped soap bubble.

Dorthy told Robot, "They're Witnesses. Those things you saw were their radio telescopes. I think I know what happened, but there isn't time to tell you. Go find a crashweb, I think we're in for a tough time."

"What I wanted to say, I have this bunch of hardcopy documents that started spitting out. Official looking stuff. The dates—"

"There's no time, Robot!"

"—just listen! Thirty two. Forty. Forty one. Forty two. Forty fucking five! We started ought two, we were gone less than a year. We're in the fucking future!"

"I know! I don't want you killed, Robot, so please. Get to a crashweb!"

"The fucking future," he said, and then he was gone and Dorthy glimpsed the escort ahead, black flecks in an arrowhead formation racing toward the tug above the cloud deck. A dozen heavily armored aircars, bellies bristling with single-shot X-ray lasers, they peeled away either side and looped back, holding just above and a klick behind. There was a moment of streaming whiteness as the tug pierced the cloud deck, and then the ocean was below and the coast was a brown stain at the horizon, rushing up at her.

The fat Witness said, "We see your contrail, Citizen. Overshoot the Island three klicks. There's an airfield. Use it."

Indicators were flashing all along the base of Dorthy's vision. The tug couldn't find the spaceport. She reached for the attitude stick and kicked in override, felt the stick come alive in her hand. The horizon tilted, steadied. She said, "I should warn you I'm not too good at atmospheric flying. We used to be part of the science crew." The stick trembled as the ship dropped through mach one.

The Witness told her, "It would be better for you if you crashed than missed the airfield."

Airspeed was down to a couple of hundred klicks per hour now, altitude so low Dorthy could make out the whitecaps on the lines of breakers that marched shoreward. The aircars were still astern: the ship was the apex of their vee formation. She could feel her heartbeat in her thumb and fingers where they rested on the pistol grip of the stick. Shoreline, then scrubby trees, glimpses of ruined buildings among them.

No time to wonder how old the ruins were. A wide river channel, a silver glimmer off to the south, fat cigar shapes (airships!) clustered ahead, suddenly caught among a forest of thready red lights that stabbed upward into the clouds.

The Witness said, "That's where you land, Citizen."

"Of course," Dorthy said politely, and hauled the stick diagonally back and kicked in the tug's reaction motor.

Then she saw only sky ahead of her and the tug's contrail twisted behind, and black specks scratching smoke trails as they fell out of the sky, burning. Robot and the Witness were yelling different things at her and there was a colorless flash and her vision grayed out for a second, came back with red damage reports scattered all over it, went away in another colorless flash. She was slammed against the couch's restraints as the tug's generated gravity cut out for a second; saw a blurred rush of burning treetops through a haze of red code strings, pushed the attitude stick all the way forward. The tug climbed, listing to port. She saw the ocean far behind her, beyond a haze of smoke. For a minute she thought she had made it. Then there was another flash. The tug's frame shuddered. Half the lifting surface gone, it began to lose speed.

Dorthy leveled out as best she could, hand sweating on the stick, trying to let the tug glide in to any sort of landing. Everything kept changing angles, as if the tug were a live thing trying to throw off her control. She glimpsed sky, a wide brown river snaking through level green, sky again, and then the horizon rising to meet her. Proximity alarms were blaring in her ears. Trees, then what looked like grassland. She had time to think that if the generated gravity cut off again, the impact of the crash would probably kill her, shoved the stick all the way back to try and get stall speed, and with a long rending shudder the tug plowed the earth . . . and stopped.

When Dorthy reached the airlock she found all three of its doors open. The fresh air of the Earth blew in her face. Vivid greens stretched out before her, tipped at forty-five degrees, all of the world a hill to the tug's gravity field.

Robot, standing at an angle beneath the hatch, shouted up to her that she better jump, the ship was on fire, more than one place. Crab-things clattered around him, their crusted carapaces verdigrised bronze, tarnished silver.

Dorthy took a breath and jumped, but gauged it wrong. The hill became flat ground that slapped her ribs and hip and knocked all the wind out of her. She had to be supported by Robot for the first couple of hundred meters. Earth was cold under her bare feet. Lush wet grass soon soaked her coveralls to her waist. The crab-things had vanished into it somewhere.

"A gun," he kept saying. "That's what I should have got. All I could think about were the fucking crabs, and after I got them out, jumped down after them, there wasn't any way back. But I should have got a gun."

"What would you do with a gun," Dorthy managed to say at last. "Come *on*, Robot, let's try going a little faster. The reaction motor blew our escort away, but the Witnesses will have other aircars. They'll be all over here any minute."

Behind them, smoke was pouring from the stern of the tug (where its blunt arrowhead would have attached to a shaft, if it had been a real arrowhead); its thick, greasy black column rose into the darkening sky. It was early evening, here. The air had a chill edge to it.

Dorthy couldn't help looking back every few seconds: it was strange not to be able to see behind her head. A haze of smoke rose above the horizon, forest set alight by the Witnesses' weapons. Grassland saddled away south and north, only shade trees breaking its green sea; ahead, to the east, was the liquid gleam of water, the wide river Dorthy had glimpsed from the air. The Mississippi, she supposed, or one of its tributaries.

She tried to remember how far that meant they'd be from Galveston, but her head wasn't working properly: nothing would cling there for more than a few seconds. Her fear, suspended since the Witness had chipped into the ship's communications, was finally breaking through. She had a stitch; her knees felt unhinged. Robot soon forged ahead of her, and so it was he who found the road.

It was unpaved, a wide strip of packed red dirt raised above a deep ditch Dorthy had to jump over. She fell down on the other side and winded herself all over again. "I'm too old for this," she said, picking herself up. "Too old and too pregnant."

Robot was looking up and down the road. He said, "I can't see those little fuckers anywhere. Do you think they followed us?" Then he said, "Listen, you hear something?"

And before they could move, the wagon came around the clump of trees in the elbow of the wide road's curve, its driver rising from the bench as he hauled back on the reins of the two horses.

The wagon driver's name was Sugar Jack Durras; he came from a place called Kingman Seven. "Soon as we saw the flashes," he said, "we knew something was coming down our way. I saw where you came down and thought I'd better take a look before the Witnesses got here. Didn't think I'd pick up honest to God spacemen. Begging your pardon, ma'am."

"My name's Dorthy, Dorthy Yoshida. And I was born right here on Earth, in Australia." Dorthy and Robot were squatting down behind the driving bench, beneath a heavy, oiled canvas, leaning against each other to steady themselves against the wagon's jolting vibration. None of this seemed real to her, and she was fighting the urge to burst out laughing. From spaceship to horse-drawn buggy inside thirty minutes, it had to be some kind of record in transport devolution.

Durras looked over his shoulder. His black hair was wound in a greased braid that reached all the way down the back of his patched, white cotton shirt. He said, "You're the local contact for your friend, then? I hope you unloaded your stuff before those bastards got you, because otherwise they'll have it in just a few minutes now."

Dorthy said, "We're not smugglers either." She remembered what the Witness had said to her. "Or freetraders."

"Six of one," Durras said, "half a dozen of the other."

Robot asked what the date was, the first time he'd spoken since they'd climbed aboard Durras's wagon.

"November twentieth." Durras was looking up at the sky. "Oh shit," he said, "there's one of their flying machines. Stay under that canvas, you hear? Sooner we get you holed up, the better it'll be for everyone. We'll hide you folks out a couple of days while the Witnesses look for you. With any kind of luck, you'll be out in time for Thanksgiving. And you can stay a while after if you like,'cause I reckon you must've one hell of a story to tell."

2

In the end, Dorthy and Robot stayed at Kingman Seven well beyond Thanksgiving, past Christmas and the New Year, and into the beginning of spring. They were suffering from retroshock, from having been plucked out of the Galaxy's core and the virtual reality of the interzone between universes and plunged into the mundane backwoods of what had once been the North-East Mexican Gulf States, the Badlands.

The little township of Kingman Seven had been founded on the site of an old agricultural station; centuries-old remains of hydroponic ponds could still be found in the scrubby forest that circled its fields. Fewer than a hundred people lived there, a dozen families whose ancestors had settled there during the Interregnum. There were thousands of communities like it in the Badlands, clinging like lichens to their patch of the Earth, old and resistant and slow to change.

They were the people among whom Dorthy had once wanted to go, the people to whom she'd wanted to tell the secret history she'd glimpsed on P'thrsn. And here she was, and she knew so much more of it now, and yet somehow it didn't matter. Nothing was as real as the cluster of wooden houses and the white-painted church and the rhythms of the township's life, slow as the seasons.

Besides, the people of Kingman Seven already knew something of the secret history. How could they not, after That Day, after the Revelation almost fifty years before, when every human everywhere in urspace had been touched by Talbeck Barlstilkin's feverish vision?

It seemed that Talbeck Barlstilkin had won after all. The Federation had started to disintegrate immediately after the

Revelation. The governments of the Re-United Nations of Earth, having been shown to have hidden the secret of the hypervelocity star and much else from their own peoples and from the governments of the rest of the Ten Worlds, had fallen one after the other. There had been riots, marches, rallies. The president of Greater Brazil had committed suicide, or had been assassinated, it was never very clear. Novaya Rosya had seceded from the Federation, Serenity had followed a hundred days later. Then Elysium, Ruby. The puppet government the RUN had installed on Novaya Zyemla had gone the same way as their masters.

And on Earth the Witnesses had seized the moment. They had taken the fiery transcendental images of Talbeck Barlstilkin's dying vision, of things like gods at the core of the Galaxy, as their own. The government hastily formed by the long discredited opposition in Greater Brazil had foundered and had been almost instantly resurrected, and half of its cabinet had been Witnesses. For a few years, their aims had coincided with the wishes of the mob, who had wanted nothing of Earth's nascent interstellar empire. Spaceports had been closed; most had been ransacked, burned to the ground. Orbital installations had been evacuated, and finally the Federation Navy had torn itself apart, RUN loyalists battling with Witness cadres. The Solar System's first and last space battle had been fought in cisLunar space. Side maneuvers had made most of Eurasia uninhabitable all over again, and Earth had suffered a year without summer, shrouded in dust clouds that had reached all the way to the troposphere. Five billion people, half of Earth's population, had died of starvation.

And after that, the Witnesses had ruled Earth, or what was left of it, with remote, careless authority symbolized by the huge airships that patrolled the skies. They cared little for the peoples they dominated, beyond ruthlessly quelling any signs of insurrection and overturning anyone who tried to set himself up as warlord or baron. They governed by division.

For the Witnesses believed that there was a far greater matter than governing Earth. Their theology had undergone a prignogenic leap after the Revelation. Instead of seeking out godlike aliens, they now sought to appease the gods of the core, without realizing that They were mostly fragments risen out of Barlstilkin's disintegrating self at the moment of his death. But that They had been printed in every human brain on That Day perhaps made Them as real as the angels or the marauders. To the Witnesses, They were more urgently real than Earth itself. Their prayers constantly poured out of huge groundbased radio telescopes that were aimed squarely at Sagittarius, at the heart of the Galaxy. The Witnesses believed that by the time these signals reached the gods, humanity would have purified itself, would have risen above its base animal origins.

Would be ready to receive godhood.

Meanwhile, most of Earth had reverted to a kind of anarchy. There was no money, but there was trade by barter; no law but the rough justice of town councils; no nations but those made by individual men and women. For most people, things were very little changed. Their masters were as remote and capricious as ever, less important than the seasons of planting and harvest. Earth had become what it had been for most of human history, a world of peasants. History continued, but elsewhere. For Earth, history had come to an end.

Dorthy and Robot learned the story of the years after the Revelation piecemeal, from the few inhabitants of Kingman Seven and nearby settlements old enough to remember them, and from those who had heard their parents' or grandparents' tales. If anyone had recorded these grace notes of Earth's civilization, Kingman Seven did not possess that book, although it did possess many others. As well as being Kingman Seven's brewer, Sugar Jack Durras was also its librarian, and publisher besides. He used a battered but still functional hardcopier to transfer filed books to sheets of smooth creamy paper laid down by one of his strains of genemelded bacteria. His wife bound the volumes for trade with other communities.

Dorthy learned from Cochina Durras how to prepare leather—mostly deer hide—for binding, and spent her days scraping flesh and hair from fresh hides and trimming and stretching those which had been tanned in a pungent extract of sumac and oak bark. She soon became adept with currying knife and raising board, slicker, and pommel. Tanning liquor hardened new calluses on her palms and fingers.

It was the least she could do to repay Kingman Seven's hospitality. Robot sometimes stirred himself to fix some piece of pre-Revelation machinery, but for the most part he sat on the Durras's porch, the communal center of the settlement, sipping Sugar Jack's moonshine with his contemporaries, good old boys and girls who were living out the last of their years.

Dorthy and Robot had both lost their urgency, their momentum. But Robot had also lost Machine, and all his manifestos were suddenly irrelevant. Sometimes he broke down and cried deep into the watches of the night, bitter tears of self-pity for the works of art he would never now create. All Dorthy could do was hold him. They had both been taken far out to sea, and cast back on a shore grown strange and wild.

After the turn of the year, people started visiting Kingman Seven in twos and threes, never staying longer than a night, casually passing through on their way to somewhere else, or so it seemed. Young people mostly, representatives of shadowy anti-Witness groups whose acronyms probably contained more letters than the groups contained members. They came to see Dorthy and Robot, having heard something about their adventures through some kind of bush telegraph. Mostly, they came looking for support, for magic formulas that would banish the Witnesses overnight, for power. Dorthy told them the truth, and mostly they went away disappointed: the truth was not enough, it seemed. But a few understood, and listened gravely and thanked her. She wondered what seeds she was sowing, but she could not keep silent. Her story and her unborn baby were all she had left of her great adventure.

The seasons wore from winter to spring, and Dorthy's child quickened in her womb, but otherwise time seemed to have stopped. As on the shore between universes, she and Robot were suspended in a moment stretched between one swing of the pendulum and the next.

When time began again, it began with a dream. Dorthy woke with it still vivid in her mind, mixed with the velvet darkness of their room, the sound of February rain on the shingles of the roof, Robot breathing quietly beside her.

A dream of a beach that was not the shore between universes . . . yet somehow like it. A sweeping expanse of black grit beneath a pink sky. Walking, or running, at the edge of shallow waves, somehow her childhood self again . . . yet not, not quite. And yet there had been whales: but not the dead hulks stripped of hide and blubber as in the flensing yard where her father and Uncle Mishio had worked. These were alive, their great backs scything green ocean, spouts flinging fountains of diamonds high above the waves. And one hung at the top of its leap in silhouette against a huge reddish sun, twisting as gracefully as a shadow dancer. . . .

Dorthy laid a hand under the swell of her belly, and felt her child shift within her womb. Shadow dancers. . . .

Then the noises which had woken her, a quick scrabbling, a multiple ticking like a fall of metal coins on wood, came again. She dared reach for the lamp, twisted it on. Harsh light flooded her eyes. Robot stirred sleepily beside her, lifting his augmented arm to lay its banded plastic over his face.

"Wake up," she said, and pushed at his shoulder. "There's something in here with us."

" . . . What?"

"I don't know. It's silly, I'm scared to look."

"Oh shit," Robot said sleepily, and pushed up against the bolster. His breath smelled of acetone, residue of that evening's jug of Sugar Jack's moonshine. Dorthy could still taste it in her own mouth, a residue of their lovemaking: being pregnant had made her as sexy as hell, she couldn't get enough of it.

The noise came again and Dorthy gave a little squeak, half real alarm, half amusement at her cowardice.

"Shit," Robot said again He leaned across her to see, then almost fell out of bed. He said, voice muffled against the flannel blanket, "They're back!"

It was the crab-things. There seemed to be more of them than Dorthy remembered, and many of them seemed smaller, too. Robot noticed it. He lay on his belly, bare ass luminous white in the lamplight. "I guess something ate, or killed anyhow, some of them. And some of the others had babies. Look there, see the little ones crawling around the spines of that big old fucker? How do you think they found us? Smell, maybe?"

"No. I know what it is. The shadow dancer templates in my head. I'm sure of it. I was having the strangest dream, Robot."

She told him about it, and they sat up most of the night discussing what to do, while the crab-things rattled around the floor and finally settled in a heap in the safe shadows beneath their bed.

The next day, Clary Rosas said, "Only place you can be sure of finding freetraders is Evangelina. That is a town on the Gulf. Perhaps a long journey for a woman with child, Dorthy, in this or in any season. And Evangelina is not a good place, either."

Cochina Durras said, "I have a cousin in Evangelina, and she is not a bad woman."

"A place can be bad," Clary Rosas said, "yet still good people may live there. It is famous for its murders and its crooked deals, Evangelina."

Dorthy said, "Well, but how often do these freetraders pass through here?"

"No one can say for sure," Clary Rosas said. "Some do not trade, they simply take. Loot the ruins of the cities, pillage the ecology. . . . They are all pirates, after all, some more so than others. It has been six years since one was anywhere near us." Her shrug was carelessly eloquent. She was a small, dark woman, alive with barely contained energies, her black hair braided with white beads that rattled about her face as she gestured, her jerkin fine deer hide supple as cotton, her boots (cocked on the porch rail) black snakeskin. Clary Rosas was the most traveled of all the inhabitants of Kingman Seven, still unmarried at the scandalously late age of thirty. She added, "Perhaps one will pass by again, perhaps not. Who can tell?"

"There's my answer," Dorthy said. "I can't wait for a freetrader to show up. I'm six months along, and last week my belly button popped out. I'm a small woman; I don't know if I can travel well with a full-grown baby inside me. So now's the time."

"But surely when the child is born," Cochina Durras said, "it will be easier for you."

They were all three sitting in a corner of the Durras's porch, sharing a pot of coffee. Dorthy had watered hers down for the sake of her unborn child, but hadn't been able completely to kick her long-ingrained habit. Rain beat on the sheet iron that roofed the porch; blowing silvery curtains half-obscured the other houses scattered among trees and fenced paddocks. Pennants left over from Fat Tuesday hung limp in the downpour. Late February, it rained almost every day, slanting out of the gray sky and soaking the rich, red alluvial earth. First planting was almost over.

Dorthy said, "After it's born it will have to be weaned, and then I suppose I should wait until it can walk, or until it can ride a horse. Before I know it, I'll be a grandmother here."

"Which is no bad thing," Cochina Durras said, smiling, Her third grandchild had been born a month before.

"Which is no bad thing," Dorthy said, returning the smile, "but not what I had in mind for the rest of my life. I still have this thing to finish, Cochina."

"Of course. But without your flying machine it will take you two months at least to reach Evangelina. And the Witnesses still look for you. It might be better to wait here."

"Perhaps," Clary Rosas said, "but it is unlikely, I think. The freetraders at Evangelina have a kind of sanction with the Witnesses. They bring technical goods the Witnesses cannot make for themselves, take away cotton, tobacco, corn, anything they can find. They have passage through the Witnesses' defenses, and those grow stronger with each year, as you yourself found out, Dorthy. Farther north you may find a rogue freetrader, but here, now, I do not think so. It is too dangerous for them. The one who came by six years ago had been on Earth for months after she landed, but never in one place for more than a few days. Rogues are always in disguise, and so they are difficult to find."

"But not in this town. Evangelina."

"Of course," Clary Rosas said, "any freetrader will want payment in return for her help."

"When she learns who I am and where I've been," Dorthy said, "she'll know she'll be guaranteed whatever price she asks."

Cochina Durras said, "And what of your husband? He may not want you to travel."

Dorthy had never got around to telling Cochina that she and Robot weren't married, that in fact the child she carried was not his. She said, "We talked about it. He agrees we should go."

"You must remember how differently they do things on other worlds, Cochina," Clary Rosas said.

Cochina Durras said, "I may well be a toothless old grandmother who's never stirred a step outside her home, but I know more than you would think!"

But Clary Rosas was telling Dorthy, "I'm thinking of taking another trip in a week or so. Not as far as Evangelina, certainly, but some way toward it. You come with me, Dorthy, husband or not. Husbands are good for only one thing anyway."

And so it was decided, in the roundabout way most things were decided in Kingman Seven. Dorthy, Robot and Clary Rosas set out on a cold but clear morning, the first day of March. Robot had spent the last few days rerigging the township's ancient solar-powered generator in payment, although no payment had been asked, for the horses and supplies they had been given.

It took them ten days to make the two hundred klicks west, to the little town at the river crossing point that was as far as Clary Rosas was going, that trip. They parted in the huge market near the mouth of the bridge, hawkers crying their wares, crowds dressed in a hundred different styles surging around the stalls. The white bow of the suspension bridge shone in clean spring sunlight, shadowed at the far end by the bloated shape of a Witness airship.

Clary Rosas hugged them both and bade them Godspeed, and Dorthy and Robot paid their toll and rode over the bridge, above the swift-moving brown waters of the Mississippi. The crab-things were shut up in a small square crate slung behind his saddle. Robot had taken off his augmented arm. Dorthy wore a voluminous blue cloak that hid the swell of her pregnancy. The Witness standing on a platform at the far end of the bridge hardly gave them a glance as they rode past.

3

It took Dorthy and Robot more than two months to travel downstream to Evangelina. Although it was only five hundred klicks by river, long detours forced by swamps and oxbow lakes more than trebled the distance. Dorthy and Robot couldn't risk taking passage on the white, stately, triple-decked riverboats, for there were always Witnesses aboard; and the host of smaller boats that used the river only traveled short distances, and couldn't take their horses.

They traveled a land written and rewritten by history, sometimes along roads that followed the route of interstate highways dating from the Age of Waste, sometimes along train tracks which, after the Revelation, had been uprooted for the monocrystalline iron in their magnetic spines. But most often they took country roads that could have been ten years old or a thousand, dirt tracks that ran straight through the checkerboard of rice fields, pasture, and pecan or rubber or banana plantations (Dorthy had developed a craving for green bananas, and devoured a dozen a day if she could); or twisted through cypress swamp or blue pine forest, following the natural contours of the land.

The journey was lengthened by the need to earn their keep at the little settlements and towns through which they passed; there were always more than enough gadgets in need of repair to keep Robot in employment for a year if he chose. In one town he earned enough to buy a rifle with a broken laser scope. After he fixed it, Dorthy was able to pot small game—coneys, armadillo, grouse, turkey. Wild rice was there for the taking, and fruit could be gleaned from plantations; they needed to buy only salt and coffee. The crab-things were quiescent in

389

their wooden box; although Robot always left the lid off each night, it was rare for even one of them to venture out.

Now that Dorthy and Robot could more or less live off the land, their journey went more quickly, and as the rains slackened and the days grew hotter, they camped out rather than hire a bed at some inn or hospice. Once, they stayed overnight in the ruins of some great building whose crumbling walls were painted everywhere with the swirling graffiti of bears; and woke to find half a dozen broken-necked coneys, still warm, laid beside the embers of their campfire.

And once they had to ride a night and a day through a swampy scrub of mesquite and ghostweed, dotted with the occasional dwarf willow, to escape a pack of wild dogs that remorselessly trotted after them. Mostly, the dogs kept a respectful distance, but every now and then one or two or half a dozen together would race up to howl crude threats, dodging back only when Dorthy menaced them with the rifle. Dorthy and Robot and their horses were thoroughly spooked and exhausted when the pack finally gave up the chase, at the edge of the next stretch of cultivated fields.

Rice that had been seedlings when Dorthy and Robot had started their journey was now grown tall, heavy heads bowed down in hot humid air. Then harvest stripped the fields and the air was ripe with the stench of ordure plowed into the drained paddies; and then for a week it seemed that every flooded field Dorthy and Robot rode past had a line of men and women and children bent over their reflections as they mechanically thrust seedling after seedling into brown water.

It was at this time, two months into the journey, that Dorthy's dreams began to grow strange indeed. She would wake in the middle of the night with baroque visions fading even as she tried to grasp them. What she mostly remembered was the recurring image of the beach of black sand that had been in the first of the dreams, when the crab-things had returned to her and Robot. Black sand, pink sky, whale in midleap silhouetted against a soft orange sun. The rest had the feel of the glimpse she'd had of the vast insubstantial city glittering beyond the involuted complexities of the fractal desert—yet somehow richer, more glorious. Waking from these dreams, she would lie an hour or more in warm soft darkness or in moonlight, with the mechanical tearing sound of the hobbled horses grazing close by, and further off the susurration of rice seedlings chafing their leaves, or the whisper of forest trees and the brief thumps and flurries of hunters and hunted—small lives whose desperate diamond-sharp trajectories she glimpsed with her Talent—and once or twice the cough of a jaguar, or the howl of a banshee, twisting like a jagged wire kilometers away in the deepest part of the night wood. But at last Dorthy would fall asleep, and awake to find her memory of the dream, like last night's fire, gone to ashes.

And so they traveled, until at last the land dipped and fields and forest gave way to a lacework of slow streams and muddy islands and mangrove swamp, and at last they came to Evangelina.

It was a port town, sprawled on a low ridge above one of the delta's long, muddy inlets. The good quarter, really not much more than a single street that paralleled the kilometer-long docks, was of white clapboard buildings raised on stilts two meters high, with covered verandas and balconies railed with rusty iron lacework. More than half were bars or whorehouses or hotels; most of the rest were given over to trade: chandlers, culture masters, assayers, notaries, and the like. Behind the shabby commerce of the waterfront, a stew of shacks and tents straggled away among swampy patchwork fields. And beyond the seaward point of the docks, a couple of Witness airships floated against the vast sky, tethered near the tilted bowl of a radio telescope.

Dorthy and Robot arrived in early evening, with the sun going down through streaks of cloud across the Mississippi. Dorthy had been feeling little cramps all up and down her belly that day, and her usual backache had sharpened to a knife blade pressing between her kidneys. As she guided her horse through dockside crowds, in the tangled shadows of the hollow cylindrical sails of barques and cavels, and cranes that like gigantic herons rose above them on slender spars, she felt a sudden heavy spasm that seemed to expand to fill the whole world—or push everything else aside. Gasping, she reined in her horse and leaned on her saddle's pommel.

Robot, one-armed again, managed to get his horse beside hers, asked if she was okay. Dorthy said, "I think it's time. We'd better find this cousin of Cochina's."

"And a doctor, right? I guess I can boil water, but apart from that I'm not going to be much use."

"Doctors get the man to boil water to give him something to do. I don't know much about this, but I think you'd better hurry."

The address Cochina Durras had given them was a small inn with a shabby facade but a clean veranda with a floor of polished mahogany, red and pink geraniums trailing down from hanging pots, and an iron rail painted blue and red. When the innkeeper saw Dorthy's condition, he brushed aside the letter of introduction that Dorthy offered and started to tell her and Robot that friends of his wife's cousin or not, they couldn't have a room, he didn't want that sort of trouble, making so much noise that his wife bustled out to see what was going on.

She didn't even glance at the letter but took Dorthy's arm at once and helped her through a narrow, dark lobby and up the stairs. She was a fat, sensible woman, black hair oiled and wound into braids above her ears. "Don't you worry dear," she told Dorthy, "I've had six myself, and not one of them died. If your husband can't afford a doctor, I reckon it won't make much difference. Oh dear! Well, never mind, we're nearly there."

Dorthy's water had broken, drenching her thighs. The cramps were coming every other minute, waves that each seemed to build on the fading pain of the one before. She hardly noticed as she was laid on a bed, her dress cut away from her. Someone was making a fuss in the doorway, but the hotel keeper's wife shooed him away.

"It's the most natural thing in the world," she said, her plump fingers probing Dorthy's swollen belly, "and men are the most unnatural, to my way of thinking. How far are you along, not more than seven months I'd say, and this your first? Eight is it? Well, you'll have no trouble, then. What's your name? Dorthy? From the south, are you? Eyes like that, I thought as much. I'm Maria, but I suppose Cochina told you that. How is she? We were both born south of here, but not as far as you, I wager. That's it, shouting gets the pain outside you."

But the pain stayed where it was, wave after wave. Sweat burst over Dorthy's entire body with every contraction. She tried to get her breathing in sync with the contractions, it was the only thing she could think about. They came every three or four minutes, not quite enough time to relax before the next one so that she was being gradually worn down. Each time it was like a hill she was sure she couldn't quite climb, but each time she somehow managed to get on top of it. She kept asking Maria if it had started yet, and the woman kept telling her that she mustn't worry, it was hard but she would get there. There were more people in the room, she wasn't sure how many. A lamp burned in one corner, and it was night beyond the window; darkness turned its glass to a mirror, reflecting the people and the woman, herself, struggling on the bed. Maria laid cloths soaked in ice water on Dorthy's forehead; some time later Robot gave her a glass of something cold and clear, scented like cloves. She managed to tell him that he'd been right when they'd crashed, if not guns, they should at least have saved the autodoc.

"I was right when I said that we never should have come down in the first place. Except I didn't know it."

Whatever had been in the glass sent Dorthy out of herself a little. The room seemed a long way away, a small square of lamplight at the end of a long tunnel. She was in the room and somewhere else at the same time, rocked and compressed by violent unstable pressures. An old, black woman, the nap of her white hair thin as a worn rug, was asking her about the contractions, and she was trying to answer through the blur of the drug; and she could hear the rumble of the voices, and tried to turn to where light glowed red through the quaking press.

When she came back, she was riding atop the biggest contraction yet, yelling at the top of her voice. Robot eased her head back down on the lumpy bolster that was by now sodden with her sweat. He said, "I hired a doctor. She's going to cut the baby out. It might have got tangled up with the cord. They have some kind of painkiller, but it still might hurt."

"The baby's alive," Dorthy said. "I can feel her, in my head."

"A daughter, huh? Yeah, don't worry about her being dead, they were listening to her heartbeat just now."

"I don't want her to be a monster," Dorthy said. "All that radiation, the marauders' weapon. Robot, if she's a monster, promise you'll kill her."

"Hey, it's okay. She's got two arms, two legs, one head. Doctor knows that much."

Coldness on her swollen belly; the white-haired doctor was painting a clear gel over it. When the next contraction came, Dorthy could feel her muscles knotting, but it didn't hurt anymore. Robot was still leaning over her. She told him, "The dreams I had. I thought they were from the shadow dancer templates. I was wrong, I think. They were from my baby."

"They're gonna cut your belly open now. Don't look if you don't want to. How are you feeling?"

"Like shit. Lift me up a little."

The doctor told her she would feel nothing, that there would be a scar, but not a large one. She was passing steel instruments, first one way, and then the other, through a little box that leaked a high whine. "Now we'll just prep you up," she said, and rubbed Dorthy's belly with grain alcohol, palped and prodded, and listened again to the baby through a little silver tube, her head close to Dorthy's skin. "Your daughter's upside down. Doesn't know the way out. So we'll help her along. Don't be afraid, now."

Dorthy wanted to say that she wasn't, but the room was going away again, or darkness was growing all around it, so that it was like a little lighted window looking out across a night as profound as that between galaxies. Clear and remote, Dorthy saw the doctor make a quick deep incision in her belly, Maria blotting up the sudden tree of dark red blood. She felt no pain, but she could feel skin and muscles pulled apart, feel pressure lifting, harsh light pouring in, rough hands cradling, pulling, as the doctor got the baby's head, wrinkled and purple, up through the incision, and then the rest of her lifting free, laid between Dorthy's breasts, heavy and wet and hot, covered in slime and blood, the cord trailing from her belly back into the incision.

The doctor bent over the baby and turned her head, cleared mucus with a finger and blew gently into her mouth, scratched the soles of her tiny feet. Dorthy tried to lift her arms, but they were too heavy, weighed down with darkness. The baby made a little choking sound, drew her first breath. But she didn't cry.

Eyes still wrinkled shut, she tried to turn her face to Dorthy's. Her first attempts at words were thick and gummy, little more than clotted gasps. She worked her tiny mouth, tried again.

"In me," she said.

The doctor walked backward until she hit the wall, bloody fingers pressed over her open mouth. Maria was calling on the Lord Jesus Christ; Robot's hand clenched on Dorthy's shoulder, and the pain brought her back into her own head.

Her daughter drew a small rattling breath, dribbled mucus and saliva. Her small wrinkled face, covered in drying blood and mucus, looked a thousand years old. "Shadow dancers," she said. "In me. In me!"

4

THE FREETRADER WAS A TALL, SKINNY MAN DRESSED from head to foot in black: scuffed zithsa-hide boots; black stockings and black knee breeches belted with a wide band of black leather; loose black shirt with a kind of short cape around his shoulders. His eyes were ringed with kohl: skull's eyes in his pinched white face. He said, "You're really from the *Vingança*, there's no problem. But see, how do I know?"

He was sprawled in the room's only chair. He looked at Dorthy, who sat on the bed cradling her daughter, at Robot, who stood with his one arm across his chest, hand on his empty shoulder socket.

"You've seen my arm," Robot said. "You've seen the crab-things."

"Your arm's an antique. Earth is full of antiques. And for all I know you got those crabs from the local swamp. More weird creatures on Earth than any other world I know, and I've been on a dozen. Anything else for me, or I been wasting time?"

"Go on," Dorthy said to her daughter.

The baby said, as she had practiced, "The *Vingança* went all the way to the center of the Galaxy. That's where I learned to talk."

The freetrader's mouth shut with a click. "I heard about this," he said, "but didn't believe it until now."

"Don't believe in *you*," Dorthy's daughter said, and pushed her face between her mother's breasts.

"You know there's a reward out for you," the freetrader said. "Witnesses want you real bad. Why I'm interested."

Robot said, "How much will you get for being the person to rescue from Earth the only survivors of the expedition to the center of the Galaxy?"

"Not going to turn you. Even if you weren't what . . . you say you are, wouldn't do that. Trade with Witnesses, doesn't mean I like the wasters. Besides, you're more valuable as cargo." The freetrader couldn't stop looking at the baby. "She really only three days old? Get her to say something else."

"I'm not a *trick*," the baby said crossly, muffled against the cloth of Dorthy's dress. Her diction was getting clearer, but she had a tendency to lisp. She batted at her mother with a tiny starfish hand. "Hungry!"

"Hush, child. When we've done our business." The baby writhed in a fit of temper, and Dorthy held her tightly until she subsided. "I'm sorry," she said to the freetrader.

"Don't hold it, Seyoura. Raised kids myself; I've a son, back in the collective on Bradbury. Guess maybe you wouldn't know Bradbury, settled after your time. Third planet of Al Nasl." He scratched above the curve of his prominent cheekbone. "Guess you don't know the star, either."

"I know of it," Dorthy said, "although I know it better as Lambda Sagittarii. But I suppose you don't know the Archer, Seyour, as you're not from Earth. Your home is, what, a hundred light-years away?"

"Hundred twenty-four."

Robot said, "Dr. Yoshida is an astronomer."

"Comes back," the freetrader said. "Yoshida. Part of the P'thrsn expedition, back in the Alea Campaigns. Brought up on stories about the Campaigns. Grandfather died in those, singleship pilot at BD Twenty. Been flying ships in my family a *long* while."

"So go look her up in a text," Robot said. "Check us out all you want. But you're interested, right?"

The freetrader said, "Don't remember anything about you, though."

"Look me up under art history," Robot said.

Dorthy felt Robot's unease, mud stirred up from the bottom of a deep pool. She said, "He's a situationist."

"Don't know anything about art. Look, know how we work? There's an outpost on Titan, where I'll take you first. *If* I take you."

"That's okay," Robot said. "I know Titan. I did some of my best work in Urbis."

The freetrader said, "Urbis was something back when, but it's frozen ruins now. Way station is a couple of arcology domes, little corner of the old spacefield. Check you out better there."

"I'm glad you're taking us, Seyour," Dorthy said, gently joggling her daughter, who didn't trust the tall, thin, unsmiling man at all.

"Haven't quite decided that. If I do, you better had check out. Otherwise you rot in Urbis, far as I'm concerned. Work hydroponics to earn passage off. Shouldn't take more than thirty years."

Dorthy understood that he was worried that this was all some sort of Witness plot, that he was being set up.

She said, "You're not being set up."

"Something else I'm going to check," the freetrader said. "Already started, in fact. Wouldn't be here, otherwise."

Robot talked with him just outside the door for a few minutes, while Dorthy gave her breast to her daughter, holding a cloth to her other nipple to sop up the sympathetic flow. When Robot came back in he said, "Maybe I should get some of that, too."

"Don't be crude."

"I think he'll take us."

"So do I. But I also think he might have second thoughts, and turn us over to the Witnesses."

"I'll admit it crossed my mind. Maybe we should move out of here, if your daughter can travel. If you can, without your belly falling apart."

"I'm sore, but I'm healing."

"When are you gonna find a name for her, huh?"

"I wanted to call her Hiroko, but my precocious daughter doesn't like the name." Poor Hiroko, surely dead, now. Or an old, old woman. And her daughter's father still on the *Vingança*, which if it had survived its transfer orbit around the singularity and reached relativistic velocity was even now leaving behind the close-packed stars of the Galactic core, twenty-eight thousand light-years from home. Time dilation would mean that Valdez would age no more than a handful of years, but Dorthy and their daughter would be dead almost three hundred centuries before he returned.

The baby released her nipple and said, "Stupid name,'roko. Stupid. I choose."

Dorthy wiped milk and drool from the baby's chin. "Then you had better hurry and choose one before one chooses you."

Robot said, "Know what? The guy asked me, just as he was leaving, if the Witnesses were right. If there really are gods in the center of the Galaxy."

"Not yet," Dorthy's daughter said, and returned to suck.

They left late that night, riding slowly through the crowds that milled up and down the wide dockside, beneath balconies where whores, men and women and creatures that could have been either or both, leaned on scrolled iron railings and called down to prospective clients. When they had paid off their room, Dorthy had glimpsed a half-formed plan to betray them to the Witnesses uncoiling in the innkeeper's mind. She had drawn aside his wife, Maria, and asked her bluntly to try and make sure that they'd at least have time to get away from the town. Maria, who appreciated plain speaking, had told her not to worry; her husband couldn't leave the inn until the bar closed early in the morning, and she'd make sure that he didn't send any of the potboys off with a message.

"But you must know word will get to the Witnesses soon enough," she'd said. "They don't take much notice of what goes on in the Strip, but a baby that can talk from birth is something different. Poor mite. I wish you could stay a little longer. It's hard on you as well as on her."

"I've been in worse places," Dorthy had said, and Maria had embraced her and given her a paper parcel of pressed dried fruit, and led them out around the back lane.

But for all of Maria's assurances, Dorthy felt happier as she and Robot climbed the wooded slope away from Evangelina, and felt Robot's relief, too. The baby slept inside the sling Dorthy had made, cozied up to her breasts: she was dreaming about the shadow dancers, their graceful weaving dance among the scoop-shell encrusted pillars of their lagoon.

They made camp inside a grove of squat old cypresses, well away from the unpaved road. Insects made noise all around them. Far down the slope they could see the dim fires of Evangelina's shantytown, the ribbon of light that was the Strip. Running lights of ships on the river were like small constellations. Just south of the town the two airships of the Witnesses were lighted up, each brighter than Luna's tipped fingernail-paring crescent. Like certain deep-sea fish, their skins were transparent, revealing shadowy skeletal structures, gas bags like luminous organs. The bowl of the radio telescope bowl was rimmed in white light: an unsleeping eye.

Dorthy's daughter woke, cranky and hungry, and Dorthy fed her while munching handfuls of sharply sweet dried fruit; they didn't dare start a campfire. After a while Robot stood up and casually announced that he was going to ride back into town, see if he could find the freetrader.

"Be careful, now."

Robot said, "It's not really me they're looking for." And there was that touch of black mood again.

Dorthy said, "Hurry back," meaning, *come back, don't run*

away. Because that was what she was frightened of, Robot's vanishing into the hinterlands of his childhood, leaving her and her baby daughter stranded on anarchic Earth.

After Robot had gone, Dorthy lay on fragrant cedar needles in the warm humid darkness, with her daughter lying between her breasts. Her belly slack and aching, like the shell of a scooped-out fruit. Well, that would pass. She had her daughter, warm, smelling of sour milk and pee and something undefinable that stirred her heart. How often she had cursed her fate for being born a woman—echoing her father's despair at having no sons: she hadn't realized that before—and yet men could never have this.

Her daughter slept again, and woke and complained about her dirty diapers. Dorthy changed her in the dark and held her again, trying out names for the baby, none of which she liked, then asking her how much she remembered, curiosity and airy fear mingling. Just what was this changeling she'd carried, full-bellied with the wanton wind of lust, hers and Valdez's? How human was she? How human would she be?

But her daughter didn't understand, or confused her vivid dreams with the smothering reality of the womb, beat her tiny hands in frustration because she couldn't explain this to her mother, and then abruptly relaxed into sleep.

Dorthy dozed, too, and woke with the sense of people growing nearer. She called out, sleepily thinking it was Robot, returned with the freetrader. Then she knew it wasn't, but before she could get up light hit her from four directions at once, and a man said, "Stay right where you are, Citizen."

5

THE WITNESSES WERE AS POLITE AS COULD BE; IT WAS AS IF there were a space around Dorthy and her daughter they dared enter only after careful ritual appeasement, saying *Careful now, Dr. Yoshida*, or *Let me just take your hand a minute*, as they helped her out of the groundcar, guided her along white gravel paths that wound between huts and Quonset domes. Beyond, the two luminous airships and the scaffolding and huge, light-ringed bowl of the radio telescope rose against a sky so black it appeared to be solid.

There were half a dozen Witnesses, dressed in loose tunics and trousers of various primary colors, each with a representation of the Galaxy's triple spiral, a synthetic ruby sparkling in its center, hung from a fine chain around his neck. All men and all very young, handsome in a clean-cut, gangling, vacuous way. Accustomed to obeying orders unquestioningly. Just the sort of cannon fodder a jihad requires.

They had tried to take her daughter away from her, but Dorthy had grown fierce despite their pistols, and they'd given up, shrugging. It didn't matter to them. They had all the time they wanted.

They put her in a little room furnished with a table and a couple of straight-backed chairs, the iron frame of a bed with a wire mattress. There were old, dark stains on the white floor tiles around the bed frame. An odd looking apparatus, a black box with a handle and long wires hanging from it, was bolted to its head.

The Witnesses left her in the room a while, two standing impassively either side of the door. The baby woke and demanded food and Dorthy fed her. "Bad men," the baby

401

remarked, when she had finished, then fell asleep again. Little bubbles of milky saliva rose and ebbed at one corner of her mouth, in time to her damp breathing.

Time passed. After a while, one of the Witnesses brought Dorthy a stainless steel jigger of coffee. She was still sipping it when two more Witnesses marched in, honor guard for a compact man who looked hardly human, dressed all in white.

His name was Paul Marquira. He was the demiurge in charge of the Evangelina station of petition. "We have all the time we need," he told Dorthy. Both of his eyes were artificial, and there were inserts in his shaved skull, transparent windows that showed blue blood vessels snaking over smooth cerebral folds. He belonged to one of the more extreme Witness sects, one which believed that immortality could be attained by such mutilation. Marquira basked in Dorthy's curious gaze, told her boastfully that half his organs were implants; his blood was an artificial plasma in which silicon-bonded haem carried oxygen; his metabolism had been radically rejigged so that for nourishment he needed only a simple nutrient solution. All that was really required was the brain, he said, and even that wasn't necessary, as the ancients had shown. Full transference of both mind and anima to machine intelligence was the next stage in human evolution, long delayed but inevitable.

Dorthy played along with Marquira. She didn't need inserts to glimpse his thoughts. She was a prize, a trophy. Possession of someone who had visited the Galaxy's core and heard the voices of the gods would hugely increase the standing of Marquira's sect. Strictly speaking she should have been sent directly to Galveston, but instead they were waiting on an airship crossing the Gulf, bringing the leader of Marquira's schismatic sect. She would be debriefed, as Marquira put it, by friendly hands.

Dorthy said that she would tell him anything he wanted to know, right here. "I have no secrets, Seyour. I saw what I saw, and I want people to know about it. It is why I came back to Earth."

"And why then are you trying to leave it?" Marquira sat across the table from her, his hands folded over the bulge his belly made in his lavender tunic. His restructured metabolism had swollen his liver fourfold.

Robot, Dorthy thought. Robot had sold her out. Him, or the freetrader, or both of them.

Marquira's implanted eyes were silver, with smeared black pupils that dilated independently. They glittered spectrally in the harsh light of the little room. "We've been keeping watch on you ever since you arrived in Evangelina. We keep watch on anyone interesting who arrives here. We are not as disingenuous as the people believe, although we like to keep a low profile. Those who give us trouble we make disappear. Without fuss, without trace. It is not our main task, but we are thorough."

"You don't have to justify yourself to me," Dorthy said. The coffee had nerved her up. "I've seen what you've done here."

Marquira shrugged. He'd heard it all before. "We need Earth for the moment, as a platform for our petitions. After the Revelation, only we had the organization, the willpower, to resist the wave of anarchy that swept the Earth. Our present position is a simple historical inevitability."

"Not one of the people you pretend to rule asked for your rule. You're all just a bunch of opportunistic vigilantes."

"Billions of people died after the Revelation, Dr. Yoshida. Literally billions. But billions more survived, because of us. Because we were prepared to make a stand."

"What are you going to do with us? Are we going to be part of this historical inevitability of yours?"

"You have been to the core of the Galaxy. You have seen the glory that people on Earth only glimpsed."

Dorthy thought that she knew what was coming. She told Marquira that his Revelation was no more than the dying babblings of a psychotic Golden with nothing left to live for but revenge, told him that if there ever had been things like gods, they had gone away an aeon ago, that the human race was just a pawn brought into play in history's endgame.

Marquira heard her out impassively, silver eyes glittering. When she had finished, he nodded slightly, and Dorthy barely had time to flinch before the two Witnesses behind her jerked her upright, one snatching her daughter as the other rabbit-punched her.

Raw white pain wiped everything away. She was on her hands and knees, feeling bits and pieces of herself float back together as the pain ebbed. Her spine was a rod of fire.

Marquira stood up and came around the desk. "You're tired, Dr. Yoshida," he said, "tired and confused and upset. You think that you hate us, so you think that you can hurt us by repeating the kind of baseless rumor that's lately been floating through the population here. In fact, you cannot hurt us at all, but we can hurt you. And we will, until we get at the truth. It may be a hard, dark road, but we will get there in the end. You will recant your heresy. And then you'll be in a position to tell everyone about what you learned, at the core. Only then: not now."

They left Dorthy alone with her daughter after that. The pain did not go away, although after a while she was able to get off the floor and sit on one of the chairs. She desperately wanted to lie down, but the floor was too hard and she couldn't lie on the wire mattress, knowing all too well what it had been used for.

The baby fretted in Dorthy's embrace, aware of her mother's pain but unable to do anything about it. Her eyes kept trying to focus on Dorthy's face, and her little hands twisted and fumbled and patted. "All right," she kept insisting. "All all right. Sleep."

"There may be comfort in dreams, child, but you always have to wake from them, and find the world unchanged. Dreams are only a reflection of the world; they don't work on it."

"*Mine* do," the baby said.

"The shadow dancers are asleep inside you. That's why you see them in your dreams. We can't wake them here."

"We'll see," her daughter said, and fell asleep, after a while waking long enough to say, "They know." And then she was sleeping again, a queer deep REM sleep that would draw Dorthy down into it if she let it.

Dawn came, quick and vivid. It began to grow warm in the little room. There was no environmental conditioning. It was just a concrete box with a white tile floor and a high ceiling Dorthy couldn't reach even when standing on the chair she'd placed on top of the desk. There'd been a writing screen set in the desk once, but it had been taken out and the hole neatly patched. There was nothing but little rolls of dust in the sliding drawer, nothing else in the little room she could use except perhaps the whiplike wires of the machine bolted to the head of the bed frame; but she couldn't bear to touch those.

Standing on the chair, she could look through the room's high, narrow window, but all she could see were the ragged crowns of a clump of palms framed against blue sky.

Most of the time she sat zazen on the desk. Time was marked by the patch of light projected from the window against the far wall, slowly traveling upward as Dorthy tried to order her thoughts and ignore the sweat that ran all over her body, the dull pain in her kidneys (she'd had to relieve herself twice, furtively, in a corner of the room; both times, her piss had been tinged with blood). What it came down to was that she could not let herself be used. Not this time. She could not fool herself that she could resist torture. That one blow had already left its mark on her psyche. And blows were the least of it. There were ways out; there were always ways out. She had tried them once or twice after particularly harrowing sessions at the Kamali-Silver Institute (once with bleach; once with a knife; and once she had tried to drown herself in the teardrop swimming pool at the Institute's weightless heart). Tried and failed, but she'd only been a child, then.

But there was her daughter. Dorthy couldn't leave her behind, but to take her as well (if she could) would be to betray the hopes of an entire race. The Witnesses knew that. Perhaps not overtly, but they knew it all the same, with the kind of instinct that lets a wild dog pick out the weakest member of a herd, the one that can be brought down with the least effort.

That's what the Witnesses were, Dorthy thought, or less than that. They were carrion creatures picking over the bones of history, possessed of enough snarl and swagger to chase off lesser creatures, but without the necessary gram of courage to make a kill of their own. Even if they did brainwash her into confirming their beliefs, they were still wrong, still superseded. Lies would not make their faith any more real. They'd continue to inflict misery on Earth; but because their religion forbade the desecration of space by anything other than their prayers, they would not spread elsewhere.

The shadow dancers, frozen potentials inside the tender curve of her sleeping daughter's skull, could not be allowed to die stillborn in this universe, for all that they still swam in the ocean of the interzone. She would save them if she could, her daughter and the shadow dancers. She had to stay alive, alert to whatever chance there might be. All she had was all she had ever had: a slender raveling thread of hope.

The glossy patch of sunlight reached the angle between wall and ceiling and began to decline, losing its sharpness as it fell. When it was no brighter than the gridded glotube that had never been turned off, a Witness brought a steel tray into the room, pale squares of vat-grown slop, a glass pitcher brimful with tepid, cloudy water. Dorthy took the pitcher and said she didn't want the food, but could she please have a change of diapers for her daughter.

The Witness took the food away without a word, amazingly returned with a stack of starched and pressed towels. Dorthy changed her sleeping daughter, who slept on, still dreaming of swimmers of dark seas under pink skies. There was only darkness beyond the window slit when Paul Marquira returned, and told her it was time to go.

A new airship was tethered beyond the radio telescope, caught in the glare of crossing searchlights. It was small and black, its cruciform vanes silvered along their edges. Red and green running lights winked either side of the cabin tucked beneath the phallic swell of its envelope. Dorthy and Marquira were the head of a wedge of Witnesses moving across scrub grass toward it.

"There is a place we have on the far side of the Gulf," Marquira told Dorthy. "You'll go there; it'll be safer."

"For me, or for you?"

"For all of us," the Witness said. The inserts in his skull flashed in the lights ringing the edge of the radio telescope as he looked from side to side. Dorthy didn't need her Talent to sense his fear. He said, "You have brought much trouble with you, Dr. Yoshida. If I had—"

And then all the lights went out: the searchlights playing on the airships; the lights of the radio telescope; the lights of the buildings and the perimeter of the compound.

Dorthy stopped and someone stumbled into her, nearly knocking her daughter to the ground. A kind of stir went through the clumps of palmetto grass all around, although there was no wind. The baby started to fret and Dorthy lifted her onto her shoulder. She was the center of a circle of panicky Witnesses. There were only the running lights of the airships, brilliant constellations swaying against the scatter of fixed stars in the sky.

And then stars began to fall, trailing streaks of fire as they slanted toward the ground, erupting into stuttering comet trails of golden fire or bursting into hurtling traceries of sparks which each blossomed into a white flower. Overlapping patterns of livid light caught the Witnesses around Dorthy in a variety of absurd postures. Then there was a terrific thunderclap and a dragon writhed across the starry sky, breathing out fire that struck the black airship amidships and clung there.

6

"**F**OOLS!" MARQUIRA SHOUTED. "IT'S ONLY FIREWORKS!"

But already some of the Witnesses were running back toward the buildings. The dragon's scribbled outline, fading, was dimmed by the glare of the burning airship. Fires had started on the ground, too. Acrid smoke swirled waist deep around Dorthy and the remaining Witnesses. Shadowy phantoms moved through the smoke, cast by the pyre of the airship, by the flares which still hung between earth and heaven. One of them was real, Dorthy realized. He was trying to tell her something, but didn't know how to form the image, and she was distracted by the communal panic of the Witnesses.

Then Marquira drew his pistol and told the others to keep together, he'd shoot the next man to break ranks. The burning airship sank to the ground, crumpling into a V as its spine snapped. A shadow hung above the leaping light of the airship's pyre, then slowly slipped sideways. Marquira raised the pistol and for a moment a line of light as bright as the sun swept through the sky. Thunder followed.

Marquira grabbed Dorthy's arm and pulled her with him. "We will get back to the buildings. They won't dare fire on us as long as we have Yoshida and her baby, and help will come for us soon enough. They'll have seen this display all down the coast." He glared at Dorthy. "And while we wait for help I'll find out from you who your friends are. Oh, you will talk, that I promise."

"I'll tell you anything," Dorthy said. She was trying to concentrate on Marquira's unstable anger and the unvoiced message at the same time. Then two things happened at once. One of the Witnesses sprawled full length. He twisted to grab at what had caught his leg and howled as he drew back bloody hands. And Dorthy's daughter, who had watched everything with equanimity, suddenly wailed and said, "More light," and squeezed her eyes shut just as a column of red fire shot up in front of the group.

Robot stood amid swirling smoke. Little black goggles covered his eyes. He held out his augmented arm, the palm of its hand upward. Something fizzled in it, and Dorthy then realized what he'd been trying to tell her and turned just as the flare ignited, throwing blue-white glare far across the scrub.

Through blotchy green-yellow afterimages, Dorthy saw Witnesses pawing at their eyes as they staggered in frantic circles or fell to their knees. No, not all of them. Marquira stood still. The flare hadn't affected his implanted eyes. He raised the pistol, centering it precisely on Robot's chest—and a clot of darkness fastened around his leg and then he was on the ground, trying to push away the big crab-thing that scrambled up his thigh. It made a metallic whir and scythed off his fingers.

Dorthy clutched her daughter to her chest and began to run toward the descending singleship. She could see it clearly now, outlined against burning wreckage. Robot matched her pace. A tide of crab-things scampered around them. They reached the leaf-shaped ship before the humans. Robot clambered onto the singleship's lifting surface, took the baby from Dorthy and passed her to the tall, skinny pilot. Dorthy grasped Robot's hand, and stepped off the Earth.

The moon rose behind Earth's half-globe: the double planet visibly dwindled. Robot pushed the screen away and kneaded his biceps with his prosthetic hand. The crashweb had raised red welts during the brutal minutes of acceleration. They were in free-fall now. Dorthy's daughter turned and turned in midair, flapping her chubby arms and gurgling with delight. Dorthy watched her indulgently. Crab-things clung together in the rear of the cramped cabin, shifting over each other with metallic rattles and clicks.

"You knew all along," Dorthy said to her tumbling daughter. "You have the eyes of your friends, I know you do." She caught her daughter and frowned fiercely at her. "And what else? What else do you know, child?" And thought, *Do you hear, feel my wonder, my fear?*

But the baby only waved her hands. Bubbles of saliva drifted from her cupid's bow mouth. "More," she said. "More more more!"

"We were pretty sure that the Witnesses had taken you," Robot said, "even without the crabs leading us on." He knuckled smoke-smudged cheeks and asked for about the tenth time, "How about that show?"

"You could have been killed," Dorthy said. "Walking in there like that. . . . I would have got away. I was just waiting for the right moment."

"All I ask is a little acknowledgment. Last performance I'll ever give on Earth. Shit, I had to be right in the middle of it."

The pilot said, "Still not sure if you people are for real. Not even sure if what we just *did* is for real."

"We're real," Robot said.

"You'd better be. Didn't have time to close a major deal on wild-type maize genes, and guess I won't be going back. And didn't realize those crab-things of yours were coming along. You sure they're harmless?"

"Mostly harmless," Robot said. He told Dorthy, "They understand me, I think. Came right along with me, after I overloaded the power systems."

"It wasn't you they were following." Dorthy was still staring at her daughter, eye to eye, wondering just how much the baby knew, how much she had been changed. By the angels. By the shadow dancers. But the baby only squinted back at her, cross-eyed, and blew bubbles.

" 'The fairy-land buys not the child of me,' " Dorthy said, at last. "We've a lot to learn about each other, you and I." And spun the baby round, laughing at her innocent delight, while on the unwatched screen the double star of Earth and Moon shrank to a single point, was lost against the diamond drifts of the Milky Way's four hundred billion stars.

·∧·∧·∧·∧·∧·

Coda
Eternal Light

WHEN THE GROUND-EFFECT MACHINE CAME ASHORE, Dorthy was on the beach, walking on wet black sand while the child ran ahead of her, scampering back and forth through lines of foam that tirelessly unraveled in the same direction. The evening before she had seen the white boat anchor off the east point of the bay's wide curve, beneath the high promontory where the marine station perched, and assumed it was only a fishing expedition put in for repairs. Fifty kilometers offshore, upwelling currents brought rich nutrients from the dark, cold depths. Huge fish, the largest in any known ocean, gathered there to feed on vast blooms of plankton or on each other. Fishing boats visited the marine station perhaps a dozen times in season, but usually their clients thought nothing of the house on the far side of the bay—or if they did, they didn't trouble its occupants.

But now a small GEM swerved out from the boat. Dorthy shaded her eyes to watch as it scribed its wake straight across the bay: a blue bead riding its cushion of air, booming through the surf and skimming up the beach to slew to a halt in a spray of sand beneath the end of the lawn that slanted back to the long, low house.

By the time Dorthy and her daughter had returned, the visitor had already installed himself on their veranda, lounging at ease in one of the cane chairs, his legs cocked on the rail. For a moment, Dorthy didn't recognize him. His hair was black, tied back in a long twisted rope, and his slant-cut silk shirt and baggy pants were elegant and expensive. But then her daughter ran up the steps to him and Robot rose and caught her and whirled her around, his augmented arm gleaming in orange sunlight.

Later, in the last of the sunlight, they sat on a flat slab of rock beside a tidal pool, talking about the past and the future

413

while Dorthy's daughter dived for quartz pebbles. The girl swam with fierce grace, her bare body flashing and turning in the deep, clear water, her eyes wide and a tracery of bubbles trailing back through her long black hair as her starfish hands searched out treasures from ribbed black sand, from crevices in the tilted rocks.

"Her friends leave them there," Dorthy said. "There must be a vein out to sea somewhere. Inshore, it's all metamorphosite."

"I was hoping to see the shadow dancers," Robot said. "But the people at the station said they were farther west."

"If you're fishing, you might see them."

"To be honest, I joined the boat a day ago, and I fly back the day after tomorrow. You heard about the expedition?"

"No, and I'm not going to look in your head to find out what it is. Those days are more or less over, for me. My daughter probably knows, though. She's something, Robot. A natural Talent, the first. No training to bring it out, and no implant to regulate it. She does that herself. I've turned down a double lifetime's worth of credit from the Elysium Kamali-Silver Institute for exclusive rights to her."

Robot shifted his zithsa-hide boots—already cracked and salt stained—as the child surfaced right at the lip of the slab and added another glittering pebble to her small cairn. Hair was pasted in knives to her forehead. Then she dived again, bare rump flashing as she effortlessly shimmied down through the clear water.

Robot said, "I didn't know what you were doing here. I heard about the times you went back to Earth, those semicovert diplomatic missions. But that was all. . . . Partly why I came, Dorthy. To catch up. Been a long time. Six years."

"And partly something else. What are you up to, Robot? You've changed."

"I'm not as crazy as I was, you mean." He grinned. "I wrote a substitute for Machine. Dumb as a box of rocks, but he keeps me steady. You've changed, too. You're not so . . . well, driven."

"I've grown up. She helps me. We live here, and learn marine biology together, and help out as best we can with the shadow dancer program."

"And stir up trouble on Earth."

"That's not how it is at all."

He grinned. "Yeah, I know that. You haven't quite lost all your edges, I see."

"The revolution will come of itself, Robot. We don't need to do anything to encourage it but tell the truth. The Witnesses can't hold on forever. Mustn't. Because every second that passes, the hypervelocity star is seventeen thousand klicks nearer to wrecking the Solar System. Twelve hundred years seems a long time, but there are billions of people on Earth. It will be the greatest and most difficult evacuation in history, but it must be done."

They talked about the Witnesses and the slowly growing resistance to their rule, and Dorthy's missions to contact clandestine governments that had survived fifty years of Witness rule. She, too, was a witness: at last she was free to tell the story of the Alea and the angels and the secret history of the Universe to anyone who would listen. And they talked about the problems of hatching and rearing to adulthood the shadow dancer cysts the crab-things had carried, of trying to alter their biochemistry so that, like the killer whales that were for now the shadow dancers' surrogate bodies, they could live in the oceans of Iemanja. The shadow dancers had problems adjusting to the strange, streamlined bodies of killer whales.

"You could try manta rays," Robot suggested.

"Not enough cranial capacity."

"Not even with hardwiring? But I guess you've already thought of stuff like that. It's good to see you've found a place, a career."

"My life has never been normal, Robot. I brought a lot of trouble on myself fighting against that instead of accepting it. Rejoicing in it, even. I was a nasty piece of work, when I was younger; I'd cut you open as soon as look at you. This, now, is as normal as it ever will be, I think. Teaching half-million-year-old alien ghosts to use killer whale bodies, watching my daughter grow into something wild and strange and wonderful."

"She still doesn't have a name."

"She's had a dozen this year alone. But she doesn't have one at the moment." Dorthy watched as the girl swam through deep dappled shadow among boulders at the bottom of the pool. Her tireless mermaid. "She frightens me sometimes, Robot. She knows that, and tries to comfort me. But still, she frightens me. We were all changed, but she was changed most of all. And not just because she could speak from birth. They've heavy weaponry out at the marine station, not all of it to keep off hive sharks. I do wonder what she will grow into, this daughter of mine."

"I've been thinking about that, too," Robot said, "among other things." He had an arch, almost Mephistophelian air about him, not at all the wild, despairing young man Dorthy had known and loved all those nights when they'd been fugitives on Earth. He crossed his elegant boots, brushed at the puffed sleeves of his raw-silk shirt, leaned back on both elbows. "You know that I was closer to the angels than anyone else, except perhaps Talbeck Barlstilkin's bonded servant. I've been thinking about that a lot. Especially since Little Machine took up residence."

"And you've come to certain conclusions. You want my opinions about them."

"I do keep forgetting about your Talent."

"Oh, Robot, I don't need what's left of my Talent to tell me you're up to something."

"Did you ever wonder what the angels are? What they really are?"

"Changelings. Thinking creatures once like us, or like the shadow dancers, or the Alea. Creatures of flesh and blood who'd turned themselves into something else. Pure thought, Gunasekra once said. He liked that idea. Living on like the dead people who were read into computer dumps before the Interregnum. But with their animas." Dorthy smiled. "You don't think that at all."

Robot said, "Perhaps their masters are like that. But I don't think the angels are. You know that they only ever spoke through me or Machine, or through Talbeck's servant."

"They spoke to me, when they took me wherever it was, so that I could speak to that combat pilot."

"Suzy Falcon."

"Yes. And they spoke to Abel Gunasekra too, I suppose. . . . I wonder if they still do?"

"They could speak to you because you were all inside my dream. When the angels first took us, Suzy and me, I was put to dreaming the, well, metaphor I suppose. The interzone between the strange virtual reality of the angels and our own perceptions. Meanwhile, Suzy thought she was talking to me, but she was really talking to Machine. And Machine was closer to the angels than me, that's why he went a little crazy I think. That and the neuter female."

"You mean, the angels were machines? Serving something else?"

"What's a machine, Dorthy? Something to do work. A lever, an orchestra, a combat singleship, a subroutine in a circuit. I think that's what the angels were. Subroutines at the interface. We never saw their masters at all. They were too far from us. To try and talk to them would have been like trying to stand inside a star."

Out in the middle of the pool, Dorthy's daughter surfaced with a cry of triumph. Then she was swimming strongly to the side. "Another!" she said, and tossed her prize to her mother before heaving herself onto the slab of rock, gasping like a beached seal.

Dorthy turned the quartz-veined pebble over in her fingers, handed it across to Robot.

"Pretty," he said. "You've found a whole bunch, huh? The shadow dancers find things like this for you?"

The little girl shrugged and stretched out on her belly, resting her sleek wet head on her mother's bare feet. She closed her eyes and seemed instantly to relax into sleep.

"The crab-things bring them," Dorthy said. "Rub your thumb over it. Go on."

Robot did, then frowned and transferred it to his prosthetic hand, turning it around and around, brushing it with fine sensory wires that extruded from the joints of the elongated fingers. "Engraving," he said. "So small, so dense. . . . Does it mean anything?"

Dorthy wiggled her toes under the weight of her daughter's head. "You know, don't you? Only you won't say. Like a lot of things."

"Do you know who the angels' real masters were?" Robot

asked. "I bet you do. I think I do, too. I knew them, once, like you."

Dorthy said, "She won't tell you whether she knows or not. And if she knows, she won't tell you *what* she knows."

"I'll tell her what I know, then. Or what I think I know."

"So that's why you came here, really. To ask her. It's been tried, Robot. Many times."

"To see her, to see you. Those were fine times we had, on Earth. Kingman Seven. I guess it hasn't changed."

"I remember the cold, and the rain. And your getting drunk a lot. And don't try and get around me, Robot."

He smiled. He shrugged. He said, "I came to tell you a couple of things, too."

"That the angels were only machines, only subroutines. Servants to something else. You figured this out by yourself?"

"They told me some of it. I just took a while to understand. A while, and with some help from Little Machine. It was all inside my head, but we needed to write our own algorithms to be able to read it. 'In the realm of light there is no time.' No future, no past, not as we understand it. Just this eternal now, eternal light. If there is a God, that's what She must be like, outside our time, outside clocks, outside entropy. Eternal and unchanging, like a standing wave at the horizon of a black hole. I've been hanging out with physicists lately. Been trying to think their way." Robot grinned crookedly and tapped the left side of his head. "Little Machine, he understands a whole lot better than I do. We manage."

"So that's why we came out when we did, fifty years in the future."

"That's something else I want to tell you about."

They talked on while, out beyond the rise where the house stood, the huge soft orange sun sank toward the horizon. The child seemed to sleep on; although Dorthy knew that she was not asleep, or not as anyone would understand it.

Robot tried to explain the history that had been dumped in his head, past and future all mixed up. There had only been one real intelligence in the Universe, just as the weak anthropic principle had proposed all along. Everything, hundreds of billions of galaxies, each with its three or four hundred billion stars, had been necessary, just enough room, for this one species to evolve intelligence. Only it had happened early on, at a time when the galaxies were still close together; or perhaps even earlier, in the era before galaxies, the era of supermassive stars and black hole formation, the era when most of the Universe's light had been created. A time when the Universe was only a few hundred million years old, a few hundred million light-years in diameter. Had to have been that early, because the masters of the angels had been all through the Universe, Robot said, living in the center of every galaxy. He thought that perhaps they had lived somehow in the accretion disks of black holes, or maybe at the event horizon itself, nourished by the welter of Hawking radiation, virtual particles that crossed into this Universe while their antiparticles, that should have been born and died with them, stayed trapped inside the singularity.

"I think I was shown what they looked like, but I can't remember it. Couldn't understand it, maybe, so it didn't stay with me. But I don't think they were like us, or the Alea, or the shadow dancers. That's what my physics friends say, too: the Universe that young, there wasn't time for carbon-based life to have got much past the bacterial stage, if that. I was at this symposium last year."

"The symposium on possible information-processing life forms? I had an invitation to go to that."

"All sorts of weird stuff there. Weirder than art, you know. Those guys just wigged me out. Anyway, whatever the angels' masters were, they didn't stick around. The Universe won't last long enough to suit them and its energy density is changing in the wrong direction. So they built machines to take them somewhere else. The place we glimpsed. They worked out a way to get between universes and went through it and would have pulled it in after them, but the Alea came along. Meat intelligence, planet-bound intelligence. . . . A freak thing, in this one galaxy, out of all the billions there are . . . maybe there were other freak things elsewhere, but we won't know about them. The only reason we know about the Alea is because we happened because of them."

The child murmured, "It's a vacuum diagram."

"Huh? What she say?"

Dorthy said, "One of my daughter's gnomic remarks. Sometimes she even explains them. Then it wasn't a lie, about the Alea being infected with some kind of intelligence-forming template? Strange, because I always thought that it was."

"There were some terrific arguments about that at the symposium. The main thing seems to be that if the high local density of intelligent races is isotropic, then we shouldn't be here, because something else would have got here first and colonized the whole Universe. Or we'd just be their slaves. Instead, the deal is that intelligence in this galaxy is, what's the word . . . ?"

"Anisotropic. Grainy. Like rock, or wood."

"It's anisotropic, a little lump formed around the Alea family that happened to settle on P'thrsn and around BD Twenty. Us, the shadow dancers . . . maybe the Elysium aborigines were a failed attempt. And the thing is, it's like that all through the Galaxy."

"Because the Alea families that fled the marauders are all through the Galaxy," Dorthy said, thinking of the secret history *she'd* been shown, on P'thrsn. The arks fleeing outward, dropping through the gas clouds circling the bright, densely packed stars of the core, vanishing into the wide reaches of the Galaxy's spiral arms, vanishing among the billions of unremarkable field stars.

She said, "That's why you're going back there, isn't it?"

"Partly." Robot ran the extensors of his prosthetic hand down his braid, translation of a gesture Dorthy remembered so well. He said, "Want to walk me back to my little waterbug? The boat's due out on the turn of the tide, and if I'm late the rest of the party will hang me from the bowsprit, or whatever it is they do to show disapproval."

The child scrambled to her feet and said something about showing them, and then she was off, leaping like a pale gazelle from rock to rock to the beach, scampering through pinkish level light which glittered on the shallow swell of the sea, on the myriad pools and rivulets scattered down the long, long black beach.

As Dorthy and Robot clambered down after her, a whale

broached the surface, leaping high, its arched body silhouetted against the sun's huge disk before falling back, vanishing soundlessly into burning water.

Dorthy stopped, struck with an ice-cold sense of déjà vu. In stepping from rock to sand, it was as if she had stepped into a dream, the dream her child had dreamed while still in her womb. . . .

Robot said something, and Dorthy smiled and walked on beside him. But still the feeling held her, a cold grip across her shoulders, cold fingers at the base of her spine. Robot was talking about his expedition, and she forced herself to listen. Someone had found a way to use the wormholes, how to navigate them. Half a dozen ships were returning to the hypervelocity star, would pass through one of Colcha's wormholes to the core. And Robot was going with them. He said that he was going to find Suzy Falcon.

" . . . But she'll be dead, surely. All those years. We don't even know if she survived the marauders, managed to get down onto the surface of the Spike! How will you even find her grave in those trillions of square kilometers?"

"The thing we found out about wormholes, Dorthy, is that when you travel through one you travel through time. In some cases it's a loop, so you come out at the same time you went in: in others the loop remains open. You go forward. That's what happened when we were sent back to Earth. We came out in the future. I'd like to think it was because the angels don't have any sense of time. But I know they planned it that way, don't ask me why. . . ."

Robot was squinting down the curve of the beach, through layers of fading sunlight and reflected glitter. "I think your daughter's found what she wanted to show us. She's jumping around up there fit to bust." He said, as they went on, "There's a little more. We're going to try and map the wormholes of the planetoid at the core. We're going to look for intelligent species that evolved close to the hiding places of the other Alea families that fled the marauders. We know there must be more: there was that species that built the ship we found on the surface of the planetoid, for instance. Hey there! What is it you've found? Just look at those things!"

Dorthy heard the chitinous rattling before she saw what caused it. The child was running about at the edge of the retreating tide, leaping around the crowd of things crawling there. There were hundreds of them, thousands, ribbed carapaces jostling, scrolls of their cephalic shields bumping blindly as they moved this way and that in the surf, climbed over each other with blind driven persistence. Strings of white mucus surged and fell all around them, twisting in the waves.

Dorthy let out a sigh of relief. "I forgot. The moons are in syzygy. It triggers their mating cycle. They come up here, away from predators."

"What are they?" Robot turned a stray over with the tip of his boot. The creature's many-jointed legs, each hooked with a single claw, wriggled frantically as it tried to right itself.

"Trilobites." Something splashed loudly farther out in the surf. Probably an amphibian, come to feed on the swarm. "Don't you get in the water," Dorthy told her daughter.

"For a minute there I thought they might have been my old friends."

"The crab-things hardly ever come ashore, these days. They're much farther out, using technology we gave them to build what we think is going to be a data store. We're having problems getting the scoop-shells established in open water."

Robot righted the trilobite he'd tipped over. "Horrible-looking things."

"They have their place."

The child had stopped her capering. She looked at Dorthy and Robot and said, "They are like us. We still have a long way to evolve, too. Take Talents with you, Seyour Robot, when you go and look for the other races. We're the beginnings of the link that will bind us all at the end of time, when the Universe falls in on itself toward the place it came from and we will know everything, and live forever.

"You don't believe me, Mother. Didn't you ever wonder where the fast star came from? The angels couldn't leave the place between universes when you met them, nor could they ever. And the oldest ones had long ago vanished, leaving nothing but the shadow of their substance and a few abandoned machines. Just as we exploded the star that caused the death of the Alea's home sun, so we sent the fast stars out. You can travel back, as well as forward. The angels are our servants, or the servants of what we'll become, all of us, at the end of time.

"Seyour Robot, it's true they are subroutines at the interface, but from the outside in. They are an attempt to communicate with the oldest ones, in a place outside the realm of light, outside time. They were there to guide you, but you had to choose. Your free will stopped the loop of the vacuum diagram from collapsing on itself. Don't you see? There is no beginning, and no end."

Dorthy dared a step forward. "I know who's speaking. I thought you'd vanished when your task was done! How dare you go into her head!"

But the child shook her head. "It's not the old Alea. It's only me. Really it is." She was smiling. "You look so scared, and it's only me! I've thought of a new name."

"What . . . What is it, child?"

"Lucia," the child said, and then she was off, running pell-mell down the beach toward the house.

Dorthy would have run after her, but Robot put a hand on her shoulder. "Hey," he said, "calm down."

"I'll have to take her to be checked again, Robot. I thought those days were over. So many things in her head, and she's so young."

"She's very special. Do you think those things were true?"

"She reads all the time, all sorts of texts. Cosmology, scientific romances. I think it's just something she picked up. Everything coming together at the end of time, a single mind like God's, living forever in the eternal light of the final singularity? I remember something like that from an old, old book. I'm sure that that's where she got it from."

But she wasn't sure at all.

Robot said, "She knew something I was trying to tell you. It is possible, theoretically at least, to use the wormholes to travel back in time as well as forward. It's not generally known outside the circles I seem to move in these days, because people worry that the Witnesses will try and use it, to change the way the last battle for the *Vingança* came out, for instance. They say that kind of paradox is impossible, or would simply create a local parallel universe we wouldn't even notice, though they're not a hundred-percent sure. But your daughter knows. The other thing we're going to do with the wormholes is manipulate one to travel back in time. Go back to a point just after the battle for the *Vingança*, after the Revelation. One year, maybe two. I'm flying the mission, going to look for Suzy. And I know she'll be alive, Dorthy. She was dumb, in some ways. But she was a fighter. She'll be there."

"And so will Machine."

"Yeah, him too."

"You loved them both. I understand, Robot. One thing I've learned is to understand. My daughter . . . maybe not. But I know other people. When you get back, I'd like to meet Suzy Falcon. We only had a little time together, and we did so much."

Robot said, "'Free will,' Lucia said. So Suzy chose, and saved the Universe. Will she be pissed when I tell her!"

They walked on. At last Dorthy said, "One thing I do know about my daughter. She has already grown beyond me. Soon I'll have to let her go, let her go on to wherever she's destined to go." She laughed. "And I thought I had troubles, Robot, when I was young! My poor daughter! Poor little superwoman! The changes she'll have to go through!"

Dorthy squinted into the last light of the sun, suddenly wanting to see where her child had got to. But there was so much light dying out of the sky, and the beach was so long, and so full of light flashing from pool to pool, that she could not even see if it had an ending.